The
Script

ALSO BY GENE STIRM

THE MYSTICAL PATH TO MYSTIQUE

AS A SHAMAN DREAMS

THE ART AND CRAFT OF COVER DESIGN

CO-AUTHOR
OSCAR GOES CAMPING

The Script

A novel by

Gene Stirm

Published by:
        Way West Production
        Tehachapi, CA 93561
        Phone: 661-823-8343

ISBN- 978-0-9826828-3-8

First Edition
First printing, May 2015

DEDICATION

To my beautiful wife Patricia, daughter Malinda Möller
and granddaughter Bethany.

ACKNOWLEDGMENTS

First to my wife Patricia, who puts up with my odd and long hours of writing. She is my muse, inspiration and sometime exasperation, without her love and support, this book would not have been written.

To my daughter Malinda in Germany for the hours of phone conversations about this book and hundreds of other fanciful ideas and her husband Stefan Möller for loving her. To Natalia Tapia, for her critique and Sally Larsen, whose untiring eyes helped so much. Thank you all.

FOREWORD

From where does a story come? It starts as an idea, a seed that may lie dormant in one's brain until some set of circumstances cause it to germinate. Then it must be fed, watered and nurtured until it, sometimes slowly, matures. So it was with this story. The moment of germination came during a screenwriter's workshop, hosted by the Writer's Guild, Hollywood, in 2001. The assignment was to write a short screenplay 10 to 15 minute in length, a compelling story in proper screenplay format. The seed that sprouted was what if each individual human life was written like a screenplay before they are born and played out over their lifetime?

The class was about both style and proper acceptable submission format. I did my assignment, 12 pages typed in standard screenplay format. However, the seed once germinated continued to grow. Slowly it matured into the work that is before you today, far beyond the 90 to 120 pages of a standard film script.

FORMAT

I mention format, because screenplays are written in a strict physical form. Though most are now written on computers, the preferred font is still typewriter style, Courier Final Draft. The margins, indention and line length are strict for scene heads, descriptions and dialog. For instance, when a new character is introduced in a script for the first time, their name is typed in all capital letters. There is a standard list of abbreviations as well, such as FX for special effects and V.O. for voice over. The reason behind all this strict format formality is that when used properly, a page of a script translates approximately into a minute of screen time. In the busy world of movies and television, a producer can turn to the last page of a newly presented script and determine exactly how many minutes a film will run. Believe me when I say, the last page of a script is the first page most producers looks at.

Outside the film industry, few people have ever read or even seen an accrual-formatted screenplay. Since the heart of my story is the script itself, I chose to constantly, but subtly remind the reader of the importance of the script to the story by starting each chapter in script format for a few lines before switching to traditional book format. The body of the book is set in Georgia.

ENJOY

PART ONE

CHAPTER 1

BEFORE

"It isn't a question of what you have. It's what you do with what you've got that matters."

Anders stopped reading aloud and rubbed the back of his neck. Riveted by the film script he had been reading for the past three-hours, his backside was rebelling. The chair in the private lounge was comfortable, but he simply had to stretch. Arms out, he twisted his torso before starting to pace. It took a minute to shake off his stiffness. He grabbed a bottle of water from the refrigerator and stepped out to the balcony. *Fresh air*, he drew in a deep breath. It was pleasant outside. The balcony faced out across a great azure sea that stretched to the horizon. Fifteen stories below, gentle waves found their way upon the uninhabited beach to kiss the snow-white sand before they retreated. A stray breeze softly stirred the grasses that turfed the gradual slope separating beach and land. A scent of freshness drifted upward.

He had been here before, more times than he wished to remember. He hated this part of the audition process, but he knew he had to face it. *Just a part of the business.*

Even at the balcony's level, the majestic building towered above him. It reflected both land and sea in flawless harmony. The structure was a marvel, more glass than metal. The panes set like Pavé-laid diamonds in pure platinum.

Anders rolled his shoulders. The velvet greenery that spread across the hills to the soft horizon, failed to calm his nervousness. He wondered why he couldn't tap the peace and stillness that permeated the air. The serenity so prevalent he felt that he could reach out and hold it in his hands. From where he stood, he could not see roads, highways, cars or parking lots, and for that matter, other buildings or even a single power pole. Like him on that vast balcony, the great structures stood alone, but it was tranquil. *Why the nerves?*

Embraced by the warm afternoon sun, Anders chose a comfortable lounge to recline upon and returned to reading the script. When he sat, he caught sight of his sky-blue suit reflected in the mirrored glass. Seeing his reflected figure concerned him. He was Scandinavian with silver-blond hair and pale blue eyes, yet the script called for a brown haired, brown-eyed actor. *Makeup can fix that with dye and contacts, I guess.* In his mind, he was already starting the process of assimilating the role. *You're getting ahead of yourself boy, you haven't finished reading the script, nor has the big guy signed you.*

Until now he had only read the pitch, outline and a few scenes, this was his first complete read-through. Anders' other concern were the two graphic sex scenes. *Show off, you were the one who suggested full nudity.* He was never ashamed of his body, but from previous experience, performing simulated sex in front of a camera and crew, made him feel vulnerable and in need of a long shower after the day's shoot. However, he knew the need of the scenes to tell the full story. *You'll just have to suck it up and enjoy yourself. And stay clear of the donuts on the craft services table.* He sank back into the lounge as he read. *I wonder who'll play the girl.*

Transfixed by the storyline, he read like the relentless tide below. Suddenly he stopped and started scanning quickly forward through several pages. *What?* He counted the pages. *Thirty-four pages and my character can't speak, can't even move. Man, that's crap. That's a lot of screen time.* He sat up as he read the pages, pausing only now and then to ponder a line. *This will take more balls to do than ten sex scenes. Wow, whoever wrote this has to be out of their friggin mind.* He sprung to his feet. *This is a killer. I don't know if I can pull this off, but I sure as hell want to give it a try.*

Too excited to sit, he started pacing as he read the final pages, so engrossed he didn't take notice of the sky's first flashes of sunset. *The end,* he flung the script to the floor in excitement. *Holy shit, what an ending!* He blinked, reoriented and sucked in a breath to yell to the setting sun. "Yes! I want it!" Ecstatic, he strained to force himself to calm down. He gazed wild-eyed at the sunset, took another deep breath, and gradually gained control of his emotions.

Confident in his decision, he pulled the door open and stepped back inside. He noticed the color of his suit reflected in the glass and looked at his sleeve. *Strange, in this light it looks brown.* He walked down the long empty hall to the central reception area. The walls of the corridor were translucent. Within them appeared vast prisms of light, seemingly drawn in from the setting sun. The colors stretched all the way to the reception area.

When he approached the receptionist, she smiled up at him. He returned her smile.

"I see you are going to take the role."

"How do you know?"

"Look at yourself." She pointed to a full-length mirror on the wall.

Transformed, his platinum hair had turned auburn with wavy curls and his eyes had changed to chestnut. He appeared to have grown in stature too, with wider shoulders, and a cleft had appeared in his chin. He had become a rugged, French-German, thirty-four year old.

"How do they do that, some kind of trick mirror?"

The receptionist's smile broadened. "FX. You can go in, he is waiting for you."

"Thank you."

"Good luck sir," she added. "I hope you get it."

Suddenly the realization kicked him. He didn't have the part yet. *Damn I hate this.* Anders rotated on his heels and stared down the long passage to his final obstacle. He clenched his teeth, cracked his knuckles, stuck out his chin and declared, "This is it."

With determination in his stride, he was on the way to his last hurdle. *Three screen tests, six months of screwing around with the casting director, meeting with writers and arguing with my agent, all their games and so far all I have is, 'it looks promising.' Now, it comes to this, the meeting with the big boss.* Stopped in front of the massive carved oak double doors, he filled his lungs. *Let me get this, please.*

The doors open. The breath pushed out of his chest. Trying not to tremble, he stepped into the odd angled, cathedral sized office. The bronze colored iridescent walls dwarfed him. Before him, windows from floor to ceiling overlooked the sea. In front of the windows, an enormous, sleek, marble and glass desk was set like an altar. Behind it, a huge chair faced the windows. On the glass top of the desk was a leather-bound book, and beside it a gold and rosewood fountain pen. *That's a good sign, I hope.* Facing the desk was a single metallic and black leather chair with a matching side table set with a tea service. *The hot seat.*

Anders nervously approached the desk with his scruffy script in hand, stopped and waited acknowledgement. His focus drifted to the huge mahogany bookshelves filled with an endless number of identical leather-bound books, *scripts,* all named and numbered with gold Roman numerals on the spine. *Wonder just how many he's produced?* Anders forced himself to stand still, stop clutching his fists, and even harder, quiet his thoughts. Patience was not his greatest virtue.

Slowly the imposing chair turned. Anders heart pounded in his ears. *Don't let him see you sweat.* An elegant, gray haired gentleman in a dark business suit, sat in the chair. His dark eyes focused on him and his gaze scrutinized him from head to foot before acknowledging him with a nod. Thereupon, he turned back to the windows and the sunset, leaving Anders standing. The light cast gold and red hues throughout the huge office. The walls, floor, and ceiling reflect a mixture of dazzling sunset color.

"I never grow tired of it." His surprisingly gentle voice remarked.

Anders remained silent. Slowly, the chair turned back again. Anders stood motionless until the man's noble hand gestured with a, "Please, sit down."

"Thank you Sir," Anders sat attentively on the edge of the chair.

"I can see you have made your decision. You have read the final script. I think we got everything added you suggested from the outline. I had the writers make some changes to fit your unique talent and put in a couple of extra scenes just for spice. You might as well have some fun with this while you are at it." With a raised eyebrow he jokily added, "I hope we don't over expose you, if you know what I mean." He chuckled a moment, before his expression sobered. "So are you completely satisfied?"

"Yes Sir, it is little more graphic than I expected, but I'm okay with it." He couldn't hide a grin. "I practically have it memorized." Anders added, in an attempt to impress. "It is a difficult role, I didn't expect some of the twists your writers added, but I am ready for it Sir."

"Yes, it is a difficult role. Please call me Max." He scrutinized Anders again, as a father-of-the-bride inspecting a prospective son-in-law. "Few can handle such a difficult challenge. However, you have done extremely well in your previous roles."

"Thank you Sir — Max, for offering this to me, I hope I prove worthy."

"I have every confidence in you," Max smiled, "Please help yourself to some tea. I think you will like it."

"Thank you, Sir." *Oops, remember to call him Max.* Anders laid his script on the table and poured his tea, picked up the cup and saucer, and proceeded to sip it with the grace of an English aristocrat.

"So, you have studied the script well?" Max questioned again.

"Yes S — Max, every detail." It was hard for Anders to contain his excitement. Focused on Max, his hand quivered when he put the cup and saucer down on top of the script. *I hope he didn't hear the cup rattle.* About to jump out of his skin, he hoped his eagerness was not too evident. *Be cool. Act, baby, act! Remember your training.* "I especially liked the scene where he meets his future wife."

Max's smile broadened. "I thought you would." He leaned back in his great chair, his eyes brightened. "Are there any questions?"

"No Sir!" *Darn, did it again.*

"Even the ending? Are you okay with the ending?"

"Yes — Max." *Nailed it.* "Even the ending." Anders looked up with a big grin and they both chuckled. "Some ending all right — didn't see that coming."

For several moments Max stared at him. Finally, a gentle smile filled Max's expression. "Good, I see you will have an enjoyable time with this role. As you know the more difficult the role the more an actor grows and the sooner one reaches their goal."

"Yes Max, I know what you mean.

Opening the leather cover of the script on his desk, Max looked down at the title page. "So from here on, you shall be called John, Jonathan Zachary Michaels," He picked up the pen and made a notation on the page, blotted it, and gently closed it. "You are cast."

For an instant, Anders thought his heart had stopped. His body went limp. He had to catch himself before he fell out of the chair.

Max slipped a contract out from under the script, a single sheet of parchment paper, and held it out along with the pen. "Please read and sign this."

Anders read the contract in silence until the last line. 'I, Jonathan Zachary Michaels, understand the consequences of accepting the starring role in, *The Incarnation of John Michaels*, and I hereby accept the role of Jonathan, known as John, of my own free will.' He glanced up at Max. "Excuse me, but this part reads, 'I, Jonathan Zachary Michaels'. Shouldn't it read Anders — ?"

"No son, from now until the final wrap at the end of shooting, you are John Michaels.

He grinned as he prepared to sign the contract. He watched the gold tip of the pen scroll out effortlessly, Jonathan Zachary Michaels, in a handwriting he had never seen before. He gazed at the document a moment before returning it.

"Please keep the pen, you may find another use for it someday." Max blotted the signature and tucked the contract inside the leather cover.

"Thank you, I will cherish this always." John put the pen in his pocket.

Max looked up, and once again rotated his chair to the windows. They both gazed at the magnificent sunset. The colors continue to change with the fluidity of a watercolor painting.

"Beautiful, isn't it?" Max asked.

"I will miss it," John replied. He stood and continued to enjoy the view.

"There will be others John, you'll see." Max assured him without turning back. After a long pause, he said, "Now John it's time for you to go."

"Yes Sir." John took one last look around the room. "Well Max, thank you again." *John, I've got to get used to my new name.* He waited for a moment, but when Max did not move, he reached for his copy of the script. Moving the teacup, he saw the stain it left on the blue coversheet. An immense surge of excitement engulfed him as he picked up his script and started for the door.

"I will keep an eye on your progress."

John turned back once more. The colors of the sunset had changed to a brilliant yellow-gold. The sun was now at the horizon and shafts of radiant light created a sunburst behind the great chair.

The doors opened behind him. Beaming, he strode toward the receptionist sitting at her desk. Upon his approach, she eagerly greeted him with her brilliant smile.

"Congratulations Mr. Michaels, everything is ready. Please step into the elevator on the right."

Mr. Michaels? Oh now I get it, getting me in character. "Thank you! Thank you, thank you," John shouted. He leaned over her desk and kissed her on the cheek.

She blushed and put her hand to her face. He took her other hand in his and said one last, "Thank you," before he turned and bolted for the elevator.

"Oh, Mr. Michaels, I'm sorry, but you will have to leave that copy of the script with me." She had followed him and was holding out her hand.

He stopped and looked at the script before reluctantly giving it to her. "I guess I'll have to do a lot of improvisation."

She took hold of the script. "That's the way the boss likes it, spontaneous. If needed, the script girl will prompt you." She clutched the script. "Thank you John, I'll keep it safe for you. We'll be watching."

He stepped up to the elevator. Immediately the doors opened and he stepped in, turned and waved. "See you." The translucent metallic doors of the elevator swished closed and he was alone.

To the right of the doors of the cylindrical elevator car was a panel with only three buttons. The bottom button was marked BEGIN, the second STOP, and the top button was marked RETURN. Adrenalin pumped through his veins. Anxiously, he wrung his hands, filled his lungs and pushed, BEGIN.

The elevator started to move with a faint whizz in a quick smooth descent. The downward movement was visible through its walls. It accelerated. Abruptly the elevator car passed out of the shaft and into space. Stars streamed passed, faster and faster, blurring, until he had to close his eyes to keep from getting dizzy.

The speed of the elevator's car increased. He felt weightless, and sensed his clothes beginning to evaporate until he stood stripped of everything. In the dim light, he was naked and entirely alone. Disoriented, his thoughts clouded, fear overcame him and he folded to the floor. The elevator car moved faster until there was no longer a sense of time or speed. "Oh God, what have I done!"

Overwhelming panic gripped him moments before his last memories evaporated.

CHAPTER 2

A LIFE BEGINS

THE INCARNATION OF JONATHAN ZACHARY MICHAELS

FADE IN:

INT.-THE GREAT VOID-DAY-APRIL 11, 1963

An undulating sea of dark deep red tones fills the screen. SFX, muffled sounds of a hospital delivery room and unintelligible voices.

OPENING CREDITS

> MALE NARRATOR (VO)
> A solitary soul slumbers alone in the perpetually dark life-giving sea of a womb. A sole sperm and a single egg have found each other and formed a being far greater than its parts. It called out to the infinite universe for an essence, that entity called a spirit, to join it and when it did, it became a human life.
>
> Rudely disturbed by a dull thud and a strange gurgle, that human's peaceful slumber suddenly ends. He looks into the dim red glow. Voices mumble unclear words in a yet unlearned language. He senses the impending event. So far, his environment has been warm and comfortable, but recently a sure and steady pressure has been building.

> Abruptly there is a burst of pres-
> sure, unbearable pushing in all di-
> rections. The unsuspecting infant
> panics. Restrained and unable to
> breath, he kicks. The darkness turned
> to a brilliant red glow accompanied
> by jarring crashes of some ancient
> cymbals, shattering all his senses.

CUT TO:

INT.-DELIVERY ROOM-SAN JOSE, CA.-CONTINUES

> DOCTOR AND NURSES busily delivering baby JOHN.
> SARAH, the mother is on the delivery table, STEVE, the
> father, in medical gown and mask, holds his wife's
> hand.

> SARAH (screams)
> Oh God, help me. Oh! No, God, do
> something!

"Here it comes." The doctor announces. "Okay. Now Sarah, one more push."

"No! Oh no, I can't, damn it, I can't," The frightened mother screams.

"Good, now push." The dispassionate doctor commanded.

"I can't, oh God, I can't." Sarah shrieked, as her insides seem to give way.

Steve's panic shows in his eyes, Sarah squeezes his hand.

"Watch the daddy!" An observant nurse from across the room yelled.

"Got him covered." A nearby nurse answered.

"Here it comes!" The doctor's voice echoed with reassurance. "Here it is. It's, it's . . . a boy."

The noise of the delivery room surged to the crescendo of an orchestra tuning-up. Over the noise, Sarah heard the slap of the doctor's hand giving her newborn son a merciless swat on his flushed bare buttock, a barbaric welcome to the harsh reality of life on Earth.

The baby belted out a cry. Sarah, herself a nurse, understood this chaotic, distorted, upside-down world of the delivery room that greeted her son as he drew his first breath. Now with lungs freshly filled, he proclaimed with displeasure, his arrival.

Between the nurses, Sarah could see someone put drops into her son's eyes. She looked up to her husband while he watched in awe, as his son was washed with a harsh cloth, scrubbed dry by a ruff towel, unceremoniously examined, poked, weighted, measured, diapered and finally wrapped in blanket. Steve's joy filled the room.

Sarah, still drenched in the toils of giving birth, looked up into the eyes of her beaming husband. The surgical mask had slipped revealing his broad rugged face and dimpled chin. They smiled at each other and tears of joy filled their eyes. A nurse placed their son in Sarah's arms. Steve cautiously reached out and touched his son's soft cheek with the back of his index finger. His large hand dwarfed the tiny child.

"He's your son Steve," Sarah whispered. "Are you pleased?"

Steve looked down." Tears dripped from his chin as he struggled to speak. "He's perfect — you're perfect — my Madonna and Child. I love you so much . . . ."

"Have you chosen a name?" The nasally nurse interrupted.

Sarah looked up at Steve and smiled. "Yes, John, his name is Jonathon Zachary Michaels."

"That sounds like a sturdy name." The nurse replied.

"Yes, John is after my father and Zachary after my partner." Steve added.

"That must be some partner."

"He is," Sarah added, "The very best."

"We will get the new momma and son back to their room, if papa will excuse us for a while." The nurse instructed. "If you will wait in the waiting room, I will call you as soon as we are ready."

"Yeah, sure, will you be all right?" He asked his wife. "Oh of course you will." He answered himself. "I'll be right outside if you need me."

"We'll be fine. Go get some coffee and call the folks, tell them they have a grandson." Sarah directed Steve, over the nurse hustling him out of the delivery room.

"You know, we are just beginning to allow fathers in the delivery room for the birth." The nurse told Sarah "He did well, only thought we would lose him one time."

"He's a cop. He's pretty good at keeping himself together."

"I'm impressed, he's going to make a great father I'm sure."

"So am I."

"We'll take you back to your room in a few minutes. Meanwhile I need to take Mr. John to the nursery."

"Oh, can't I hold him just a little longer?"

"You will have plenty of time to hold him. Right now the pediatrician needs to check him over."

"There's nothing wrong with him, right?"

"Heavens no, it's just routine. Someone will bring him in for his first feeding. Meanwhile you need to rest."

*   *   *

With her dark blond hair pulled back and her bright blue eyes still a bit puffy, Sarah felt like a well-used dishrag, wrung out and tossed in a hospital bed. Drained, she still beamed at the bundle cuddled in her arm. Baby John slept in innocence. Exhausted, the new mother couldn't hide her joy and the pride.

"Hello there little guy." Steve cooed. He had ditched the hospital garb for a blue plaid shirt and khakis. "Welcome to your new family little guy." He gazed intently at his son, smiling and shaking his head in wonderment. "Oh God, Sarah, he's beautiful."

"He looks like you." Sarah replied.

"Do you think so? I think he looks like you, all pink and sweet."

"He's got your brown eyes."

"How can you tell?" Steve questioned.

"A mother can tell."

"But he's got your nose. He kinda looks like your father in some of your Mom's old pictures of him."

"You think so?" Sarah smiled.

"Yes, I think he looks like his Grandpa and his mommy." Steve assured her. "He's got your funny little turned up nose, not the Michaels' schnozzle, like his father."

Sarah reached up to Steve with her free hand, the IV drip still attached and pulled him to her, gave him a kiss, before she ran her fingers across his nose. She whispered, "I don't see anything wrong with your nose." She kissed him once more. "I love you."

"Oh God, I love you too," Steve managed to get out, before tears welled up in his eyes again. He kissed Sarah, then his son's forehead, and Sarah once again.

All of a sudden, the door opened and someone thrust a large teddy bear into the room. The oversized stuffed bear bounced up and down at the end of a long arm, a voice boomed from the hall and declared, "Happy Birth Day, Baby Michaels."

Zach, Steve's partner, a teddy bear of a man himself, burst in the hospital room, in police uniform. Suddenly in the moment of his exuberance, he realized that he might be disturbing the newborn. Cautiously, he tiptoed to the foot of the bed and grinned. He looked at the newborn in Sarah's arms and then the huge teddy bear in his. "Maybe it's a little big." He sat the bear on the foot of the bed. Sarah watched his eyes study the sleeping baby before turning to Steve and finally back to her. He asked, "It's all right, I mean everything is all right, isn't it?"

"Yes." Sarah answered.

"It's a boy, we named him, Jonathan," Steve said, with an almost teasing smile.

"Good name," Zach agrees.

"After my father," Sarah added.

"John Zachary," Steve went on.

"Zachary, after a very special friend." Sarah added quickly.

It took a moment for it to sink in, and then Zach gasps. "Oh my God, me?"

"Yes you." Steve grinned. The two men give each other a hug, a deeply shared moment between two friends. After Zach pulled away from Steve, he leaned over and kissed Sarah on the cheek.

"Do you want to hold him?" She asked.

"Oh yes." Zach reached out but stopped and looked at this hands and his uniform, "Not now, I've been at work all day. Let me get cleaned up. Besides, he's sleeping. Nadia and I will come back later, if that's okay?"

"Sure. We were wondering, hoping, that maybe you and Nadia, ah — ." Steve hesitated and glanced at Sarah. "Will you and Nadia be his Godparents?" Steve asked.

"Of course, we'd be honored to be little John Zachary Michaels' Godparents."

"I want somebody I can really trust to be there if something should happen."

"Stop it Steve. Nothin' is gonna happen to you."

"I know" Steve said unconvincingly "It's like an insurance policy. You hope you never need it, but it's nice to have just in case."

"Is he like this about everything at home?" Zach asked Sarah.

"Yes, he has insurance on everything, and he's always full of what ifs." Sarah saw the hurt expression in Steve's eyes. "But I wouldn't want him any other way."

"I just thought he was that way at work." Zach grabbed the stuffed teddy bear off the foot of the bed. Animating its arms, he gave the stuffed toy a voice. "Hey Little John, sometimes your dad acts like a big worry-wart." Zach glanced at Steve, his disapproval obvious. "But, you can tell us apart. He's the one with the big frown on his face."

"It's not funny."

"I'm not trying to make fun of you. Just trying to tell you, lighten up a little."

"I'll try, I promise."

"Good, well I'm gonna scoot, see you later." Zach put the bear back on the bed.

Steve watched Zach leave then turned his attention to Sarah. "Do you really think I worry too much?"

"A little. But, I mean it. I wouldn't want you any other way. I love you just the way you are."

"Oh Honey, I love you and John so much. I just want us to be a happy family forever and ever. But sometimes this fear creeps over me and I — ."

"I understand, but we can't let it spoil our day."

The couple beamed at baby John, asleep in Sarah's arms. She felt the power of love and their joy fill the room.

"I promise you, I will never desert my family."

CHAPTER 3

THE CHRISTENING

INT.-FIRST PRESBYTERIAN CHURCH-July 14, 1963

Family and friends of Steve and Sarah Michaels fill
the first several rows of pews in the stately old Los
Gatos Church. The regular Sunday service has ended and
the anticipated christening of Jonathan Zachary
Michaels is about to take place. Zach and his wife
NADIA stand beside Steve and Sarah with baby John in
her arms at the baptismal font

    The voice of the minister, PASTOR PATTERSON, a
wily old Scotsman, echoes through the vastness of the
church.

                  PASTOR PATTERSON
        Our gracious and merciful heavenly
        Father, we present unto Thee this Thy
        servant. Clothe him we pray, with the
        whole armor of God--.

"How much longer is this guy going to go on? Steve whispered to Sarah.

"Shush, behave yourself." Sarah managed to give Steve a discreet elbow to the ribs, he ex-haled a puff of air.

A precocious two-year-old standing on the third pew, slipped off, landed on the floor, and let out a loud cry. Only her pride injured, she quickly climbed back up and stood quietly, for the moment, by her father.

Granny, Steve's grandmother, in a conservative dark dress and hat, smiled with amusement and winked at Steve.

Granny's hanging in. Steve spotted Sarah's father yawn. *Give a preacher a few new faces in their pews and they will preach them in to submission.* Steve let out a soft moan and whispered to Sarah. "He'd get more new members if he talked less. I'm getting hungry. I'm sure everyone else is too." Steve quickly leaned out of elbow range.

The Pastor placed his hand on John and continued, "Zachary and Nadia James, I charge you before God and this Congregation, as Godparents, to take on the responsibility of this child's spiritual upbringing and to uplift this family in prayer and vigilance against all evil. Do you so swear?"

"We Do." Zach and Nadia answer in unison.

The Pastor directed Sarah to hold baby John so his head was over the font. In a flurry, Pastor pulled up the sleeves of his robes, put one hand under the infant and with his other hand, dripped water onto the infant's forehead. In a resounding voice he declared, "Jonathan Zachary Michaels, in obedience to His command, I now baptize you in the name of the Father and of the Son and the Holy Ghost. Amen."

Baby John fussed as the cold waters dripped across his brow. Taking a small towel, the Minister patted the excess water from the baby's face. Sarah gently cuddled him to her and he quieted. The Minister nodded to the organist, and with the introduction to *Amazing Grace*, he waved his hand for the congregation to stand.

Sarah looked up at the pipes of the organ. The sunlight streamed through the striking stained glass window and flooded over the joyful gathering. Women in hats and gloves, and the men in suits, little girls in white dress and boys in jackets with short pants, all sang with gusto.

The hymn ended on an all stops pulled cord from the organ, sustained longer than anyone had breath. Straightway the Minister offered his final benediction. "The Lord Bless you and keep you: the Lord make His face to shine upon you, and be gracious unto you: the Lord lift up his countenance upon you, and give you peace. Amen."

"A — men." Steve's voice rang out above the Pastor and the congregation.

A buzz rose from the people. They greeted each other and the beaming parents, grandparents and Godparents. Children, overlooked by their parents busy with handshakes and hugs, darted between the adults, releasing their pent-up energy. The guests worked slowly up the aisle toward the back of the church, poured out the great doors, down the steps, to come to a stop on the sidewalk.

Everyone had cameras and insisted on taking pictures. Steve and Sarah Michaels along with Zach and Nadia patiently stood and posed, but baby Michaels began to show his impatience with the whole affair. It is now passed feeding time by a good hour and his fussing was about to turn to all out displeasure with a loud vocal protest.

"We need to get going." Sarah insisted as John continued to fuss. "You have all afternoon to boast."

"I'm not boasting." Steve muttered through his teeth to Sarah.

"Well whatever, John-John needs his diaper changed and a bottle."

"I'll get your folks and we'll go." Steve agreed.

"Open the car door first," Sarah, instructed. She stood with baby, diaper bag, and purse in her arms.

Frenzied, Steve felt for his keys, checked and rechecked his pockets. He started to panic. Sarah pointed, "They're in the ignition. Some cop."

"Oh no." He moaned grabbing Sarah's locked door. They were Sarah's keys. He had lost his somewhere at the house that morning. "Some cop all right." He muttered.

Sarah only smiled. Forgetfulness was only one manifestation of excitement over the birth of their son. Sarah has been constantly amused at Steve's recent behavior. She had reassured him that he is not the first man in the world to have a son. Nevertheless, she was pleased he thought he was.

Sarah could see through the window that the driver's door button was up. "Your door is unlocked." She said relieved.

Without a word from either, Steve quickly stepped around the car, opened his door, and unlocked Sarah's door. He sheepishly returned to help mother and now loudly complaining son into the car. Sarah's parents arrived at the car and climbed into the back seat.

"Honey, will you get out a bottle?" She asked, before Steve slid in behind the wheel.

"Where are they?"

"In the diaper bag."

"Are you feeding him enough?" Sarah's mother asked.

"Are you kidding?" Steve replied. He passed Sarah a bottle. "He's eating us out of house and home."

"Well, I don't think he's getting enough solids, doctors don't put babies on solids soon enough these days," Sarah's mother continued. "He's a big baby, like your brother, and he gets too hungry between feedings."

"Yes mother." Sarah acknowledged and put the nipple in the hungry mouth.

Steve started the car, pulled away from the curb, sounding the horn. The remainder of the gathering, still visiting in front of the church, started for their vehicles. Leisurely, Steve drove away while an impromptu caravan followed. Baby John struggled to stay awake and suck his bottle, but the drone of the motor soon put him asleep. The eventful morning had caught up with him.

"How many are coming to the house?" Sarah's mother asked, looking out the back window at the increasing motorcade.

"About forty-five," Sarah answered.

"Oh dear, where are you going to put them?"

Keeping his eyes on the road ahead, Steve assured his mother-in-law, "I got it covered. I've setup the yard and rented extra tables and chairs. I think we have enough room. Dad, can I call on you to kinda tend bar? Keep an eye on things, you know, ice, glasses, and stuff, it's self-help. Zach will take care of the keg. Most of the guys are beer drinkers."

"Whatever you want me to do?" Sarah's father agreed, a kindly man with a full head of white hair and penetrating sad eyes.

"Mom you can help Sis with the salads," Sarah suggested.

"That will be fine, but don't you over do it, you hear?

"Yes, Mom."

Steve turned onto the expressway and sped up. In a few minutes, they would be home.

*   *   *

"I'm tellin' ya Steve, now's the time. You can't do better than now." Bob insisted as he tended the barbeque, a homemade unit built from a fifty-five gallon drum. The grill sizzled with chicken, tri-tip, and hot dogs for the kids. Bob was round, not fat, but round like the Pillsbury Dough-boy. A veteran cop of twenty-five years, he was about to retire and start a second career in real estate.

"I'll think about it." Steve agreed.

"Listen, it's time for action, a thirty-five hundred square foot, semi-custom house on a full acre and a half, for under thirty-four grand Steve, what's there to think about?" Bob turned and stood with his hand on his hips and waited for an answer.

"I don't want to get into any shady real estate deals."

"This isn't a shady deal. They're offering a legitimate discount to cops and firemen, because they want to build a good community, that's all."

"But it's so far out."

"Out? It's Camden Avenue. It's 1963 man, in ten years Cambrian Park will be the heart of the Santa Clara Valley."

"Okay, I'll talk to Sarah and maybe take a look, but no promises."

"You won't be sorry."

"Steve!" Zach yelled from across the yard. "I need you over here for a minute."

"I'll catch you latter." Steve assured Bob and hastily retreated in Zach's direction. "What'd you need Zach?"

"I thought you might need this." Zach handed Steve a cold beer. "And a break from the sales pitches."

"Thanks." Steve took a drink and looked at his twenty-year-old, ticky-tacky house, a small two bedroom one bath, a postwar baby boom-ers deluxe. He and Sarah bought the house as a starter five years before on a GI loan. He knew it was time to trade up.

"I was leading him on a bit," Steve confided. "I've been talking to Aaron Futter. He's getting into real estate law and financial planning. He thinks the Cambrian Park project would be a super investment. I've picked out a large lot. It's at the end of a cul-de-sac. Aaron's found out that someone goofed with subdivision plans on the lot next door. They didn't map a county easement, so a home won't fit on the lot properly. Aaron is talking with developers. They are willing to sell the odd lot at a big discount. We are waiting for an okay from the county planner to merge the lots. That will give me three acres."

"You fox. But isn't Aaron a public defender?"

"Yeah, but he's getting out of that, going in to financial and business law. Sarah and I have already decided to put our house up for sale. I believe that with what we have in savings and the sale of our house, we'll be in great shape. I'm going to tell Bob next week. He'll get full commission."

"You just want to see him dance a little longer?" Zach said with a wicked grin. "Maybe sweetening the deal a little too?"

A group of kids playing tag ran between Zach and Steve. One little guy hid behind Steve, grabbed his leg and peeked around. When he looked up and realized he didn't know Steve, he ran off.

"This place is too small to raise a family. I'm going to provide my wife and kids with the biggest and best house I can possibly afford. Something I can be proud of, and live in the rest of my life. And if something should happen to me, Sarah and John will never have to worry. I've got it all fixed up through Aaron. Never want my family to go through what my mother and I did. I'll make sure they always have a roof over their heads."

"Good for you." Zach poured a beer for himself. "Can you trust Aaron?"

"Sure, known him for years. We went to high school together. After graduation I went to Korea, he went to Stanford."

"Good choice — for him. Need a refill?"

"Good choice for me too. You can top it off. Thanks again for standing up with me today. Promise me, if anything happens you will be a father to my boy."

Zach frowned. "I keep tellin' you, don't talk like that, nothing's going to happen to you."

"Promise, I don't want my son to be without a father. Promise and I promise I'll never bring it up again."

"You know I will always be there for John."

Guests were arriving by both the front door and back gate. The backyard with its ample shade was abuzz. Tables and chairs sat in the shade with a long serving table near the barbeque. Sarah and her mom were in the house sending the guests that came in the front way to the backyard. Everyone knew everyone well enough that formal introductions were not needed. With this group, you couldn't be a stranger for long anyway. Two of Steve's co-workers had skipped the christening and worked on their specialty, barbeque. Now the party was shifting into full gear and Steve was pleased.

"You have a fine looking son Steve. Congratulations!" Jane said. She and her husband Bill had just come through the gate.

"It took you long enough. Six years?" Bill harassed. He had been a classmate of Steve's at the police academy.

"Yeah, well thank you, but it was worth the wait."

"Is he gonna be a cop like his ol' man?" Bill asked.

"God, I hope not." Steve quickly responded.

"What, bein' a cop ain't good enough for him?"

Steve saw the defensiveness in Bill's eyes. Even he was surprised at his quick answer. The truth being, with all his planning, the thought of John following his example hadn't even entered his mind.

"I didn't mean it to come out like that." Steve paused to gather his thoughts for a moment. "I want him to be, whatever he wants to be."

"That's a copout. There're a lot worse things than bein' a cop." Bill waited for a response.

"Yeah, I know, but there are something's better too . . . . I just want him to be the man, the Big Guy wants him to be."

"I don't think, God's wants, have anything to do with it."

"Now Bill, don't start that." Jane interceded by taking her husband's hand.

"I don't know," Steve smiled, "I think it's all planned. Life is more than just chance."

Steve knew Bill was holding his tongue. Everyone knew there would be hell to pay from Jane if he didn't. He was notorious for starting arguments with anyone, about anything, but when Jane was around he was a pussycat.

"How about a beer, Hon?" Jane suggest, directing Bill toward Zach and the keg with a little push. Once she was sure, Bill was heading in the right direction she turned to Steve. "I must say, you sure picked a great day for a barbeque. Is Sarah in the house?"

Steve nodded. "Yes she's——."

"Well I'll talk to you later." Jane's voice trailed off as she scurried across the yard toward the back door.

Steve looked back at the house just in time to glimpse the dark figure of his Granny, looking at him from the kitchen window. His grandmother on his father's side, Granny was a fine old French woman from New Orleans. He lifted his glass and smiled at her. She waved back before disappearing into the room. She and his mother were the only living members of his family. His father, a U.S. Army MP, died in the Pacific near the beginning of World War II, leaving him and his mother to fend for themselves. They lived with Granny for several years before his mother got a decent job with Lockheed and they could move to their own apartment in Sunnyvale.

*   *   *

"He's beautiful Sarah," Lisa cooed. She sat in a chair next to the bassinette, stationed in the middle of the tiny living room. Lisa was a substantial woman and the only one of Sarah's schoolmates from nurse's training that was not married.

"Thank you, we think we'll keep him." Sarah joked.

"Are you going back to work soon?" Lisa asked.

"No, Steve wants me to wait at least until John is in kindergarten."

"That's a good dad. But can he swing it on a cop's salary?"

"He thinks he can."

"John's got his father's beautiful brown eyes," Joan spoke up from across the room.

Fussed over far too much, John let's out a wale in protest.

"And his mouth too," Lisa kidded.

"He looks just like his father did at that age." Granny observed, in her velvety gentle voice that carried just a hint of a southern accent. She had settled into a rocker near the bassinette.

"Well I can see some of Sarah in him too." Sarah's mother added, not wanting the Miller family excluded.

"Thank you mom, but I don't mind him taking after his father. I think he's a pretty swell guy."

Sarah's mother picked up Baby John and cuddled him. "He's handsome as his father and sweet as his mother. Do you want to hold your great-grandson, mother Michaels?"

Granny held out her arms and Sarah's mother handed her the baby. Sarah watched Granny cuddle baby John, rock him in her arms and smile. The old woman suddenly froze and looked deep into the child's eyes. Abruptly the room dimmed. Out the window, Sarah saw a small white cloud has passed before the sun. Granny and baby looked at each other, Sarah could see a sadness come over the old lady's countenance. The cloud passed and the sun once again streamed in the window. Granny trembled and held out baby John for Sarah. Sarah took her son, kissed him, and held him safe in her arms. She saw that Granny was still trembling and looking fearful.

"What's wrong Granny?" Sarah asked with concern.

Granny stared off into space but didn't answer. Sarah, concerned, called out the window. "Steve, Steve, can you come in here? Quickly please."

Steve responded to Sarah's call and dashed into the house. "What's wrong?" He asked rushing to Sarah. He looked at his son then back to Sarah for the cause of the alarm. "It's Granny," She motioned with a nod of her head.

Abruptly, Granny raised her arm, pointed her finger into space, and began to speak in an unusually loud voice with a strong southern drawl. "Whoa Lord! Tis dark, tis very dark."

"What's dark Granny? What do you see?" Steve questioned.

"My, my, 'dis child has chosen a dark and difficult path. A path o' heartache and sorrows, such as no man should have ta walk." Suddenly she yelled out to an unseen presence. "Why? Why, you let 'im choose 'dis way Lord? Why?"

She fell back in the chair in a swoon. Steve rushed to her side, took her hand and patted it. She quickly recovered. Baby John started to cry. Sarah comforted softly. "Hush, hush, it's okay."

"Are you all right Granny?" Steve asked.

"Oh my yes Son." She answered in her usual gentle woody voice.

"You have given us a little start there." Steve said.

Sarah saw the concern in Steve's expression. He studied the old woman's face. "Can I get you anything?"

"Yes." She gazed slowly around the room, took a somewhat embellished breath, leaned over to Steve, and whispered. "Can you get me a beer?"

Steve chuckled, looked up at Sarah and smiled. Patting Granny's hand, he said, "Anything you want Granny."

*   *   *

By the time Steve returned with the beer, Sarah had convinced most of the guests that it was time to make their way to the backyard to eat. Baby John was sleeping peacefully in his bassinette and Granny was sitting quietly in her chair.

"Here yeah go Granny."

"Ah, thanks!" She reached for the paper cup of beer with both hands and held it like a communion chalice for a moment before taking a respectable drink. "That hit the spot." She licked her lips and then grinned.

Steve sat on the footstool in front of the dear woman, and smiled. Granny has always liked her beer, he remembered. "So now, what was all that about?"

"Steven, you have a very special son."

"I know."

"He's got a tough road ahead."

"Why do you say that?"

"I can't say why, I just know, he has chosen a tough life. You mind me, you teach him well." She wagged her boney finger in his face. "Do you understand?"

"No! I don't understand," Steve admitted.

"You have ta trust in the Lord and you teach him well, right from wrong, about love, no secrets, show him how to be a man and he'll make it all right. That's all I got to say." Granny sat back in her chair and took another drink of her beer.

Steve was used to her insights, and sometime strange pronouncement. On the night his father died, she got up at three in the morning, dressed in black, and at three-twenty-two, on the dot, began crying, "My son is gone. My son is gone." She refused food or solace for three days. That day the Army notified the family. It turned out she began crying the exact instant he died.

"I got somethin' for you son." Granny gingerly placed her near empty cup on the end table and started fishing for something in her oversized handbag. "Tain't right the little one gets all the gift's." She pulled a brown paper wrapped package from her bag. "Here, this is for you. Someday you can pass it on to John."

"Thank you." Steve knew by the feel it was a book. He carefully removed the wrappings. He was right. It was a brown leather bound, book with a gold stamped title on the spine, "Great Expectations," he read aloud and opened the book. "The pages are blank." He looked up a Granny puzzled.

"Read the title again, carefully."

"Great—Greater, Greater Expectations. Author, Michaels."

"That's for you to fill in. The expectations and the outcomes."

"I don't know that I'm much of a writer, but I'll try."

Steve stood, placed the book on the end table and extended his hand. Granny placed her right hand in his. He could feel her twisted arthritic bones through her thin skin. "Now, are you ready for some lunch?" He helped her to her feet.

"I've been smellin' that barbeque cookin' all afternoon. Reminds me of the old days in New Orleans. I'm so hungry I could eat a whole chicken, all by myself."

"Give me your arm." They started toward the kitchen. Granny clung to his side more for comfort then help. *It just wouldn't seem normal, if Granny didn't have some sort of vision.*

They made their way gradually across the kitchen linoleum toward the backdoor. He looked back over his shoulder at his son sleeping in the living room. *I wonder what she saw.*

*   *   *

"Steve, can you come here a minute?" Sarah called from the living room window.

"Just a second, one last table to fold up and I'll be done."

Sarah looked at her mother's list of christening gifts, and who had given what. She repeatedly checked all the cards herself. There was definitely no match.

Steve came through the kitchen. "There, all done, the yard's cleaned up and everything is put away. So what's up?"

"There is a gift that I can't match with the giver. I've checked every-thing over several times. It's sure a strange gift for a baby."

"What is it?"

"This." She held out a small box.

Steve looked at the folded card attached to the box and read it aloud. "To baby Jonathan Zachary Michaels." He turned the card over. There was no name. He looked at Sarah, puzzled. "It's not signed."

"I know. Look inside."

Steve opened the box. Sarah could see by his expression, he was as mystified as she was.

"Who would give a baby a fountain pen as a christening gift?"

"That's what I thought. It's beautiful. I think it's solid gold and may-be rosewood. But it's not a baby's gift."

"Well maybe somebody thinks he'll use it someday."

CHAPTER 4

ONE COOL DUDE

EXT.-MICHAELS BACKYARD-14 YEARS LATER-MARCH 19, 1977

Two teenage boys in swimsuits sit in a private corner
of the yard near the pool of the Michael's upper-
middle class suburban, Cambrian Park home. Beach
towels are draped between the fence and a lounge for
privacy. In their seclusion, the boys huddle over a
stag magazine. John Michaels now thirteen, mature,
ruggedly good looking, reads the magazine. ALVIN
ZAPPA, a mousey looking kid, immature thirteen year
old with dark saggy hair and thick black rimmed
glasses sits next to John. The boys are best friends
and classmates. SANDY a yellow Lab, lies beside them.

                    ALVIN
        Turn the Page.

                    JOHN
        I haven't finished reading it yet.

                    ALVIN
        You're not reading it. You're just
        looking at the pictures.

"I am too reading it."

"Look at the next page."

John turned the page. "Oh you got to be kidding."

"I told you there were some neat pictures in it." Alvin said, and
grinned, clearly pleased with John's interest in the magazine.

"Do you have it memorized? Where did you get it?"

"I snatched it from my brother's stash."

"Where did he get it?"

"A liquor store over on Third Street." Alvin, by habit, pushed his glasses up on his nose. "You got to be eighteen to buy them."

"Boy they show everything." John felt his unruly member responding and discreetly made an adjustment.

Sandy perked up his head, let out a bark and ran to the side yard.

"Hey Dude." A voice yelled from the side gate. "Dude, you back there?"

"Yeah Butch, open the gate and come in."

"Did you invite him?" Alvin asked with a disgusted look on his face.

"He sort of invited himself." John stood and yelled. "Come on back."

"Why can't you ever say no?"

Butch moved into the neighborhood over Christmas vacation. John tried to befriend him at school, feeling sorry for the new kid. Butch wasn't the type that fit in anywhere. His hair was so white he looked albino and with pale gray eyes, the kids called him, 'The Ghost.'

"I can't, your dog won't let me." Butch yelled.

"Sandy?" Alvin got to his feet. "He won't bite. Just open the gate. He wouldn't harm a fly."

"I can't dudes, I can't. She's trying to bite me."

Alvin glared at John. "If he bit anyone, I can't think of a worthier soul."

"We better go let him in."

When they got to the gate, Sandy was bouncing around wagging his tail. "Stay Sandy." John opened the gate and Butch, a tall stray tomcat of a kid, timidly entered. Sandy bolted at him to sniff his greeting. Butch recoiled, with raised hands. "Down Sandy, get down." John pulled him back.

"Why do dogs always have ta sniff ya there?" Butch asked in his Midwestern drawl. John was aware that Butch, a year older than him, always tried to play the tuff guy, even though he didn't act that brave.

"Just dogs I guess." Alvin answered.

"Come on back." John walked in front of Butch while Sandy led the way. Alvin followed. Did you bring your suit?

"Naw, too cold to swim."

"The pools heated."

"That's a big pool."

"My dad likes to swim."

"Nice place. Your ol' man must be rich."

"Naw, he just got a good deal. He bought the house thirteen years ago and put in the pool five years back. I though you knew, he's a cop."

"Cop?" Butch faltered in his step slightly."

"So keep your nose clean." Alvin piped up from the rear.

"You call your dog a he. From here it looks like a girl?"

"Sandy's a male. Why do you ask?"

"Well he ain't got no balls."

John stopped and looked back at Butch. "He's been neutered, so we won't have pups."

"Hope nobody cuts my balls off 'cause they don't want me to have kids."

"That's not a bad idea." Alvin stopped behind Butch by several feet, "Where are you from?"

"Nebraska." Butch answered without looking back at Alvin.

Alvin just shook his head. Holding out two fingers, he made a scissors action to John from behind Butch.

John and Alvin giggle all the way back to where they had been sitting. John could tell Butch didn't have a clue. The three settled and Sandy stayed near. John and Alvin decided to soak in the spa and let Butch entertain himself with Alvin's magazine.

Seeing Butch's interests were occupied, and certain that the sound of the spa drowned out their voices, Alvin quietly asked. "Why did you ever make friends with him?"

John shrugged his shoulders. "We're not really friends." He didn't have a good answer, "I felt sorry for the guy I guess, now I wished I'd kept my mouth shut."

"Live and learn."

When both the boys started to resemble lobsters, they pulled themselves out of the bubbling water and joined Butch. Soon all were engrossed in the magazine.

"Yum, yum, I'd like to bite those tits." Butch declared with an exaggerated lick of the air.

"Do you think those are real?" Alvin asked.

"Sure they are." Butch authenticated without hesitation. His constant sneer lent authority to anything he said about sex, the only subject he appeared to know anything about or at least pretended too.

"How do you know?" Alvin challenged.

Butch rose above the screen of towels for a precautionary check of the house then ducked back. "Look, I got a cousin you see, he knows this dame——poses for one of these magazine. He said they can't retouch or fake nothing in these pictures. None of them——it's the law."

"No Shit?" Alvin questioned wide-eyed.

"Honest ta god. I swear it." Butch crossed his heart with a melodramatic emphasis.

"I don't believe it." Alvin said, and pushed up his glasses.

"If yea don't believe me go ask his dad, he's a cop, he'll tell ya."

"Yeah sure." Alvin said. "He's going to ask his dad if the pictures in porno magazine are for real."

"It's true I tell ya," Butch contended, "It's like——like a Truth in Advertising Law."

The argument ended for the moment but John wasn't convinced. The three continued to look through the magazine, keeping watch for uninvited visitors.

"That's the way I like it." Butch pointed to a picture of a woman astride a man.

"I like it that way too," Alvin agreed.

"Crap, I bet you never had sex with a woman."

Alvin didn't respond. Another spread revealed a guy with two women. "Look at the size of that guy's——." Alvin pointed out.

"So?" Butch remarked nonchalantly. "That ain't so big."

"Yeah, right, I suppose yours is bigger." Alvin said with a laugh.

"It is——whole lot bigger." Butch gave Alvin a shove that knocked off his glasses.

"Knock it off." John jumped to his feet and stood between Butch and Alvin. "Like shit. I don't believe you. Prove it." John demanded.

"Pervert. Ya just want to look at my cock?" Butch sprang to his feet and glared down at John.

"If it's all that big, drop you pants and prove it." John stood defiantly.

"What, so you and pimple face can ogle?" Butch met the challenge.

"If you're the man you claim, prove it." John was not intimidated by the larger Butch.

Alvin pushed up his glasses and looked up at Butch and John facing off.

"It'll cost ya, twenty bucks."

"Ah, shit, you're full of it."

"That's the deals. Twenty bucks if ya want ta take a look. I might even let ya feel it——both of ya.

"You're so full of shit, you know." John tried to figure a way to end the argument without backing down.

"What's a matter, no balls like your dog?"

Just then, John's mother called from the sliding glass door of the family room. "John, is Butch out there?"

"Yeah." the three chorused.

"Butch, your mom called, she said your father's on the rampage looking for you. So you'd better get home, now."

"Ah, Gees." Butch turned, and headed for the side gate. About half way there, he turned back and after checking to see that John's mother was back inside with the door closed, he yelled. "Anytime you got your twenty bucks, give me a call." He pantomimed opening his pants and exposing himself, before he flips the guys the bird with both hands.

"What a Jackass." John murmured and sat on a lounge.

"You better believe it." Alvin joined him on the next lounge. "Thanks for stickin' up for me."

"Don't mention it."

"All that braggin', and all that stuff about girls he's done it with, do you believe him?"

"No."

Alvin sighed. "Big doesn't run in my family."

"I don't think it runs in Butch's family either. I think Butch's dick is about the size of his brain and that ain't very big."

"You got that right." Alvin tried to mimic John's father deep voice. "It isn't a question of what you have."

"It's what you do with what you've got that matters. John finished the quote and started to laugh, "But I don't think that's what he had in mind."

"Well it fits."

The two boys reclined on the lounges without speaking for a while and enjoyed what was left of the sun. A small white puff of clouds scampered across the expanse of blue like a lost pup.

"Why do you put up with all his bullshit?" Alvin finally asked.

"I don't know, kind of felt sorry for the sap. I probably shouldn't of tried to befriend him in the first place. From now on, I'll just ignore him."

"That's not you John. And you're not going to tell him to take a hike either. You're just too nice a guy to tell a jackass like that to take a hike."

John didn't answer. He knew Alvin was right.

Alvin turned to John. "You can keep the magazine."

"Thanks." John tucked the magazine under the lounge pad. "Want to hit the spa again."

"Nah, too cold." Alvin pushed at his glasses and drew a breath. "What do you think is wrong with Butch?

"My dad says that when guys are real horny they quit thinking with their brains and start thinking with their dick."

"Well my brothers are dick-brains for sure. Can't think of nothing but sex."

"Maybe it's like they say, sex will make you blind."

"What are you boys doing?" Steve asked.

John jumped at the sound of his father's voice. He stood only a few feet away. *How long has he been there?* "Just talkin'."

"Just talkin'." Steve mocked. "It must be some serious stuff you're talkin' about."

"It is." Alvin squeaked out.

"Sorry to interrupt your great conversation, but it's getting close to dinner." Steve looked at Alvin, "Are you staying for dinner? Sarah will call your mom if you'd like?"

"Sure Mr. Michaels, I'll stay."

"Well you fellows better hit the showers." He pointed at the towels. "What's this for?"

"Dryin them." John explained.

"Oh! Okay." Steve gave a knowing look at John before starting back to the house. "Take your blinds——towels in with you."

"Your dad is so cool." Alvin assured.

"Ya think so?"

They grabbed the towels and headed for the house. Once inside the bathroom John slipped off his wet trunks and got in the shower first. Alvin sat on the counter between the double basins.

"What are we gonna do about Butch?

"Hope he finds somebody else to bother." John answered.

"Yeah, I thought that would be your answer. Who would want him for a friend? He's like a damn fly, always pesterin'."

"My dad says things like that have a way of working themselves out." John stepped out of the shower, leaving the water running. "Your turn."

He chuckled to himself about Butch, as he toweled off, that Alvin wanted to ditch him too. John suddenly sobers. He felt he was reliving a moment in time.

Alvin shut off the water, gave himself a quick wipe with a towel and then wraps it around his waist. John was still looking in the mirror. "Are you wishin' or dreamin'?" Alvin asked.

"Neither. I thought I saw something—someone—not me, in the mirror. Déjà vu kinda like."

"My grandma says déjà vu is God tellin' ya, you're on the right track. Doin' what you're suppose ta be doin' in life."

"Spooky." John wrapped his towel around his waist, picked up his trunks, and opened the door. A burst of steam preceded the boys out of the bathroom. They raced down the hall to John's bedroom. Once in the bedroom, they started sorting out their clothes piled on John's bed. John's room has two single beds. One John used and the other was for a guest, Alvin being the most frequent visitor.

Neither had a chance to dress when there were two quick raps on the door. Steve stepped in, obviously angry and pushed the door closed. He tossed the stag magazine on the bed and stood with his fists on his hips. "You gentlemen forgot this." There was a cop's sternness in his voice.

The stunned boys froze. Their eyes bulged. They look at each other and back at the magazine. Eventually, Alvin bleated out, "It's mine—Sir."

"No it's not, it's mine. He gave it to me." John insisted, not willing to let his friend take the blame for his forgetfulness.

"Well whoever's it is, I don't want it lying around where you sister could find it. Is that understood, MEN?"

"Yes Sir!"

"Yes Mr. Michaels."

"Good. Now you gentlemen get dressed, dinner will be ready in ten minute." Steve turned to the door. "You know those magazines exaggerate everything. They use trick photography and airbrushing. Things aren't necessarily how they appear."

Steve closed the door behind him. John let out his breath. Alvin visibly shaken, sat on the bed.

"I told you the photos were doctored."

"If that was my ol' man, I wouldn't be able to sit-down for a week." Alvin said.

"Oh, I'll probably hear more about this."

"How did he know that we were talking about those pictures with Butch? Was he spyin' on us?"

"Dad? No, he just knows."

"Your dad is so cool."

"Yeah, but he's still a dad." John pulled on his jeans. "We'll see how cool he is." He picked up the magazine, took it to his dresser, placed it under his shirts, grabbed a blue t-shirt, and pulled it over his head. Alvin hadn't moved. "Get dressed."

*   *   *

At the dining room table Sarah, Steve and Tess, John's eleven-year-old sister, waited. Sarah has prepared a spread of meatloaf, mashed potatoes with gravy, kernel corn and a tossed green salad. John and Alvin took their usual places. Once settled, they all bowed their heads for the blessing.

"John, will you say grace?" Steve asked. John could see his father watching out of the corner of his eye.

"Lord!" John's voice cracked. His voice seldom cracked any more. Now it only happened when he's excited, nervous or under pressure.

Tess giggled. Steve cleared his throat and John knew it was his way of telling her to behave. John swallowed and tried again. "Lord, ah . . . we thank you for your blessing this day . . . and ah for our family and friends, and . . . we ask you to bless this food we are about to receive. Amen!"

The Michaels were not an especially religious family. They attend the Presbyterian Church now and then, usually around Christmas and Easter. However, Sarah insisted on grace before meals, more as a matter of manners than religious conviction.

The meal started in silence. John sensed the tension. *Is he really mad? Was Tess the one who found it?*

Tess, not accustomed to such quiet at dinner started to sing as she passed the corn to Alvin.

"Tess." Sarah whispered softly, shaking her head, no. The tension clicked up a notch.

They finished serving their plates and began to eat. The quiet emphasized by the clatter of utensils meeting china. Steve remained sober faced and the boys kept their heads down to avoid eye contact. Steve placed his fork at the side of his plate. He took a drink of water and cleared his voice for attention. "There is something we need to discuss with you boys." Steve's deep booming voice shatters the silence.

Oh God, not now. In front of Mom and Tess. John cringed at the thought and then spotted the panic look on Alvin face. He looked as if he was going to duck under the table.

"Tess, may I have some butter please?" Steve asked. The dagger stuck in John's gut, twisted. Steve slowly buttered a slice of French bread. "I was wondering——." He took a bite, chewed and swallowed before he continued. "Easter vacation is coming up in two weeks, is it not?"

"Yes," John answered cautiously.

"I was thinking, we men should go fishing for the week, if you would like?"

What? Fishing? A flood of relief washed over John.

John was too stunned to say anything. He looked at Alvin who was looking at his father like a deer caught in the headlights.

"So, would you like to do a little bass fishing?" Steve asked. "Or would you prefer spending you Easter vacation reading your magazines by the pool?

"Yeah, fishing." John couldn't help but grin. Relieved, he knew that all was okay and his dad really was one cool dude.

"Me too?" Alvin asked.

"Yes you too Alvin. I said boys. I've already checked with your folks and it's okay with them. Is there anyone else you want to bring along? Butch maybe?"

"NO!" John and Alvin answered in unison.

CHAPTER 5

THE BIRDS AND THE BEES

```
EXT. SQUAD CAR/STREET-SAN JOSE, CA-DAY-MARCH 21, 1977

Zach is driving S.J.P.D. black and white and Steve is
riding shotgun. It is a sunny spring day and they are
on a routine nuisance call.

                    FEMALE DISPATCHER (OC)
            One-twenty-six, what's your location?
```

"We are on San Carlos Boulevard, heading west at Fourteenth Street, over." Zach confirmed.

"What's your ten-twenty?" The dispatcher's voice squawked back.

"Approximately fifteen minutes, over."

"Ten-four."

"Ten-four, over and out." Zach hooked the hand mike on the dash. "So you caught little Johnny and Alvin in the backyard reading a stag magazine?"

"I didn't actually catch them with it. Butch was there. I suspected something fishy was up when I saw they had made a blind with some towels. When Alvin and John went in to change for dinner, I checked around. That's when I found it."

"Did you take it away?"

"No."

"No? I sure as hell would have."

"I figure that if they are mature enough to know what was going on in the picture they were mature enough to keep the magazine. If they aren't, taking it away would just make them more curious." Steve took a deep audible breath that was somewhere between a sigh and a moan, "He's growing up, damn near as tall as me and shaving at least a couple of time a week."

"Do you think they actually know what's goin' on in the pictures, or just hopin'?"

"It's hard to tell, isn't it? I mean, at fourteen he knows, but how much? Does a kid honestly understand sex at that age? Any age for that matter. I know at his age I thought I knew it all. Actually, I was as dumb as a stump."

"I hear ya. It scares the shit out o' me," Zach confessed. "With two girls, I don't know what to expect."

"You've got time. They're what, six and eight? Give them five years." Steve shook his head. "What pissed me off was he left the magazine in the backyard. Tess could of found it. I have no clue on how to explain something like that to her."

"I'll leave that for Nadia."

"Your time will come Papa." Steve said and laughed. "John keeps both Sarah and me hopping with all his questions. I think of myself at his age. With hormone ragging, every thought was sex related somehow. And I didn't have a man to talk to, just my mom and grandma. That's why I decided I'd be frank about everything."

"Even sex?"

"Especially sex. I answer his question truthfully and as openly as possible. I just don't want him to get careless. You know, do something stupid. Get himself in trouble. It's not that I think that every woman is a Delilah. God knows I don't. But sometimes a little flirting and a little promise can make a boy think he's in love. When he wakes up, twenty-years later he's married with a half-dozen kids."

Zach stopped for a red light.

"I'd like to keep him and Alvin away from that Butch kid. He's a little too old to be hanging around the boys. I keep hoping something will shoo him on down the road." Steve looked up a side the street as Zach drove. "I wish you could come fishing with us?"

"Sorry, Nadia would nail my hide to the garage door if I missed her family's reunion."

At the next corner, there was a group of teenage girls standing. When Zach stopped for a light, Steve notices them watching him, and smiles. They start to giggle. "Goosey Girls."

"They probably think you're flirting with them." Zach brightened up. "Hey, I got an idea. I was going to get rid of my old VW Bug. Why don't I give it to John? It needs a ton of work. It'll keep him busy for a year."

"Yeah, that's the next thing, driving. You got to let me pay you something. What about your girls?"

"Forget it, I don't want it sitting in my driveway that long and they'd never be able to keep the thing runnin'. He's my Godson, remember."

"Yeah, but he should pay you something. Have some skin in it."

"It will cost him enough to fix it up. He'll have plenty of skin in it before he's through."

"I think I'll spring the car on him during the fishing trip. Tell him it's his birthday present from you."

"Maybe you'll get him interested in car magazines."

*   *   *

John was in the open garage stuffing the last of his gear in a duffle bag when a car pulled into the driveway. Blinded by the headlights, he couldn't see who it was. But when someone jumped out and yelled, "Hey, guess what?" He recognized the voice. Alvin danced around in front of the car like a three-year-old needing to pee.

"Hey!" John yelled back, shielding his eyes from the glare.

Alvin's mom left the motor running, bounded out, flung open the car's trunk, quickly deposited the contents on the driveway and hurried back to the driver's seat and in a frenzy, backed out into the street. Before she pulled away, she yelled out the window, "Be good and mind Mr. Michaels."

"Yea Mom." Alvin grunted.

"And, remember to change your underwear."

Alvin spun around to John. "Did you hear? Did you hear?" He was too excited to stand still.

"Hear what?"

"About Butch."

"Butch? No, what?"

Miss. Hill the librarian caught him jackin' off in the AV room."

"No shit?"

"Yeah." Louie and Mike were with her when they went to get a projector. She opened the door and there he was, with his pants down beating it."

"For sure?"

"Honest ta God! Louie and Mike saw the whole thing. Mike called me this afternoon. They had to go to Vice Principal Stevens' office and tell him what they saw."

"No shit." John started laughing so hard, tears ran down his cheeks. "I bet there wasn't much to see."

"Mike said Butch was expelled, gonna have ta go ta Middleton from now on."

"Isn't that a shame? Maybe he'll quit hanging round here."

Steve stepped out the service door. "What's happening?"

Alvin was too bashful to tell and John was laughing so hard he couldn't. Finally, John gain enough control and blurted out, "Butch got expelled!"

"Expelled?"

He got caught playin' with his thingamabob, in the AV room at school." Alvin's voice was higher than usual.

Steve looked at John confused.

"Jackin, off, Dad."

"Oh, you mean . . . that's too bad." Steve said. He turned his back to the boys but couldn't conceal his laughter.

"What's all the commotion?" Sarah questioned, as she brought an armload of bath towels out of the house and handed them to Steve.

"I'll tell you later." Steve said. He took the towels and stuffed them in a duffle bag. When he turned to the boys, he was still grinning. "Have you got everything?"

John giggled for a moment longer, relishing the moment. Unable to keep from grinning, he asked. "Should I pack some rain gear?"

"If it rains, we'll just come home." Steve answered, clearly trying to keep straight faced.

John looked at his full backpack. "I think we'll skip the parkas."

"Good decision." Steve looked at Alvin's pile of stuff at the end of the driveway. "I have an extra duffle bag and a backpack for you Alvin."

"Oh thanks, but are we gonna have ta hike?"

"Maybe." Sarah seemed to sense there was an inside men's joke and let it pass. "John did tell you this was primitive camping?"

"Yeah, but I didn't know what he meant."

"It means no table, benches or even a toilet," Sarah explained. "It's el natural, not even a shower, that's why it's a boys only trip. Oh, did you remember the toilet paper Steve?"

"Yep, we got it." Steve patted his backpack and looked at Alvin. "It's a private lake on some acreage out of Mariposa. It belongs to a friend at the precinct."

"You boys better turn in, if you plan to leave by five."

"Good night Mrs. Michaels." Alvin said and ducked in the door.

"Good night Dad, Mom." John went to kiss his mom on the cheek, but she grabbed him and gave him a hug.

*   *   *

Bright sun danced on the surface of the small lake and a spring breeze moved the oak trees gently on the otherwise quiet afternoon. Camp was basic, a stone fire ring with three sleeping bags on the ground nearby and a folding table for food prep with a large ice chest. Rope strung between two trees held towel, clothes and anything else that could hang. A prominent bush held several roll of toilet paper for necessary walks in the wood.

The lake water was too cold to enjoy swimming, so their days were spent fishing, pitching horseshoes, tossing a Frisbee or just relaxing in the three folding chairs near the fire ring.

In the afternoons, Steve brought out his pistol for some target practice. That day John fired several rounds with his usual deadly aim. His father had started teaching him to shoot at the police firing range when he was ten. Zach said he was a natural marksman. So far, Alvin had declined Steve's offer to try the gun, but today he accepted. After about twenty rounds, the kid hadn't hit the target once.

Steve reloaded. "Okay, let's try it again. Look at the target. Think of the gun as an extension of your hand."

"I can't do this Mr. Michaels." Alvin's frustrations were beginning to show.

"Yes you can." John insisted.

"Look at the target." Steve's spoke calm and slow. "The gun barrel is your finger, point at the target. Keep your eyes on the target. Now gently pull."

The shot rang out. He missed.

"He did it again Dad. He closed his eyes."

"I can't help it. I try to keep them open, but I just can't help it." Alvin lowered the gun and turned to Steve. "I've had enough."

"Let me shoot." John took the gun from Alvin and quickly fired five rounds. All the bullets cluster in the bull's-eye. "See, it's easy."

"I don't think I'll ever get the hang of it." Alvin walked to the smoldering fire and dropped in a chair.

John handed the gun to his father and hurried to Alvin. "Don't be discouraged." He sat next to him. "Keep trying you'll get it."

"That's just it. I don't want to get it. I don't like guns."

John sat silent. He couldn't imagine anyone not liking guns.

Alvin looked up at John. "My Grandpa says, 'A man that lives by the gun, will die by the gun.' I can't get it out of my head."

"All those who take up the sword, shall parish by the sword, book of Matthew." Steve stood behind John.

"Sword, gun it's all the same." Alvin looked up at Steve. "Isn't it?"

"You may be right."

*   *   *

Sun angled through the majestic oaks creating streams of light in the drifting smoke that hung in the air from the campfire. Alvin poked the fire, and then put on another chunk of wood. In a large iron kettle, Steve's prize winning chili bubbled gently. Alvin checked it and gave it a stir.

Boy am I glad we are sleeping outside. John remembered the effect of his father's chili from before. He sat next to Alvin and they watched Steve work his way around the lake casting for bass.

"I wish just once, my ol' man would take me fishin'." Alvin spoke as though he was simply thinking aloud. "Or once just look at me the way your father looks at you."

"What do you mean, how does he look at me?"

"You dummy, you can't see the love in his eyes?"

John didn't answer.

"He has so much love for you even I can feel it." Alvin paused. "Well, at least I get to share in some of it."

"I've never really thought of it . . . . Yeah, I guess I am lucky, real lucky." John watched his father.

Steve whipped his fishing rod to set the hook. His pole bent and he started to play his line. The reel chattered as the line pulled against the drag. "I got a big one!"

"Hang in there." John yelled back. "It's about time you caught something. I'll bring the net."

Reeling the fish in the last few feet, Steve fought to keep his trophy from tangling in a root. Grabbing the net from John, he stepped knee deep into the water and netted a beautiful three-pound largemouth bass. Before he could boast, the mud stuck to his feet. When he tried to take a step, he lost his balance and fell backward, but managed to keep his fish. However, in the process he had drenched John with mud and pond scum. He struggled to the shore. The two looked at each other and burst into laughter. Steve put his arm around his son's shoulders.

John looked at his father. Thanks to Alvin, he noticed the love in his father's eyes that he so often took for granted. He was proud of his father and wanted him to know it.

"I guess we need a bath."

*   *   *

Pops and crackles of the fire accompanied by the songs of crickets were the only sounds that filled the night. There was a slight nip in the air and the three sat, jackets zipped, and bellies full of fried bass and chili, staring deep into the flames.

"Your mother and I have been thinking." Steve's voice cut through the night, startling John. "You'll be driving before long. Zach has this VW bug. It needs work, and . . . well, he wanted to give it to you for your birthday next week. I thought we could work together, and rebuild it. By the time you're ready to drive, we'll have it working. How does that sound?

"Oh Dad, really?"

"It might give you somethin' else to occupy your time besides reading stag magazines and thinkin' about your——thingamabob."

"Oh Dad."

"Yeah, oh Dad." Steve mocked. "I was your age once, believe it or not." He added, teasing John's hair with his hand.

"That will be so great. Can we paint it red? When can we get it?" He turned to Alvin. "What do you think?"

Alvin didn't answer.

John jumped on Steve, almost knocking him and chair over.

Steve let out a howl.

"Sorry Dad."

He hugged his father, kissed him on the cheek before he caught himself, and pulled back, embarrassed. Steve stood and John threw his arms around his father again and hugged with such might, John could hear the wind forced out of him.

"Slow down a minute I can't breathe." Steve gasped.

"Oh wow, my own car. Oh God, Dad, you're the greatest dad ever."

"I think your pretty good too Son." Steve held him in his arms. "I wonder how many more times I will get to do this?" He said softly clinging to his son, "If only I could make this last forever."

"It will." John assured him, but he was already letting go. John quickly turned in Steve's arms. Alvin sat, in the fire light and John could see tears running down his cheeks. "What's wrong?"

"Nothing. I'm happy for you, that's all." Alvin said quietly. "Your dad is so cool."

"Thank you Alvin, being cool means a lot to a dad." Steve accepted the compliment.

"I think I'm going to turn in now, I'm kind of sleepy," Alvin said.

"But wait, don't you want——."

Steve had stopped John by gently grabbing his hand. John looked at his father questioning, and then understood.

Steve sat and directed his attentions back to the fire, his son soon joined him. Some time had passed with no more talk of the car, only a few empty words about the stars and the loud crickets.

"What ya thinking about?" Asked Steve.

"Ah, nothing."

"I know you have something on your mind. I see those wheels turning. Your brain is going a mile a minute isn't it, thinking about the car?"

"Not really."

"What then? Look Son, whatever's on you mind, I want you to feel free to talk to me. You can ask me anything, man to man. I don't care what it is, go on, and ask me."

John sat forward and stared into the fire. Deliberately he turned to his father. His eyes were bright and full of fire. He sat up straight and gathered the courage to ask his father. "What's it like to make love?"

"What? I thought you and Alvin were well read on that subject."

"I'm not talking about the sex part. I know you can have sex without love. It's the love part I don't understand, like you and Mom."

Steve closes his eyes and in a soft, almost apologetic voice, sighed, "You must think I'm Solomon."

John watched his father face in the light of the fire.

Steve sat for a time before he spoke. "Well Son, you are right there is sex for pleasure and self-gratification and there is making, sharing love. When it's with the right person, someone you truly love, it's like giving the perfect gift and receiving it all at the same time, your bodies join and its paradise."

Steve looked at John and then took along deep breath. "And when it's not the right person, it's just sex."

They returned to their vigil of the fire. A log sparked with a loud pop and a few stray embers flew in the air and disappeared.

*   *   *

John put another log on the fire. Steve jolted. "Sorry Dad didn't mean to startle you." Steve grinned. John smiled back, before he returned his gaze to the fire.

"I hope there are no more questions." Steve said. "I wonder what all goes on in your head sometimes. Thanks for letting me in." He looked up to the stars. "I've been given quite a son. I pray, the universe is pleased with how I've raised you so far. I pray I can lead you onto manhood giving you all the tools you need to be a success."

"Whoa! Did you see that?" John shouted, "A shooting star." He stood and pointed at the sky.

Steve stood and put his hand on John's shoulder.

"Dad I don't know what God thinks, but I liked your prayer."

John slipped his hand inside his father's and the two just looked at the stars. Finally, through a yawn, Steve said, "I think it's past my bedtime. Don't you think it's about time to turn in too, or dare I ask, any more questions?"

"No more . . . . For now." There was reluctance in John's voice.

"Give that brain of yours a rest, Son. This won't be our last fishing trip."

"Yeah. Sleep well Dad. I love you."

*   *   *

John undressed quietly and slipped into his sleeping bag. In the fire-light, he could see his father settle down in his bag. *God he's great. What would I do without him?* He looked up at the starry night sky and felt at peace.

"John?" Alvin whispered, "I could never ask my ol' man questions like that."

"You were awake?" John asked.

"Sorry. Didn't mean to eavesdrop, I'll never say anything."

"I know."

"It seems your family is like the Cleaver's and mine is like the Bunker's meet the Brady Bunch. Thanks for sharing him with me."

"You're welcome."

"Someday John, I don't know how or when, but I will repay you."

"No need, just be my friend."

"I will, forever."

CHAPTER 6

A LUCKY SHOT

EXT.-MICHAELS HOME-MORNING-JUNE 13, 1977

The third bay garage door was open, an older, beat-up, charcoal gray, VW beetle, sits on blocks. John's over-sized feet stuck out as he examines the underside of the car. Steve comes out of the front door on his way to work.

                    STEVE
        "Are you asleep under there?"

John, startled by Steve's voice, lifted up and smacked his head on the underside of the car with a loud thud, and then fell limp.

"Are you okay?"

Slowly, John slid out from under the VW on the mechanics creeper holding his forehead and trying not to cry.

"Sorry, I didn't mean to startle you. That must hurt. You okay?"

"Ah — Yeah, I'm fine."

"You don't sound fine." Steve stood and studies John's forehead. "What were you doing?"

"Just lookin'."

"Well slow down, we have plenty of time."

"I know," John whined. "But I was——."

"We've had it here less than a week and you're wearing a groove in the cement from sliding in and out under it."

Bummed, John stood up and brushed his hair out of his face. When he touched the rising bump on his forehead, he winced. "Am I bleeding?"

"No, but you better put some ice on that. I don't want to be accused of child abuse." Steve kidded.

Feeling the spot gently, he agreed with the need for ice. "Yeah, I think I will." John started for the house.

"Say Son." Steve stopped him. "We need to work on the back fence tomorrow morning. I need some eight-penny galvanized nails. Will you stop by the hardware store and pick up at least five pounds of them sometime today?"

"Yeah, no problem." John squinted back at his father. "Anything else?"

"I think that will do, but take care of that knock on your noggin." Steve peered at his son's head and made a sympathetic face. "Ice it. See ya tonight."

"Yeah Dad."

"You won't forget the nails?"

"No Dad."

"Behave yourself."

"Ga — bye Dad."

"I love ya knot head."

*　　　*　　　*

"How's the kid doing with the bug?" Zach asked between bites of his burger.

"He's got the bug all right. He'd sleep with it if I let him." Steve took a chomp out of his burger and a glob of catsup dripped down the front of his uniform. "Crap." He wiped it quickly with a napkin.

"I'm glad he's excited."

Steve covered the front of his uniform with a napkin before he took the next bite. "I didn't think he would be that excited." Another glob of catsup drips down, on the napkins this time. "Ah crap, I always make a mess when we eat in the car — looks like I've been shot."

"He's fourteen now, it's either sex or cars," Zach teased, finishing his burger without any problems. He had mastered the art of eating and driving at the same time. "Yes sir, when a boy reaches that age, all they think about is sex or cars."

"What scares me is when it changes to, sex in cars."

"It usual takes a couple of more years to put the two together, and a bug is a little small to be much of a sex-mobile." Zach was now into the fries.

"Isn't it called the *Love Bug*?"

"Oh Yeah, I guess you're right." Zach picked up his shake. "Stick a straw in it for me?"

"So now that school's out, want to do a fishing trip? A family outing this time."

"Not a guy's only? What's a matter Pop, don't want more embarrassing questions?"

"How would you like your daughters asking you what's it like to make love? The questions he asks will make you hair stand on end."

"So what makes you so sure he won't ask more questions on a family trip? Then we can have a real family discussion." Zach looked at Steve and laughed.

"Yeah go ahead and laugh, your time will come."

"So far I've been spared those kinda questions. I know I wouldn't have an answer."

"Zach?" Steve looked at his partner seriously. "Promise me something?"

"What's that?"

"Look after Sarah and the kids if something happens to me."

"Damn it Steve, nothing is going to happen to you." Zach slammed on the brakes and glared angrily at Steve. "I don't want to hear any more of that kinda talk. You're a damn fool for talkin' that way. You promised me years ago you would quit asking me that. You could put a jinx on yourself."

"Especially John." Steve continued. "I worry about John, if something should happen to me. I've taken care of them financially, but a boy has it rough without a father, particularly a kid like him."

"Quit talkin' that way." Zach demanded. "It gives me the creeps."

"Promise?"

"Yeah, sure, I promise. Now shut-up about it."

*   *   *

The frighten sales clerk yelped like a kicked pup.

"HANDS UP!" The first of two robbers yelled rushing through the door.

Isaac dropped his pliers and looked up from his jewelers' bench. Two men with nylon socks over their heads pointed handguns at the clerks. The clerks quickly thrust their hands in the air. Isaac stood slowly, his hands high and crept sideways toward the cash register.

"Stretch the guy." The fat man pointed his gun at Isaac.

"Don't move."

Isaac froze. His foot only inches from the button of recently installed silent alarm.

"Pull out them trays and dump 'em in the satchel." The muscular robber instructed the two clerks. "Durk, lock the damn door." He commanded without turning.

Durk locked the door and started pacing nervously.

The nervous ones are always the most dangerous. Likely to panic and shoot. Isaac tried to remain calm and remembered what Chief Bates said after the last holdup. He used the punk's momentary distraction to step on the alarm button.

The satchel swallowed the last tray of rings. Stretch turned back to Isaac. "Now you, empty the register." He poked Isaac hard in the ribs with the barrel of his 45, before slipping it in his back pocket. He held the satchel with both hands in front of Isaac. "Put the cash in, all of it." He sniffed and took a quick look at his partner.

Isaac started to empty the contents of the cash register into the bag unhurriedly, recalling the Chief's words. *In a robbery, demonstrate a willingness to cooperate, but stall as much as you can.* He watched the guy called Stretch.

"Hurry up." He sniffed again.

There was a crude tattoo of a snake on Stretch's forearm. His twitching muscles made it seem alive. *A prison tattoo. Not this punk's first holdup.* Isaac looked up at the fat one. Beads of sweat seeped through the nylon stocking and dripped off his chin. *First time for the fat slob.* He placed the last of the cash in the bag.

"Now open the safe." Stretch yanked Isaac from behind the counter and shoved him toward the backroom. "Durk, keep your eyes on the bitches." He motioned Isaac to the back with the point of his gun.

"Keep your hands up where I can see them." Durk ordered the women. Isaac could see the gunman's hand tremble. "Hurry up Stretch, goddamn it, hurry up." He moved closer to the door and looked out. The clerks huddled together behind the counter.

"Quit gawking." Stretch pushed Isaac through the door to the backroom.

Isaac felt the gun in the small of his back. *Stall.*

*　　*　　*

"What was your first car?" Steve asked. "Do you remember?" He had gathered up the trash from lunch and stuffed it in a bag.

Zach turned north on Fourth Street. "It was a dark green '38 Chevy coup. I could never forget it. I loved that old car.

"All unit, silent alarm at Robert's Jewelry, corner of First and Santa Clara, code three." The Radio squawked, repeating. Zach turned on the rack lights and siren, and hit the gas.

Steve picked up the hand mike, "Car one-twenty-six in response, ETA five minutes."

Zach turned a hard left up an alley then on to Third Street, going south. The tires squeal. He accelerates. "Four blocks." There was exhilaration in his voice. "I bought Nadia's rings at Robert's."

*　　*　　*

Isaac, on his knees, fumbles with the combination of the old safe. "Quit stalling." Stretch gave Isaac a painful poke deep in the right kidney with the barrel of his handgun. The jeweler gasped but didn't speed his efforts. Finally, with an audible click, the last tumbler fell into place. Isaac reached for the handle and gave it a pull. The heavy safe door swung open. Half filled with papers and several empty shelves the safe contained two trays, one of gold and platinum settings and the other glittering with unset stones of all sorts and diamonds, most neatly wrapped in paper squares. Isaac carefully slide out the tray of settings and dumped it into the waiting satchel. He returned to the safe and drew out the second tray and looked down at a half million dollars in loose stones. He stood and turned toward Stretch, then faked a stumble, dumping the stones on the floor.

"Asshole!" Stretch bellowed. He swung, striking Isaac on the left cheek with the barrel of his gun. Isaac tasted blood immediately. "You old fool." Stretch raised his gun and brought the handle down on Isaac shoulder with a bone-shattering thud. The old man fell backward.

"Sirens!" Durk yelled in a panic.

One of the clerks screamed. Stretch spun. He rushed through the door yelling. "Shut up!" There was a moment of silence. "Goddamn it. The back! Out the back."

"Cops!" Durk yelled.

Stretch ran to the backroom and danced around trying to decide what to do. Barricaded against intruders from the outside, the backdoor was secured with a chain, a crossbar and dead bold. He fumbled to open the door.

They made it. Thank God, they made it. Isaac watched Stretch battle to get the door open. Then sunlight streamed in. He turned to Isaac. Their eyes met. "You bastard. You sounded the alarm." Without hesitation, he fired.

The bullet grazed Isaac flesh on his left side just above his belt. Stretch ran. Isaac could see his blood start to stain his shirt as he lay among his diamonds and jewels. He grinned.

*　　*　　*

In front of the building, Steve jumped from the vehicle before it came to a stop. He heard the shot. Steve yelled. "Cover the front, I'll take the back." Already at a full run with weapon drawn, he rounded the building.

Zach scrambled out of the vehicle gun drawn. The two women rushed out the front. Once outside, the young women collapsed into the older and they both crumpled to the sidewalk. "Stay down?" He yelled. "Crawl around the side of the building and stay down, backup is coming."

"I think they shot Mr. Roberts, he's in the backroom."

Grabbing his radio, Zach confirmed that backup was on its way and requested an ambulance. He crouched and started for the front door.

*　　*　　*

Steve ran into the alley. The suspects emerged through the door. He jolted to a stop and yelled, "Halt or I'll shoot."

Stretch slowed, whirled around and fires one shot on the run. The bullet struck Steve in the chest. He looked down and saw a small entry wound just to the right of his badge. He dropped to one knee and fired.

The bullet hit Stretch's right knee, shattering it. He went down hard. The gun fell from his hand and slid several yards up the alley. Jewelry and money scattered onto the pavement.

"I'm shot! Oh God, I'm shot!" Stretch grabbed his leg and started to scream.

Durk stopped, turned around and started firing wildly. Steve fired three rounds, each struck Durk in the chest, but Durk managed to squeeze off one more round into the air. He tottered for a moment then fell forward onto a trashcan before rolling onto the pavement.

*   *   *

Zach emerged from the back door and saw Steve still kneeling. He turned his attention to the gunmen on the ground and ran to disarm them. The fat one was dead, but skinny one was lying on the pavement bellowing for help.

"I'm shot. Call me an ambulance." The robber demanded, like a bratty child. "I'm shot," His leg dangled from his knee with his foot pointing backward. Zach cuffed him then retrieved the gun. With the scene secure, he turned back to Steve.

"Fuckin' pig! Help me ya goddamn pig."

Zach ignores his ranting. He heard the sirens of backup. Black and White's pull into both ends of the alley, squealing to a stop. Police fanned out over the scene.

Steve was still on one knee with his weapon draw, he had not moved. Zach sensed something was wrong. "Steve?" He called. Steve didn't answer and Zach started to run. "Steve, are you okay?" He asked as he approached. Steve looked up at him. Zach could see the bullet wound and small amount of blood on his chest. He bends down for a closer inspection. Steve looks down at the hole.

"I think I got hit with something," Steve said. As he spoke, a small trickle of blood came from the corner of his mouth. He rubbed the back of his left hand over his mouth. "In the mouth too, I guess."

Zach could see a pool of blood at Steve's knee and circled behind him. The exit wound had ripped through his shirt on the right side of his back. Zach knelt behind him. "Lay back Steve." Zach pulled Steve back against his chest. "Officer down!" He bellowed, "Steve's been hit. Call for an Ambulance."

Zach gently took the gun from his hand. Bewildered, Steve looked at Zach, then at the wound in his chest.

"No, I'm okay." Steve protest. It's just catsup.

"You've been hit Steve."

"A lucky shot I guess." Steve tried to sit-up. "It can't be much. It doesn't even hurt."

"Lay still 'til some help gets here." The blood was spreading. Zach knew Steve was bleeding badly and frantically shouted for medics.

"Look, it's quit bleeding." Steve insisted as he pointed to his chest. It was like a bee sting, but now I don't feel anything."

"Lay still."

"Will I be okay?"

"Sure Steve, sure — now lie still."

"It's getting cold, I'm cold."

"Get me a blanket or jacket, anything." Zach yelled.

"I feel funny," Steve said. He began to shiver it Zach's arms.

"Hang on Steve." Zach yelled in frustration. "Where's the goddamn ambulance."

Steve looked up in the sky. Zach knew Steve was going fast. Steve leaned his head back and looked up into Zach eyes. "Oh God, Steve, hang on."

"Remind John about the script. Zach, please tell John to remember the script."

"What script, what are you talking about?"

"Never mind, just tell him." Steve pleaded, raising his hand to Zach's chest. "Promise?" He coughed blood.

Zach took Steve's cold hand in his. "I promise."

"What's wrong with me? I feel dizzy."

Zach knew Steve's lungs were filling with blood and he was slipping away.

Steve looked beyond Zach, his eyes brighten and he smiled. "Look at all the lights. Look, it's beautiful, Zach, beautif . . . ."

There was a moment when Steve's eyes suddenly cleared, then seem to reflect a golden sunset. Zach turned and looked at the sky, but saw nothing but blue. He felt life drain out of Steve, his hand went limp and his eyes clouded.

"No! Steve, hang on." He pleaded, and then began to cry like a baby. Zach knew the signs of death. He fell over Steve's lifeless body, touched his forehead to Steve's as if somehow he in some way could give life back to him. "No, Steve no, you can't go, you can't. Oh Steve."

A medic stepped up behind Zach. He looked up. "It's too late. Leave us alone a little longer, please."

Zach held Steve's lifeless body and cried. His face pressed against Steve. Finally knowing there was nothing more he could do, he kissed his friend gently on the cheek, one last good-bye.

*   *   *

It wasn't unusual for a Black and White to be parked in front of the Michaels home. However, when John spotting a patrol car parked at his house this day, it made him feel uneasy. A nervous acting uniformed officer stood near the door and when he saw John, he froze. John rode up the driveway, jumped off his bike and hurried up to the officer.

"What? What's going on here?"

The young officer shook his head no. "You need to go inside."

"Is something wrong? Something is wrong. What's wrong?" John yelled. He began to beat his fists on the cop's chest. The officer struggled to grab John's hands and restrain him, but John succeeded in pull away. "What's wrong with you, can't you talk to me?"

The young officer gestured for John to go in the house. "Please John, go inside. Zach wants to talk to you."

John ran to the front door and into the living room. His mother, Tess and Zach were sitting on the sofa. Zach looked up and the muscles in his cheeks tense, their eyes lock. Then John looked at his mother and then his sister, they are crying. Nausea hit him is his gut like a fist. "He's dead."

John started shaking his head, no, slowly at first, then with a force that shook his whole body. Zach stood and extended his arms, but John didn't accept his invitation of comfort. Inside him somewhere deep, a groan started. Primal in origin, it increased in volume as it moved up like a wrenching vomit and exploded into a shriek, "NOOOOOOO!"

CHAPTER 7

IN THE LINE OF DUTY

EXT.-LOS GATOS MEMORIAL PARK-MORNING-JUNE 18, 1977

An overnight weather front left the morning cool and overcast. Large groups of mourners, police, fire and civilians have gathered for Steven Michaels' funeral. Filled to capacity, the cemetery is a sea of uniforms for the interment. They stood around a smaller group of family and dignitaries seated under a canopy. John, his mother and sister sit in the front row center along with Zach. The MAYOR, CHIEF OF POLICE and LIEUTENANT GOVERNOR, sat beside the family. TV News crews from the local and the networks were covering the graveside service.

Reverend Paterson walked slowly back to the portable podium. He nods to the seven-man rifle squad. Three volleys of gunfire cracked the air, followed by bugler playing *Taps*. A squad of police helicopters flew over-head in the missing man formation. After *Taps* was finished, a bagpiper, off in the distance played, *Amazing Grace*.

> REV. PATERSON
> Forasmuch as it has pleased Almighty
> God to take unto Himself the soul of
> our brother, we bear his body hence
> to this place, that ashes may return
> to ashes, and dust to dust, and the
> imperishable spirit may be forever
> with the Lord.

A single drummer beat a cadence as the Honor Guard ritually folded the American flag that had draped over the coffin. One of the Color Guard carried the folded flag to John and stood in front of him. John looked up at the officer then to his mother and after some hesitation struggled to a stand to attention. The officer handed John the flag and saluted him, holding the salute he waited its return. John stared at the guard with a blank gaze. A hush fell across the cemetery, Zach could see John tremble for a moment, and then with great effort, returned the salute. The officer finished his salute, pivoted on his heels and marched back to his position. John held a long salute, and finally crumpled back into his chair.

The Honor Guard stayed at attention behind the coffin, and Reverend Paterson stood with his head bowed at the podium. There was absolute quiet. One of the funeral directors stepped up to the family. Zach, in dress uniform, sitting next to Sarah, now stood, took her hand and walked her to the coffin. She placed a single white rose on the oak casket and began to cry. Zach tried to console her. Another uniformed officer stepped up to Tess and walked her to the coffin. She laid her flower next to her mother's rose. Sarah put her arm around Tess's shoulder and hugged her.

A third officer stepped up to John and stood, but John refused to move. Finally, the officer nervously looked around for direction. Zach gave the questioning officer a nod. With a quick salute, the officer stepped from John to the Lieutenant Governor and walked him to the coffin. The rest of the assembled group began to follow. It took thirty minutes for the procession of mourners to pass the casket. The entire time John remained seated.

*   *   *

From where Zach stood, he watched and waited for John. Most of the mourners were gone, only a few small groups lingered. The Police Honor Guard dismissed and funeral workers packed up around John. He continued to sit with the folded flag on his lap.

Alvin stood near the canopy under a large pine tree. He too looked numbed by the loss, and clearly pained, as he observed his best friend. Slowly he approached and sat beside him. With no words to comfort his comrade, he reached out and put his hand on John leg.

"Get your hand off me and leave me alone." John blurted. His eyes flashed with anger. "Get away from me. I don't want to see you."

Alvin recoiled. Tears rolled down his cheeks. It appeared as if the last thread that held his heart together ripped apart. His chin fell to his chest and he cried. Eventually, he wiped his eyes, and nose with the back his hand pushed up his glassed, stood, and started to walk away.

"Alvin, I didn't mean that." John said, with a restored gentleness. "I just need to be alone."

Alvin stopped, gave his buddy a slight wave of his hand, a silent signal that said he understood.

Nearby, leaning against the mortuary's limousine, Zach watched John and Alvin. He turned to the black vehicle. "You and Tess go on home." He instructed Sarah through the open window, "I'll wait here with John."

"Thank you Zach," Sarah patted his hand.

Zach knew he had one more duty to perform before he could be alone to mourn the loss of his partner and best friend. "We'll be along soon."

The limousine drove away. From a distance, he could see John stand and walked to the casket. In an apparent rage, he pushed the flowers aside and threw himself over the coffin. His body shook with uncontrollable sobs.

"I can't understand. Why? It's not fair."

Zach stepped up behind John and put his hand on his shoulder. "Come on son, it's time to go home."

"No, leave me alone." John refused to lift his face from his father's casket.

"We can't change it." Zach could see John's tears spatter onto the polished oak lid of the casket. "We have to go." His voice cracked. "We have to go on . . . . I know it's hard to understand, but listen to your Uncle Zach."

"You're not my uncle." He reared up, nose to nose with Zach. "Leave me alone."

"No!" Zach shouted. He stood firm in response to John's anger. The two stared into each other's souls. Zach knew if he backed down and allowed John to sink into his sea of pity, he would drown.

John bolted off through the gravestones and Zach started after him. John ran until he reached the massive front gates of the cemetery, where he stopped and looked at the street before him, apparently confused. After a moment, he sat down on the curb.

Not to set him off on another run, Zach quit his chase and slowly approached, and quietly sat on the curb next to him.

Eventually John lifted his face to Zach. "I'm sorry."

Zach put his arm around John and held him. John bent his head to Zach's shoulder and they cried, neither moved for a long time.

"It's normal at a time like this to hurt and want to hurt others out of our pain." Zach consoled. "To dull the pain, our natural reaction is anger. Anger at the person that caused the loss, anger at those around for not being able to stop the pain, anger at ourselves for our inabilities to change things, and anger at God, for whatever reasons left."

"I don't believe there is a God anymore." John's face was cold and hard. "I think we're all on our own."

"I hoped for more, but I kinda have to agree with you." Zach found a hanky in his pocket and gave it to John. "Steve didn't have a need for structured religion or a personal God. I remember him saying once during an argument about God at the precinct, 'Whenever you name or try to describe God, that's not God, you can't put God in a box or a book'."

"Isn't that about the same?"

"Your dad had a belief. He believed that there is reason for things, a reason for life, and some kind of master plan." Zach paused and fidgeted with his utility belt. "Your father left a message for you. I don't know what he meant. It may have just been . . . you know . . . he was dying. It was his last words. The last thing he asked me . . . he said to tell you, to remember the script. That all he said. 'Remember the script'."

John looked at Zach with a frown and slowly leaned toward him. The two hugged and just sat on the curb for a while. The cemetery had returned to a state of quiet normalcy. On the street, traffic flowed and all around them, life went on.

CHAPTER 8

TIME TO MOVE ON

INT.-JOHN MICHAELS' BEDROOM-EVENING-DECEMBER 10, 1977

The guest bed has become a catch all of books, both clean and dirty laundry, and other junk. John has made a small shrine to his father on his dresser. A framed 8 X 10 photo of Steve Michaels in uniform with his badge affixed, sits on the dresser and a collection of memorabilia clutters the rest of the dresser and the wall behind. The folded American flag lay beside the photograph.

John lies on his bed fully dressed, hands folded behind his head as he stared at the ceiling. He has not had a haircut in sometime. He is pale and has lost weight.

SFX off screen - Muffled voices - There is a knock on the bedroom door.

                    SARAH (OC)
          John, you awake, can you come out
          here a minute?

                    JOHN
          Yeah Mom.

     "Meet me in the dining room."

John rolled slowly off his bed, pushed his hair out of his eyes and looked at his father's photo. The pain and sadness that came over him the day of his father's death has not left him, even for an instant. Since that moment, he has walked in a fog where nothing mattered. All he could do was hash and rehash, why, until he had pushed all other thoughts from his mind.

John drew in a deep breath, held it for a moment and then let his chest simply collapse, before aimlessly heading to the door. From the archway to the dining room, he saw a stack of file folders, on the table, with a separate stack of official looking papers and a lockbox. At the table his mother, Tess and Zach sat. Silently he took a seat, folded his arms across his chest and looked down.

"Your first quarter report card came in the mail today." Sarah began.

"So?"

"So . . . you didn't do too well."

"So?"

"So' it's time we talk. This is not going to be easy. I'm just going to start. It's been six months — it's time to move on. I've decided to go back to work. No, we don't need the money. It's for me. I'm going to start next week in Dr. Longley's office. I'll work weekdays."

John looked up at his sister then back to his mother. "Why?"

"For my sanity. I've got to get out of the house and do something. I know you're hurting. We've all been hurting." Sarah pulled a folder in front of her. "You father seemed to sense, to know he would die young. He had more insurance than even I was aware of, including mortgage insurance, the house is paid for, your college is paid for, and there is a sizable trust fund for you and Tess.

"That still doesn't answer why. Why he had to die."

"Listen Son, your mom and I can't answer that." Zach looked John in the eyes. Only you can — maybe — someday. Right now we just have to accept that he is gone and make the best of it."

Sarah turned to her son. "I don't know if your father talked to you about his theory of life."

"No, I don't . . . maybe . . . his thing about. 'It's not what you have, but what you do with it — '."

"No son." Sarah reached over and took John's hand. "Your father believed that life is like a movie script that is written before we are born. We each choose our role in life's drama. What happens to us in life is preplanned. Who our parents are, if and whom we marry, if we have children and even when and how we die. He would say, it's like a movie, that the actors, director, cinematographer and the rest of the production crew can interpret the script and make it their own so to speak, yet they are bound to follow the script."

"Sort of predestination." Zach added.

"Predestination?"

"He never spoke a lot about life being like a script. Kept most of his idea to himself." Zach continued. "But from the time you were born, he made me promise over and over to take care of you. Look after you if something should happen to him. It was an obsession with him. Sometimes I'd get so damn mad at him." Zach shook his head. "I threatened to request a new partner, if he didn't stop talkin' about it. I even suggested he'd see a shrink. He said he had, but it didn't change anything. I know the two of you talked about everything under the sun. I was sure you knew when he was so adamant about me tellin' you, to remember the script when he, he . . . ."

John just sat, listening. Inside his gut ached, the same ache that had dominated his life since his father's death. *Are they telling me this nonsense to make me feel better?* He felt his hot tears drip down his face. He had tried repeatedly to free himself from its grip.

"Sometimes I remember him holding me." John didn't look up. "He would just hold me and look at me. When I got too big for his arms, he would grab my leg or take my hand and look as if he wanted to say something, but couldn't. I'd ask him what. He would just say, he wanted me to know how much he loved me."

"I'm going to leave these papers here on the table. I want you to look through them in the next few days. They may help you understand what he felt, what he thought, what he believed." Sarah opened the lockbox. "There is something else. I forgot all about this until I started going through these papers. There were two gifts in this box, from your christening. One was to your father and other one we think was meant for you. His was a diary from Granny. You probably don't remember her. The other was this." Sarah handed John the box with the fountain pen. "That's exactly how it came to us."

The box felt heavier than expected in his hand. He examined the card and then the outside of the box. There was an eagerness and fear about opening, as though opening a sacred relic from the distant past. Lifting the paper-hinged lid, it took him a moment to recognize what it was. He took it from its box and it felt familiar to his fingers. Unscrewing the cap, he studied the strange gold tip a moment before he touched it to a scrap of paper. "It doesn't work."

"It's a fountain pen. You have to fill it with ink. I think its fourteen karat gold and rosewood, probably quite valuable." Sarah said. "Take care of it."

He held it in his hand as if he was about to write and it felt good. "It's like a gift from my Dad." The moment he said the word it struck him, it was the first time he spoke the word, dad, since his father's death. For some strange reason, the longer he held the pen, the better he felt. He closed his eyes and began to feel at peace.

"There is something else," his mother continued. "You Granny gave this book to your father, for him to pass to you."

John picked up the book and opened it. "The pages are blank." He looked at his mother questioningly.

"It's meant as a diary. But your father just made a couple of entries."

John found the bound-in ribbon bookmark and opened the page, then turned to the beginning. On the first page was an elegant but slightly shaky hand inscription, 'To Steven Michaels, may the joy of this day be forever in your heart, Love Granny.' John turned to the spine, *Great — Greater Expectations*. The handwriting on the next page was unmistakably his father's.

'July 15, 1963. Yesterday was my son John's Christening. The birth of my son was the greatest day of my life. I will never forget it. He is my joy and my life and truly my Greatest Expectation. My hope for him is that he will be whatever he chooses and to that end, I will try to provide the building blocks I can. I will never fill him with falsehoods, but let him explore life unfettered. My Goal is to provide him the ~~money~~, the opportunities, love and freedom to be his own man and someday experience the joy of fatherhood, and if in his script, a son of his own.'

John remembers their last fishing trip. How his father held his hand. The closeness they had. And Alvin pointing out how much his father's love showed. John continued reading.

'August 13, 1963, made an offer on a new home today. Excited, I believe this is a once in lifetime buy. Also opened a bank account in John's name, for his college education.

'September 25, 1965, Brought Theresa, named for her Granny, home from the hospital, mother and daughter doing fine. I was afraid that I couldn't love a second child as much as I did John. I was wrong. I love my whole family.'

John reread the diary several more time as he went through his father's other papers. When he looked up, he was surprised to find he was alone at the table. The grandfather clock in the living room struck the half-hour. It was ten-thirty. He took the pen and the book and retired to his room, placing them on his nightstand and readied for bed.

That evening, the fog in his mind crept in and pushed away the blanket of sleep as it had every night since his father's death. He felt his tears, the loneliness and the pain. *Will it ever change?*

"Only if you want it to." The voice spoke gently.

John sat up and turned on the lamp on the nightstand. There was no one there. Assured it was only his imagination, he lay back down and stared at the ceiling for a long time before turning out the light. It wasn't long before he felt a presence in the room, yet he knew no one had come through the door.

Who or whatever it was seemed to stand near the foot of his bed. He felt the pressure of someone sitting on his bed and he could detect the faint but distinctive scent of his father. He stared wide eyed into the darkness. Slowly his eyes adjusted and he recognized the shape, an unmistakable shape. "Dad?"

"Yes son."

John froze. Comforted, but confused. "What — why — how?"

"Don't ask or try to reason, just believe for a moment."

"But you are dead?"

"Yes."

'Then how?"

"There is but a thin veil between this world and the next. I so wanted this moment with you, but until you called to me this evening, it couldn't happen."

"Oh Dad why, why did you have to die?"

"All who live on this earth must die Son. The how and why is written before we come. What we learn and what we do with what we have in this life is the reason we live. On the other side we are spirit, on earth spirit and body unite. This is where we can experience love, joy and happiness."

"Even if it causes pain and misery to others?"

"Even so. We come to experience good as well as pain, grief, sorrow and death that we may live. The sages of old called it the perfection of the soul. Your pain and sorrow can destroy you or make you a better man. It's your choice. Embrace life, all of it, the good and the bad."

"How can I live without you? What is to become of me?"

"I'm not at liberty to tell you that, the answers are for you to discover. You can lie here in your bed and waste away. Never fulfilling your destiny, doomed only to repeat it, or get up and face life and all its challenges. Live each day."

"I can't do it without you." John sat up. He felt his father take him in his arms.

"You can and you will. It is the life you chose."

Feeling his father's presence and his love, the pain began to fade.

"Tomorrow, I want you to take down that shrine. Don't keep me bound in the corner of your room. Put away the keepsakes. As long as you focus on the past, there can be no future."

"What about the pen. Is it from you?"

"No, it's not from me, it's from a friend, take good care of it, you will need it someday, it's in your script."

John stayed cradled in his father arms until sleep came.

*   *   *

At first light, John awoke alone. There was still a pain in his heart, but there too was also the knowledge he could overcome it. He began the task of straightening his room, putting away his clean clothes and hampering the dirty. With determination, he turned to the shrine and began pulling down the souvenirs of a lifetime, leaving only the photograph of his father with his badge pinned to the frame. The pen and the book he placed in his nightstand drawer.

There was a gentle rap at his bedroom door. "John, are you awake?" His mother asked.

"Yes, you can come in." He answered. His voice sounded different to him, deeper, stronger and cheerful.

Sarah looked around the room and then to John, questioning. "You cleaned up."

"You were right, it's going to be hard, but it's time to move on." He threw his arms around her, hugged her and gave her a kiss on the cheek. "I love you Mom."

"And I love you too."

"I've got to call Alvin."

"That's what I came to tell you. He's here."

John quickly showered, dressed and ate a hearty breakfast, with Alvin at his heals every step of the way. Like everything else, John had shut Alvin out also.

At ten o'clock, Sarah knocked on John's bedroom door. "John, Alvin," She spoke through the closed door. I'm taking Tess Christmas shopping with me. Do you think Alvin will help you get the Christmas decorations down out of storage in the garage?"

Alvin opened the door, "Sure thing, Mrs. Michaels."

John didn't hesitate. "Let's go." He raced Alvin down the hall with Sarah hurrying after them.

"Wait. Let me get the car out first. Tess, are you ready to go?"

They all caught up in the garage. Sarah and Tess were getting in the car when Alvin asked. "Where's the Bug."

"Oh, ah——." Sarah looked at John.

"Mom had a shed built out back. We put it out there for now along with some of Dad's things we want keep."

Sarah smiled and got in the car. "Open the garage door, Son. Shall Tess and I pick out a tree while we are out?"

"Sure Mom. And maybe bring home some pizzas and we can all decorate the tree this evening, altogether."

Sarah backed out and drove off. Alvin and John made quick work of getting the decorations down and stringing up the outdoor lights. When they finished John got them a couple of Cokes and went to the family room. Alvin flopped on the sofa and grabbed the remote. "Want ta watch the game?"

"Sure." John stood at the sliding glass door and gazed out across the backyard. The newly built shed stood at the far corner near the creek, partly obscured by the trees."

"So what happened? Why the sudden change?"

John's attention, still fixed on the shed, took a moment before answering. "I can't explain. I just guess it's time to move on."

CHAPTER 9

THE BACKYARD VILLA

EXT.-THE MICHAELS POOL-AFTERNOON-OCTOBER 3, 1983

John has matured into a good-looking, physically fit, twenty year-old man.

The scene opens with John swimming laps. At the house, the sliding glass door from the family room opens and Alvin steps out, dressed in slacks and white shirt. His straight hair is shaggy and over his ears and still wears black framed glasses. He carries a brief-case, puts it on a patio table and steps to the side of the pool. John sees Alvin, but keeps swimming laps as they talk.

> ALVIN
> Tess said you've been back for two weeks.

> JOHN
> Made it back in time for her birth-day.

> ALVIN
> How was it over there?

> JOHN
> Great.

```
                    ALVIN
        Did you spend the whole year in Hei-
        delberg?
```

"No." John turned and continued swimming back to the other end of the pool. "Two months each——in Paris and Rome——the rest Germany, mainly Heidelberg." John reached the end of the pool, flipped and pushed off.

John's mother has died after a long battle with cancer during his first year of college. Before her death, she had asked her sister Carrie, a widow, to come and live with Tess and John as long as needed. John decided to spend his second year of college studying in Europe. With a reduced study load, he spent a good deal of time pulling himself together.

"You should try——studying in Europe." John made another lap turn.

Alvin started walking alongside the pool while John continued to swim. "Can't afford it——time or money."

"Yeah, it did put me behind some. But you get a completely different kind of education. Got your letter——and the prospectus, before I left Germany."

"Well what do you think?"

"Don't understand all of it."

"Oh? I thought it was pretty clear."

"What?" John kept swimming.

"I thought it was clear." Alvin spoke louder and walked faster trying to stay up with John. "How much longer are you going to keep this up?"

"Twenty minutes. Why don't you have a cola? In the fridge, by the barbeque."

Alvin helped himself to a cola and paced around the patio before working his way back to the table to wait for John. He opened his brief-case and shuffled through some papers. From the pool, John could see Alvin getting anxious. He wanted him to sweat a little.

When John had stretched his swim for as long as he thought Alvin could handle it, he stopped and hung onto the side of the pool, to catch his breath. Alvin stood and started toward him. "Stay seated, I'll be right there."

Alvin stopped and stood by the table. John jumped out of the pool, grabbed a towel and a cola. He draped the towel over his shoulders and with a smooth unhurried walk approached with hand extended. Alvin put the can of cola on the table and they shook hands.

"It's been awhile. You're looking good." John said.

"Thanks, but talk about looking good, you look great. What's in the water over there? I thought you would a least have a beer belly or love handles or something."

John felt uncomfortable by the compliment, even from an old friend. He still saw himself as skinny and awkward. "Please sit." He wrapped the towel around his waist. "So explain this deal to me."

Alvin sat, looked up and pushed up his glasses. "I want to start a software company. Designing and selling 3D CGI PC interactive games."

John raised his eyebrows. "You've spent too much time at Berkley with the rest of the computer nerds. Give it to me in English."

"Games, computer graphic games for personal computers. Listen John, in a few years, everyone will have their own personal computers. They will link together. People will send electronic mail, collaborate for work and play computer games, either alone or linked on line."

"Games!"

"You've got to get with it. It's the computer age."

"Games? How are you going to make money playing games?"

"I'm going to create and sell the software to play games with."

John leaned both his hands on the table. "I'm teasing you a little." He chuckled and then smiled. "I must admit though, I'm not up on the latest when it comes to computers. But I talked to a friend that thinks that there is money to make, creating computer games. Big money." John tilted his head and looked at Alvin's notes. "So how much do you want me to invest?"

"Well, I can rent an eight-hundred square foot shop in an industrial park in Santa Clara for around eight grand a year. Add some additional equipment. I've almost everything I need already. And some part-time help . . . . I figure twenty-thousand will start it out and get me through the first year. If I can get some investors to put in a few grand each, I can get it started."

"Number?"

"Say . . . two——five thou." Alvin looks up at John.

John frowned. "Okay. Questions?" He ran his fingers through his hair and took a swig of cola. "When do you look to start this——whatever you call it business."

"This January."

"So why, Santa Clara. Wouldn't it be better in Berkley, closer to your school?"

"I get my Bachelors in Computer Science at the end of this year. I'm moving back home."

"This year?" How did you get so far ahead of me?"

"I haven't been playing the rich playboy."

"I assure you, I am neither rich, nor a playboy."

"Well from my perspective it looks that way."

"Trust me." John shook his head. "Okay, I think it's a good idea and I'm willing to put up some money."

"Aren't you getting cold? You make me shiver just looking at you."

"Not really. But let me grab my day planner and a shirt if that will make you more comfortable." John started toward the house. "Help yourself to more soda."

When John returned, he was dressed in a blue-striped t-shirt, tan pant and sandals, letting his head of naturally curly hair, do its thing. He pulled another can of cola from the patio refrigerator, sat at the table with Alvin, and opened his planner and a notebook. "Now you're going to tell me someday they will make computers the size of notebooks."

Alvin just grinned.

"I have been thinking this over for a few days. Would you consider a silent partner?"

Alvin gave John a blank look for a moment. "You mean you? Absolutely."

"I have a few stipulations. I hope that is all right with you?"

"Sure, shoot." Alvin took a pad and pencil out of his briefcase.

"I want you to do this right. I've talked to Aaron Futter. He's my attorney. He will setup a corporation."

Alvin looked up concerned.

"He'll do it pro bono. Set it up with you as principal shareholder, fifty-one forty-nine percent, if that's okay?"

"Perfect." Alvin excitedly pushed up his glasses, again.

"I asked Tess to design a logo and I want you to get business cards and stationary. No second rate anything. Understand?" John took Alvin's glasses off his face, examined the bent and glued together frame. "And for Christ's sake, get new glasses."

"But——but——costs."

"No but's. Here." John handed Alvin a check.

Alvin's eyes bugged. But——but——."

"No buts, I said.

"This is for fifty-thousand do——dollars."

"If we are going to be partners in this, I want it first cabin."

Alvin leaned back and put the palm of his hand to his forehead. "Are you sure? What about yours and Tess's education, the house and expenses."

"Alvin, Dad and then Mom's life insurance came to more than two-million dollars after everything was paid. So if you need more, let me know. No scrimping, understand. I can't write code, but I have a little dough and can write checks."

"This will do fine. And the company is going to pay you back every penny. With luck, I'll add three zeros to this."

"I'm not worried about that." John straightened up. "Let's go get dinner. Celebrate Alvin and John Software." John gave Alvin a reassuring pat on the back.

Alvin tossed everything in his briefcase and jumped to his feet. "John and Alvin —— no, J & A Software Incorporated." He hurried to catch up with John. "And you say you're not a rich playboy."

*   *   *

Alvin leased his industrial space in January and hit the ground walking faster than he planned. The extra boost of capital let him hire a 'gofor' and a classmate who wrote code. By spring, they had their first product on the market. It was something Alvin had been working on for a couple of years and just needed finishing and packaging. It was the start.

After his year abroad, John had difficulties settling back at Stanford. His head said law, but his heart didn't have a direction and as usually happen in such matters, the head wins and the dreams are put in the circular hold file. John decided he couldn't go wrong with a law degree.

By the end of the spring semester, he felt he was back in the groove. Now, with summer break starting, he planned a building project at the house. A little addition, he came up with the idea while in France. On a patio table, he spread the blue prints and excitedly paced in circles around them. His dog Sandy followed him for a while, but when they weren't going anywhere, gave up, found a cool spot and took an afternoon nap.

Tess, in green Bermuda shorts and light yellow top, strolled out on the patio drinking a soda. "Hi, still making changes?"

"Too late. Start construction Monday."

"I'm not sure why you want to build a French Villa in the back yard."

"It's not a Villa. It's a small three room guesthouse."

Tess arched her eyebrows. "Two-thousand square feet, with a French twist. I know big brother, it's all right to have a few dreams come true."

"How was rehearsal?" John asked settling on a lounge with a beer.

Tees made a face. "Rehearsals, for what? Walking across a platform for a worthless piece of paper takes no talent. I'm just glad high school's over."

"I wish you were sticking around for the summer."

"Can't, I want to find an apartment and get settled in before school starts."

"My little sister moving to the Big Apple."

"NYU's been my dream."

"You ever plan moving back to California?"

"Are you kidding? That's why I turned over the house to you. She looked across the yard to where John had staked out the foundation for the guesthouse. "And when I come for a visit, I'll have a French Villa to stay in."

"You are still going to do the interior decorating for me?"

"I'll come back winter break just for you." She sat on a lounge next to her brother. "You going to be okay, living here all alone?"

"Why shouldn't I."

"Say, why don't you plan on spending Christmas in New York, with me this year? Then I'll fly back with you and we'll do the Villa."

"I'll think about it, and it's not a Villa."

*   *   *

Tess and Aunt Carrie flew to New York, the week after her graduation. Carrie was happy to be going back home to Maryland, to her own home, family and especially her grandchildren. John made the trip to New York for Christmas and checked out how his sister was doing. Now, as promised, she was spending her semester break, decorating the guesthouse.

Tess stepped out of the great room of the guesthouse when John came across the patio. At the opening in the low, cut-stone wall that delineated the separate sitting area from the rest of the yard, she threw up her hands to stop him. "No, no, no. No peeking until I'm done. You agreed."

"Just came for an update."

"We are finished with papering and painting. George is doing some touchups now. Tomorrow we'll start bringing in the furniture. Give me three or four more days"

"You know this is killing me."

"I like to see you suffer. Tess turned and looked back at the guesthouse. "I must admit, it looks fantastic. When you first told me your plans, I thought you were crazy."

"Zach said the same thing."

"I envisioned a Vegas style monstrosity, not the simple clean lines and soft Earth Tone colored stucco and stone building you designed. With all the multi pain windows and doors, the interior is going to be gorgeous. I think you are wasting your time studying law."

John beamed. "I'm glad you like it." He put his arms around his sister. "It means a lot to me." He swung her around to the house. "Wait until you see what I have planned next. A whole new wing on the house, maybe a second story with a balcony."

"I don't want to hear about it."

"I put a fresh pot of coffee on. Let's get out of the chill and have a cup."

"Last one there is a rotten egg." Tess bolted and they raced for the house.

Tess took her coffee to the family room and sat. "Don't you feel like you are rattling around in this place all alone?"

"Yeah, it's a little empty right now." He joined her. "But I'm looking forward to having a family."

"You'll need a wife first."

"Details."

"Is your sex life improving? Dating anyone special."

"No one special."

"Just sleeping around." She gave him a knowing grin and he returned an impish smirk.

"I swear the gal that snags you will have to have plenty of tricks up her skirt or a bat, maybe both."

John, embarrassed by his sister's frankness, let out a chuckle before taking a sip of coffee. "So what about your love life? Anyone?"

"Yes there is. They went home for the Holidays or I would have introduced you." Tess glanced up into John's eyes. "There is something I need to tell you. I don't know if there is any other way to put this — I'm a lesbian."

"I know."

"How?"

"Just do. I confirmed it when I was there Christmas."

"Does it bother you?"

"No."

"I love you John."

"I know. I love you too."

*   *   *

"All right, everyone ready for the unveiling." Tess announced standing in front of the guesthouse doors.

Zach and his wife Nadia, along with Alvin and Sandra, the girl that started as his go-for, stood in a row facing Tess. John filled their glasses with champagne.

Zach eyed Tess's glass. "I didn't see that."

"Welcome to Villa de Mont-Jean." Tess led the toast. She ceremonially untied the sash she had put on the doorknobs and opened the French doors to the great room. Pivoting, she bowed to usher the group inside.

"This is the great room." She started her tour. "French Country styling, featuring a sitting room with fireplace." Proudly leading on, she pointed. "Behind there is a dining area with a kitchenette and wet bar across the back wall. The Artwork, all French, collected by art connoisseur Monsieur Jean, that's French for John. On your left is the blue room with double queen beds and featuring contemporary German art. And on the right the green and red room, again, a double queens but this time classic Italian Renascence art."

Everyone applauded and told Tess how great she did. With more champagne, they hit the buffet spread on the dining table.

John came up to her and kissed her on the cheek. "Thanks Sis, you did a magnificent job."

"Well you're very welcome." She took of sip of her champagne. "You are looking sharp, like you stepped off the pages of GQ. How come no date tonight?"

"No time, too much studying, but thanks for the compliment."

"You've got to be the most eligible bachelor on campus."

"I'm becoming aware of that. I'm trying to keep a low profile."

"Is it working?"

"So far."

"Is that a blush I see?"

John grinned and took a drink of his champagne.

Tess pointed at Sandra. "You better keep an eye on her. She and Alvin are looking pretty serious."

"I've been noticing that."

"Maybe you can rent the Villa to them for a honeymoon."

"It's not a Villa."

PART TWO

CHAPTER 10

THE SETUP

INT.-STANFORD UNIVERSITY LIBRARY-OCTOBER 28 1986

In a secluded reading area off the old main hall, John
Michaels, AGE 23, sits alone at a table studying. The
space is cutoff from the rest of the library by new
construction. The area has four old style tables each
with six chairs. Next to John is a table with three
Asian students studying together and at the far side
of the room two women sit, KATHLEEN O'MALLEY, career
student, a foxy thirty-one-year-old redhead and JULIE
DAVENPORT, younger, out of style brunette, Kathleen's
good friend. Kathleen is trying to catch John's attention.

> JULIE
> Who is he?

> KATHLEEN
> His name is John, John Michaels. He's
> here every Tuesday night, like clock-
> work. He's the guy I'm going to mar-
> ry.

"Has he asked you?" Julie studied him for a moment. "He is cute. I
love his eyes. Maybe a little young."

"He's twenty-three." Kathleen declared, not that age was any deter-rent to her. "A senior, prelaw. And no, he hasn't asked me—we haven't really met yet."

Kathleen had attempted to get John's attention, but so far, she only managed to annoy the Asian students. Becoming frustrated at her failed endeavors, she scribbled, HI SEXY on a sheet of paper and wadded it up into a ball. "Besides, young ones are easier to train." With a toss, the wad of paper sailed high over the Asians, crossing twenty feet and with deadly accuracy hit John on the forehead.

He jumped. The paper wad bounced off him and landed on his open book. Stunned, he looked up for the source of the ambush. Kathleen smiled. He smiled back for a second then turned his attention to the paper. Un-wadding it, he looked at it and then back at Kathleen with a blank expression. She winked and she could see him blush before turning his gaze back to his book.

"Have you been following him?" Julie asked. "God, he's turning as red as a beet."

"Kinda, and checked him out a little." Kathleen continued to stare at John. He took another quick glance up at her. "He graduates, BA this spring and plans to start Stanford Law in the fall. His father was a cop, killed in the line of duty. Left him fixed up quite well."

"Did you hire a detective?"

"No, I just used him for a class project." Kathleen's smile broadened each time John glanced up at her. "He's in my Criminal Psychology class. I've been trying to get his attention. Until now, all I've managed is a smile and a nod. Tonight I'm going to get his full attention."

"I think you have."

"I'm going to get more than a shit-eating grin out of him."

It was apparent that John had lost his concentration on his studies. Each time he looked up, Kathleen continued to flirt with him. He would smile back, blush a little more and turn his eyes back to the book in front of him.

"Did you do a background check on me too?"

"I'm not marrying you."

"You sure are presumptuous." Julie glanced at John then back to Kathleen. "He looks shy. You're embarrassing him to death."

"That's okay. I may embarrass him a little more before the night is over. Got to set him up for the kill. Tonight he'll notice me."

Cautiously, he looked up again and when he did, she put her finger to her lips, licked it sensually, and then blew him a kiss.

"Kathleen, you're a devil, you're distressing him to no end. He's glowing like a stoplight." Julie whispered. Kathleen blatant flirtation was getting awkward for her.

"Ah he loves it." Kathleen insisted. "Probably sitting there with a hard-on. Another ten minutes and he'll cream his jeans."

"Kathleen!"

"What? What's wrong with having a little fun with the guy? He loves every second of it."

"Your embarrassing him, see he is starting to fidget."

"He's had to adjust his pants three times. Watch."

Kathleen continued to flirt as Julie observed, before long, John reached under the table obviously pulling at his jeans. Julie and Kathleen put their heads together and giggle.

"See, what did I tell you."

John looked up and smiled, but just then one of the Asian students shushed the women and John quickly looked back at his book.

"How do you know what the guys thinking?"

"I have three older brothers. Horniest bastards you would ever want to meet. When they were younger they always had a hard-on, always playing with themselves, one-way or another. Say the word sex, and they'd go ballistic. For them, cherry pie took on a new meaning. And from the time I can remember they tried to make it with every girlfriend my sister or I had over."

"I should have known you then." Julie sat up and tried to compose herself.

"Believe me you don't want to know my brothers. Besides, two are married now. One's a doctor and the other's an attorney." Kathleen started gathering her things together.

"And what about number three, is he still available?"

"I guess I could arrange a date, but he's a priest, blessed Father O'Malley.

"Oh, I guess I'll pass then."

"Let's go over and really turn him on."

"You sure?"

Kathleen stood up, picked up her books and purse, and waited for Julie to gather her things together.

*   *   *

John glanced up as the women stood and felt disappointed that they were leaving, saddened and relieved, he didn't know how much more flirtation from the beautiful redhead he could take and stay sane. She looked familiar, but it wasn't until she stood that he recognized her from class. When instead of leaving, she started toward him he panicked, sat-up and tried to control his urge to grin.

"Hi, mind if we join you?" Before he could answer, she sat in the chair across from him.

"Ah, Hi." John squirmed in his chair, his usual good manners would have had him stand, but in his present situation, he remained seated.

"I'm Kathleen and this is Julie." Kathleen said, and extended her hand.

With a wipe of his sweaty hand on his jeans, he reached out and shook it. "I'm John."

Julie dropped her things on the table with a loud plop. "Nice to meet you." She extended her hand and waited to be acknowledged.

"Oh——Hello. Please sit-down. I'm John."

There was a brief awkwardness. The three looked at each other and giggled. In a huff, the Asian students picked up their things and left, loudly expressing their irritation to each other in what sounded like Chinese. Kathleen rolled her eyes and made an apologetic face at John. "I hope we didn't disturb them."

"I don't think so." John couldn't quit grinning.

"You've got a great smile," Kathleen told him. The two looked at one another. "Want to go for some coffee?" she asked.

"Gee, I don't know." John was beside himself at Kathleen's forward-ness, but at the same time taken in by her. "I have so much work to do." Her red hair and flashing green eyes fascinated him. *Say yes stupid, say yes.* He fidgeted, his nervousness released by a right foot bounce.

"A coffee break might do you some good." Kathleen looked directly into his eyes as she spoke. "I've been watching you. You haven't been doing much studying."

"I don't know. I've got so much work and a test tomorrow." He felt the fire return to his face. Befuddled, he scanned the books and notes he had spread out on the table before him. "How about a rain check." When he heard his own words come out of his mouth, he felt the blood suddenly drained from his face. *Oh God, how stupid*. He wished he could retract his words. *Rain check? How dumb. Idiot.*

"Suit yourself." Kathleen said in a way that told John she wasn't the kind that took no for an answer. She spread out her things, indicating she was not going anywhere soon.

Julie looked at Kathleen for a moment then did the same. John was pleased that they were staying. He was at a loss for words however, so the three just exchanged somewhat awkward glances.

John's nervousness began to subside when he heard Kathleen kicked off her shoes noisily under the table. Next, she opened her book and apparently began to read. John stared at the page in front of him, but his eyes refused to focus on the words. Regretful of his refusal, he tried to figure a way to accept the invitation for coffee without looking like a total moron. Without a doubt, there would be no further studying tonight. Kathleen, the most beautiful woman he had ever met, had enchanted him.

Unexpectedly he felt Kathleen put her foot on his chair seat between his legs. He jolted upright. *Oh my God!* The top of John's head felt like it was about to blow off. Her bare foot pressed into his crotch. *Oh God, she's not.* Modesty, passion, shyness and desire scrambled his brain. Julie glanced at him questioningly. *Does she know?*

Sure that he must appear obvious, John nervously looked around, expecting everyone's eyes to be on him. In their secluded location, no one could see them. His mind raced for words, nevertheless his mouth was dry and the words wouldn't come. He was afraid that if he didn't say something encouraging, she might stop altogether. Agonizingly hoping she wouldn't, he was only able to emit a barely audible whimper. Her foot teased him. Frenzied, his mind went blank. An involuntary jerk caused the front legs his chair to bounce off the floor. The loud bang alerted

Julie. Her eyes darted between the two, questioning. John trembled. He tried to keep control, afraid that at any moment he'd lose it altogether.

"Now, are you sure you don't want to come . . . with us for some coffee?" Kathleen asked again, in a low sexy voice.

"I'll come." He squeaked out. Invitation accepted. About to surrender completely, he realized Julie was gawking at him, apparently with no idea of what was happening under the table.

A newfound boldness suddenly kicked in. Restraint abandoned, he reached under the table, took hold of Kathleen's foot, pressed it firmly against his erection, and looked her in the eyes. "You want me to come . . . now, or later?"

"It's up to you. We can go for coffee now." She pressed her foot hard against him. "Or just sit here and see what comes up."

"I'd like to sit here all night." John was near eruption. He glanced at Julie an instant before fixing his gaze on Kathleen. "But, I think we better go now."

"If you insist, we can carry on this wonderful conversation at the coffee shop."

"I'd be delighted too." He agreed.

With incredible dexterity, her toes teasingly slid slowly down the length of his shaft before dropping to the floor. John used every bit of control he could muster up to keep from going over the edge. While Kathleen stood and coolly began to gather her things, John sat in misery, left hanging.

Confused, Julie looked at John then back to Kathleen. Her expression indicated she had missed something. For obvious reasons he wasn't about to stand. He just sat and looked pathetically at the two women preparing to leave.

"Aren't you ready?" Kathleen asked.

"I . . . need to gather my . . . things." He quickly surveyed the table before glancing back at Kathleen. "I'll meet you at the north entrance in a couple of minutes."

"We can wait," she said, in an obvious tease, acting as though she was about to sit back down.

"No, no, please go on." He was catching on to her game. "I've got to remove a footprint. I'll catch up."

Kathleen turned to Julie. "Shall we excuse the gentleman?" She asked.

With a bewildered expression, Julie nodded and they started to walk away. John's shoulders drooped and he gave a sigh of relief. When the women were a safe distance, he quickly gathered his books and papers, stood, carefully concealed the front of his jeans and sprinted for the men's room.

*　　　*　　　*

Kathleen watched him make his mad dash, with amusement she snickered. "That got his attention."

Julie looked on confused. "What did you do to him?"

"A little footsies under the table."

"You what?" Julie gasped and dropped her books.

"Shush, keep your voice down." Kathleen waited for Julie to pick up her stuff.

"Do you think playing footsies with a man will get him to marry you?"

Kathleen arched her eyebrows. "It's part of my plan. First, you've got to get his attention, from there is relatively easy. Just make him happy."

"What if you get to the happy and you find out you're not in love him? Are you still going to marry him?"

"Definitely. A women doesn't marry for love, she marries for security. If love happens along the way, it's a bonus. It's the man that marries for love, or thinks he does."

"So you think you can make him fall in love with just a little titillation. Kathleen, you've been reading too many French novels."

"He's a man. I guarantee I can make him fall in love with me."

"I'll believe that when I see it."

"I'll invite you to the wedding."

"You sound so sure of yourself. What if he doesn't even ask you for a date, how are you going to get him to marry you?"

"Stick around and take notes." Kathleen glanced around. "Now here's what I need you to do. Stay with us tonight. When I work it around to him walking us to our apartments, I want you to stay with me, understand?"

"Stay with you?"

"No matter what, stay with us. Be like a shadow until we walk you to your door."

"That's going to get him to marry you?"

"That's the start. You'll see."

*   *   *

John dropped his books on the shelf above the basins in the empty men's room. He cupped his hands under the faucet and splashed cold water in his face. Raising his face to the mirror, he watched the water drip off his chin. *Boy, did you get lucky tonight or what?* He wiped the excess water off his face and flung it on the floor, then grinned at his reflection in the mirror. With a swagger, he paced back and forth trying to gain his composure. "Yeah." He answered himself. "And it feels good, real good." *But what if it turns out like another prom night?*

John spun on his heels, looked at himself in the mirror, and pointed. "Fuck you, that was five years ago"

He strode to the condom dispenser. Though he often thought, making condoms readily available on campus was dumb, especially in places like the library. He pulled a handful of change out of his pocket and began stuffing quarters into the vending machine. Halfway out the door he remembered his books and returned. He did a final check in the mirror. *Looking sharp there Johnny boy. Got a hot one tonight.*

*   *   *

It was a quarter to midnight and Dregs' was still busy. The owner of the trendy coffee shop had dropped out of Stanford in his junior year and started the place in an old storefront that had hosted a number of businesses. It had become the hippest new coffee shop in town. With a blend of retro sixties with new yuppie chic, it was more popular than anyone could imagine.

"And would you believe it . . . ." John laughed at his own joke so hard he could hardly get the punch line out. "He ate the whole thing, and didn't get sick."

Kathleen and John had been laughing it up the last hour. She appeared to hang on his every word. Obviously, bored, Julie sat quietly at the table. John tried to include her, but his real focus was on Kathleen and she seemed to like it that way.

Finally, Julie stood, took some money out of her purse and tossed it on the table. "I think I'm going to skip dessert Kathleen and go straight to bed, I don't think there's enough for three anyway."

"Dessert, what dessert?" John questioned.

"John." Julie said. With a grab of his chin, she looked directly in his eyes. "Pure and foolish little boy, good luck, Parsifal, Kunday is calling." At that, she gave Kathleen a disgusted look.

"Julie?" Kathleen glared at her.

"I'm sorry Kathleen. It's late. I'm tired, good night." Julie turned to John. "Nice meeting you."

Kathleen jumped to her feet. "Wait a minute, we'll walk you home." Julie stopped and looked back at Kathleen.

Shock and confused by Julie's outburst John insisted, "It's not that late." He was not ready for the night to end.

"It isn't?" Kathleen leaned over to John and whispered. "We'll walk Julie home, then, get a drink or something?"

"Oh, okay, any suggestions?" John muttered. *Skip the formalities. Tell her you want to take her straight home to your bed.*

"Your place or mine?" She asked.

"Oh." *This is too easy.* "All I got at my place is some beer." *Damn. Why did I say that?*

"I'm not much for beer." She made a pouty face. "My place is just across the street from Julie. I have some nice cognac."

Score. Ya, I am going to get lucky. Encouraged, John leaped to his feet and pulled whatever cash he had out of his pocket and tossed it on the table. In his haste, two packaged condom flipped out between the bills and landed on the table. Kathleen quickly picked them up and handed it back to him.

"I don't think you want to leave this for a tip, you might need them."

John stuck the condom back in his pocket. There was no question in his mind where this night was going. He took Kathleen's hand and they started for the door, feeling like a teenager again on his first hot date. Julie was waiting just outside the door.

The walk to Julie's apartment didn't cool the fire raging in his jeans. John waited at the sidewalk while Kathleen walked Julie to the door of her apartment building. There was a quick exchange between the two women that ended with laughter. Kathleen hurriedly rejoined John, looped her arm in his and they walked on.

Her apartment building was across and just down the street. They took the elevator to the fourth floor. At her door, they stopped and she turned and kissed him. It immediately turned into a mutual exploration with hands and tongues. John's mind fuzzed.

"Let me check if the coast is clear." Kathleen whispered.

"What?"

"Make sure my roommate Stacy isn't home." She slipped in the door, leaving John standing in the empty hall.

Roommate? She didn't mention roommate. Just then, the elevator doors opened. He turned his back and leaned against the door casing. An apartment door opened and closed behind him, he was alone again in the hall. *Come on Kathleen. Come on.*

Kathleen stepped out into the hall. "Sorry, my roommate is home. We have an agreement, no night visitors when the other is home."

"Wha——."

Her lips slammed into his, her tongue thrust into his mouth. There was a fury of touching and feeling. She pulled back. "Here's my number." He felt her slip something in his front pant pocket. "Call me tomorrow. Sorry, got to go." She disappeared into her apartment and closed the door.

John let out a groan. He pounded the wall. In a whimper, he dropped to his knees.

*   *   *

"I just closed the door." Kathleen told Julie then sipped her Coke. They sat at an outside table of a campus sandwich shop. "I heard him moan and hit the wall."

"No, you didn't, poor guy."

"I heard the elevator a little later and when I checked the hall, he was gone. He called this morning. We made a date for burgers and a movie tonight."

"So he asked you out?"

"You better believe it. It's part of my plan. Tempt him with promises, but not deliver until he is crawling, begging."

"So what's your game tonight?"

"I already called and left and message on his answering machine, re-scheduling for tomorrow night. I'll give him a call about midnight and whisper sweet nothings in his ear."

"Oh, poor guy."

"Tomorrow night we go to the early show. We'll sit in the back, I'll give him enough encouragement he won't remember the movie. After, I'll invite him to my place. That's where you, Stacy. Bill and Nathan come in. When the end credits start, all of you need to hurry to the lobby and wait near the exit. I'll keep him occupied a little longer. Then on our way out, surprise, surprise. Look who we've run into. Stacy will suggest an im-promptu party at our place. After the party, he'll be sent home with the rest. Sorry not tonight Charlie."

"Oh that is cruel."

"Ah, but it gets better. I can't see him this Friday, that's Halloween, I'll think of an excuse to put him off until Monday. Plan to meet for dinner at Escoffier's on El Comino. Tell him we'll go to his place for dessert."

"So you're going to spring your man trap, then?"

"Nope. My father is coming into town that day. He's joining us for dinner and I'll just have to drive Daddy back to his hotel. Regretfully sorry Johnny."

"He may give up the chase."

"Not on your life."

"But what if he's not interested in girls, what if he's gay?"

"He's not gay, I've checked, maybe a little naïve, but not gay. With my tease, he'll be so horny he'll walk through fire to get in bed with me. I'll arrange dinner at his apartment Friday night. By then he will be hamburger, and by Sunday meatloaf. The hook will be set."

*　　　*　　　*

"Dammit Alvin, this has been the longest two weeks in my life." The phone cord hung up a moment on the way to the balcony of his apart-ment. He straddled the lounge. His bicycle, a cafe table and two chairs occupy the rest of the space. "She's the hottest, most exciting girl I've ever met. I've run more miles and taken more cold showers in the last two weeks than I can count. I think she's the one. Like you and Sandra."

"We knew each other a year before we even dated."

"But now you're married."

"I don't see the similarity. How do you know she's the one after a couple of date?" Alvin asked. "That weren't much of a date if you ask me."

"I just know. I can't think about anything but her."

"Sound to me as if your dick's, doing the thinking. Remember what your father said."

"It's not that way at all, honest. We haven't even made it yet."

"That's my point. I hope she's not just stringing you along?"

"No, it's not like that, she wants it as much as me. We just keep getting interrupted. I guess you can call that bad timing. I'm telling you there is real chemistry there."

"Are you sure it's not just biology?"

"Biology——chemistry, who cares? Tonight she's coming here and it will be fire. I assure you there will be no interruptions. I'm so horny it feels like my balls are hanging to my knees."

"Just be careful she doesn't lop 'em off."

"Well if it doesn't happen tonight, I might lop them off myself out of frustration.

"You are desperate."

"You better believe it."

CHAPTER 11

PARADISE FOUND

INT.-JOHN MICHAELS' APARTMENT-NOVEMBER 7, 1986

THE APARTMENT is a comfortable third floor one bedroom
a few blocks from campus. The bedroom has a double bed
flanked by nightstands with lamps and one has alarm
clock. On one side of the room is a highboy dresser.
In the living room is a black leather sofa and chair
with a large TV and VCR on a stand. A counter bar with
two stools separate the kitchen area and small round
oak dining table with four matching chairs sits near
the sliding glass door that opens onto the balcony.
The furniture shows quality, the walls are off-white
except the one behind the sofa, its deep burgundy with
a modern female nude in tones of red.

John paces from the bedroom to the kitchen, checks the
oven and turns it down. He wears pressed jeans, laun-
dered at the drycleaners and a crisp blue and dark
gray striped short-sleeve shirt. He steps out on the
balcony.

The phone rings, John jumps and hurries to answer.

          JOHN (out of breath)
    Hello.

            ZACH
    John, is that you?

            JOHN
    Oh hi, Uncle Zach.

"Are you okay? You sound a little funny."

"I was outside." John took the phone out on the balcony where he could continue to watch for Kathleen's car.

"Where have you been keepin' yourself? I haven't seen you in at least a couple of months now."

"Been busy with school, it's my heaviest semester. After this, I'll only have two more classes to graduate."

"Good for you Son. You know Nadia and me are real proud of you."

"Thanks."

"Listen, we were thinking, this will be about the last good weekend for a barbeque before we button up for the winter. I've invited some of the guy's and their families from the precinct and since you know most of them, I thought you could join us."

"Sounds good, but . . . ." *Think of something fast.*

"You could drive down this evenin' and we can have two whole days, we can watch the game on Sunday."

"Ah . . . ah, I've already got a date tonight."

"Well drive down in the morning, it's only twenty minutes."

Oh gees, think, think.

"John, you there?"

"Yeah Zach, I'm here."

"Good, I thought I lost you. So can you make it?"

"I'd like to, but I have a big test next week. I planned on hitting the books all weekend."

"Oh."

John could hear the disappointment in his voice. "Thanksgiving is coming up, how about then?"

"Sure, that'll work."

"I can get us tickets for the big game on the Friday after."

"Hey yeah, that sounds great."

"Nadia too?"

"No, that's Black Friday, she's got plans."

"Well if any of the guys want to go, I can still get up to six tickets." Just then, John spotted Kathleen's car pull into the guest parking area. "Well you let me know the first of the week and I'll see what I can do. Got to go now, somebody's at the door. Bye Uncle Zach."

"Ya sure, bye and good luck — ."

John left the phone on the lounge and made a beeline for the bathroom for another piss and a quick check in the mirror. In the middle of his apartment, he stood for what seemed an eternity, his heart pounded with excitement awaiting Kathleen. At last, he heard the elevator doors followed shortly by a knock on his door. *Hold it, hold it, don't act to eager . . . go.*

"Hi, you found it okay. Come in, welcome to my humble abode."

"Nice pad." Kathleen looked around then handed John a bottle of wine. "Here, I hope you like white."

"Sure, it will go good with dinner." Struck by her red hair that appeared brighter complimented by her Kelly green blouse, John realized he was staring. "Ah, dinner, I fixed lasagna and antipasto salad . . . from the deli." He took the wine to the kitchen and started opening it. He could see Kathleen was checking out the apartment.

"How long have you lived here?"

"A little over a year. My sister Tess helped me fix it up. She's studying fashion design in New York."

"She did a nice job."

"Thanks, I'll tell her."

"I like your painting."

"I bought it from the artist. He was selling his work in a park near the Berlin Wall. We weren't supposed to paint the wall, but Tess did it when I was in class." John stepped up behind Kathleen with two large stemmed glasses of wine. "Here . . . cheers."

"To whatever tonight may bring." She smiled and they touched glasses before taking a sip and then ran her tongue slowly across her upper lip.

"I got spumoni— ."

She looked at him inquisitively.

"Spumoni, ice cream, for dessert."

"Nice." She stepped closer. John retreated until his calves touched the sofa.

Pointing to the sofa he asked, "Would you care to sit down?"

She gave him a slight push and he sat. She quickly knelt on the sofa beside him and looked into his eyes. He fidgeted with his wine glass, and then took a drink. In a quick move, she took his glass and placed both glasses on the end table. Without a word, she turned back to him and planted a kiss on his mouth. Fingers of one hand ran through his hair as the other slid down his chest to ignite his groin.

He fumbled with the buttons of her blouse with both hands. Once unbuttoned, she slipped it off and let it fall to the floor. Together they undid his shirt and her bra. She leaned over him and let him kiss her nipples. They harden at the teasing of his tongue. He hardened in response. Nimble fingers unfastened his belt and unzipped his fly. With a lift of his hips, she slipped his jeans to his knees. There was no need for words. Each knew what the other wanted. He kicked off his pants and carried her to his bed.

In the frenzy, he managed to grab a foil condom packet from his nightstand, but she took it from his hand and opened it. He rose up on his knees as she unrolled it on him slowly. Then she lay back and with a smile, opened the gates of Paradise to him.

*   *   *

John cracked his eyelids. The morning sun peeked through the window of his bedroom. Amidst empty condom wrappers, the digital alarm clock glowed 6:23. He rolled over. Kathleen lay asleep next to him. Slowly he became aware of the agony of his ecstasy. Every muscle ached, he felt like the survivor of a huge car wreck. Staring at the ceiling, he pleasantly recounted all of last night pleasures. Sore to the core, his need to pee forced him out of bed.

Tossed clothing littered the apartment, marking the path from the sofa to the bed. John snagged his jeans off the floor and slid into them. He staggered to the kitchen, found his way to the coffeemaker, put on a pot and sat on a counter stool to wait. For a moment, he thought he heard her stirring and checked, but she was still asleep. A wave of anxiety rose and he forced it away. Soon the coffeemaker gurgled its last and beeped. Coffee in hand he stepped out onto the balcony, sat on the lounge and sipped his brew.

The morning air nipped at his bare chest, he drew in the fresh breath and looked at the phone, wondering if he dare call Alvin this early on a Saturday. Finally, he grabbed it and dialed. On the fourth ring, a bewildered voice answered.

"Hello"

"Hi guy." John spoke in a hushed voice.

"Hey Dude . . . what's up so early. You singin' soprano?"

"Does it sound like it?"

"It sounds like you may have dropped an octave."

"That ain't all that's dropped. I just woke up and can hardly walk."

"You alone."

"No, she's still here. She's asleep."

"Well I guess that's a good sign. Did you wear her out?"

"Tried, but she turned the table. I'm so sore you'd think a horse kicked me."

"Complaining or bragging?"

"Oh good God, Alvin, it was paradise."

"Bragging."

Just then, the slider opened and Kathleen stepped out with a cup of coffee, wearing only John's shirt. "Kiss and tell?"

"Ah . . . NO——!"

"No, not bragging or no not kissing and telling?" Alvin asked. "I take it she's up."

"Yeah, got to go. Catch you later, bye."

John hung up and looked up at Kathleen from the lounge. She straddles him sitting on his lap. "Naughty boy, bragging to the other boys? Why not tell me?"

"Oh Kathleen, it was the greatest night of my life."

"If you thought that was, wait until you find out what I have in store for you later."

"What?"

"Oh, I'm going to keep it as a surprise for now." She leaned over and kissed him. "Now would you be a dear and run down to my car and get my overnight bag off the back seat."

After a couple of more long kisses, she let him up and walked him to the door. Handing him her car keys she said, "It's the red Camaro."

"I know."

*   *   *

Shirtless and shoeless, John was whistling on his return with Kathleen's suitcase. He was ecstatic when he found her in the shower. "Where do you want your bag?"

"Anywhere. Come join me. You can scrub my back."

"Gladly."

After a long hot shower, they dressed in sweats, and spent the rest of the morning with small talk before enjoying an early lunch of overcooked lasagna and wilted antipasto salad. Kathleen stepped out on the balcony. John opened the refrigerator door and asked, "Would you like a beer?"

"No thanks, I'm fine."

John got himself a beer and then joined her at the rail. She leaned against him. After several minutes, he reclined on the lounge. Kathleen sat between his legs and rested her head against his chest, running her hand up under his sweatshirt. Long fingernails teased at his nipple. "Take off your shirt."

He acquiesced, and dropped it beside the lounge. She began to play with the patch of hair below his bellybutton. The fall afternoon sun flooded the balcony. The carillon in Hoover Tower sang before it tolled three o'clock. He felt good.

Exploring finger slid under the waistband of his sweats. He groaned his approval. "Take 'em off." She whispered.

Several apartments in the next building had a view of the balcony. For a moment, he entertained the thought of insisting to moving inside, but a little gentle persuasion from her caressing fingers dispelled the thought. With a quick look across the way to assure they had no obvious spectators, he slid off his clothes. He suddenly realized his nakedness. He had unashamedly undressed in front of her, made love to her repeatedly and showered with her, but suddenly, exposed as they were he felt vulnerable and self-conscious, but her reassuring caresses made him relax, heightening the experience, he felt sensual and free.

Kneeling on the lounge between his legs, and with reinforced expectation he watched her fill her hand with body lotion. He trembled when her warm hands spread the smooth cool cream across his chest, belly and down all the way to his knees in a long fluid motion. Reaching up with firm fingers, she started kneading his right chest with both hands. Slowly, sensually, she worked his muscles. He closed his eyes. "Oh God, that feels good."

Shifting her weight forward she began working her finger magic on his neck and shoulders. Slowly inch by inch, she worked her way down over his torso. The tower clock struck the half-hour. With anticipation of what would happen when she reached below the naval, he started to fantasize.

"You're gorgeous." She said. He opened his eyes and followed her gaze. She held him at her mercy. "So big and firm."

Only briefly uncomfortable at the scrutiny, he was pleased by her admiration.

Through previous experiences, he recalled a few superlatives used to describe it, but gorgeous was never one of them. *She certainly knows how to inflate a man's . . . ego.*

Abruptly he felt a sharp pain on his right pectoral. He winced and opened his eyes. Kathleen had sunk her teeth deep into his flesh. The pain forced him to let out a yelp and pushed her away. Her teeth broke the skin of his chest.

"Just a little love nip. What's love without a little pain? It makes the loving better."

It was more than a love bite. Blood had begun to flow. She gently kissed the bite. The sting of pain melted under her lips. Gently she took him to new heights of passion and he forgot the wound. Skillfully she lavished upon him more pleasure than he ever imagined possible.

The tower clock sang, tolling the fourth hour of the afternoon. His tower stood equally as impressive as Mr. Hoover's tower, he assured himself. Then like the Mother Goddess, she rose over him and took him in her womb. Of all the metaphors, he thought of to describe that moment failed. She just fucked his brains out. When at last they collapsed, wet and exhausted, she curled up on him. The tower clock the tolled fifth hour and he drifted into sleep.

*   *   *

When he awoke, it was dark and she was still in his arms. She had found a blanket and pulled it over them. He began stroking her hair and she stirred. His hand touched her cheek. She pressed his fingers to her lips and kissed them. "I love you."

"I love you too." She echoed.

John filled his lungs with the night air. "I've never been so——so happy."

"Is that what you call it, happy?" Her hand slid up his chest as she spoke.

"I call it paradise."

"That's more like it."

CHAPTER 12

WHEN YOU KNOW, YOU KNOW

```
INT.-DREGS' COFFEE HOUSE-MORNING-Nov. 17, 1986
```

Julie is waiting for Kathleen when she rushes in, dropped her purse, shopping bags, and sweater on a chair.

                    KATHLEEN
          Sorry I'm late.

                    JULIE
          That's okay, no classes until this
          afternoon.

"What are you drinking?" Kathleen asked, grabbing her wallet on the way to the counter. Dregs' offered counter service only, during the slow part of the day.

"The house decaf."

Kathleen ordered two house blends, one a decaffeinated, and two brand muffins. Kathleen gave Julie a grin while she waited for the order. "They had your favorite muffins." She said returning to the table with the coffee and muffins on a tray.

"Oh thanks." Julie helped herself to the coffee and muffin. "I haven't seen you since last Thursday. Do you let him come up for air?"

"Sometimes, I finally had to send him to class to get some rest, but I'll make him do our homework as soon as he gets home, before I let him do his own."

"So I gather you're keeping him interested."

"He's asked me to move in with him."

"You were serious."

"Damn right I was serious. I'll move in over this weekend. Stacy is pissed. I told her I would pay my half of the rent until she finds a new roommate."

"My, that was fast. At least you'll have a place to go back to when your boy wakes up." Julie tore the rest her muffin into small pieces. "Do you know what you're doing? Or do you just think you do?" She put a piece of muffin in her mouth and washed it down with coffee. "What about him? You can't be in love. You hardly know him."

"He thinks he's in love with me, that's all that counts. Love is just a state of mind."

"Honestly, I don't know how you can do this. How can you live with yourself?"

"It's easy. I knew what I wanted and went for it. I'll keep him happy, he's easy to please, and he pleases me, for now."

"So you are going to marry him?"

"When he asks."

"And if he doesn't."

"He will, when I'm ready."

"He wants to wait until he finishes law school before marriage."

"That sounds logical."

"I already told my sister about him. Her only concern is that he isn't Catholic."

"That's the least of any ones worries. Does she know how old he is?" Julie asked.

"Not yet."

"And what about you, I know I've asked, but do you love him at all?"

"That's irrelevant."

"I don't know what kind of marriage you are going to have if you don't love him?"

"Remember, love has not been the criteria for marriage for most of human existence. I'll manage to love him, in my way."

"I hope so, for his sake."

"I am being honest." Kathleen sipped her coffee and finished her muffin. With nothing more to say, she looked at her watch, "I've got to scoot." She gathered her things. "We'll have to do lunch soon."

"Remember next week is Thanksgiving, I'll be going home for a few days."

"Then we'll do it this week, say Thursday, I'll call. I've got to go pack.

*   *   *

"Gees Son, I wished you'd of talked to me sooner." Zach said. He sat across from John at a small table at Sammy's Donut Hole, the twenty-four hour police hangout up the block from the station. Zach was on his morning break.

"You know Uncle Zach, I love you and Nadia and respect your wisdom and love, but I'm not asking your permission. Kathleen is moving in with me."

"I'm not saying you can't do that. But have you considered school and your future? It's all so sudden."

"It's a different age now. We are just living together. If it works out, somewhere down the line we'll tie the knot. If not, we go our ways, but I don't see that happening."

"I understand. Keep your focus on school is all I ask."

"I've got two classes left to complete my bachelors and I can start on my law degree this spring while I finish them, if I really push it I'll graduate in two-and-a-half years. I'm not planning marriage until then."

"That's good. Please Son, take it slow. When do we get to meet this girl?"

"I'll bring her Thanksgiving."

"Well I guess you've got it all worked out."

John put his hand on Zach's. "Don't worry, I won't do something stupid."

"Well then there's not much more I can say."

"Thank you."

"So ah . . . with the two of you living together . . . are you using birth control."

"Yes Uncle."

"Condoms or is she on the pill, if you don't mind me asking?"

"Condoms."

"Condoms are not always reliable. You should have . . . Kathleen check on the pill.

"She tried it, too many side effects, makes her sick as a dog. And the pill's not one-hundred percent reliable either. Kathleen is very careful. She's not ready for children."

"She sounds sensible."

"Oh she is." John picked up his coffee. "If something happens then it's meant to be."

"You sound more like your old man all the time."

"Thanks, I think." John reached into his shirt pocket and pulled out an envelope. "Here are your tickets for the game." John stood. "I've got to run, meeting Kathleen this afternoon."

Zach stood up, banging his revolver against the table. "After all the years of making us cops fatter, you would think Sammy would enlarge the booths." Zach reached out his arms and the two hugged. "So we'll see you and Kathleen Thanksgiving."

"That you will."

*　　　*　　　*

John sat at a table in Drag's, looked at his watch and continued tapping his fingers impatiently. The bright fall sun streamed through the windows. He opened a book and tried to read, but couldn't concentrate. At the sound of the door, he looked up to see Alvin. He stood.

"Hey Alvin, your late." Alvin had put on a few pounds since he married, but still looked skinny and a bit disheveled, he did however sport new wire frame glasses.

"Don't know why I let you talk me into coming today. I should have guessed the Saturday before Thanksgiving the traffic would be bad. Stop and go all the way."

"Can I get you some coffee?" John asked, already on his way to the counter.

"Sure." Alvin followed at John's heels. "So stud, what's this all about?"

"Kathleen's moved in with me."

"When?"

"Yesterday."

"Yesterday — that was quick. You still on that kick?"

"It's not a kick, I am serious." John paid for the coffees and they returned to the table.

"Ok, so it's not a kick? You called, what three maybe four weeks ago——tell me you met this girl you've got the hots for. Next day you call again——it's paradise. A week later, you call——we've got to talk. Now you tell me she has moved in with you. She moving alright, I think you need an ice pack in your pants."

"I don't know how to explain it, but this is the real thing. I am absolutely, positively sure."

"It sounds like you're trying to convince yourself. You need to let your balls, cool down——start thinking with your brain again. How can you know? Who is she? Where's she from? Where's she going? You sure she's not just a gold-digger taking you for a ride——playing you for a fool. You know you have a lot at stake here."

"Slow down. Listen to me. I'll tell you what I told Zach. I'm not asking your permission."

"But how do you know this is right?"

"I know." The determination in John's manner put an end to the inquisition. He took a sip of coffee. "I can't explain it, but I know." He looked Alvin in the eyes. "When we marry. Now I'm not saying right away. In a couple of years or so." John paused. "I want you to be my best man. I'll understand if you say no."

"You know I can't refuse. I'm glad you're going to take a few breaths before you plan to tie the knot. Make sure they are very deep ones."

"I don't know why you and Zach aren't more excited for me."

"Just want you to be happy. We don't want you to get hurt."

"I've got to take this chance, if I get hurt, so be it."

"If you are sure, I'm with you a hundred percent." Alvin played with the stir stick in his coffee. "This is a real kick in the pants, you know." Alvin grinned. "So tell me about her. More than she's paradise."

"Well . . . she is funny and bright and of course beautiful." *Should I tell him she thinks I'm gorgeous too?* "She's Irish, from Chicago. Her father is a big-time criminal attorney. She has an older sister and three older brothers. Her sister and one of her brothers are attorneys and one brother is a medical doctor."

"You better mind your p's and q's with a family of ambulance chasers. So what's the other brother a politician or a thief?"

"He's a Catholic Priest."

"Oh brother, I see some friction there. Is the whole family Catholic?"

"I think so."

"That, my dear friend, may be your nemesis."

* * *

John stood at the open window and watched the rain. It had started sometime after midnight. He had lain sleepless most of the night listening to the rain and thinking about how happy he was. The emptiness that had hung over him since his mother's death, was at last gone. His thoughts, his wistful imaginings and sleeping dreams were of the future. His home, Kathleen and children, a son, maybe two or three, like the old Fred MacMurray sitcom, *My Three Sons,* he would be the perfect dad. The past few weeks were a blur. In the span of one short month, he had met and fallen in love with the most wonderful woman in the world and now they were living together.

At daybreak he got up and quietly made coffee, letting Kathleen sleep. He watched the rain and the clock for nearly an hour. Still in his white t-shirt and briefs, he stepped out on the balcony with the telephone. Though it was a bit on the chilly side, he didn't care and the overhang kept the balcony dry. He dialed and waited for Tess to answer. "Hello." A sleepy voice yawned.

"Hi Sis. How are you?" He was pleased as always to hear his sister's voice.

"Why are you calling so early? What time is it?"

"Nine your time."

"Oh crap."

"Yeah. And I'm doing fine too."

"Sorry. I over slept." She paused. "Good morning dear brother, glad to hear your voice." She yawned again. "Sorry. What are you doing up so early, isn't it still dark there?"

"Not quite. I've met a girl."

"A——oh, this sounds serious. What, is it Groundhog Day or something, you finally crawled out of your hole. Where did you meet her, the library?

"All right, don't be funny, I'm serious. Her name is Kathleen. Kathleen O'Malley, she's from Chicago. I met her a few weeks ago. And yes, in the library. She's a law student too. She is simply fantastic. I'll send some pictures."

"Are you serious?"

"Yes, you can meet her when you come out for Christmas."

"Oh, I've been meaning to tell you, a group of us from school are planning a little ski trip Christmas break, to the French Alps with a few days in Paris. You're not disappointed."

"No . . . ." John twisted the phone cord in his fingers. "Why would you think that?"

"I know you brother. You probably have Christmas all planned."

"We are living together." He said softly. "I told you it was serious."

There was a long silence. "I didn't see that coming. This is my brother John Michaels I'm talking to? I'll cancel the trip."

"No, no, we're not getting married, at least not for now."

"I would hope not."

"You don't sound excited?" John questioned.

"Maybe it's because I'm not sleeping with her." There was another silence. "You caught me . . . by surprise." There was an extended pause. "Congratulations."

"What, what's wrong, aren't you happy for me?"

"It's not that, it's . . . ."

"John, who are you talking too?" Kathleen asked from the sliding glass door.

"Listen Tess, I've got to go, I'll write and sent you those pictures. Talk to you soon. Love You." He hung up the phone without waiting for her response.

The sky darkened and the rain started to fall heavier.

"Was that your sister?"

"Yeah, she's real happy for us."

Kathleen quietly came up behind him and kissed him on the neck. She slid her hand across his chest. He rolled his head toward hers and smiles.

"You're freezing. You'll catch your death out here in your underwear. Come back to bed." She whispered in his ear. "I know how to warm you up."

John needed no further encouragement. He picked her up in his arms, kissed her, and carried her back to bed. He pulled off his t-shirt, the scab and bruising visible, she turned her mouth towards the bite. John tensed. He felt her warm lips, a gentle kiss and then she turned her lips to his.

"You left your mark on me."

"I guess that means you are my possession — forever."

CHAPTER 13

A FAMILY INSPECTION

EXT./INT.-TAXI-CHICAGO SUBURBS-DAY- FEBRUARY 17, 1987

Kathleen and John are in the backseat of a taxi on
their way from O'Hare Airport to the O'Malley's home
in Arlington Heights. It has snowed for three days
straight, starting late Valentine's Day, and driving
conditions are bad.

                    JOHN
          Look at all the brick.

John was amazed at the bricks used in home construction. It's his
first trip to Chicago. "They don't build houses with brick much in California, too many earthquakes."

John could see the taxi driver looking at him and Kathleen through
the rearview mirror and heard his grumbling. "First, it was the snow, now
it's the bricks. I'm glad we're not going downtown. I never heard anyone
talk so much, he's giving me a headache."

Just then, they slid to a stop in front of the O'Malley's home and the
cabby popped the lid of the trunk from the dash. "Twelve-seventy-five on
the meter."

It was obvious the cabby wasn't getting out in the snow, so John
handed him a twenty and got out. Kathleen followed, but instead of John
getting the luggage, he just stood and looked up at the snow with his
arms outstretched.

"Come on, get the bags." Kathleen's words snapped him out of his awe. "I'm freezing."

Still watching the falling flakes swirl, John grabbed the luggage and closed the lid. Apparently anxious to beat a hasty retreat, the cabbie pulled off as soon as the trunk lid slammed, spinning his wheels on the ice in his getaway.

Kathleen took the overnight case leaving the two large suitcases for John. Two inches of new snow had accumulated on recently shoveled walk. Fresh snow crunched under their feet as they made their way toward the front steps. Before they had crossed the porch, the door flew open and Kathleen's mother bounded out to greet them.

"Come in. Come in." Katie hugged and kissed Kathleen with a warm greeting."

"Hi Mom."

"And you must be John?" She turned to hug John, but froze with her arms extended and looked at him. He was soaking wet from melted snow and now with a fresh layer, it had turned him into a walking snowman. "Look at you, you must be freezing."

"I've tried to get him in, but this is the first time he's seen it snow."

"You've never seen snow?"

"I've seen snow," John tried to explain, "I've been skiing, and it snowed in Germany, but not like this. It's beautiful."

"Well you will see plenty of it here. Welcome to our home. Get inside and warm up before you catch your death."

"Thank you."

"Now Kathleen, take him downstairs and get him out of those wet clothes before he catches a cold. He's in the basement guestroom and you're in the upstairs sewing room."

"That will be cozy." Kathleen said under her breath preceding John into the house.

Katie stepped to the edge of the porch and looked at the snow while John and Kathleen waited.

"What are you doing Mom?" Kathleen asked from the door.

"I'm trying to imagine what seeing falling snow for the first time would be like." After a moment, she shivered and started for the door, shaking her head. "All I see is plain old misery."

*   *   *

Katie gave the contents of a huge kettle a stir and adjusted the heat. The kitchen was large, but comfortable with a breakfast nook. Off from it were the family room in one direction and the dining room in the other.

Perched on a stool at the kitchen counter, Kathleen sipped a fresh cup of coffee. Katie returned to the sink, she looked a little like Kathleen only shorter and a few pounds heavier, with a touch of gray in her reddish-brown hair. "It will be a couple of hours until dinner, would you like something to snack on in the meantime?"

"Oh no, I'm fine."

"How about John, do you think he's hungry?

"He might be."

"I'll fix him a sandwich. What does he like?"

"Anything, he's not fussy?"

"He's not like your brothers."

"Heavens no."

"I'm glad you insisted he take a shower to warm up." Katie poured herself a cup of coffee. "He looked like he was wet clear to the skin."

"He was so wet and full of snow at the airport, I didn't think the cab driver was going to let him in his cab."

"How did he get so full of snow at the airport?"

"He went out in the street and stood watching it come down." Kathleen poured herself some more coffee. "He's like a big kid in the first snow."

"He is a kid."

"Mom, let's not start that, he's twenty-three."

"And you are thirty-one."

"There is nothing wrong with that."

"That's eight years. Couldn't you have found someone a little older?"

"Mom," Kathleen's Irish temper flashed, "We've gone over that on the phone and you promised."

"All right, all right, I've said my piece. I won't mention it ever again."

"Promise?"

"I promise."

*　　　*　　　*

John came up from down stairs. He was wearing his favorite jeans, and a Norwegian ski sweater in browns and tans. "Promise what?"

"Oh. I promised Kathleen that I'd make her favorite fruit salad for dinner, since she couldn't make it for Christmas."

"Mom, we've been over that too."

"Fruit salad's one of my favorites." John sat on the stool next to Kathleen and looked around the kitchen. "Your kitchen is bigger than our whole apartment."

Katie glared at Kathleen with the expression of an inquisitor. John realized that she didn't know he and Kathleen were living together. "Will Mr. O'Malley be here tonight? I enjoyed our visit last November."

"No." Katie turned quickly back to the stove.

John sensed he said something else wrong and looked at Kathleen questioning. She shook her head no. "Dad is in New York. He has a branch office there and has to spend a lot of time there keeping things going."

John decided he better keep his mouth shut.

There was a loud slam of the backdoor. From where John sat, he could see a man through the mudroom door wearing a fedora and black overcoat. He brushed off the snow and unbuttoned his coat. Beneath the coat, he wore green hospital scrubs. With effort, he hung up the hat, but the coat dropped on the floor. It appeared he was having some difficulty getting the coat to stay on the hook. He made several attempts before he could get it to stay.

"It's my brother Jake." Kathleen told John.

Katie paid no attention to the commotion made by her son in the mudroom. "How about some coffee John?"

"No thanks, it keeps me awake if I drink it this late in the day."

"Maybe the man would like a real drink." Jake said. He charged at John with his right hand extended. "Hi, I'm Jake, I've been hearing a lot about you." He seized John's right hand and pumped it. John started to stand. "Sit, sit."

"Pleased to meet you." John could see the family resemblance. Jake a small framed man, that John guessed him to be at least a half-head shorter than he was. "I've heard a lot about you too."

"Rumors I'll assure you. All rumors." Jake stopped shaking John's hand, but didn't let it go.

He appeared to try to focus on John's face. His narrow chin, black curly hair and sparkling dark eyes, gave him the appearance of a leprechaun.

Jake finally released his hand. "I'll give this back to you." He spun to his mother, giving her a loud kiss on the cheek.

"Pee-you, you've been drinking." Katie waved her hand in front of her face fanning away the fumes.

"I stopped in at the Shamrock." Turning, he froze and looked at Kathleen as if she just appeared out of nowhere. "Hi Sis." He grabbed her and gave her more than a brotherly kiss on the mouth. Lifting her off her feet, he swung her around the kitchen in a full circle. When he let go, she laughed. He pivoted to John. "Now John, how 'bout a whisky? Irish of course."

"Sounds good."

"Isn't it a little early?" Katie asked, clearly sounding her disapproval.

"It's what the doctor ordered, and besides where's our Irish hospitality."

"You." Katie looked like she wanted to stay angry but couldn't. He smiled. His Gaelic charms were infectious.

"Anyone else?"

"I'll have one," Kathleen added.

"You're not pregnant?"

"Jake." Katie gasped.

"I hope not." Kathleen said with a smile.

Jake slapped John on the leg. "With this stud, it's possible."

"You would be the first to know." Kathleen told him with an ominous sounding laugh.

"Jake, you know I don't like that kind of talk."

Jake ignored his mother. "I bet Mom's got you in the basement too."

With that, Jake bounded to the wet bar in the family room ready to fix their drinks. "How do you like the snow?" He set up three glasses and began filling them with ice out of the refrigerator under the bar.

"It's great. We don't see much snow in our part of California. I guess everyone thinks I'm crazy because I like the snow."

"He stood out in it at the airport until I didn't think the cabbie would let us in his cab." Kathleen said, and then gave John a kiss on the cheek and whispered. "Big kid."

"Stick around here and you'll get sick of it in a hurry. You're lucky the plane could even land." Some of the ice cubes slipped out of Jake hand and dropped on the floor, sliding across the room. "Oh shit."

"Jake, mind you mouth." Katie insisted.

"Where are Christine and the kids?" Kathleen asked.

"Kelly has a dance recital this afternoon, they will be over after." Jake scooped the ice cubes in the large tumblers using his finger. "Hope ye don't mind the fancy tongs. The whisky will kill any germs." He then proceeded to pour the largest whisky's John had ever seen.

"So how did you escape the hospital?" Kathleen asked.

"I hid in a laundry cart and paid an orderly to push me out the back door."

"Jake. Don't be so smart-alecky," Katie grumbled.

"I did thirty-six hours straight, so I got sprung." Jake brought the drinks in, two in one hand, gave one to Kathleen and passed the other to John as he stood. "Let's see, we got to make a toast." Jake stood next to John and put his arm over his shoulder. His shortness showed. "I want to bend your ear a little too, before the madhouse starts." He looked up at John. "Christ, how tall are you?"

"Six-one." Kathleen answers. "Madhouse?"

"You know——girl talk." Jake looked at John. "Are you sure? I'm five-seven and you make me feel like a shrimp."

"Maybe it's the boots." John turned his foot to show the heel of his boot.

"Cowboy boots, California. I should've guessed it. Where's your horse?" Not waiting for an answer, Jake stepped back, and held out his glass. "An old Irish toast." He lifted his glass to John. "To the cowboy and his snow. He may be a little doffed. But his eyes are bright and his heart be warm. May he learn to come in from the snow——before his balls freeze off."

"Jake." Katie yelled. "You're embarrassing our guest."

"Naw. Come on drink up." Jake had downed half his drink in one gulp then turned to John.

"If he wants to fuck an Irish gal he'll have to take an Irish ribbin'. Right John?"

"Jake!"

"Dar you go again Mommy." Jake seized John by the shoulder. "You are fucking my sister? If you're not, there's sure as hell somethin' wrong with ya."

"I ah, I . . . ." Pathetically, John felt his face flushed and looked to Kathleen for help.

"Jake O'Malley, if you can't talk with a civil tongue in your mouth, I will shut your trap for you, and you'll be eating your stew through a straw." Katie picked up a large wooden spoon and shook it at her son.

"I'm sorry Mommy." He gave her a kiss and she whacked him lightly on the back with the wooden spoon. "Ouch."

"Don't apologize to me, apologize to this fine young man you have just met and humiliated in front of his girlfriend."

"Look John, Kathleen, I'm sorry, I'm a little shitfaced, and I didn't mean to offend. Okay?" He finished his drink and sat the glass on the counter then hugged Kathleen. He held her close with his right hand to the back of her head and pressed her cheek to his.

"Oh it's okay." Kathleen assured him with a pat on the back. "We still love you."

Jake continued to hug Kathleen, until she finally pulled away.

Jake looked at her with his little boy grin until she smiled back. At that, he turned to John, spreading his arms out for a hug. "Forgiven?"

"Hey, no problem." John hesitated a moment before he wrapped him arms around Jake.

The men hugged. John felt Jake slide his left hand over his butt and pulled them tight together. John quickly released Jake expecting him to do the same. When he didn't John looked at Kathleen over Jake's head for help. All she did was start to laugh. Jake continued to hug John. Kathleen seemed to be enjoying Jake's antics. Shocked, John felt Jake grab his crotch and take a feel. Angered at the personal invasion, John jerked free with his fist clenched.

"No wonder Sis likes you." Laughing, Jake turned his gaze to Kathleen, swaying unsteady on his feet, he added, "I can imagine what he looks like naked." His head wobbled. "I'll bet his is a damn good screw."

"Damn you Jake." Kathleen's hand made a loud slap when it hit Jake's face. Sobered only slightly by the blow, Jake fought to maintain his balance. They all stood frozen in silence.

Obviously angered, Jake took his glass from the counter, staggered to the family room bar, generously refilled it, and then disappeared into the living room.

"Irishmen, always with the joking," Katie muttered. She lifted the lid of the stew and nervously checked it.

"I'm sorry. I don't know what's got in to him." Kathleen apologized. "Please forgive him. I've never seen him behave like that. It must be the stress at work."

John was both angered and humiliated. "Too damn much——Irish Whiskey," John assured her, "If he tries anything like that again I'll—— I'll——."

Kathleen kissed him, took his clenched right hand in hers and rubbed it gently until he relaxed it. She whispered to John. "I've never seen you angry before, it's sexy." With a kiss to the back of his fingers she begged, "Please forgive him, he's drunk." She glanced toward the family room, then to her mother, and back to John with a pleading look. "I think I need to talk to him." She let go of John's hand and followed after her brother.

Left alone, John felt awkward in the kitchen with Katie, who busied herself at the range. He took his drink from the counter and downed it, and sat back on the stool to wait for Kathleen's return.

"Do you like tongue?" Katie asked John without turning from the range.

"What?"

"Do you like tongue, pickled beef tongue, to eat?"

"I don't think I've ever had it."

"I was wondering if you wanted a sandwich, I have some tongue chilled. I'll make you a tongue sandwich. It's an old family favorite."

"I can believe that." John stood, looking for Kathleen. "I think I'll pass, I'm not hungry. I'm going to see how Kathleen is doing."

Katie turned quickly to John. "I think you better wait here, she can take care of her brother." The sternness in her voice stopped him.

John settled back on his stool and looked at his empty glass. *I could sure use another one of these.* Somehow, the situation suddenly seemed funny and he began to relax. An image from the movie, *Tom Jones,* came to mind, the scene where the Squire checks out the new bull. *I guess I checked out. That was an odd way to get the family's stamp of approval. Odd family. Can't wait to meet the rest.* He smiled to Katie and waited for whatever might come next.

"Jean and her family should be here soon." Katie worked with her back to John while she spoke. "You'll like Jean, she's an attorney. Kathleen and Jean are planning to practice law together, if she ever finishes law school."

"Oh is that so." At first, the words didn't register. "Oh, you mean law, here in Chicago?" His surprise must have showed.

"Yes, for as long as I can remember she's been talkin' about it. Hasn't Kathleen told you?"

"No, she hasn't mentioned it." *What next?*

"The girls plan to join their brother and take over their father's office here in Chicago. I would expect Kathleen to join Jean when she graduates, whenever that is."

"That's strange." Now John truly needs another drink. "Kathleen has never said anything about returning to Chicago to practice law." Deciding to help himself, he picked up his glass, but before he got far, Kathleen returned from the living room, they met at the bar.

"Need a refresher?" She asked.

"I think I do."

She filled his glass and they both returned to their stools, clicking glasses before they drank.

"He is out like a light on the couch. I took his shoes off and covered him," she reassured her mom.

"He's been going for thirty-six hours straight, then had a little too much to drink at the Shamrock." Katie declared. "Irishmen, do two things better than anything else, drink and fight. But just because he's a wee bit tipsy, is no excuse for his behavior. He just wanted to see if he could rile you a bit, I'm a guessing. Didn't mean no harm."

Teasingly Kathleen putted her hand on John's leg out of the line of sight of her mother. "His little medical exam did rile you didn't it, honey?

It was free." She ran her hand up his leg as she leaned forward, kissed him and gave him a friendly little squeeze.

Through clenched teeth, John growled. "I almost, freed him." Then he kissed her back.

"That's all you get for now," she whispered in his ear.

"I will be glad when he finishes his residency and can start his own practice. Working so many hours is driving him crazy." Katie said, continuing her work on dinner.

"Later." Kathleen whispered in John's ear, while giving him another loving squeeze and moaning in his ear. After a long moment, she took a deep breath and turned her attention to her mother. "Does he still plan to partner with Dr. Collin here in Arlington Heights?"

"I don't know what his plan is. It changes with the wind."

John reached for his glass of whiskey. Rapidly becoming aware of the whiskey's effects, he just ran his finger around the rim

"Speaking of partners and practices, your mother was just telling me about Jean's and your plans."

"Oh that was just girl talk."

"Girl talk?" Katie questioned.

"Yes mom, just talk." She took John's hand. "John owns a nice home near San Jose and he plans to practice there, when he finishes school. His father was a police officer in San Jose too."

"Was he, I bet he'll be proud."

"He's dead Mom, killed in the line of duty. Remember I told you."

"Oh, I'm sorry, I forgot. Bless his soul."

"It was a long time ago, but I made a promise to myself——." John began to explain.

"Have you told your sister about this, just talk?" Katie interrupted.

"We'll talk this week."

Katie put a plate of cheeses and finger sandwiches that she had been preparing on the counter. "I guess we all have a lot to talk about. Help yourself, dinner is not until seven. Try the pickled tongue sandwiches."

John looked at the little triangle shaped sandwiches. *Pickle tongue. This family has its thing about pickled tongues.*

CHAPTER 14

A MATTER OF PRINCIPLE

INT.-THE O'MALLEY DINING ROOM-LATER THAT EVENING

The O'Malley's clan is gathered around the dining room table with the kids tucked away at their table, safe in the breakfast nook. Recovered from his nap, Jake has showered and changed into a gray pinstriped suit that his wife had brought him. CHRISTINE, Jake's wife, blond straight hair and blue/green eyes, is a dutiful Irish Catholic wife of seven years. She and Jake have three children and she is pregnant again. She sits quietly across from him at the table. Her face reflects sadness and her demeanor indicated that Jake is an asshole at home too.

JEAN, fuller than Kathleen, a taller version of her mother, sits next to her brother Jake, and across from her husband PATRICK, her husband and the father of their four children. Balding and with horn-rimmed glass, Patrick is quiet and puts up with the antics of his brother-in-law. Kathleen's Brother CONNOR and his wife ROSE are near the end of the table. Connor and Rose are both redheads, and their six kids all sport the same mops of bright red hair.

The surprise of the evening was the arrival of the oldest of the O'Malley children, FATHER RYAN O'MALLEY, a Catholic priest. He takes his place at the end of the table. Katie sits at the head of the table, the matriarch, flanked by Kathleen in a deep green dress and John in a dark blue suit.

The dinner has proceeded quite well and John is slowly getting to know his new noisy prospective family.

Jake, still a little groggy from his nap and more
whiskey, has so far behaved himself.

The somewhat peaceful dinner is shattered when SEAN,
Jake and Christine's oldest son, a skinny dark-haired
boy, runs through the room and circles the table yelling. Two of Connor and Rose's girls are chasing him
and yelling. Both girls are a head taller than the
boy.

                    JAKE
          At it already Sean? That a boy. Keep
          on running. Don't let those wild
          wicked women get ya.

                    KATIE
          Children settle down. Why don't you
          turn on the TV? (To Jake) Don't en-
          courage them.

"It's on." The tallest of the three yelled as they make their third lap.

"Then sit down and watch it." Jake yelled back. He poured himself another glass of red wine. "Why don't you see if you can settle them down?" He barked orders to Christine without looking up.

The obedient wife got up and ushered the three children into the other room without saying a word. Kathleen watched her go and John could see her anger build. Obviously irritated, she threw her napkin on her plate and looked at her brother with an almost lethal stare. "You're such an asshole Jake. Why don't you ever take care of the kids for once?"

"Me?"

Patrick took the hint. "Excuse me, I'll check on the kids."

Jake sat with his elbow on the table and sucked at his wine. He wait-ed until Patrick was out of hearing before he commented. "Henpecked husbands!"

"Jake O'Malley, you are breeding a scab on your nose if you're not careful." As usual, Katie was ignored.

"Yeah little brother, what makes you so holier-than-thou?" Jean bristled as she came to the defense of her husband.

"Because my job is to work my goddamn balls off at that fucking hospital and hers is to take care of the brats." Jake emptied his glass and poured another.

116

"Haven't you has enough?" Katie asked.

Jake slammed down his glass. Wine spattered over the table. He stood and pushed his chair back, with his legs. "I gotta take a piss," he announced, "Ya want ta come and hold it for me Mommy?" The room fell silent as Jake stormed out.

Ryan stood. "Please excuse me." Irritated, he followed Jake.

Connor jumped to his feet and followed his brothers.

Katie's eyes puffed with tears for a moment, her only visible emotion. Allowed only an instant to her display of feelings, she took a drink of water and composed herself. "I'm sorry you had to see that John. He's under a lot of pressure, you will forgive him?" The silence hung in the air like a bad smell.

John and the women returned to their dinner in silence.

"Yes, well let's get back to what I was saying." Kathleen broke the quiet gracefully and tried to change the subject. "I want to take John to see Saint Patrick's while we are here."

"You rang?" Patrick teased returning to the table. Jean gave him a loving, don't get smart look, as he sat.

Christine came in from the kitchen. "Did I miss anything?" She glanced at the empty chairs. "Where are the boys?"

"They took Jake out to crucify him in the snow." Jean quipped.

"I wish, but he's not worthy of it." With her head down, Christine admits quietly. "He's getting to be a bear." Obviously, her husband's behavior embarrassed her.

"Kathleen wants to take John to see Saint Patrick's." Katie was in control of dinner again and determined to put an end to the airing of the families' dirty laundry.

"Oh, how lovely." Gratefully, Christine took the cue that the subject had been changed.

"Are you Catholic?" Patrick asked John.

"Not hardly!"

"Are you interested in Catholicism?" Patrick looked at him questioning. "Saint Patrick's Cathedral is beautiful. It's over a hundred years old. Are you going to become a Catholic?"

"I don't think so." John felt himself start to bristle.

"What's wrong with becoming a Catholic?" Christine asked.

"Well, I don't believe much in any religion."

Katie dropped her fork. "You don't believe in God?"

"I didn't say that."

"Well we can't have an atheist." Katie flushed.

"Mother, let the man speak." Jean advised Katie in her counselor at law voice. Then she looked at John with cold eyes. "So what do you believe?"

"Well, I'm not an Atheist."

"Oh thank the Lord."

"Mother, please let him talk." Jean glanced at Katie out of the side of her eyes then back to John.

"I just don't believe in the Catholic concept of God."

"Oh Saint's preserve us." Katie blessed herself with the sign of the cross.

"That's okay!" Returning from the other room Ryan came unexpectedly to John's rescue. Standing at the door he leaned against the casing with his arms folded. "It isn't what you believe. It's what you are that counts. Most Catholics don't believe in all the doctrines and teaching of the Church, or even know what being a Catholic is all about. They are just born Catholics and so stay Catholics, fulfill their Holy Obligations and go about their lives." He stepped to the table and leaned forward with both hands on the back of his chair. With intensity, he looked at John from across the table with his piercing eyes. His black suit and Roman collar gave him authority, but uniforms or symbols of authority didn't intimidate John. "So, the thing is, if you're thinking of get married to a Catholic, it's best if you are a Catholic or willing to become one."

"Well, I don't see that happening." John didn't blink as the two men stared at each other.

"Oh, Holy Mother of God!" Katie blessed herself again. She has obviously had enough confrontations for one night.

"No offence Mrs. O'Malley." John felt his jaw tighten as he glared back at Ryan. "I just don't think I'll ever become a Catholic or a member of any church for that matter. John's sudden bristling show of fortitude brought silence to the room.

Kathleen stood and started clearing the table. "Let's get the dishes going before we are here all night."

"Good idea," Jean agreed, "The kids have school tomorrow."

When Kathleen picked up John's dish, she whispered to him, "We'll talk about this later."

"He's out like a light I think, on the living room sofa." Connor announced, returning to the table.

The women got up and started clearing the dishes. Kathleen put her hand on John's shoulder, indicating for him to stay seated. "You're a guest tonight."

Patrick and Connor remained seated as the women cleared the table. Father Ryan stood and waited until the men were alone, and then in the newfound quiet, Ryan sat across from John and looked squarely at him. For the first time, John felt apprehensive. He knew Ryan was not only a priest, but also the father figure in the family and if he were to marry Kathleen, he would have to get past him.

The men faced off. John remembered the rule. *He, who speaks first, loses.* Try as he might, he couldn't read Ryan's face, but he was determined not to yield. He loved Kathleen, and was willing to fight to his death for her, but on this issue, there would be no compromise.

Ryan's penetrating stare slowly began to soften and the glimmer of a smile appeared. "I can see the power of your conviction, good." He turned to his brothers and Patrick. "If you will excuse me, I will say goodnight. I have early Mass in the morning." Turning back to John, he extended his hand. "It was a pleasure meeting you, goodnight John. Let me know when you're going to Saint Patrick's, I'd be honored to join you and give you a tour. "

John stood and they shook hands and without another word, Ryan left the room.

"Man that took balls." Jake had returned and apparently been standing in the doorway listening. "I think I might get to like you yet." Jake reached out and shook John's hand. "Brandy?"

"I thought you were passed out in the living room." Connor said as he looked up at Jake.

"Just a catnap, it got too quiet."

*   *   *

With all the help, the kitchen whipped into shape in no time. The kids, bribed with cookies and dishes of ice cream ate as quietly as kids do anything. Katie had started the dishwasher and they stood wondering what to do next. Discussion of religion was defiantly not on the agenda. In fact, the whole cleanup was rather quiet. Kathleen was a little surprised when Ryan came and said his good nights, and then left without comment. Curiosity grew as to what was transpiring in the other room. There was an outburst of laughter from the dining room and then as if on cue the men sauntered in with brandy snifters in their hands, new bosom buddies.

"Well look who's showed up now that the work is done," Kathleen kidded. "Did you save any of that for me?" She looked at John. She was dying to know what Ryan had said. She finally mouthed, "What?"

"I'll tell you later." John whispered.

"You remember where the brandy is Sis." Jake replied. He walked over and gave Christine a kiss on the cheek that was not well received. She finally gave him a slight smile and a nod of acceptance before busying herself with the kids. She left Jake standing in the middle of the kitchen.

"Anyone else for a brandy, Mom, Jean, Rose, how about you Christine?" Patrick asked, receiving silent negative responses.

"No thanks." Christine turned and looked at Jake. She smiled openly, took his hand and the chill lifted.

"I think we need to start thinking about getting home with the kids." Jean said.

"So what have you and John got planned for tomorrow?" Christine asked Kathleen.

"Jake is taking John sightseeing and Jean and I are going shopping."

"Oh' is that right." Christine's eyes flash at Jake. "So why wasn't I told?"

"Just a little guy time." Jake tried to placate the oversight. "Patrick and Connor are joining us for dinner and we are picking up a game or something."

"If you ever get passed the Shamrock." Christine was obviously pissed.

"I don't remember asking your permission." Jake's voice rose. He went on the defensive.

"Neither do I." She turned to the table. "Kids, get you coats, we're leaving."

"But Mom." Sean whimpered.

"Now."

Christine gathered up the kids to their protests and herded them off to the mudroom for their coats. Calmly, Jake turned to the counter and sat on a stool, leaned on an elbow and swigged his brandy.

"Jesus Jake, that's cruel. What is the matter with you?" Conner started to lecture.

"Fuck her! And fuck you too." Jake headed for another brandy.

Jean glanced at John. "Don't take lessons from our brother." She advised, in a voice loud enough that Jake could hear from the other room. "He's a prick! A goddamn prick"

"Jean!" Katie, shocked by her daughter's outburst was in a dither, apparently ashamed more by John's witness to Jake's behavior, then the behavior itself. "Don't mind us."

"Well he is mother," Jean insisted. "He's become nothing but a drunken prick."

Jake stepped in from the bar and toasted them all. "To me, the big Irish prick." Smirking, he downs his drink. "Do you mind if I sleep in my old room tonight Mom?" Glaring at Christine as he spoke. "We don't have a dog house." Not waiting for an answer, he staggered off to the basement.

"I'll talk to him in the morning," Katie assured them. "Well get it worked out, don't worry about it, just you kids get home safely."

Christine looked at Kathleen, to hurt to cry, and too proud to if she could. Silently, she gathered her brood together, bundled them up, and herded them out the back door. Her sad eyes said more than any words. She gave Kathleen and John a goodnight wave.

*   *   *

John stood at the door and watched Kathleen turn on the lamp beside the single bed in the front upstairs bedroom, the room doubled as Katie's sewing room.

"Your brother can have this bed and we could sleep down stairs." John suggests. "My room has a queen size bed.

"No way, Mom would die first."

"This is ridicules, she knows now we are living together?"

"She knows, but she won't let us sleep together in her house. Not under her roof." Then she mocked her mother. "Why, what would the Church and the Priest think?"

"Well whatever." He sat on the bed beside Kathleen. "Do they always carry on like that?"

"Sure, haven't you heard of the Fighting Irish?"

"I thought that was a football team."

"They took the expression from the O'Malley's."

"And why did everyone go hush-hush when I mentioned your dad."

"Dad's been living in New York for several years, with his mistress. You can call it, divorce Irish Catholic style.

"Well we're not going to be like that." John gave Kathleen a kiss. She put her arms around his neck and they fell back on the bed. He continued to kiss her, but was not happy about the sleeping arrangement. "I think your family is a little crazy."

"So do I, big crazy." She began undoing his tie. I like you in a suit. Her hand ran across his chest. "Mm." They kissed. She pinched his nipple as she kissed him, and then rolled him over and looked in his eyes. "Why don't you get undressed?"

"Will your mother approve?"

"I'm not asking her."

'My condoms are down stairs."

"I have some in my makeup bag, in case of an emergency."

"This is an emergency."

CHAPTER 15

SPURS THAT JINGLE JANGLE

```
INT.-HALLWAY OUTSIDE KATHLEEN'S ROOM-THAT EVENING
```

John, in his trousers and t-shirt and with his suit jacket, shirt, sox and shoes in hand, creeps out of Kathleen's room, closes the door and starts toward the stairs. The down stairs hall light illuminates the steps. Katie's bedroom is across from the landing. There is light coming from under her door. The steps squeaked as he started to descend. When he is halfway down he hears Katie's door open, and looks back. The door is open a crack.

                    KATIE (OS)
          Goodnight John, sleep tight.

                         John
          Good....

Katie's door closed. He descended the stairs, turned out the hall light and, closed the basement door behind him. This wasn't a basement like any he imagined. A fully finished level of the house, the stairs ended in a huge game room, equipped with a wet bar, TV viewing area and pool table. *'It be the boy's lair'*. John remembered Jake called it. Off the main area were three bedrooms, a full bath and separate laundry. The only way you could tell it was a basement was by the small high windows. Furnished in a dark masculine, but somewhat dated style it had been the bedrooms and den of the O'Malley boys. Now two of the bedrooms where used as guest rooms mainly for the grandchildren's sleepovers. The third room was locked and never mentioned. John presumed it had something to do with Mr. O'Malley.

John's room was large with a queen size bed, and sitting area complete with sofa and chair and writing desk. On his way to his room, he saw the door to the other bedroom was open and Jake in his underwear was sprawled on the bed, asleep or passed out. John turned out the light and retired to his own room. He left his door ajar. The near windowless rooms made him feel claustrophobic. He wondered what it would be like to grow up in a basement, while he neatly hung his clothes in the closet. With his shaving kit in hand, he went into the bathroom. *How ridiculous, sleeping in separate rooms.* He looked at his reflection in the mirror. *That Jake has a real drinking problem. Wonder what the old lady thinks about that? Naw, she would never believe that. Not her Sonny Boy. Pity his poor wife.* With a shake of his head, he stepped up to the commode. *I'm sure as hell, not gonna become a Catholic just to please this bunch.*

Back in his room, he looked in his suitcase for his pajamas. *How could I've forgotten pajamas?* "Crap." *I know I got them out to pack.* John checked his suitcase again. *Maybe I stuck them in Kathleen's bag.* He didn't actually care, because he never slept in them anyway. That was Kathleen's idea. *The proper thing.* He preferred to sleep in the nude.

*   *   *

Something woke him. The haze of deep sleep, left reluctantly. John felt that someone was watching him and opened his eyes, raised up, and looked around the unfamiliar room. The room was warm and stuffy and during the night, he had pushed off all the blankets, keeping only the sheet over him. A nightlight near his suitcase and a small amount of daylight that bled in from the small heavily draped window were the only source of light. He remembered he was in Chicago and lay back and folded his hands behind his head. The Egyptian sheets felt good against his skin. Images of Kathleen, all alone upstairs, filled his head and he allowed himself to indulge his fantasies.

"It's a little late to be thinking about that." Jake's voice shattered the moment. "She's already gone."

John jumped at the sound of his voice. In the dim light, he could barely make out Jake leaning against the door casing with his usual smirk.

Jake flipped on the light, with his bloodshot eyes he scrutinize John. *How long has he been standing there?* Without another word, Jake turned around and headed across the den to the refrigerator. John looked at his jeans on the stand with his suitcase and was about to make a dash for them when Jake returned with two bottles of beer, stood at the door and looked in John's open suitcase. John felt even more uncomfortable with his visual inventory of his personal effects.

"I'm sorry about yesterday afternoon and last night, what I can remember of it." Jake sat on the foot of John's bed and handed him a beer. "I kinda made an ass out of myself."

John hesitated before taking the beer. He was amazed at the minimal effect the huge amount of booze he consumed had on him.

"Kathleen and Jean have already left for downtown, about an hour ago. I heard them leave when I went upstairs after some coffee. You know women when it comes to shopping. Kathleen said she didn't want to wake you."

"What time is it?" John looked for his watch on the nightstand.

"Do you always sleep in the nude?"

"Most times." John pulled the sheet up. *What's with this guy, some kind of closet queer?*

"It's almost eleven." Jake informed him as he kicked at John's boots. "So, you really love her?"

"Yes."

"You got spurs for these boots?" He looked John in the eyes. "She's gonna be a ruff filly to tame."

"What do yea mean?"

"You'll find out." Jake put his hand on John's leg and John tensed. "Hey I didn't come to have sex with you. But if I were so inclined you wouldn't be a bad catch." Jake grinned and abruptly stood. "Just toying with ya me boy, just toying." He moved to a chair. "You think, maybe you're a little young for her?"

"No, we're only three years different."

"What? You're twenty-three, right? How old do you thing Sis is?"

"Twenty-six."

"Damn kid, she's thirty-one. What else don't you know about her?"

John didn't have an answer.

"You know Sis is a little on the spoiled side. She was always Daddy's little darling. Got everything she ever wanted. Stanford is her fourth university. She doesn't want an education. She just likes the action, as long as Daddy is paying the bills, and why not. I don't think she wants to be a wife and mother either, especially a mother."

John sat up in bed and propped a pillow behind his head.

"I hope you've got what it takes to keep her happy, and I'm not just talking about in bed." Jake finished off his beer and stood. "You're a good kid." He said quietly. "Too good for this family. We've got some problems, real problems."

"I can see."

"You haven't seen anything, yet." For a moment, John watched Jake look at the large picture of the Sacred Heart, that hung above the bed as if he'd never seen it before, then look back at John. "We live in a different world, we do, being born in this clan."

"I'm not going to be a Catholic. I just can't be something I'm not."

"I understand and admire you for that. See I wasn't that drunk." He winked. The Irish charm started bubbling up as he smiled. "It takes balls to stand up for what ya believe or don't believe. Just remember blood is thicker than water and some secrets should never see the light of day. Be warned. Gonna grab me a shower now. Then off to home and take care of a wee family problem." With that, Jake started for the bathroom, but stopped at the door. "Unless you need to use the facilities first."

"No, I can wait."

Jake looked at John for a moment longer. "I'll be out of here in a minute and give you back your privacy, but I'll be back at two to pick you up for the grand tour and the game. In the meantime, enjoy the rest of your mornin'. Only one here is Mommy."

"Okay, I'll be ready."

Jake shook his head. "If I were you I'd run, fly like a bat-out-of-hell away from her, all this mess and forget about marriage."

*   *   *

"So, are you sure you want to go through with it?" Jean asked.

"I'm sure." Kathleen sipped her coffee. They had stopped in at a Michigan Avenue coffee shop near the water tower.

"But he's a kid, he's just a pup."

"Pup hell, he's all man."

"I'm confident he's got the hardware, but he is still a kid. I know it's no use saying it, but I thought you were on the hunt for a rich man."

"I said I wanted a man that was well-off. He's got more than enough."

"Is that so? He's a student with at least two plus years of law school ahead of him, are you going to get a job and support him?"

"He was left a nice home, paid for, a healthy chunk of insurance money that's been well invested, and has family educational trust that could provide good educations for the whole damn O'Malley clan, all inclusive. He's worth at least four-and-half million, give, or take a few hundred-thou.

"I know, but that's not rich in this day and age," Jean assured Kathleen.

"It's enough to make life comfortable. That's what I mean by well-off." Kathleen put down her coffee cup. "Rich men judge their worth by bank accounts and their sexuality by the number of eighteen-year-old fashion models they've got in the back seat of their limo."

"You've got that right," Jean agreed.

"Don't worry. He's young enough to be trained and rich enough to keep me comfortable. I don't want a man like our father."

"Well then the only problem I see is his religion or lack thereof. What's with him?"

"He says, that when his father died he put his religion in a box, and then when his mother died, he threw away the box. That's the extent of the discussion."

"Well!" Jean sat up. "If you're thinking of marrying him, you and Jake had better get hold of him by the ears and drag him down to Ryan's rectory, for conformation classes. There are a few rules in this family that we don't break. And marrying outside the Church is one of them."

"He's a sweet guy, but he doesn't drag well."

"I noticed that last night. Your pussycat has a little tiger in him. Maybe Ryan will have to grab the Bishop's crosier and hit him on the skull. Then all of us can stick his head in the Holy Water Fount until he gives in and professes the faith."

"I don't think we will need that drastic of measures." Kathleen laughed. "He'll be a hard nut to crack, but I know how to soften him up."

"Oh my!" Jean looked at her watch. "We need to get going, I want to stop next door."

They grabbed their things and headed out the door. The sun was bright and the sidewalks clear, but the previous day's snow was evident. With temperatures in mid-twenties, the downtown was busy. Kathleen and Jean walked toward the door of the gourmet cookware's store. About to enter, a man in a suit and dark overcoat stepped out and nearly ran into them.

"Excuse me." He muttered and then looked up. "Kathleen? I'll be. What are you doing here?"

"Scott?" Kathleen was surprised at running into him. He's a big guy with an even bigger ego. They've had a hot and cold relationship for years. It ran especially hot before, during and after his fourth marriage. "How nice to see you." Kathleen was genuinely pleased.

"I thought you were in college out in California." He gave her a hug and a kiss on the lips.

"Just visiting." She stood and looked at him a moment. At forty-six, he looked sharp with just a touch of gray is his jet-black hair. "You know my sister." She added without shifting her gaze.

"Jean!" His salesman's charisma gushed. "Good to see you again." He shook her hand, and then turned his attention back to Kathleen. "You're looking good woman."

"Thank you, so are you."

"So what's new?" Scott asked.

"Kathleen's here with her——."

"Visiting." Kathleen interrupted. "I'm here visiting family. And you?"

Jean acted irritated by Scott and even more so with her sister and went on into the store alone.

"Well you know, still traveling a lot. I like the freedom. So how long are you in town?"

"Until the end of the week."

Good, maybe we can have drinks, dinner or something."

"I'd love to, but I'm really booked up."

He pulled out a card, wrote a phone number on the back, gave it to the Kathleen, and then opened his address book. "And what's your number in California?"

Kathleen took the book, wrote her address and number, and with a smile handed it back. "And when you are in California, give me a call, discreetly."

"Of course, discreetly. What's the saps name?"

"John."

"You going to marry this one?"

"Maybe."

"Are you sure I can't buy you a drink. I'm free."

"Let me tell Jean."

*   *   *

A polished waiter brought the second round of drinks at the Ninety-Fifth Floor Bar atop the Hancock Building. They sat near the window but weren't interested in the view. The small talk had given way to long silent looks. The sun was slowly dipping toward the horizon.

"So do you really think this guy is mister right?"

It was the first time Scott mentioned John since they met in the street. She wasn't thinking of John and certainly didn't want to talk about him.

"You know, if you just want to get married, you could marry me." Scott said.

"You know you're not the marrying kind. You've proved that."

"So my record isn't very good." Scott took a sip of his scotch. "Have you told him about us?"

"He doesn't need to know everything. Do I hear a hint of jealousy in that question? You don't have anything to be jealous about."

"Is he the usual young buck? I know you like them that way."

"Young bucks are no match for experience." She inconspicuously began making circles on his leg with her finger. "It's the seasoned bull that gets the heifers."

"My apartment is two blocks from here."

"Is that a proposition?"

"It's an invitation."

CHAPTER 16

A CLOSE CALL

INT.-JOHN'S APARTMENT-EARLY MORNING-MARCH 11, 1987

In the subdued light, Kathleen is seen laying on the bed and starring at the ceiling. John sleeps soundly next to her. She turns to him and with a slow deliberate movement slides her hand over his belly.

> KATHLEEN (V.O.)
> Am I really ready to make this commitment?

She slowly smiles as she affectionately teases John, deliberately trying to rouse him.

She felt his response to her fingers, but impatient as always, she wanted him awake. Aggravated, she rose up and lightly blew in his ear. Still asleep, he reacted as if a bug was pestering him and swatted at it, so she blew at his ear again. It worked. He awoke, turned his sleepy face to her and smiled. They kissed. She pulled herself close to him, and they lay still for a moment in each other's arms.

With a yawn, he stretched and as he did, she continued her loving caress. With approval, his smile widened. Now more awake, he lifted up, kissed her passionately on the mouth, and wrapped his arms around her. She noticed him glance up at the clock. His eyes widen and she felt his muscles tense.

He bolted up. "OH SHIT!"

"What's wrong?" Kathleen asked, confused.

"Look at the time."

"Who cares?

"Midterms. I've got a midterm in twenty minutes. Shit." All evidence of his amorous intentioned dwindled as he jumped out of bed. Clothes flew. He dug for something clean to wear.

"John, come back to bed."

"I can't, I'm late. It's my last day of midterms." With a turn, he grabbed the alarm clock and checked it. "I was sure I set the alarm last night."

Kathleen sat up in bed, her passion turned to irritation. She watched John hurriedly trying to dress.

"You haven't made love to me all week. Don't you love me anymore?"

"Since when is three days a week? It's the midterms. I've had to cram for midterms." He pulled on the jeans he's worn the past four days, poked himself in and buttoned the fly. "I got behind on our trip. I've been doing catch up since." He grabs a polo shirt that only had one-day's wear. It didn't smell, so he yanked it on over his head. "We need to do laundry."

"That's not very romantic."

After grabbing a pair of socks out of a drawer, he sat on the bed to put them on. "I promise I'll make it up to you tonight. I'll be home after four.

"Promise?" Kathleen pouted.

"I swear to God." He kissed her lips with nothing more than a peck. "Tonight, all night." He swore, and then danced into the bathroom, pulling on his shoes as he went. She watched from the bed as he splashed water in his face, simultaneously stuck a toothbrush in his mouth, and applied stick deodorant under his shirt. Then he doused on some cologne and ran a brush over his hair.

Kathleen jumped up on her knees, eagerly as he came back into the bedroom. "Tell me what you're going to do to me tonight?"

"Fuck your brains out." He stopped by the bed to give her another quick kiss, but she grabbed the waistband of his pants and pulled him off his feet and on top of her.

"I can't wait." Wanton arms wrapped around his neck and she started to devourer his lips.

"I can't now." He mumbled and pulled back. "Tonight, I promise."

He ripped himself away. In a move to vent her frustration, she jabbed her clinched fist in his crotch. Stunned, his eyes widen as he momentarily froze. In that instant, she was not certain she hit him in anger or was simply overly exuberant in her passionate pleas for him to stay.

Instinctively, he covered his crotch with both hands and gasped for air. "Woo!" His eyes fill with tears. "That could damage a guy for life."

"I'm sorry, I'm sorry." Smothering his face with kisses, she begged forgiveness. "I'm sorry. I didn't mean to hurt you. I love you."

"Some love pat. I've got a scar from your little love nip." Still protecting his crotch with one hand, he kissed her and gave her a one-arm hug. "I got to go. Tonight. I might be healed by then." Their lips hung together as he pulled away. With a wobble in his step, he headed for the front door, careening into the doorjamb in his hurry.

Kathleen sat cross-legged on the bed in a pout. Bored, she picked up a brush from the nightstand and began brushing her hair. Not accustomed to waiting, she began to think of ways to amuse herself for the day. Housework was not on the agenda, even though their first argument was over the messy apartment. She felt if he wanted a maid, he could hire one. She had dropped all but one class. Daytime TV was a bore. Reading didn't interest her and occupying her time with anything but John, had become a challenge.

The phone on the nightstand rang. Kathleen didn't pick it up until after the third ring. "Hello," she leisurely answered.

"Scott? How interesting, I was just thinking about you." She put the brush down. "Where are you?" She smiled. "At the San Francisco airport?" She sat up. "How long." She looked at the clock. "Sure you can come by, I'll be free all day." She giggled. "You naughty boy." She rose to her knees. "If you hurry you might catch me still in my nighty." With her feet, she reached for her slippers and slid them on. "See you in an hour, you have my address."

Unhurriedly she hung up the phone. With slow deliberate movement, she turned on a Madonna album and began picking up the apartment.

*   *   *

Kathleen had straightened up as much as she was going too. She had changed into a light lavender negligee with matching robe, and sat at the kitchen table reading a romance novel. The stereo played softly.

Startled by the sound of the phone, she hastily picked up. "Hello." She answered hesitantly. "Yes this is Kathleen O'Malley." She grew serious. "Who?" She quickly put down her book. "Oh yes, Dr. Levin." She took a slow deep breath. "You're sure . . . . Absolutely positive?" She closed her eyes as she listened. "I'll have to think about the options. Can I schedule the abortion through your office?" She looked up at the calendar. "Before March twenty-fifth. I'll let you know in a few days." She stood. "Thank you for calling me doctor."

She hung up the phone and stared out the window a long while. Then abruptly she smiled and headed to the bathroom to put finishing touches to her hair. Shortly there was a knock at the door. Without urgency, she gave herself a final shot of cologne then flitted toward the door.

"Just a moment." On her way to the door, she spotted a pair of John's underpants, sticking out from under the coffee table, which she quickly kicked under the sofa and took one more look around the room. At the door, she stopped and took a breath before opening it.

"Hello traveler."

"Well hello yourself, beautiful." Scott had a bottle of champagne in one hand and bouquet of flowers in the other, both of a cheap variety.

"Oh you shouldn't have."

"Didn't want to come empty handed."

"Come on in." Kathleen felt his lapel. "I like your suit."

With a forced enthusiasm, Kathleen took the flowers and champagne to the kitchen and stuck the flowers in a large drinking glass. Scott followed and stood awkwardly near the kitchen table.

"I think it's a little early for this." Kathleen kidded about the champagne.

"It's nearly noon in Chicago."

"Maybe later." With that, she placed the bottle in the refrigerator.

She watched as Scott gave the apartment a quick once over then asked, "Your place or his?"

"It's his. He'll be out all day, midterms."

"Oh." Her words well received. "I thought the style a little to masculine for you. Is he anyone I know?"

"No. No more questions." Without any hesitation, she put her arms around him and kissed him on the mouth. He kissed back. Their hands explored each other.

"Okay," Scott breath quickened with excitement. "No questions."

With deliberate hesitation, Kathleen pulled herself away and turned toward the sink. "Would you like some coffee?"

"No."

There was no question what he was there for and she was ready to give it to him. She just didn't want to appear too eager. "So what are you doing in Palo Alto? It's a little off your beaten track."

"Had a meeting in San Francisco last night and don't fly out until this afternoon." He stepped up close behind her. "I had some free time and naturally thought of you."

"Naturally." She felt the tension in her shoulders at his touch, but like a skilled masseur, his hands soothed it away. "Well, I'm glad you could stop by." She melted under the commands of his sensual strokes and leaned back into him.

He kisses her neck. "You really serious about this guy?"

Kathleen turned from the sink. "Maybe."

"Why don't we get married?"

"That would never work. I told you that when I saw you in Chicago. I know you to well."

"Maybe this wasn't a good idea. Should I go?"

"No." She touched her fingers to Scott's lips.

"Are you in love with him?"

"No questions, remember?" She reminded him.

Scott stood for a moment then stepped back. Suddenly with abandonment, she threw herself into his arms and began wantonly kissing him, pushing off his jacket, letting it fall to the floor. She eagerly began to unbutton his shirt as they worked across the apartment toward the bedroom.

Scott excitedly anticipated Kathleen's moves like a dance partner as they maneuvered to the bed. She shoved him backward. Lying before her, she unfastened his belt and unzipped his pants. Scott's kicks off his shoes. With one quick move, she pulled off his pants and underpants and her eager hands reacquainted with the familiar.

The two were noisy, tumultuous lovers, reassuring one another with exaggerated groans and moans of pleasure. Thru the years they had perfected there foreplay to an art and knew just what the other wanted and willingly gave it. Among the squeals from Kathleen, answer by primal grunts and long moans from Scott, the two lovers used hands, tongues and mouths, feeding each other into a sexual frenzy.

Hung half off the bed, Scott's free hand groped for his pants on the floor. Finding them, he pulled a condom from a pocket and holding it in one hand tore the packet open with his teeth. Kathleen took the rolled sheath and started to position it. Scott rolled on his back to enjoy the process, letting the empty condom packet flutter to the floor.

Soon bedsprings begin to piston in rhythm squeaking out the old familiar hymn of fornication. Scott roared in deep long loud groans while Kathleen moaned an obbligato. Together they sang to the rafters.

*   *   *

John and a half-dozen other students gathered on the steps. Everyone had finished their midterms early and their professor dismissed the class. The discussion centered on where to have lunch.

"John, you going to join us?" Mary asked.

John's stomach growled. He looked at his watch, eleven-ten. He was hungry from missing breakfast. "Where are you going?"

"Student union."

"Sounds good." But then John thought about leaving Kathleen in a pout this morning. It was only a brisk fifteen-minute walk to his apartment. He could surprise her, eat lunch, have a quick noony, and make it back for his two o'clock test.

"I changed my mind. I'm going home for lunch."

John was almost to the main gates when he heard someone running up behind him.

"John wait." Mike yelled. "Where are you going?"

John turned. He slapped the palm of his hand to his forehead the moment he saw Mike.

"I thought we were going to review for this afternoon's exam?" Mike was out of breath.

"Sorry, I forgot."

"You've been forgetting a lot of things lately. If you have something more important to do, we can skip it."

John looks past the gates and down the street. "It can wait."

"Where do you want to go? I've got to get a sandwich or something first. I'm starved."

"The student union is the closest."

John looked up the street again for a moment. "It will do."

*   *   *

There was stillness now. The bed was made and any trace of defilement gone. Kathleen had dressed in black slacks and a red knit top. In a vase on the table, Scott's flowers sat prominently. A pair of champagne glasses sat beside them.

Looking out the window, she watched clouds break away and the sun begin to stream through the balcony door. At the sound of a key in the lock, she turned to the door and drew in a breath.

John came through the door obviously tired, but apparently glad the day was over. "Hi honey." He greeted her with a quick kiss.

"Hi, how did it go?" she asked.

"Good, hard, but I think I did well. How was your day? It looks like you have been busy. The apartment looks great. "

"Thanks, I got bored."

He touched the flowers as if to see if they are real. He asked, "What's this?"

"For you. I got some champagne too. Kathleen retrieved the bottle of champagne from the refrigerator.

"Woo, a celebration, for me?"

"For us. Here, you open it." She handed him the bottle.

With his thumbnail, he worked the foil off the top of the bottle and it fell to the floor. "I wasn't expecting this." He picked up the foil and put it in the trash. "What a nice treat." With a twist, he removed the wire, at the same time he looked at Kathleen with a big smile. She sat quietly. Impatiently he pushed at the cork with his thumbs, it popped out of the bottle and hit the ceiling, foaming champagne spilled on the table. John quickly filled the glasses and handed one to Kathleen.

"To us," he proclaimed, with a raised glass. They touched rims, and then John downed his champagne, but Kathleen only sipped a little of hers, he refilled his glass and downed it too.

"I thought we would order in a pizza."

"Maybe later." He put down his glass and started to wiggle like a puppy when its owner came home. "I made a promise this morning that I intend to keep, right now woman."

At that he picked her up in the air, she locked her legs around his waist and they kiss.

"I didn't think you would be up to it after all your tests."

With exaggerated movements, he twirled her around the kitchen. She cried out in delight. He danced her toward the bedroom, spinning first one way then the other as he carried her. "I'll show you how up, I'm up too." He dropped her on the bed. On hands and knees, he crawled over her and lowered himself, pinning her to the bed. "I've been waiting all day for this."

"So have I." She said and then wrapped her arms around his neck and sucked the breath out of him with her kiss.

They continue to devour each other with kisses while he kicked off his shoes. With the show of release from pent-up energy, he jumped to his feet and stripped off his clothes. Kathleen tried to slow the momentum by undressing slowly which only fanned John's flame. He reached to pull her onto the bed and when he did the gold band of his Rolex wristwatch scratched her arm.

"Ouch. That hurt." She cried out.

"Sorry." He took off the watch and stretched to put it on his nightstand, nevertheless, his attention was elsewhere, and it fell to the floor. "Shit." He grumbled. Sliding half off the bed sideways to retrieve it, he suddenly froze with his bare butt in the air.

"Are you okay?" she asked?

He didn't answer but slowly rose back on the bed and looked at Kathleen. "Have we had some visitor lately?"

"What do you mean?"

"John held out the empty condom packet. "This. I found it under our bed."

"What's that?" She knew instantly it was Scott's. She tried to contain a flush. "A condom wrapper?" Her heart raced and she tried to stay calm. "It must be yours."

"I only used one brand of condoms." He reexamines the wrapper. "And I've never used this kind, ever."

"It just an old wrapper you dropped under the bed, you just forgot." She knew she had to shift suspicion. "From one of your old flames."

"Natural-lamb, no way, I've never used these. Only playboys and gigolos use these."

Kathleen could see the suspicion role over his face like a cloud. She heard the hurt in his voice turn to anger when he asked. "You haven't been——.""

"Cheating on you? How dare you think that? Are you sure, you haven't been cheating on me? It probably fell out of your jeans. Something you stuffed in your damn pocket." She began a fake cry. "You probably bought the thing out of a vending machine at the Student Union, in a hurry any brand would do." Now near frantic, she threw herself on the bed, buried her face in the pillow and began to cry hysterically. She knew he couldn't stand to hear her cry.

"There, there honey, I didn't mean to accuse." He lifted her from the pillow and took her in his arms to console her.

She continued to sob. Repentantly, he ran his fingers over her back, trying to assure her. "You're right. It may have been there for some time." He assured her. By the tone of his voice, he was apparently trying to reassure himself as well.

She turned in his arms and they kissed. "Honey?" She whispers, her magic fingers made circles on his chest and she began to cast her spell. "Let's forget this waiting crap and just go to Reno."

"Reno?" He asked through a kiss. She felt him thaw. "We'll call my family and tell them we are getting married in Reno the weekend before Easter. They can come if they want."

Her charm worked, all his resistance fades. "Are you sure, that soon? I thought we were going to wait?"

Their lips touched and they melted onto the bed. "Positive, trust me." She whispered.

"We need to think this — ."

She stopped his words with a kiss. Her caressing finger fanned his passion and the fire grew until she felt him reach for a condom. "We don't need them anymore."

He looked at her questioning.

"Remember on Christmas Eve when you had your little accident with the ruptured condom?"

"I guess so."

"Well, I found out today, I'm pregnant. You're going to be a daddy."

"Oh my God."

CHAPTER 17

BELL A RINGING

INT. RESTAURANT MEZZANINE-RENO, NV.-APRIL 5, 1987

Bells rang, the synthesized notes drone a hideous tune, the slot machine's lights flash and falling coins clank on metal. The Tex-Mex restaurant, on the mezzanine between the two big hotels casinos in downtown Reno, is a buzz. In their black tuxedos John and Alvin cut through the bar rushing to the men's room.

                                        CUT TO:

INT.-MEN'S ROOM-CONTINUES

John and Alvin belly up to the urinals side by side.

                    JOHN
          Damn Alvin, I'm glad you could make
          it. How they treating you up in Seat-
          tle?

                    Alvin
          Fine, couldn't ask for better.

At Christmas Alvin had decided to take a leave from his company to work on a special six-month project for Microsoft. He left his wife Sandra in charge of the business and took an apartment in Seattle.

"Glad to be doing something more than playing games and putting out fires. I don't like being the boss all the time." Alvin confessed. "It's hell though, being away from Sandra and the baby. I fly home every weekend."

"That will keep you busy. Thanks for being my best man."

"Don't mention it. I just wished I didn't have to wear this monkey suit."

"It was Kathleen's idea. I would have settled for a fake tuxedo printed on a t-shirt. But it's nice to dress up sometimes." John straightened his bowtie.

"So where's Nadia and Zach?"

"They couldn't make it. One of the girls is sick. I also get the feeling Zach is not real pleased with our getting married."

Alvin stepped to the washbasin beside John. "That's a shame. But the whole affair was kind of fast. The last I heard you weren't going to think marriage until after law school."

"Well, ya know, when it's love, it sometimes can't wait."

"I hope you'll be happy."

"We will." John dried his hands on a paper towel.

"You guys do a prenuptial."

The question surprised John. "Ya, well kind of yes and no. Kathleen balked at prenups, so Aaron advised I leave everything in the trust, house and all."

Alvin pulled an envelope from an inside pocket." Here, it's sort of a wedding present. You can put it toward the renovations on the house.

John opened the envelope to find a check made out to the Michaels' Family Trust. He got dizzy when he looked at the amount. "Good God, five-hundred-thousand.

"I told you I'd pay you back. That's the first zero. I got two more zeros to go."

"You can't be serious. I never expected anything like this."

"It's a dividend. I talked to Aaron he said make it out to the trust."

"It's staggering to see what one simple zero will do, but I can't accept this."

"You have to, you're my partner."

"I guess I need to attend the board meetings more often. Thank you." John hugged Alvin in a long embrace.

"You know this is getting awkward."

John released him and tugged at his cummerbund. "I never could figure out what these are supposed to do."

"Supposed to make a guy look sexy."

"Or like a jerk when it rides up to look like a bra.

John made a final check of himself. "Well, you ready to par—ty?"

Alvin grabbed John's arm stopping him. "The truth man, what's the rush? You're already living together. You've only known her a little over four months. This is not like you. It takes you longer than that to pick out a new car. Was this her idea or yours?"

"Neither." John pulled away from Alvin, stepped back to the washbasin, and looked at him through the mirror.

Not to be put-off, Alvin stepped up to John and put his arm over his shoulder. "Come on John, for Christ's sake. We've known each other for damn near fifteen years. Tell me, what's the rush? I know it's not just the sex."

John took a step back. "Promise to keep it a secret?'

Alvin nodded.

"Kathleen's pregnant."

"Holy shit. I guess that's a good reason to get married. But I hate to tell you, that's a secret you can't keep for long."

"I guess not. I'm just a little confused. Actually . . . I'm scared spitless." John looked Alvin in the eyes. "I've looked forward to having children. But I don't think I'm ready."

"You'll make a great dad."

"I think I'm going to put law school on hold for a while. Join the SJPD. Don't know how Kathleen will take it. I just know I can't take any more school, not right now. I just hope I can hold together until graduation. My head's not with it. I don't know if——."

Just then, someone entered and walked up to the urinal. The conversation stopped. After a moment, the guy looked up suspiciously at John and Alvin just standing, and hastily retreated. John couldn't help but chuckle.

"Listen John, don't do something foolish. Finish the semester. Think about it. Wait until summer before you decide. Promise me you will wait until summer. Don't flush everything down the toilet.

"No promises. Alvin . . . just be my friend."

"You know I love you. You've always been like a brother. Whatever you decide I'll support you. I may kick your ass a few times, but I will support you."

"So, ready to join the party."

"Sure am." Alvin gave John a pat on the back. "Put a smile on your face, the worried look doesn't become you."

John pushed the door open and on cue, smiled.

*   *   *

Crossing back through the bar, they stop for a cocktail waitress who's serving six women seated at a table. Two good-looking young men in formalwear stand out among the usual Reno crowd and garner a good deal of attention.

"Are you boys the floorshow tonight?" One of the female patrons kidded.

The cocktail waitress turned and gave them a look and smiled.

A boisterous lady teased, "I didn't know the Chippendale Men were in town."

John and Alvin laughed and quickly headed for the safety of their table.

"What kept you?" John's sister Tess asked. "We thought maybe you fell in."

The small wedding party of Tess, Julie, Alvin, Sandra and Jean, Kathleen's matron of honor, had attended the wedding at the, Little White Chapel and were now ready to celebrate.

The spirited atmosphere of the restaurant made the intimate wedding party seem large. Other patrons were delighted with the group and shared in the happy couple's moment. Alvin arranged for a bottle of champagne to be sent to every table in the restaurant. The bride was stunning in a simple ivory satin dress and matching ribbons in her hair. John was so proud of her he was beside himself. A young man infatuated. He could scarcely take his eyes off his new bride.

"Everyone. Hey, everyone quiet." Alvin stood with a glass of champagne. "I want to make a toast. So everyone fill your glasses." There was a murmur as glasses were filled. Everyone in the restaurant stopped and prepared for the toast.

"Okay, a toast to the bride and groom." Alvin began. "Here's to the Hot Dog and his new bride." He held his glass out toward John. "Of course, I don't know what he did with the old ones." Alvin laughed at his own, not funny joke. "Okay. Okay, settle down, now let me see." He started checking his pocket. "I know I got it here somewhere." The suspense rose as he continued to check his pockets. "John gave me a list, a list of all his attributes." There was some laughter and Alvin started working the crowd. "Oh well, what I can say about John is, he is a catch, and I would have married him myself if I weren't already married."

"So would I!" A woman stood and yelled from a table across the room, "Yoo Johnny."

John laughed, embarrassed.

"He's managed however," Alvin continued, "to snag the prettiest girl on the Stanford Campus."

There were several whistles and some guy yelled. "Oh baby, you broke my heart."

Alvin laughed, and then gained control. "We love ya Kathleen." The circle watching had grown to include people in the bar area. "Stand up. Stand up so the people can see you, both of you. Stand up."

John stood first and when he did, a cheer went up. When Kathleen slowly rose to her feet, everybody broke into applauses. John and Kathleen stood hand in hand, a beautiful couple. The restaurant's photographer along with everyone that had a camera snapped pictures.

Finally, Alvin rang his glass with a spoon for attention. "So everyone, raise your glass for John and Kathleen Michaels."

They all toasted the newlyweds, amongst cheers, applause, and congratulation. John kisses Kathleen, in a long wedding kiss, and then they acknowledge the well-wishers, before sitting. But within seconds, a man at the next table started tapping his glass with a fork. Every person in the restaurant has joined in until the bride and groom kiss again.

"How wonderful." Jean remarked. "You couldn't have planned a better reception."

Of course, John was absolutely giddy. Beaming, he could hardly stay seated. Finally, he jumped to his feet, took two glasses of champagne, and handed one to Kathleen.

"To my dear precious wife." He toasted and they touched glasses. Kathleen took a sip of her champagne while John chugged his, with the encouragement from nearby tables. He held the empty glass up, and then sat it upside down on the table.

*   *   *

"Not drinking?" Jean asked Kathleen privately. "That's not like you. Staying sober for the big night?"

Kathleen sat silent for a moment then smiled and leaned over to Jean and whispered. "I'm pregnant."

"You're what? You're sure?" Jean's voice rose with excitement. "I wondered why the rush."

"Ssssh, Yes."

"How long?"

"Three-and-a-half months."

"Oh, Jesus, Mary and Joseph. Kathleen, mother and the family will shit!" She looked over at John as he sat back down. "Does he know?"

"Yes! That's why we decided on Reno."

"Wonderful! I thought it was just because he didn't want a Catholic wedding."

Jean stood up and started tapping a spoon on her glass for attention, as she prepared to make a toast. "Okay everyone, on behalf of the missing O'Malley family, I want to thank you for being here and I wish to make a toast." She lifted her glass. "John, welcome to the family, even though you're not Catholic or Irish. Now we may overlook you not being a Catholic." A distinct Irish brogue creeps into her voice. "But it be a wee bit hard to overcome the idea of ya not bein' Irish." There was a collective moans. "It does appear, however that ya have one true Irish attribute."

"He likes to fight." Someone chimed in.

"No, there is another F-word I'm a thinkin' of." Jean continued.

A big knowing "oh," filled the room.

"Fertility is the word my dear boy. John me boy, congratulation to you and yours, expectant bride, on this your wedding day.

There was a silence as the surprise announcement registered. Then a round of cheers, catcalls, and congratulation arose from the entire restaurant. John turned a deep shade red, and looked at Kathleen with a grin.

Alvin slapped John on the back. "See I told you, you couldn't keep it a secret for long."

The small combo returned from break to the bandstand and started to play, *Can't Help Falling in Love with You.* John stood and took Kathleen's hand. She rose gracefully and he took her arm and with a kiss to her hand led her to the dance floor, the happiest man in the world. People, strangers stop them along the way, men shook John's hand and kissed Kathleen and women kissed John and hugged Kathleen. Finally arriving at the small dance floor, they began to dance.

Shortly, Alvin and Sandra followed. The two couples danced alone under the colored lights of the dance floor. Alvin winked at John. "Only in Reno.

"Why do men always look so damn sexy in tuxedoes?" Jean remarked.

Tess looked up. She could see the happiness in her brother's eyes and actions.

"Of course I think your brother would look sexy in anything."

"So do I, but he's my brother . . . used to think he was kind of a nerd."

"Kathleen said that they are moving back to the Cambria Park house this summer."

"Yeah, the tenants are moving out in May. I'm going to help them with a major renovation, expanding the family room, kitchen and master suite. John already had the plans. The additions will double the square footage. Now it looks like I'll be doing a nursery too."

"That was a surprise. So I assume you didn't know either."

"No." Tess, cautiously pours herself some more champagne, making sure the waiter doesn't see. "I didn't think John would be getting married for a while, he was so intent on school for one thing and he's never been much of a lover boy either."

"Why do you say that?" Jean was eager to hear more about her new brother-in-law.

"Well, the first time he ever had sex with a girl was after his high school prom. He came home that night, told everything, and then cried because it was, 'so wonderful'. The girl dumped him the next day. I guess it wasn't so wonderful for her." She poured herself more champagne. "He didn't date for a year after that."

"Tell me more."

*   *   *

"The party atmosphere cooled a bit during the bands next break. Shortly the covey of women found it necessary to attend the ladies' room, leaving Alvin and John alone. John leaned over to Alvin. "I've made up my mind. After this semester, I'm going to take a couple of years off from school. I'm going to join the San Jose Police Department."

"Why, you've got the money and you don't have to work. Why not just take your time and finish law school."

"I just feel like I want to focus on being a father and husband."

"I don't understand why being a cop makes you think you'll be a better father."

"Just something I got to do. Kismet."

"If you feel it's necessary, do it. I doubt I can talk you out of it. But if you don't get back at it in a couple of years I'm going to start kicking your ass."

"That's a deal, if I'm not back in school in three years, I'll bend over and you can kick my ass all the way to Stanford."

CHAPTER 18

A CASE FOR GOD

```
INT.-O'MALLEY'S KITCHEN-AFTERNOON-JUNE 13, 1987
```

The Sunday dinner was about to get underway at
O'Malley's home. Christine and Jean are putting final
touches on a fruit salad and vegetables, an obviously
pregnant Kathleen watches from a nearby chair. Katie
is busy bringing her beef gravy to perfection. The men
are in the backyard drinking beer.

This is John and Kathleen's second visit to the
O'Malley's home in Chicago. Kathleen had promised that
they would come for a visit before John started the
police academy.

CHRISTINE
It's too bad Connor and Rose couldn't
be here

KATHLEEN
How does Jake like private practice?

"Loves it!" Christine answered, "He's a new man."

"That's good to hear, he was getting to be a real asshole."

"Tell me about it."

The phone rang. "Get that Christine, will ya please honey?" Katie
asked.

Christine wiped her hands on her apron and she picked up the phone. "Hello . . . . Yes, just a moment." She make an odd, I don't know face and held the phone out to Kathleen.

"For me?"

"It's a man."

"I'll take it in the living room." The women turned and watched Kathleen lift herself out of her chair and waddle out of the room. Aware of the audience, she closed the kitchen door before she answered the phone.

"This is Kathleen."

"Hello." The velvet voice at the other end said.

"I got it." Kathleen yelled, indicating to Christine to hang-up. She waited to hear the click of the receiver before she spoke. "Scott, what a nice surprise."

"Welcome home." Scott's proclaimed in his usual charming baritone.

"Well thank you, but I'm just here for a few days." There was a silence. "So where are you?"

"Home." There was another pause. "Alone."

"Oh, that doesn't sound like much fun."

"It's not. I'd love to see you while you're in town?"

"How did you know I was here?"

"I ran into Jake at the Shamrock the other day. So?"

"I can't. Scott, I'm married."

"So I hear." There was a sudden chill in his tone. "He must be some guy? I hear his shit doesn't stink. Can he walk on water too?"

"Be nice."

"Sorry."

"Don't be jealous, it doesn't become you."

"So you're gonna be popping one out pretty soon I hear, it isn't mine is it?"

"No, you've always made sure of that. I told you I was pregnant back in March. "

"Yeah, I know. But I didn't think you were going to go through with it."

"Well I changed my mind."

"So what's this fella of yours really like? Besides being kind of young."

"He is, a little young, but he's solid. He's got his feet on the ground."

"Rich?"

"Kinda. He's not poor."

"Jake says he's gonna be a cop. Only rich cops I know are crooks."

"He's sort of an idealist. Thinks he can do something for society as a cop. His father was a cop too."

"I could never understand that kind of thinking. You've got to take care of number one first."

"You're a little self-serving."

"Hey, that's the way the real world is. So, do you love him? Be honest."

"Well, kinda."

"I thought so. So now, who's self-serving? Is he that naïve?" "No, just a Romantic. Believes the best in everything."

"Well that's convenient. And I'm sure he loves you . . . . Well if it starts to wear a little thin, give me a call."

"I'll keep it in mind. Scott . . . thanks for all the good times."

"Yeah, sure." There was a silence on the phone.

"And Scott, whenever you're out in California, you can give me a call, we're in the book. Cupertino, Michaels." Kathleen could hear the women in the kitchen serving the kids plates. "We're about to sit down for dinner."

"I love you babe"

"Me too." Kathleen heard the click of the receiver. She hung up the phone and hoisted herself out of the chair, put a smile on her face and headed for the dining room.

*   *   *

The adult members of the O'Malley family were waiting, standing around the dinner table. They greeted Kathleen, but none mentioned the phone call. Jake held the chair for his mother and she took her seat, as the rest remained standing. With unusually good manners, Jake then pulled out the chair for Christine. John and Patrick did the same for their wives, and then the men took their seats at the beautifully set table. Father Ryan was the last to sit.

There was a silence. John watched as the rest bowed their head in reverence. He remembered at home, how his mother always insisted on grace before every meal. That was until his father died, after that the family never prayed before dinner again. They didn't pray at all.

"In the Name of the Father," Ryan began.

John tucked his chin down as the rest closed their eyes, crossed themselves, and joined in a unison prayer. "Son and Holy Ghost. Come Lord Jesus, be our guest."

It angered him to hear them pray. *Hypocrites.* His heart pounded in his ears.

"And let this gift to us be blessed."

Why should I be so angry at something that doesn't exist?

"Amen!" They ended their prayer by crossed themselves again.

"Oh!" Kathleen gasped with a jump.

"Are you all right dear?" Katie asked.

"Yes, just a little kick from junior."

"So when is your delivery date?" Jake asked.

"September twenty-fifth."

"So now we know why you couldn't come for Christmas." Jake quipped. "Who's gift to whom."

Jake gave John and Kathleen, a little smirk and picked up the large platter of carved roast beef. He held it for his mother as she served her plate and then he passed it to John. The others helped themselves while Jake busily poured the wine. The afternoon dinner was quiet. John had been buttering up Katie since they arrived the day before, trying to make up for the hurry-up wedding, and now Jake was fueling it again, by bringing up the baby.

"The roast is delicious Mrs. O'Malley." John remarked, in an attempt to change the subject. "Man I can't believe the weather gets so warm in Chicago."

"Have you chosen a name for your son? Christine asked.

"Steven," John answered without a second thought.

Katie dropped her fork on her plate with a clank.

"After John's father." Kathleen spoke up quickly. At the same time, John could see her give Christine a dirty look.

Christine Mouthed, "I'm sorry," to Kathleen.

"Oh — ." Was Katie's only remark."

"His middle name will be Seamus after Daddy." Kathleen tried to defuse the situation.

"That's nice." Katie said.

John remembered Kathleen promising to name their baby after her father when they found out it was a boy, trying to make up for their Reno wedding.

"I've spoken to John about coming out for Thanksgiving and letting me baptize young Steven Seamus at Saint Patrick's." Ryan said.

John recalled the conversation with Ryan in the backyard. Ryan, backed-up by Jake and Patrick had kept at him all afternoon. He felt they would resort to physical violence if he didn't promise.

"Well cheers for Steven Seamus." Jean chimed in.

"Yes, a toast." Jake grabbed his glass in one hand and the bottle of wine in the other and stood. He made sure everyone's glass except Kathleen's was full. "None for you Sis."

"Oh God, not another old Irish toast?" Jean rolled her eyes at her brother.

Jake raised his glass high. Against the chandelier, the cut crystal goblet sparkles. The beams of light showed down on the table, they turned into the hues of a red and golden sunset. The light captivated John, helped by a few beers before dinner and now on a second glass of wine, his head spun. He didn't remember the chandelier looking like that before, but for some reason the refracted light reminded him of something, a place of crystal and light. He shivered and felt the hair at the back of his neck stand on end.

"To the newest member of our family, little Steven, let his days be long with joy and his nights short of sorrow." Jake's words buzzed in John's head like the lights in his eyes. He could no longer make coherent sense of sight or sound. "Let there be prosperity, good health, and may he and we all be blessed, with length of days."

John suddenly remembered the date, June thirteenth, the anniversary of his father death.

"Is there something wrong Honey?"

Kathleen's voice brought him back. "Déjà vu." He whispered. "Just some weird thoughts. I"m all right."

"So John, Sis says you're moving into you house when you get back. What's the house like?" Ryan asked.

"My Dad bought it back in the sixties. It's a large semicustom California Ranch style on a large double lot. He bought the adjoining acreage across the creek a few years later.

"A creek?" Jean asked. "Can you swim in the creek?"

"Hardly, it's dry most of the time. But when I was ten, my dad added a large pool and spa. My sister Tess and I inherited everything after my mother died. I later bought out my sister's interest and added a guesthouse."

"We will stay in it, until the renovations are complete. Then we will have plenty of room so everyone can visit.

"I rented the house out when I was in college, too big for a bachelor. Luckily, the tenets moved out in May. So we started the remodeling. Kathleen and my sister have been overseeing furnishing. We are even adding a basement of sorts."

"John's sister is a fashion designer and is doing the interior decorating for us." Kathleen added. "You know me when it comes to that."

"I hope you don't overdo it Sis. Is your sister going to live with you?" Jake asked.

"No she lives in New York. She a student at NYU"

"That sounds like quite an estate you put together."

"I'm trying. We want all of you to come out for Christmas this year."

"Oh, I don't know." Kathie looked up at John.

"That sounds like fun, doesn't it dear?" Jean said to Patrick. "I'll talk to Connor."

"I don't think I can make it, Christmas you know." Ryan said. "The Church gets pretty busy at Christmas."

"Count us in." Jake seemed genuinely excited. "We'll drag Mom along."

"Good then, it's all settled." John agreed.

"A toast." Jake jumped to his feet and held up his wine glass. "To Christmas."

John's attention was hypnotically drawn once again to the glass in Jake's hand. All answered, "To Christmas."

*   *   *

153

The men retired to the living room after dinner for brandy and Jake and Patrick each had a cigar. For a few minutes, there was deadly silence. Even Jake was quiet. He appeared too busy sucking on his big cigar to talk. John felt that Ryan has been scrutinizing him all through dinner. Now Ryan sat in a large wingback chair in his black suit and roman collar shirt and stared at him, John was beginning to feel quite uncomfortable.

"Jake says you are joining the police department in San Jose." Ryan finally broke the silence.

"Yes, I start the Academy as soon as I get back."

There was another awkward void in the conversation. John was expecting to have to go through his reasoning again with Ryan about why he was putting law school on hold, the way he had to with Jake and Patrick, but the question never came. *The grilling would be better than the silence.* He felt like he was back in grammar school sitting in the principal's office for doing something wrong, but didn't know what.

"You know," Ryan began, "Mother is disappointed that you and Kathleen where not married in the Church. I know, you expressed your opposition before, but I am asking you to reconsider, for mother, Kathleen and especially your son."

"You're good, all of you, some setup. I told you I don't believe in your mumble-jumble." John was ready to walkout. "I'm not a theologian. I can't explain the how and why I believe as I do. I just don't believe it the way you do."

Jake leaned forward in his chair and puffed his cigar as if he were at a prizefight and the opening bell was about to ring.

"I don't believe we are born on this Earth to sit around and hope for a better something, someday after we die. That was fine in the Dark Ages, but it makes no sense today. If God gives us life and sends us here to live, then we should live and experience life and not be afraid that if we do the slightest thing wrong or go to the wrong Church or say the wrong thing or believe the wrong way, we will be damned to an eternal hell. I can't believe in that kind of God."

John surprised himself with his boldness, the brandy helped. He took another drink and leaned back in his chair. "We will not have this discussion again. Be content with me allowing Steven to be baptized in your Church. "

The room fell silent. John looked Ryan in the eyes. Jake left and returned shortly with brandy decanter and nervously refilled their glasses.

Ryan raised his glass towards John. "Well I guess you've made your case for God."

*   *   *

With the dishes finished and the children downstairs playing, the women gathered around the breakfast table for coffee.

"That John, is he always so happy? I've never seen him without a smile." Christine said.

Kathleen grinned reflective for a moment. "He's happy, most of the time . . . and always on the go. I swear, sometimes I think he is hyperactive, but he really never gets uptight, if you know what I mean. Not like a typical type A."

"What does he think about being a father?"

"The greatest thing that has ever happen to him, he couldn't be happier."

"I just can't understand why he doesn't just finish law school." Jean said. "He has enough money and even if he didn't he could get student loans and maybe work part-time. And why does he want to be a cop?"

"It's a family thing. His dad being a cop and all, it seems to be in his blood, and he feels compelled. He promised that he will work part-time on his law degree."

"But it will take him years that way. If he stayed in school now he could be finished in what, fewer than two years?"

"That's what I keep telling him, but he's stubborn. He's even hinted that he isn't sure if he really wants to be a lawyer. He says he likes law enforcement."

"Well I think we all need to keep the pressure on him to finishes school." Katie said.

"Mom, and all of you, it's not as if he's a sixteen year old thinking about dropping out of high school. He's a grown man, husband and soon to be father. It's his choice. I may not fully agree with it, but as his wife, I will go along with his decision. For now."

"Are you sure he's not Irish?" Katie asked.

CHAPTER 19

COLD WINDS IN PARADISE

```
INT.-PRIVATE HOSPITAL ROOM-DAY-SEPTEMBER 30, 1987

Hospital room filled with flowers on every flat sur-
face with helium-filled balloons floating above. Kath-
leen is in bed and John is in a chair next to the bed
holding his new son STEVEN, one day old.

John is talking to his son.

                    JOHN
          Hello there, yes hello there little
          one, yes.
```

Steven makes a face and fusses. "It's okay, it's okay, I'm just your old man, you better get used to me. Oh honey, he is beautiful." John beamed. With his right index finger, he strokes the back of Steven's tiny hand.

"Don't wear him out the first day."

"He is so little. I can't believe he's so little."

"Well they don't come out walking."

"I know." John continued to make faces and coochee-coo sounds. "I'm so happy and so scared at the same time. I've dreamed about being a father. Now that I am, it scares the hell out of me. What if I can't provide for my family? What if I'm not a good father? What if——."

"Stop with the, self-doubt. You'll be a great father."

"I can't help but worry."

Just then, a nursing attendant pushed the door open. "More flowers." She carried a blue and white ceramic baby-bootie vase filled with blue dyed carnations. "Let's see, this one is from . . . a Scott Hanson. Now where do we put it?"

"Nobody I know." John looked at Steven. "Somebody you know?"

"He was my insurance agent in Chicago." Kathleen said.

"Insurance agent." He continued to talk to Stevie. "Good guy to get to know, I guess."

*   *   *

John was sitting alone drink in hand and channel surfing in the family room of the O'Malley's home. Eight months had passed since Steven's birth. John under constant pressure from Kathleen's family and out of excuses finally relented and flew his family to Chicago for Steven's promised christening. John wanted Alvin and Sandra to be Steven's Godparents, but Ryan wanted Jean and Patrick. However, both Sandra and Alvin were born to Catholic families, were baptized and married in the Church. Though they hadn't attended church since their wedding, they were still technically Catholics and Ryan finally agreed.

Neatly dressed, Jake, in slacks, dress shirt and tie, arrived and headed straight toward John with his hand extended. John stood. "Welcome, glad you could make it. Wow, look at that California tan. Too, damn cold here to get out in the sun until summer."

"Hello Jake, nice to see you. Yeah, I can't believe it's still winter in April."

Jake turned to the bar. "Need a drink."

"No thanks, I already have one." John clicked off the TV.

"We'll get a couple of weeks of spring sometime after Easter then summer, hotter than hell. Too bad you aren't staying for the Holiday." Jake poured a drink and started for the sofa. "Sit, sit. So how are you holding up? You know this whole thing takes all of ten minutes if you stretch it, and believe me Ryan will. All this takes place in the baptistery, an alcove of the sanctuary. Only family and a few close friends will be there."

"Yeah, I got all that from Ryan. So much, fuss. Ridiculous——I don't go along with it, but Kathleen insists. I think religion should be a choice, not something pushed on a baby."

"I understand, I remember your last visit. I don't believe in it myself, but to keep peace in the family, I acquiesce. Figure it doesn't hurt, sort of like preventive medicine. I'm in enough shit with the family most of the time that I don't need to step in that one too. You're lucky you live in California. Play their games once and awhile, enough to keep you out of the doghouse and live your life the way you want. Kathleen's not interested in being Catholic any more than I am. She just does what is necessary to keep Mom and Ryan off her back."

"Thanks for the advice. I'll keep it in mind."

"What will you keep in mind?" Kathleen asked entering the room.

"Oh Jake was giving me some advice about tomorrow."

"Well I don't know how sound Jake's advice might be. Fix me a cola, please hon."

Jake jumped to his feet. "I'll do it just as soon as I can steal a kiss from my sister." He grabbed her and kissed her on the cheek. "You are looking good too, almost as good as your old man here."

"Thanks, I think." Kathleen sat next to John. "I'm bushed. Stevie's finally taking a nap in the living room and all the arrangements for tomorrow are done. Even Daddy will be there."

"Oh joy. That will make it interesting." Jake handed Kathleen her drink.

"You will behave yourself."

"I'll try." Jake said.

"Will your insurance friend be there?" John tried to remember the name. "You know a . . . that Hanson fellow, I think his name was— ya, that's it, Scott Hanson."

Kathleen shot a surprised, almost questioning look at Jake then back to John. "Ah . . . no."

Steven let out a yell. "Hon would you mind checking on him?"

"No problem." John said and headed for the living room.

*   *   *

Kathleen leaned back in her chair and took a deep breath.

"Does he know about you and Scott?" Jake asked as soon as John was out of the room."

"No, and I intend to keep it that way. I told Scott it was over the last time I was in town. The jerk sent flowers when Steven was born. I would like to have rung his neck. I guess Conner told him, they have offices in the same building. I told John he was my old insurance man."

"Don't play with fire if you don't want to get burned."

A sudden wave of nausea hit Kathleen.

"You okay." Jake sat on the sofa near his sister. "You're looking a little peaked, you getting enough rest."

"I'm not ready to announce this, but I'm afraid I might be pregnant, again."

"So that's why the cola. Stop by my office Monday first thing in the morning and we will find out."

"But John had a vasectomy after Steven was born."

"Why."

"Long story. I don't want more kids. Now this."

I got a snip job when Christine got pregnant with number four. All I could see was a dozen kids and I don't really care for the one's I got. I haven't told Christine or the family, you know their stand on birth control."

"So what am I pregnant?"

"Well you could have had unprotected sex too soon after the vasectomy. It takes a while for all those swimmers to die off. Or the doctor may have screwed up and cut the same tub twice. Or maybe it's not—."

"Oh it's John's I assure you." Kathleen took a deep breath and tears filled her eyes. "Goddamn it, this is all I need."

*   *   *

John had been wandering around the house the past half-hour with a hand full of papers. He temporarily forgot where he had put them when he put Steven to bed. Locating them in the kitchen, he grabbed a beer on his way to the bedroom.

"What are you doing?" Kathleen asked. She sat on the love seat in the sitting area off their master suit.

"I'm trying to make sense of this hospital bill."

Kathleen shushed him. "Katie's just fallen asleep."

John looked up at the basinet in the darkened area next to their bed, where three-week-old Katie was asleep. "Sorry. Do you need anything?"

Kathleen, in her bathrobe, lowered her book and looked at her half cup of tea. "I'm fine. Is there a problem? Doesn't our insurance company want to pay it?"

"Most of it, but I still need to review it. Remember some of the odd charges on Steven's bill, like the two units of blood and a few other things that we didn't use."

"Who cares as long as we don't have to pay for it?"

"That attitude is why medical insurance rates are so high."

"Whatever." Kathleen went back to her reading.

After several minutes of scrutinizing the bill, John went to his office and looked up some terms in his mother's old medical dictionary. When they renovated the house, he turned the original master bedroom into his home office.

Still uncertain as to why there was an odd charge of over $2,000.00 on the bill he came back to the bedroom, sat in his chair, and made some more notes on the writing pad. Kathleen seemed to be ignoring him, so he asked. "Do you have a minute?"

"Sure." Kathleen placed her bookmark and put her book down.

"There is a charge, it's covered, but I don't think it's right. They are charging $2,284.57, for a mini-laparotomy tubal ligation." He looked intently at Kathleen who simply looked back without a reaction. "In layman's terms, that's having your tubes tied."

"I know what it means."

John felt a flush. "Are you saying you had your tubes tied?" She didn't respond. "Why? I already had a vasectomy."

"We talked about it, remember."

"We joked about it. I didn't see the need."

"Yeah?" She pointed at the basinet. "And we still got her."

"Yes, but I don't remember us coming to an agreement about it. I thought we were going to look into it."

"Well when I went into labor you were in Sacramento at that meeting, and Katie was coming fast. The admissions administrator said that if I had it done during delivery, the insurance would pay for it, but if I waited, it could cost us up to five grand and the insurance wouldn't pay. So I signed the forms. I just forgot."

"You forgot? You forgot something like that. Why didn't you discuss it with me?"

"I was in labor. The baby was coming. You weren't there to discuss it. I did what I thought was right. It wasn't your decision, it was mine." Kathleen picked up her teacup and went to the kitchen.

John wanted to pursue her, but didn't. His emotions churned. He was angry, hurt and in a way humiliated. *She forgot to tell you.* "Damn." He finished his remaining beer and dropped the bottle in the wastebasket, then picked up the papers and took them to his office. In the dark, he sat at his desk.

Why did she need it? They knew her pregnancy with Katie was because they had unprotected sex too soon after his vasectomy. It was her making decisions without him that hurt. *It's changed. We once shared everything. In our own worlds now.* John was determined to change things, if he only knew how.

*   *   *

At first light, John found himself still at his desk. He made his way to the kitchen and put on a pot of coffee before visiting the bathroom. While the coffee brewed, John checked in on Steven. He looked down at his sleeping son, so small, so sweet, and so innocent. *What the hell, you can make a big deal of this. Destroy your marriage, your family. Maybe she did forget. You can't change it now.* He gave his son a gentle kiss as not to wake him and returned to the kitchen

With a cup in hand, he returned to his office, sat at his desk, and flipped through his rolodex. He stopped at the card for his brother-in-law, Father Ryan O'Malley and dialed. A female voice answered. "Saint Bernadette's rectory, Sister Sophia speaking, how may I help you?"

"Is Rya——Father O'Malley there?"

"He's at morning Mass. May I take a message?"

John hesitated. "No, never mind. It's not important. I'll catch him some other time, thank you."

John hung up the phone before she could respond. *You can do this on your own.*

John went back to the kitchen refilled his cup, poured a second cup carefully fixing it just the way Kathleen liked it. He grabbed a hand full of cookies and put them on a saucer, then placed everything on a tray and started for the bedroom.

*   *   *

Two days before Christmas, John finally put up the Christmas lights. Finished with the installation, but with the boxes still scattered on the lawn he plugged in the lights to check them. Happy with his work, he was setting the timer when a black Lincoln Continental pulled in the driveway.

"Merry Christmas." Alvin yelled, opening the car door.

"Merry Christmas to you too. What are you doing here? I thought you were all spending Christmas in Seattle." John greeted Alvin with a hug. "What a surprise."

"Sandra and I decided to do Christmas with our families this year. We're expecting again in May, number four."

"Well congratulation. It's good to see you. Come on in, I'll scare up something hot or cold."

"No, not today, I can't stay. Thanks anyway. I've got a list of things I got to do." Alvin looked at the lights and the boxes in the yard. "Are you putting them up or taking then down."

"I got a late start this year. With the new baby and all, time just got away from me."

"Speaking of the new baby, that's why I'm here." Alvin popped the trunk and pulled out a large box wrapped in baby giftwrapping paper. "This is for Katie. It's a stroller. Sandra picked it out. She says it's the Cadillac of strollers. If you don't need it we can exchange it."

"No, no it's perfect. We haven't got one for her and Stevie isn't ready to give up his yet."

"You two sure have been popping them out. You trying to catch up with us?"

"No, that's it, no more. We decided that two is enough."

"Did you figure out what is causing it?"

"Yeah."

Alvin studied John for a moment then shivered. "Man it's cold for the valley, and you in just a t-shirt."

"Well I've been getting used to the cold lately."

Alvin leaned against the fender of his car. "What do you mean?"

John could tell by the tone of Alvin's voice that he couldn't fool him. "Kathleen and I've been hitting some rough spots."

"You mean that a cold wind is blowing through paradise?"

"It started when she got pregnant so soon after Stevie's birth. I don't blame her, she's been pregnant nearly the whole time we've been married. I think all she could see was diapers."

"Well a little snip-snip can take care of that."

"Yeah, I had it, and we thought it's had been taken care of . . . . It just takes longer for it to be effective than we thought." John kicked a pebble back into the flowerbed. "It's fixed for good now."

"Outside forces?" Alvin asked. "Is Kathleen or are you having an affair or something?"

"No nothing like that. Just some of the luster is off the roses. Kathleen isn't real excited about me being a cop for one. Kind of sets the sparks for disharmony. I'm beginning to think she might be right. Maybe I should have stayed in school. I would probably have my law degree by now."

"Well quit the force and go back to law school. You've got the money."

"It isn't that easy. I'm taking classes, but with two kids, it's hard to study. Don't get me wrong, Stevie and Katie are the light of my life. I don't regret have them. It's just the responsibility of being a father. You're a dad, you understand. I guess I'm kind of doubting myself. Will I be a good father? Can I provide? So many questions . . . . I guess I take after my father. Maybe I'm just in a bit of a funk."

"I don't know what to say. How can I help?"

"I'll have to work it out myself. I'll make it work——for the kids' sake——I'll make it work. Whatever it takes, I'll do it."

"Can you do it by yourself?" Alvin asked, but didn't get a response. "Well, if you need to talk, I'm always available and if you need to get away for a while, our home is open and you're always welcome."

"Thanks for the offer, but I'm determined. I'll make it work if it kills me."

*   *   *

John had been planning Zach's retirement party since Christmas, a huge barbeque poolside. He knew March was a little early for an outdoor party but he made plans for every contingency, caterers, entertainment and a large tent in case of rain. It turned out that it was a sunny afternoon and even a few of the kids swam. The party was over, the caterers had packed up and the rental company would come in the morning to take down the tent and pack up the tables, chairs and bounce toys. John, Zach and Alvin were sitting near a space heater while their wives were in the house. They had followed Kathleen, when she went to check on the kids, lured by a promise of coffee.

Zach had brought a bottle of whiskey and shot glasses to the table, and poured a round of shots, not that any of the guys needed any more to drink.

"Too retirement." Zach lifted his glass. John and Alvin followed and they downed their whiskey. "Thank you Johnny for putting this together for me. It's been a blast."

The men sat quietly. The evening was pleasantly cool, but not cold. "It looks as if we are having an early spring." Alvin said. "So John, things warming up for you two, as well?" Alvin glanced at Zach and then back to John.

"It's okay, he knows. Yeah, there's been a thaw."

"Good. You had me concerned. I'm glad you're working things out. So what are you going to do without Zach telling everybody what to do and how to run things down at the precinct?"

"I don't know, we're going to miss the old fart, I'm sure."

"Oh I'm going to keep my eye on you young pipsqueaks."

Just then, the phone rang. John went to the patio phone to answer, but evidently, Kathleen had picked up before he could get to it. He waited to see if the call might be for him, but after a minute, he started back, and then stopped. His curiosity got the better of him and he picked up the phone. There was a man's voice. "Maybe we can get together?"

"John is that you?" Apparently, Kathleen heard him pick up.

"Yeah. Is this for me?"

"No dear, it's for me . . . it about mom . . . her insurance."

John could sense an annoyance in her voice. "Sorry." John hung up the phone. His head buzzed and he wasn't thinking clearly, but wondered why her mother's insurance agent would be calling her at this time, on a weekend. Then he remembered that her family didn't do anything of importance concerning her mother's failing health without all the kids involved or there would be one hell of a fight. Dismissing any further thoughts, he returned to the guys.

Alvin had already poured three more shots and he and Zach waited his return. Without a word, they downed their shots. "Anything wrong?" Zach asked.

"No, I don't think so. Sometimes I just don't know if I can trust Kathleen."

CHAPTER 20

THE PAINS OF LOVE

```
EXT.-POOLSIDE MICHAELS HOME-MAY 12, 1997
```

The renovated and expanded Michaels pool now included an island bar, waterfall, beach and grotto spa with lush tropical landscaping. At a table near the pool John and Zach sat talking and keeping a watch over his children, Steven age 10, and Katie 8, as they play in the water.

A month earlier Kathleen's mother had died and she stayed on in Chicago after the funeral.

> JOHN
> Thanks for staying with the kids
> while I'm at work. Kathleen gets back
> from Chicago tonight.

> ZACH
> Don't mention it. Retirement isn't
> what it's cracked up to be, I was
> glad to have something to do.

"Well anytime you're bored, the kids would love for you to come over and play."

"Thanks, I wish my grandkids lived closer, we could all play together."

"Would you like another beer?"

John was to his feet before Zach could respond. With the pool renovation, John added a new covered outdoor kitchen. John pulled two frozen mugs from the freezer and poured them full of draft beer from the stainless-steel kegerator. Just one of the gadgets added with the other new appliances.

"Here you go."

"Your dad would have loved this. He was so proud of this place. It thrills me to see what you've done. I know it would have made him happy."

"I wish he and mom could see it, and the kids."

"Well I'll bet they're looking down from heaven and are pleased."

John smiled, but didn't say anything. He touched his mug to Zach's and took a drink. Amanda, the family's two-year-old Irish setter, sat at his feet with her ever-vigilant eyes on the kids. John patted the dog on the head. She turned and looked up at him with her big brown eyes.

"Zach, I don't know how to say this. I don't know what I'm going to do." John looked at his kids across the pool as he spoke. "Kathleen is cheating on me."

"What! Are you sure?"

"Yeah. I'm sure."

"That's a kick in the nuts." Zach squirmed in his chair.

"And I don't think it's the first time either."

"What are you gonna do? Are you thinking of separating, divorce?"

"I haven't worked it out yet. I've got the kids to consider first, I don't want them hurt and I know that a divorce will, no matter how I try to protect them."

"I understand. What's Kathleen saying?"

"She doesn't know I know anything. I just found out a couple of days ago. I started to suspect something when I could never catch her by the phone. She was supposedly staying at her sister's but every time I called her, she was out. Jean kept making excuses that were beginning to sound pretty lame. So I called Richard Southerland, I think you know him, he use to work out of the South Precinct. He got married and moved to Chicago a few years back. I asked him to check around for me. It didn't take much looking. He called me four days ago, she's been kicking up her heals with an old flame of hers."

John stood and took a couple of steps towards the pool. Katie waved. He waved back and then turned back to Zach. "Goddammit, it hurts, it hurts like hell." He returned to his chair and put his hand to his forehead as if he had a headache. "I haven't slept since."

"You okay son?"

"Yeah . . . . You know, the signs were there since before we were married. I guess I just chose to ignore them. I guess I really was thinking with my dick and not my head. Yet, I feel a bus broadsided me."

"Life has a way of doing that, broadsiding you and you don't even see it coming. Sometimes you don't even know you've been hit. When your father died, I don't think he even knew he was shot."

"Maybe it's easier that way. Better than being run over by the bus and surviving to live like a vegetable for years."

"You will survive and recover. Pull yourself back together. You have so much to live for, your kids and who knows, maybe you and Kathleen can work it out."

Yeah, maybe . . . . I was thinking, I've got to go to the airport in a couple of hours, would you mind taking the kids for the night. I've decided I want to confront Kathleen tonight. I would rather they not be around when I do."

"You're not thinking of somethin' . . . foolish, are you?"

"No, no nothing like that, I just want some privacy, that's all."

"Of course I'll take the kids. Promise you won't do somethin' crazy."

"I promise."

"You know things can happen, Things can get out of hand. You've got weapons in the house."

"You know that's not in my nature."

"I know."

"And they're unloaded and in the gun safe. There won't be any problem. I won't do anything rash. I consider my kids first."

"I know you do."

"I haven't given up, I'm determined to try and work it out. I'll call you tomorrow when we're ready for you to bring the kids home."

*   *   *

After Zach left, John got himself another beer and went to his office. He pulled a book from his shelf of classic. *Funny, nobody actually reads the title, 'Greater Expectation.'* It had been years since his last entry, shortly after Katie's birth. The first couple of years he was diligent in making entries, but it eventually slowed to a point that he only wrote in the dairy on the anniversary of his father's death and even that gave way after his marriage to just the major events of his children's births. Half-heartedly his looked through the pages, from his father's last entry about his hope that John would not follow him into law enforcement and that his son find true love, to his one entry's about meeting Kathleen.

With the rosewood fountain, his kept in the top drawer of his desk he began to write. *When I read my father's expectation, I can see now how much of what I have done with my life would have disappointed him. I will commit to finishing my law degree and leave the police force as soon as feasibly possible. I will no longer be gullible when it comes to Kathleen. I will try, for the sake of the children, to forgive her and try to repair our marriage. However, I will not forget and I will think clearly in all matters of the heart, as much as that is humanly possible, May 12, 1997.*

John put the pen back in his desk, returned the book to its place and readied himself for the drive to the airport.

*   *   *

The drive home was quiet. Their only conversation was about, her long layover in Denver, and how tired she was. John put her suitcase on a bedroom chair and she headed to the shower. John went to the wet bar in the family room and poured a Scotch. Drink in hand, he returned to the bedroom. He noticed she had left the bathroom door ajar by a few inches. It seemed a bit strange. She usually closed the door. He thought of the many showers they used to take together and he wondered if she had expected him to join her, tonight. The desire to do so was gone, instead he sat on the sofa in the sitting area and waited for her to finish.

He had envisioned what was about to happen dozens of times in the last few days, each time coming to a different conclusion. Like with roulette, once you spin the wheel you never know where the ball is going to land. The water turned off, he took a drink and tried to steady his nerves.

Kathleen seemed surprised to find John sitting on the sofa. She loosely tied her robe. "Were you waiting to use my shower?"

"No, I wanted to talk."

"Give me a second."

She went to the kitchen. Her grace and beauty showed even in a bathrobe and he realized how much he missed her this past month. Since they met, they had not been separated for more than a few days at a time. For a moment, he thought of dropping the confrontation and letting the whole thing pass, but this time the festering in his heart wouldn't let him.

She returned with a glass of wine and sat on the sofa next to him. "So what is it you want to talk about?"

"I know about Scott."

John was determined to let her speak first. He could see a moment of panic in her eyes and a concerned look come over her face. Then slowly she seemed to regain her poise. "Is that why you've been so quiet and arranged for the children to be away?"

John looked down at his drink. "Partly." He fought to hold his tongue. He knew if he didn't stay strong, he would surrender to her charm as he always did in the past. Too much was at risk, the hurt too great, and the stakes too high.

"I'm sorry. I never meant it to happen."

John looked up. The tears already ran down Kathleen's cheeks and dripped from her quivering chin. John took her in his arms and felt her sobs.

Kathleen finally appeared to pull herself together. "He's an old friend." She began slowly through her tears. "I met him when I was in high school. He lived down the block, a car salesman then, Ryan's age. We dated for a while. He was fun, but neither of us wanted anything serious. After I graduated and started college, we just sort of drifted apart. I hadn't seen him for years."

John reached for the box of tissues. She wiped her eyes and blew her nose.

"He knows the family. He was there at mom's funeral. I only saw him from a distance. A couple of days later he called Jean's, I answered the phone and we talked. I told him that I was married and had two children and that you took them home because they had school. That I was going to stay in Chicago to help Jean settle mom's things. A few days later, he called again and asked if we could meet for coffee, I agreed. After that, it just seemed to get crazy. Oh God, John I didn't mean to hurt you or the kids. It just happened . . . . Forgive me?"

John wanted to believe her. The alternative was too much for him to bear. Although a part of him had come to doubt her every word, he made a conscious decision to believe. Faith is often blind to the truth. Even when the truth hits you between the eyes, you believe the lie, it's easier that way. "Of course I forgive you." He held her in his arms along time. Slowly the pain and the doubt drifted away.

"Take me to bed." She whispered.

*   *   *

John and George, a handyman that often helped John, had just finished fixing a sprinkler head near the walkway to the front door when Zach pulled up in the drive way. The pickup had hardly stopped when the door popped open and Steven and Katie jumped out and ran toward their father.

"Dad, Dad. Look what we made." Steven yelled, a model airplane held over his head.

John knelt and Steven nearly knocked him over with his hug, when only seconds later Katie joined her brother in an exuberant group cuddle. The children's delight in seeing their dad momentarily over shadowed their excitement about their model airplanes.

"Look, Uncle Zach helped us made them." Katie thrust her model in John's face.

"Wow that's great." John carefully examined their work. "That's super Katie and so is yours, Steven.

"Steven's flies better than mine." Katie explained. "But see . . . I painted flowers on mine."

"It's just beautiful."

Just then, Steven let his plane fly. It rose, lifted by a breeze, circled up over the garage and just when it looked like it was about to land on the roof, it cleared the eave and made a near perfect landing on the lawn.

"Great flight." Zach said. Katie just held her plane while Steven retrieved his. John stood and glanced at Zach leaning against his pickup. "Do you think I should sign them up for aeronautical engineering school?"

"I think Lockheed might want to hire them."

"Good idea, I'll send their resume's over tomorrow."

Steven and Katie looked at their father questioning. Finally, Steven caught the tease. "Oh Dad."

"Your mom's home." John said.

"Oh." Katie said as she wound the rubber band by the propeller, preparing for a try at launching her plane.

"Come on Katie. Let's go show Chuck and Gene." Steven said, starting toward the neighbors with Katie following."

"Woo, wait. Go in and say hello to your mother first." The kids stopped and looked at their dad. "Then you can go play." They smiled and ran to the open front door.

John watched them disappear into the house. He took a deep breath before turning to Zach. "Thanks. It seems like they had a great time."

"They did." Zach handed John an overnight bag. "Here's the rest of their things." There was an awkward pause. "You and Kathleen have your little talk?"

"Yeah." John didn't want to talk about it, but knew Zach wouldn't leave until he got a satisfying answer. He wished now that he had kept their problems to himself. "We're getting it worked out. The kids come first."

"You know Son," Zach stepped closer and touched John's chest with his finger. "Hurts of the heart are hard to heal."

"I know, but a little pain now and then, sweetens the pleasure."

*   *   *

The summer came, Chicago faded. Kathleen, Katie and Steven spent most of their time in the pool. The three seem to build a bond that John had not seen before. In late July, John took a three-week vacation. He drove the family up the coast to Portland and on to Seattle to visit with Alvin and his gang for several days. On their way home, they cut inland through Salt Lake City. A near perfect vacation

Even the holidays were brighter that year. It was the first time they didn't make a pilgrimage to Chicago for either Thanksgiving or Christmas. Kathleen's family felt a little slighted, but John smoothed their feathers and they all agreed that the next year, Christmas would be at the Michaels.

At the first of the year, Alvin moved his family back to Cambria Park. His business demanded he spend more time in Silicon Valley, so he purchased and renovated his parents' home. John was happy to have him nearby again. Alvin kept his promise, a little late, to make John get his rear in gear and finish law school.

It was a pleasant March afternoon, Alvin and John were sharing a beer by the pool. Alvin had called John earlier in the week with something urgent he needed to talk about, face to face.

"I will finish this fall semester." John looked at Alvin, pleased he would finally finish the law degree and have Alvin off his ass.

"Well it's about time."

"Is this all you wanted to talk about?"

"No. It's time for another zero. It should have come sooner. Since I'm back fulltime, I've made some changes and we're back on track. Here." Alvin grinned, handed John a folded check, and waited for John to look at it.

John had almost forgotten Alvin's pledge. He held the check and his hands trembled. Taking a deep breath, he looked, five-million. He didn't know how long he just sat there and stared at the number.

"Are you okay?" Alvin asked.

"Stunned."

"I told you it would come. I made it out to the trust like before, is that okay?"

"I wish Kathleen was home to see this."

"Where is she?"

"Beauty salon. This calls for something more than a beer." John dashed into the house and came back with a bottle of cognac and two snifters. "Cheers."

"Cheers. Hey I got to tell you about my gig in Hollywood."

"That consulting thing for the computer movie?" John asked.

"Yeah, I never knew it took so long to shoot a movie. It's a weird film, directed by the Wachowski guys. I got to the set. It was supposed to be a big computer room full of blinking lights and things whirling. The scene was about them hooking up this guy's brain to the computer. It took them all week to shoot two pages of the script. They would try it one way then another. Three actors and the director going over and over, should it be this way or that way, while forty or fifty people, crew, sat on the set and waited."

"Who were the actors?"

"Keanu Reeves, Laurence Fishburne and Carrie-Anne Moss, they are calling it *The Matrix*. Going to have tons of special effects. It'll be another year before it's finish. But what I wanted to tell you is, it was like you said your father talked about."

"How's so."

"They had the script. Only dialog and real sketchy descriptions. Primarily nothing more than an outline. The actors made their characters come to life. They give the script flesh."

"It all sounds a little crazy. What has that got to do with life?"

"Remember your dad said our lives are scripted. You told me about it after he died. It's our lives but it's all planned ahead, the script is written before we are born. We are all just living a script"

* * *

John walked Alvin to his car without much comment. After Alvin was gone, he went to his office and put the check in the safe. For a long while, he just sat thinking about what to do with the money. He knew he shouldn't do anything without talking to Aaron. When he picked up the phone to call Aaron's office, he was surprised to hear Kathleen on the phone. She had evidently come home and called one of her friends. He was about to hang up when the other party spoke. It was a man.

"It was good seeing you." He said.

"Thanks again for lunch. We'll have to do it again."

"It's a date. I'll call you the next time I'm in town."

"Do that. Well I had better go. John and the kids should be home soon. I love you baby."

"I love you too. Bye."

"I'll talk to you later Scott. Goodbye."

John heard the phones hang up. He sat for a time before going to the family room and pouring another drink.

"Oh, you're home." Kathleen spoke from the kitchen. "I didn't hear you come in. Where are the kids?"

"In their rooms."

"You're home early, anything new happen?"

"No." He stood at the bar with his back to her.

"Are you going to be home for dinner?"

174

"No. Got a meeting." He picked up the bottle of cognac and went back to his office.

*   *   *

Before John left that evening, he took one of his handguns from his closet and tucked it in his jacket pocket. There was no meeting, instead he drove to the secluded end of his street and parked where he knew Kathleen wouldn't spot him. He nursed the bottle of cognac and his anger until late into the night.

Around midnight, in the dark, he walked to the house and silently slipped in the back way, through the exercise room that joined their bedroom. In the dark, through the slightly ajar door he watched Kathleen get ready for bed. He stood silent. His police training took over. Slowly he raised his weapon. Even with the booze, his hand was rock study. The muscle of his finger started to tense as it had thousands of time.

"Mommy, Mommy I'm scared." Katie ran to her mother and jumped on the bed. "I had a scary dream. A bad man came to shot you and Daddy.

CHAPTER 21

DÉJÀ VU

INT.-MICHAELS' DINNING ROOM-DECEMBER 24, 1998

Close-up on the glass held high in Jake's hand, same
angle as when John experienced Déjà vu, at the
O'Malley home twelve years before. John stares at the
glass as the camera pulls back. The table with Kathleen at the foot of the table with their two children,
Steven, now age 12, and Katie, age 10. Also at the
table are Jean, Christine, Patrick, Conner and Rose.
Jake stands, as the others ignore him.

                    JEAN
          Well Sis it's wonderful you having us
          all out here.

                  KATHLEEN
          We are delighted all of you could
          come.

"Come on, isn't anyone going to join me in a Christmas toast?"

"No, you can just hold your glass up all night." Christine joked. "Are
you okay John. You look like you just saw a ghost."

"Yeah, yeah, just thought of something. I was remembering a dinner
we had years ago at your folks home in Chicago."

"My arm is getting tired."

"Well make your dumb toast." Christine said.

"Okay, lift your glasses. To a Merry Christmas, let our days be long with joy and our nights short of sorrow. Let there be prosperity, good health, and may we all be blessed with length of days."

Other than John, nobody paid much attention to just another one of Jake's toast, the third for the evening. John heard the conversation going on, but couldn't make sense of the strange feeling that had just come over him. He felt he was just thrust into a scene from a movie he had seen over and over but couldn't remember the rest of it.

"It was a lovely meal Kathleen." Patrick wiped his mouth and placed his napkin beside his plate. "I don't think I can move."

"Well then don't. Kids, you're excused." Kathleen stood "Girl's let's clear the rest of these dishes and John will get out the brandy for the men. I have champagne for the ladies."

John, still confused by the experience and maybe the wine, looked at Kathleen. "What, oh yes. I was just thinking. We are so happy it was our turn again to host the family's Christmas, this year." Everyone hesitated and looked at John. He realized he had said the same thing only minutes before. "Oh, brandy, yes I'll get the brandy."

"Great! Need a hand?" Jake offered

"I think so." John stood slowly, stepped to the sideboard, and stood.

The ladies cleared the last of the desert dishes. Patrick remained seated while Jake helped set out three brandy snifters and then turned to John, questioning. "Are you okay?"

"Yeah, fine." John returned to the table with his and Patrick drinks.

"Well brother-in-law, here's to your Law Degree and many years of successful practice. Congratulations."

"Good show." Patrick lifted his glass to John.

"Yeah, well after twelve years on the force I felt I could do more good as a prosecutor."

"I'll bet Kathleen is happy."

"Well she sees the dollar signs."

"That's Kathleen." Jake said with a chuckle. "But it doesn't look as if she does without much."

"You sure can say that. I'm impressed with all the additions you've made to the house. That new pool must have set you back a real chunk of change."

"The old pool needed more repair than it was worth so we replaced it. We had fun with the pool, wanted to make it interesting so we put in slide, beach, island bar and the spa in the heated cave so we could use it year round. You will have to give it a try."

"I didn't bring a swimsuit."

"I think we can find you one."

"It doesn't look as if you will be selling this place anytime soon." Jake added to the conversation.

"No, we're pretty happy with it."

"So when are you going to make the big change?" Jake asked.

"I'm going to leave the force in January to prepare for the bar exam. Even if I don't pass the first time, I'm not going back. I'm finished being a cop. I will just keep trying until I pass it."

"Is that why you seem a little glum this Christmas, gonna miss the old boys club."

John forced a smiled. He knew he couldn't tell his brother-in-laws the real truth about his somber mood. "No——well maybe a little."

"You seem hesitant, are you sure of your decision?"

"I'm sure, another week and I'm out of there for good."

"That soon? So when's your last day?" Patrick asked.

New Year's Day, I promised I'd work New Year's Eve. You know how crazy it gets, but at six a.m., January 1, 1999, I wave good-bye, and start a new life." John stood. "Come on. Let's go out to the patio. We have space heaters and you can see my computerized light show on the water."

*　　　*　　　*

In the kitchen, the women had finished cleaning up. Since she arrived, Jean had been questioning Kathleen about John. She felt there was something going on between them that Kathleen wasn't saying or didn't know. She made it her mission to find the underlying cause of it.

Kathleen started the dishwasher while Jean dried the roaster. She turned to Kathleen and asked. "That was a fantastic roast. I didn't even know you could cook. What have you got planned for tomorrow?"

"Well it's supposed to be a surprise, but John is planning a Christmas Luau, with a whole roast pig and all. He wants to show off the patio, pool and his culinary skills. I hope you brought your swim suits."

"Well you certainly can't have Christmas dinner outdoors in Chicago." Christine said.

"Not hardly." Jean thought of the foot of snow that fell the day before they flew out of O'Hare.

"I'll bet John can't wait to change careers." Christine added.

"He seems a little sad to me." Jean said. "Is he having some problems? Anxiety over taking the Bar Exam?"

"Not that I know. I think it's mixed emotion. He loves police work, likes the action, and you know him always on the move. When he's home I never know when he's going to rip out a wall or what he's going to dig up next. He is even trying to get a variance from the city to put a stable on the property across the creek so we can all have horses."

"He is a busy boy, how do you keep up with him?" Jean asked.

"I let him, the kids and the dog go their way and I go mine."

"Doesn't he object?"

"He is all about being a father. As long as I don't get in the way of that, he doesn't mind what I do. It took years for me to convince him that was the way he wanted it."

"Some relationship." Christine said, taking a seat at the breakfast table.

"Well it's better than being a doctor's servant and nanny." Kathleen snapped back.

"Okay Kathleen." Jean said. "We get your point. I don't think any of us have a perfect marriage. But that's how you planned it from the beginning wasn't it, a no strings attached marriage." Jean sat at the breakfast table. "It just took you a little longer than you thought to get there."

"How about some more champagne?" Kathleen asked.

Jean watched her fill her glass. "So when does he plan on leaving the police force?"

"New Year's will be his last shift."

"I think it's wonderful, John practicing law. No chance of you heading back to Chicago? Christine asked.

"Come-on, leave California?"

"That's too bad. We'd love to have you closer."

"I'd love to be closer too."

"I bet." Jean muttered to herself.

The phone rang and Kathleen answered with a quick, "Hello . . . . Oh, well hello and Merry Christmas to you too." Kathleen turned. "Excuse me, but I need to take this." With that, she walked into the darkened living room with the wireless handset.

*   *   *

Kathleen finished her chat with Scott and started back to the kitchen. When she approached the door was ajar, she heard Jean's voice and pauses. "Have you noticed it's colder in this house than an Illinois blizzard? And I'm not talking about the weather."

"What do you think it is?" Rose asked.

"I think that phone call has something to do with it."

"Do you think it's Scott?" Christine asked.

"I'm certain of it." Jean assured.

"That's dangerous."

"He's a brazen son-of-a-bitch." Jean stood, "I ought to go in there, yank the phone out of her hand, and tell that bastard what I think of him."

"Why does she keep messing around with him?' Rose refilled her glass. "Do you think she will leave John?"

"No! She just likes a little action on the side."

"Do you think John has any idea?"

"I'm sure of it. He may be foolish, but he is not a fool. She told me he confronted her about Scott when she got back after Mom's funeral."

"How come I never hear about these things?" Christine questioned.

"Maybe it's because you don't listen."

"So what happened?"

"Sis wiggled her way out of it somehow. Promised it was over and all. I can't believe he was that gullible. But when it comes to Kathleen, he has always been naïve I guess. It's almost as if they have some weird agreement, sick game, or something."

"Or a death wish."

"You heard what Kathleen just said about him going one way and she the other."

"Why don't you keep me more in the loop?"

"You've got your hands full with Jake."

"I know, but he's not a cheater." Christine went to the sink and got herself a glass of water. "John's been pensive this visit. And tonight at the table, he was a million miles away. I wonder if he knows she's up to her old tricks."

"I've been wondering the same thing, but he is hard to read. He'll make a good lawyer. I'm sure he is up to something. I just know I'm staying out of it and you should do the same."

"I will, thanks for the warning."

Kathleen stepped into the kitchen and put the phone back in its cradle.

"Kathleen, one of these days." Jean warned. "Think of the scandal, think of our family."

Kathleen held her index finger to her mouth in the silence gesture.

"What the hell's the matter with you?" Jean slapped her hand on the table. "Why don't you leave John and go live with Scott?

Kathleen calmly filled her glass with champagne. "He's a salesman."

"Well you sure are buying what he is selling. It's not his looks or charm. Heaven knows he doesn't have much of them."

"No it's none of that. There's just something I can't explain."

"Why don't you marry Scott?" Christine asked.

Kathleen let out a horselaugh. "Marry Scott? Hell, he's not marriage material.

"Is it the sex, John have problems? Maybe he should talk to Jake."

"Sex with John has been good, however it's been a little strained lately, but that's because of school. He's a perfect husband. Sometimes to perfect. No, it's not the sex. Scott's not the exceptional lover, though he thinks he is."

Jean shook her head. "If it's not sex with Scott, what is it?"

"It's sex——sort of——don't get me wrong." Kathleen looked blissfully into the air. "But Scott, his is like a fine French dessert. You know, when you're stuffed after a delicious dinner and the waiter still brings that cart, you're never too full for one of those temptations. That's Scott. You can't live on nothing but dessert, but oh every so often . . . ."

"So Scott is your Bonbon?" Jean arched her eyebrows.

"Yes, and you know how nice it is the have a box of bonbons every now and then." Kathleen said, while cuddling her arms around herself.

"Of course bonbons only satisfy for a moment." Christine added. "I'll stick to my Irish stew, thanks."

*   *   *

The men were enjoying their second brandies. A fire blazed in the fire pit and the colored lights changed patterns on the waterfall and under the pool. The small talk had ended and John realized just how little he has in common with his brother-in-laws. The men awaited the wives' to join them. John began to wonder what was taking so long.

"Connor and I are proud of you brother-in-law." Patrick said, giving John a pat on the back. "Great to have another lawyer in the fanily."

"So am I." Jake agreed. "Here come the girls."

Jean led the ladies from the kitchen. "What are you boys proud of?"

"John's going to practice law." Conner answered.

"Oh that, we were just discussing it. But as I understand it, you won't be talking him into moving to Chicago." Jean said sitting beside her husband. "I thought we would all have to twist one or both of his arms off before we'd get him to turn in his badge."

"Kathleen has been doing that for the past ten years." John brought the decanter of brandy to the table.

"Well, I for one am glad you came to your senses." Jake started to raise his glass.

"Stop him. He's going to make another toast." Jean shouted.

Patrick grabbed Jake's arm and the rest started hooting at him.

"All right, all right. I get the hint, no toast. Jesus, Mary and Joseph, give a guy a break, why don't ya."

Katie and Steven came out with their dog Amanda, who seemed to smile with her felt antlers and big red bow tied to her collar. They stood a moment and then started singing, 'We Wish You a Merry Christmas'.

By the second line, one and all had joined the singing.

John focused on his children and after they finished the last line of the song, he knelt down between them and grabbed them in his arms. "And a very happy, Happy New Year." Amanda licked John's face. "He hugged her. "And a Happy New Year to you too."

CHAPTER 22

A BRIGHT NEW YEAR

INT. JOHN'S HOME OFFICE—4:30 P.M.—NEW YEARS EVE, 1998

John sits at his desk. Zach sits across the desk from John in the wingback chair. John has a folder with several legal documents spread out on his desk.

                    JOHN
          That's it. Aaron will file the di-
          vorce paper next Tuesday.

                    ZACH
          I am sorry that it has come to this.
          But it's for the best. Nobody can say
          you didn't try.

John had finally decided to confided his plans to Zack, determined nothing would change his mind this time. "You don't know how close I came. I haven't told anyone this. Last spring when I found out, she was still at it with Scott, after all the promises. I almost lost it altogether."

Zach leaned forward. "What do you mean?"

"I got a little drunk. Got out my Glock and was going to take her out. Had my finger on the trigger and started to squeeze. Katie ran in the instant before. It gave me time to think."

"Why didn't you talked to me."

"I had to work it out myself. But I knew then it was over. Just needed to work out the details. Aaron's protected most of my assets. His son will handle the divorce. I don't give a damn anymore. I just don't want Katie and Steven hurt. Next week a whole new life begins."

"Good for you son."

"Now all I have to do is make it through tonight. Tomorrow I hang up my uniform for good."

*   *   *

John is driving the squad car and his partner Lou, is riding shotgun. Lou, Hispanic is ten years older than John. They have been partners for two year. Lou checked his watch. "It is eleven-thirty-five." There was a light rain downtown San Jose. "Quiet."

"So far. I think the rain is kind of keeping things toned down."

On the horizon, the clouds were breaking up and the moon peeking through. "It looks like it's gonna let up for a while." John made a right turn.

"Yeah, then some jackass will get his gun out and start shooting at the moon. Between the stiff new laws and the ad campaigns, it's gotten a whole lot better. You should have seen it ten, fifteen years ago, a God-damn war zone. Everybody thought they had to shoot their guns at midnight."

"I remember my dad going off about it, he hated New Year's Eve." John turned off Santa Clara Street and on to First Street. The old Bank of America building was on his left and halfway up the block on his right the jewelry store. It had a face-lift during the Downtown renovation but it was still called, Roberts Jewelry. *Well Dad I'm going to leave the force. I hope you're happy.*

"You okay?"

"Yeah . . . just thinking about my dad. That's where he got shot. In the alley behind that jewelry store."

"So how does it feel, short timer? Are you counting the hours? Six-and-a half more to go. You gonna miss it?"

"What the Force? Probably, at least some of it."

"Well I think you are doing the right thing. If I had your brains, I'd do it. You can bet your ass I would."

"Well, I got some other reasons too." John turned and drove up the alley before turning back on the main street. "If you don't mind me airing some dirty laundry."

"I don't mind. Go ahead and get it off your chest."

"My wife's been cheating on me."

"Awh, naw . . . that's the shits. Are you sure? "

"Yeah, it's been going on for some time. At first, I denied it, then tried to ignore it and finally tried to fix it. Nothing's worked." John glanced at Lou when they stop for a red light. "Zach and my attorney are the only ones that know the whole story. I've talked to Steven and he's trying to understand. I always knew something was going on but I pretended not to believe it. I hoped we could work it out."

John made a left turn and started driving into an industrial area. Once again, he took a glimpse at Lou. There was the feeling of relief at being able to tell Lou.

"You know who it is?"

"Yeah, a guy named Scott, Scott Hanson, from Chicago, a half-ass traveling salesman, a looser with four ex-wives and half-dozen kids. He's pushing sixty for Christ sake. I guess they had the hots for each other from before Kathleen and I were married.

"What are you going to do about it?"

"I needed time to think it out. I realized it was a mistake from the beginning, but mistakes are hard to admit and even harder to fix, especially when kids are involved. I have an attorney. He's going to file the divorce papers next week. I wanted to wait until the Holidays were over and I could be home with the kids. It might be tough, but I've got enough crap on her. I'm going to ask for custody of the kids too. When I talked to Steven, he cried. He's sharp, maybe sharper than I am. He knew there was something going on. He's sworn to secrecy until the papers are filed. I'm telling you Lou, I know it's going to be tough, but at the same time it's going to be a bright New Year."

"Well you've got my support and I'm sure go for the gang at the precinct too. It sounds good, and I hope it will be a bright New Year for you."

John looked out at the night sky, the parting clouds were laced with silver moonlight. He slowly drove down the vacant street of the industrial park when the glass shattered in the driver's window. At the same moment John felt a sharp pain behind his left ear.

"HOLLY SHIT! What the fuck was that." Lou shouted.

John heard Lou but couldn't seem to answer.

"John, are you okay?"

John still couldn't react. It felt as if a bee had stung him behind the ear. He stared straight ahead, the street lights dimmed and began to blur.

"John? Pull over. Stop!"

John couldn't move. He felt Lou take control of the car and pull it to a stop. All was black now and his thoughts began to fuzz. He felt Lou pull at him and turn his head.

"Oh Jesus Christ, No!"

John heard Lou grab the radio hand mike and yell. "Officer shot, officer shot . . . ."

Everything faded into nothingness.

*   *   *

Zach, although officially retired for five years was still a SJPD Reservist, and when it came to John, the first to be informed. With a call from Lou, he sprang into action, making sure that someone from the precinct was on their way to inform Kathleen and bring her to the hospital. He then dispatched Nadia immediately to take care of Steven and Katie before he rushed to the hospital.

Lou stopped pacing when Zach entered the anteroom of Santa Clara Valley Medical Center's emergency, a room set aside for police, paramedics and ambulance drivers, for breaks and to do their paper work. He knew Lou had stayed with John until they rolled him into emergency surgery. The men hugged and then sat at the table strewn with the paper work Lou had been filling out about the shooting.

"How is he?"

Lou shrugged his shoulders. "Nothing new. They said they'll let us know as soon as they hear anything."

"Who—why? Was it a stray bullet from a partier's random shot or intended?" Zach fired questions at Lou knowing, that at that moment, there were no answers."

"Investigators were just arriving on the scene when I left with John in the ambulance, but so far I haven't heard anything more. However, the way I saw it, it looked intended. Somebody deliberately shot at us, a random stupid act of violence toward the police." Lou had to compose himself, as he looked at Zach. "It's getting worse these days."

Zach could see Lou's dark eyes fill with anger prompting his own emotions to erupt, first at the senseless violence and then the remembrance of all the pain of Steve's death. He also knew firsthand the feeling of helplessness Lou was experiencing.

"I tried to call his wife." Lou forced himself to continue. "Sergeant Hammer was already there, he said that as soon as someone got there to take care of the children they would be on their way. The ER receptionist will send her back here when she arrives. I didn't get to tell her what happened."

"That's probably for the better, let the Sergeant do that. I sent Nadia to watch the kids."

At a little after two in the morning, on New Year's the ER was filling up with mostly noisy drunks. Zach could tell by Lou's actions that he couldn't take any more questions. Silently he poured each of them a cup of coffee. "How do you take your poison?"

"Black."

Zach put some sugar in his and returned to the table. Lou started to gather the papers. "Can I help you with any of this?"

"I've done as much as I can at this point."

Zach didn't need to imagine the guilt that floods a cop's thoughts when something happens to a partner. You immediately blame yourself. "How long ago did you call Kathleen?"

"It's been about an hour. She should be here soon."

Zach could tell there was something Lou was holding back. It seemed to have something to do about Kathleen. He studied Lou's face then finally asked, "Is there somethin' you want to tell me?"

Lou looked up, his eyes focused. He appeared to be weighing something in his mind. Then slow and hushed, he spoke. "Just moments before he was shot, John told me he was filing for a divorce next week. He said she didn't know, but you knew all about it."

Zach put his hand over Lou's reassuringly. "Yes I——."

Lou suddenly looked passed Zach to the door and then stood. Zach turned. An aid was leading Kathleen to the room. "Don't say anything to anyone about the divorce for now." He stood.

"What's going on?" Kathleen asked. Her cold eyes stared into Zach's.

Lou's words still echoed in Zach's head. He wasn't able to answer her immediately.

"What's going on? The Sergeant said John's been shot." Then the look of terror crossed her face. "Zach, Oh God! Is he dead, is he, is . . . ?"

"No. He's alive. That's all I can tell you right now." In that moment, Zach suppressed all his distrust for Kathleen. He tried to believe that in her heart, she still loved John. After all, she was his wife and the mother of his children.

"What? How?"

"He was on patrol and a single bullet came through the driver's window and struck him."

"Struck him, where?"

"In the head, behind the left ear."

"Oh God." Her knees buckled, Zach helped her to a chair and got her a paper cup of water. "Is he going to be all right?"

"We don't know. They took him into emergency surgery about an hour ago."

"Was he conscious? Did he say anything?"

"No, he lost consciousness the moment he was shot." Lou said.

An ER doctor came into the room dressed in scrubs. He walked up, put his hand on Lou's shoulder without much expression, and then looked down at Kathleen.

"Are you Mrs. Michaels? I'm Dr. Chan."

"How is he?" Kathleen asked. Tears were running down her cheeks.

The doctor glanced at Zach and then back to Kathleen. "We are still trying to stabilize him. Once that is done we'll just have to wait and see."

"Wait and see?"

"Mrs. Michaels, your husband has suffered a bullet wound to the head. To the back of his brain to be more precise. The first thing we must do is stop the bleeding and prevent swelling from causing any more damage. It appears to be a smaller caliber bullet or maybe just a fragment. There's no exit wound. A neurosurgeon is working on him right now. He will assess the damage and be able to give us a better picture. Once that's done, we will then simply have to wait and see what happens. The brain is extremely complex and has mysterious healing powers we are just starting to understand. You husband is physically fit and as far as the body is concerned, the wound is minor. But, as far as his brain, well we just don't know yet. Right now he is on life support."

"What does that mean?"

"He has stopped breathing on his own, but that is not unusual with this type of trauma. For the time being, we are keeping him on a respirator. We will probably keep him in an induced coma to give his brain some time to settle and then see if it can take back over normal physical functions. It might take a few days or an even few weeks."

"Will he recover?"

"Right now he faces an immensely serious battle." The doctor sat and took Kathleen's hand. "He may recover completely or he may not. I'm not going to paint a rosy picture only to see everyone's hopes dashed."

"Oh God!"

"Yes Mrs. Michael, this is the time to pray."

"What do we do, wait here?" Zach asked.

"You can or in the surgery lounge, it might be more comfortable. It will probably get crazy around here as the morning wears on. The lounge up stairs is quiet and the cafeteria is open, we will notify you as soon as we know anything, but it might be a long wait."

"I'll wait."

"We'll wait." Zach added.

"Can I see him?" Kathleen stood.

"If he makes it through surgery, and as soon as he is stable you may visit him. It will probably be several hours."

Kathleen stood when the doctor left the room. Lou followed a couple of steps and watched the Doctor hurry down the hall and disappear.

"Arrogant prick." Lou grumbled.

"He is doing his best." Kathleen said.

"Now we play the waiting game." Zach said.

"I need some coffee." Kathleen requested, looking at the coffee pot.

"That stuff is nasty. Would you like to go to the cafeteria?"

"Yes, I would like that."

CHAPTER 23

THE FIRST 24

INT.-HOSPITAL CAFETERIA-LATER-NEW YEAR'S DAY, 1999

ZACH sits across a table from Kathleen in the near empty cafeteria. In silence they sit. He watches Kathleen sip her coffee.

                    KATHLEEN
          I wish I could just see him. Did you
          see him?

                    ZACH
          He was already in surgery when I got
          here.

Kathleen closed her eyes, drew in a deep breath and let it out with a barely audible sigh. She sat perfectly still with her eyes closed for several minutes. Zach studied her face. *Is she prayin?* He hoped she was. There was genuine concern for John in her voice and action. *Was it in her heart?* For now Zach, was willing to try to believe she was genuine. Kathleen would occasionally open her eyes and drink some coffee before returning to her apparent meditative state.

   Zach finished his first cup of fresh coffee that didn't smell burnt like the stuff in the EMT's room. He refilled the cup. The time dragged. He wanted to go back and check on John, but Kathleen just sat there.

   Suddenly her eyelids popped opened. Wide eyed she glanced around apparently disoriented. She calmed, her gaze fell on Zach. "Do you think he'll be all right?"

"He's a tough kid." He returned her inquisitive look. "He's got a lot of courage, fight and spunk. I believe he'll be okay."

"Thanks for being here." She broke eye contact. "Let's go to the surgery waiting room. I want to call my family."

Zach stood, held out his hand, she took it, stood and without letting go, they walked to the elevator. She continued to cling to him in the elevator and all the way to the third floor surgical waiting room. It was empty. She released him only then, and thanked him with a smile and took out her cell phone.

"You can't use them in here." Zach pointed to the sign prohibiting cellphone use.

Kathleen went to the payphone. With a nod, Zach took a seat across the room, giving her as much privacy as possible in the small waiting area. Her first call was to her brother Ryan. It took quite some time to get him on the line. Zach could only hear bits and pieces of her conversation. Once on the phone she gave Ryan a brief explanation. After she answered a couple of apparent questions, she closed her eyes, crossed herself and listened for a long time. Zach assumed Ryan was praying with her for John. Seemingly finished praying, she crossed herself again and discussed Ryan coming to San Jose.

A little more animated, her second call was to her sister Jean. Zach could pick up enough of the twenty-minute conversation to determine that Jean would arrange with Ryan to fly out as soon as possible. She then placed a mysterious third call, turned away from Zach, and spoke in the phone with a hushed voice. Try as he might, he could not hear her words clearly nor could he see her expression.

When his curiosity finally got the best of him, he decided to get a magazine off the rack next to the phone, but just as he stood, a nurse came through the operating room doors.

Still gowned and with her mask pulled down below her chin she asked, "Michaels' family?"

Kathleen quickly hung up the phone and stood. "I'm Mrs. Michaels."

The nurse took a step toward Kathleen and then looked a Zach.

"He is a close friend of the family."

The nurse gave a consenting nod. "Dr. Hayward is finishing up now."

"Is he——?"

"It's too soon to tell, it was a difficult surgery. Mr. Michaels will be taken to recovery within the hour if all goes well."

"Can I see him?"

"Unfortunately not yet. He will be in recovery for a couple of hours. After that, he'll be taken to ICU. You may see him briefly at that time. But that won't be for several hours. You can wait here or come back when——."

"I'll wait right here."

Zach sat with Kathleen; it was already 9:00 a.m. The time passed agonizingly slow, like a bad dream. The sleepless night, terrible event and uncertainty of John's condition made the image of colorful floats of the Rose Parade on the muted TV seemed bizarre. He recalled John at his father's funeral and the struggles of a fatherless boy trying to make sense of life. Now the whole thing was repeating. He wrestled with the thought of John not making it.

For the next several hours, he prayed, paced and attempted positive thoughts. And endlessly stared at the TV, in hopes the hideous spectacle on the boob tube could dispel the darkness engulfing him.

It was a little before noon when Nadia showed up with Katie and Steven. Katie rushed to her mother's arms the moment they entered room. Steven hurried to Zach and they hugged.

"I hope you don't mind, they needed to see their mom." Nadia apologized. "I was going to take them to lunch and thought we should stop by. Any news?"

"No." Zach answered. "He should be out surgery, but it's going to be some time before we know anything."

Nadia glanced around the empty room. "Where's everybody. The emergency room downstairs is going crazy. It took me forever to find someone that knew where you were."

"Only emergency surgery's today. I believe John was the only one right now." Zach turned to Kathleen. "Why don't you take Katie and Steven to lunch in the cafeteria?" He suggested. "If there is any word, Nadia or I'll come get you immediately."

Kathleen hesitated a moment and looked at Zach as though she didn't comprehend. He was about to repeat his suggestion when she responded.

"Oh yes. Kids, how about some lunch?" She gathered herself, her purse and the children. "We won't be long."

"Take your time, if we hear anything we'll come get you."

Zach watched them make their way to the elevator and disappear behind the closing stainless-steel doors. He turned to Nadia and smiled. "Thanks for coming."

"I wasn't sure, but they needed to be with their mother. Steven overheard the conversation on the phone. They know their father was shot. I had to bring them."

"You did right."

"And you, how are you doing?"

"I'm trying to hang in there. It's hard."

"I know. Any news, any hope?"

"He is alive, so there's hope, but I think it's grim. I have a bad feeling."

"What about Kathleen? How is she taking it?"

"Come sit." Nadia sat beside Zach and held her hand. "She's cried a little, but no tears. She spent some time praying on the phone with her brother the priest. Then she called her sister Jean. They just seemed to chat. She is flying out with Ryan, tomorrow."

"Does she have any idea that John was planning on filing for a divorce next week?"

"I don't think so, John wasn't going to tell her until he filed." Zach ran his hand across his forehead. She made another call. I don't know too who. She spoke hushed. I couldn't get any hint of the conversation. It was obvious she didn't want me to hear."

"Do you think——."

"Right now I don't want to think anything. I'll give her the benefit of the doubt. John may walk out of here in a day or two and be able to take care of his own affairs."

"And he may not."

"Then it becomes a whole different ballgame. I'll cross that bridge if I come to it. Right now, I am focused on him making it through the first twenty-four hours. But I will keep my eyes and ears open, wide open."

*   *   *

Kathleen and the children spent a little over an hour at lunch. When they returned to the waiting room, there was still no news. Zach and Nadia went to lunch leaving Katie and Steven with their mother. Nadia took the kids home at two. There was yet no word, other than a couple of nurses assuring them they would know something, soon.

Kathleen finally reclined on a sofa and tried to get some sleep. Zach dozed in a chair, but the moment he fell asleep he was awakened by internal voices calling for help. Sometimes it was John's voice and other times John's father Steve. He remembered Steve in his arms when he died, the feeling of his life ending and his odd request to remind John about the script. The scene forever etched in his memory. However, this time it was different. A group of spectators stood behind him.

"Cut!" The director yelled. "Check the gate."

Zach looked up to face the director, camera operator and assembled crew watching. The camera operator yelled, "Gate's clear."

Suddenly Zach felt Steve stir in his arms, then sit-up. The script girl in a chair next to the director turned a page back, looked up at the director and pointed at Steve. "That's not in the script. That part about, 'remember the script'."

"That's all right, I liked it, adds a bit of mystery. Make a note of it. I'll work it in later."

"But what if he doesn't like it."

"I'm the director."

"Yes Sir, but he's——."

"Well if He doesn't like it, we'll fix it in post. Print it. Moving on."

Zach snapped awake at the sound of the door, confused. *Was I dreaming?* Zach looked around. *Moving on, what the hell does that mean?*

A man stepped through the door gowned in green. Both Zach and Kathleen stood immediately. The man began to speak, stopped, apparently realized he was still wearing a surgical mask, and pulled it off his face.

"Is he going to be okay doctor?" Kathleen asked.

The man hesitated a moment and glanced at Zach before answering Kathleen.

"I'm not the doctor . . . ah I'm Father Reyes, the hospital Chaplin. Your brother, Father O'Malley, called me. I've just come from the recovery room. Dr. Hayward will be with you momentarily."

"Did you see John, is he . . . is he——?"

"He is alive, but unconscious. He is in quite serious condition. The doctor can explain. Your brother asked me to pray for him and be with you until he gets here."

"How . . . how serious?" Kathleen asked.

"I just administered Last Rites."

Kathleen collapsed into Zach's arms. "Please Father, get her some water."

"I'm okay." Kathleen stood. "I just wasn't prepared for that."

"He's not a Catholic." Zach said.

"I'm aware of that, but Father O'Malley asked me too, anyway."

The inner doors sounded and seconds later, a doctor in scrubs stepped through the waiting room doors. "Mrs. Michaels, I'm Doctor Hayward." He looked at Zach still holding onto Kathleen. "And you are?"

"A close friend," Zach looked at Father Reyes, "And John's Godfather. Zachary James."

"Please sit." Dr. Hayward pointed to the sofa.

The doctor sat across from them and Father Reyes took a chair at the end of the sofa. The young Priest appeared to be in silent prayer that at first annoyed Zach, but after a moment, it seemed comforting.

Gently, Zach took hold of Kathleen's hand, and waited for the doctor.

"As you know, your husband is in serious condition." The doctor began slowly addressing Kathleen. "He has sustained a gunshot wound. The bullet entered three-point-five centimeters behind his left ear and lodged in the back of the skull. The bullet and bone fragments caused damage to the Occipital Lobe and Cerebellum. We have removed the bullet and bone fragments and stopped the bleeding. The bullet seems to have come from a small caliber rifle, shot from close to medium range. It has been sent to the forensic lab for further analysis."

"What does all this mean?" Kathleen asked. "Can I see him now?"

"He had a rough go in recovery. It took longer than anticipated. They are transferring him to ICU now. It will be an hour or so before you can see him. He is unconscious. We will keep him in a medically induced coma as he starts the healing process."

"Just how serious is he Doc? Will he be all right?" Zach questioned.

The doctor took a deep breath, looked at Zach and then at Father Reyes before he turned his attention back to Kathleen. "Each brain injury is unique. The foreign matter is removed and blood vessels repaired . . . but, and at that's a big but, we don't know how the trauma and bruising will affect the outcome. We have removed a segment of his skull to prevent any further damage from bruising, which will be replaced later. The induced coma will further protect the brain from swelling. He is fortunate that he was treated quickly. Now it's a matter of wait and see."

Zach felt Kathleen's grip tighten as the doctor spoke. Now for the first time tears streamed down her face. Father Reyes handed her several tissues. The men sat in silence while Kathleen dried her tears. Once composed she turned again to the doctor.

"That's it, wait and see?"

"I wished I could offer a clearer prognosis."

"How long will he be in a coma?"

"That will depend on how he heals. He is young and in good physical shape. We will monitor the swelling and as soon as we are sure the crisis has past, we will take him off the coma inducing medication. We will of course watch for infection. During this time, we will keep him on a ventilator. This could be for two or three weeks or maybe longer."

The doctor paused. Stone faced, he looked directly at Kathleen. "Your husband is in critical condition. He arrested three times, twice during surgery and once in recovery. We had to resuscitate him. I want you to be prepared when you go in to see him. We performed a tracheotomy, placed a nasogastric tube, head drain, urinary catheter and there are numerous monitoring devices connected to him. I assure you, we have and will continue to do everything humanly possible to keep him alive and restore him to his former self. However, sometimes, it is beyond our control. I have asked the Chaplin to be with you when you first visit your husband."

The doctor's chest swelled from drawing in a breath. He turned his tired gaze to Zach. Hope seemed distant.

"If there are no more questions, I'll check on the transfer."

"Thank you Doctor." Zach said, stood and shook the doctor's hand. The doctor walked the few steps to the door and retreated into the operating suites. Through the small window, Zach watched the doctor vanish through the next set of doors.

On the TV, another encore of the Rose Parade streamed silently past, the only color in the otherwise sterile waiting room. Father Reyes stood, made the sign of the cross over Kathleen and began to pray with her.

Zach left. He hurried through the lobby, desperate for a breath of fresh air. Outside He took a deep breath. The first day of the New Year was turning into twilight. He cried.

*   *   *

Another two hours past, Father Reyes had excused himself to attend pastoral needs in the ER. When he returned he was in a suit and Roman collar. He escorted Zach and Kathleen upstairs to the ICU. They had to gown up and then wait a little longer before a nurse came to escort them in, for their five-minute visit.

Zach didn't even recognize John when he approached. In the bed was John laying lifeless. Wires were attached to his bare chest and temples, tubes protruded from nearly every orifice of his body and some places where no previous opening existed. Banks of machines wheezed and beeped, maintaining moment by moment the little life that remained in John.

Zach with Kathleen in his arms, looked on in disbelieve. Kathleen reached out and touched John's unresponsive hand. Tears blurred his vision.

"He's made it this far." Father Reyes whispered. "The first 24 hours are the most critical."

Is that all it's been, Zach wiped his tears. *Twenty-four hours.*

Gene Stirm

PART THREE

CHAPTER 24

CHANGE IN THE GAME

INT.-JOHN'S ATTORNEY'S OFFICE-JANUARY 6, 1999

Attorney AARON FUTTER, in a dark blue suit, sits at
his desk across from Zach. His office is large, classic 80's style, with books, awards and signed photos
of politicians and a few celebrities on the wall, a
modest bar in the corner, the office a testament to
his years of successful practice.

                    AARON
          Everyone at court is concerned about
          John. Thanks for filling me in. The
          newspapers just said he was in seri-
          ous condition. I had no idea how se-
          rious.

                    ZACH
          I thought you needed to know. With
          the trust, and you filing his divorce
          papers this week.

"Well, I'm not in family law per say, my son is representing John in
the divorce, but it's all in the same office. However, this certainly changes
the game. We can't file for divorce if he is incapacitated. We did all the
preliminary papers before Christmas and planned to file this week."

"He showed me a copy." Zach leaned back in his chair. "He was expecting a fight, especially wanting full custody of Steven and Katie. We suspected Kathleen would contest and with her family of lawyers, she has plenty of backup."

"I know. He hoped that it wouldn't get too ugly for the children's sake, but he has quite a dossier on her and her gentleman friend Mr. Hanson. He was ready for the fight. Now until he is capable, we can't file."

"What if . . . ."

"He dies? She will get the children of course, but you are the trustee of his estate and executor of his will. Nevertheless, for right now let's think positive and hope he will be back to his old self in no time."

"I have been with Kathleen almost constantly the last six days and her concern seems genuine."

"Sometimes a crisis like this brings out the best in people."

"Let's hope so."

*   *   *

With Kathleen's family taking up the daytime hours, Zach began spending his nights at John's bedside. It was a little before six in the morning, when Zach slipped out of the ICU, strode to the elevator and pushed the call button. When the doors open, Lou, in full uniform, stepped out.

"Zach, I was hoping I'd catch you." Lou gave Zach a hug. "How is he doing?"

"As well as can be expected, but what are you doing here at this ungodly hour?" Zach was surprised but even more pleased to see Lou. He knew Kathleen and her family had unfairly pushed Lou aside. Zach got the distinct impression they blamed him for the shooting.

"I'm on my way home. I've stopped by several times, but with the family here, I haven't been able to see him. I thought this early, I might get in for a minute, but if they're busy." Lou looked Zach in the eyes. "Any change?"

Zach directed Lou to the small ICU waiting area across from the elevators. "No, but we aren't expecting much for another week or so."

"Week or two? It's been three weeks."

"It takes time."

Lou sucked in a breath. "Are you here every day?"

I come in at eleven. The night crew lets me stay. I usually take off before the morning shift comes on, there's a lot of commotion then. Kathleen comes in after she gets the kids to school. Jean or her brother Ryan usually spends the day with her too." Zach could see Lou's stress. "How are you doing?"

"Going through a lot of, what ifs."

"There is nothing you could have done, but I understand. The, what ifs, just about drove me crazy after Steve was shot. It's not easy, but time will help."

"I hope so. How did you manage to stay with it after Steve?"

"I really don't know."

Lou looked out the window. "I'm thinking of quitting the force." He quickly glanced at the ICU door then at Zach. "How is . . . she holding up?"

"Kathleen? She is doing all right, but it's taking its toll on her. She has family staying at the house with her, so she is not alone."

"What about the divorce?"

"Everything is on hold for now. I'm kind of hoping things will work out . . . for the kids' sake if nothing else."

"Good . . . . Do you think they will let me see him, just for a second?"

"Sure, I'll talk to the night nurse. She is pretty lenient, as long as we don't get in the way."

*   *   *

Little changed in the next two weeks, John was still on life support. The ICU staff let Kathleen stay with John longer in the evenings. She often sat with John from after dinner until Zach showed up. There was nothing more anyone could do, but to hope, wait and pray,

The overhead lights were dimmed. Kathleen looked up at the clock, ten-fifteen. The endless cacophony of beeps, buzzers, breathing machines and babbling voices overwhelmed all but the most resilient. In the dim din, Kathleen took hold of John lifeless hand.

The following morning she would meet with Dr. Hayward for an update. She wanted to come alone, but every one of her family had a reason why they should be included in the meeting. In the hope for peace, she finally gave in and told them they could all come. She definitely was not looking forward to the meeting.

The rhythmic rising and lowering of John's chest to the hum and hiss of the ventilator was the only sign of life. The hand she held felt like a warm plastic dolls. "Oh John I'm sorry." Tear rolled down her cheeks. "I love you. I'm sorry I haven't always been the faithful wife. From now on, I will do better. Come back to us, Katie and Steven need you. We all need you."

*   *   *

The family has assembled in Dr. Hayward's office. Kathleen sat across the desk from the doctor, flanked by Jean on her right and Ryan on the left and behind them stood Patrick, Jean's husband and Kathleen's brother Connor.

"I wish I could bring you more information." The doctor began slowly. "Physically he is healing better than expected. His heart function is strong and he has been stable. He has come through the crises with no infection and the brain swelling has receded. The drain has been removed from his skull and we will portably replace the area of bone we removed by the end of next week. He is no longer in a medically induced coma."

Kathleen looked at her sister then back at the doctor. "We were just there. He is still in a coma."

"Yes, but it's no longer induced. The latest EEG is showing a small increase in brain activity, however, we don't know when he will regain consciousness. As of yet, he hasn't resumed the swallowing reflex and until he does we will keep him on the ventilator. We started introducing food through the nasal tube and his gastro-intestinal system is responding. He is holding his own. I feel he can be moved from the ICU to a private room in a week or so, probably shortly after the skull segment is replaced.

"How long might he stay comatose?" Ryan asked.

"The brain injury is causing the coma. There is no way of knowing when he will come out of it, or even if he will." The Doctor paused and looked from face to face. "We have to wait and see."

"Wait and see? Is that your only answer?" Kathleen stood. "In the meantime, what are we supposed to do?" She stepped to the door.

"I know it's difficult. In a case like this, we have to go on the best we can. Hope that he might wakeup today, but prepared for what may be a long battle."

Ryan stood. "And what if he never wakes?"

"It's far too soon to face that question. We just have to give him some more time?"

"How much time Doctor?" Kathleen stepped up to the desk. "Maybe he is dead already and it's just your machines making him appear alive. Maybe we just need to pull the plug?"

"Right now that's not the case. We mustn't get ahead of ourselves."

Ryan put his arm around Kathleen. "We must keep our faith. Let's leave the Doctor to his work. I'm sure he has much to do. Let's go to the chapel and pray."

"We, you forgot to say, we." Kathleen rushed out the door.

*   *   *

"Kids, ten minutes." Kathleen called from the kitchen. She poured herself another cup of coffee and joined Jean at the breakfast table going through a stack of legal papers.

"Why didn't you show me this before?"

"I just ran across them last night. That bastard." Kathleen took a sip of coffee. "After the wonderful news we got from that damn Doctor, I thought I better look in his desk to see if there was something that needed attention, that when I found it. That bastard."

"Calm down, calm down."

He's been acting a little strained lately, but I thought it was because he was planning to leave the force. I didn't think he was planning this. That sneaky little bastard, I ought to just pull the plug. That would be a divorce all right."

"Are these allegations true?"

"Well——."

"Well, are they true?"

"Sort of."

"I thought you learned your lesson years ago." Jean pushed several pages toward Kathleen. "This is a no fault state, but he's got a damn good case here to get the kids and avoid alimony, It appears as if he has witnesses and plenty of evidence to back it up too."

"What can I do?"

"Well fortunately right now, this can't go forward, but if he recovers and he pursues the matter, you are screwed. He will probably get the divorce on his terms. Adultery in today's divorce courts is still a serious charge."

"Adultery?" Ryan questioned. Kathleen hadn't notice Ryan enter from the guesthouse, already dressed in his black suit and Roman collar.

"Yeah, John was planning on suing our dear sister for a divorce, requesting full custody of the kids on grounds of adultery."

"Oh Kathleen O'Malley, say it's not true." Ryan shook his head in disbelief. "I need some coffee."

Jean grabbed the keys from Kathleen. "I'll take the kids to school. You tell Ryan what's going on."

Kathleen's mouth hung open. She glared at Jean on her hurried way out of the kitchen. She sat with her back to Ryan. She could easily deal with the rest of the family, but to have to face Ryan was something she truly had hoped to avoid. Ready to get it over with, she braced herself and looked at him.

Ryan showed little emotion. He poured his cup of coffee, doctored it with milk and a little sugar. "I know, I know, sugars not good, but something's can be forgiven."

The first jab. Kathleen knew it would be brutal. She watched as Ryan slowly worked his way to the table and sat across from her.

"Now." Ryan paused and took a deep, somewhat dramatic breath. "Tell me what is going on."

"I found some papers in John's desk. He was going to file for divorce."

"And?"

"He is alleging I committed adultery."

"And . . . . Dear Kathleen is there any truth to that allegation?"

"Well . . . ."

"I see. Well, since you were not married in the Church, your marriage is not recognized by the Church, but in a court of law it is."

"I know that."

"This is serious, sin is sin and adultery is a grievous sin. May I assume it was Scott?" Kathleen didn't answer. She was ashamed, but Ryan's preaching angered her.

"When you play with fire," he continued, "expect to get burned."

"I don't need this." She felt her face flush.

"I believe you need this more then you realize. What are you going to do? Just walk out on twelve years of marriage. Leave with your legally lawful husband in a hospital, not knowing if he is going to live or die. And the children, what are you going to do about the children or have you even thought about them. Or were you just planning on life as usual, and just go and play house with Scott every now and then?"

Kathleen felt her hot tears running down her face. She was both enraged and humiliated by her brother. She leapt from her chair, rushed to the family room, hurled herself on the sofa and bawled like a baby.

Her love for John had grown through the years, yet she never could resist the thrill of Scott. Near hysterical, her thoughts muddled. However, to be alone with time to think was not an option.

Relentless, Ryan stood over her. "You know you've sinned against God, your children and most of all, you betrayed the man who truly loves you."

Through her tears, she could see Ryan's shoes. She dropped to her knees and grabbed his legs. "Father forgive me, for I have sinned."

*   *   *

That afternoon the family regrouped. Kathleen managed to put the shattering events of the morning behind her. Her Act of Contrition satisfied Ryan and the others acted as if nothing ever happened, something the family was good at doing. Their focus was now on moving forward. Jean and Connor had volunteered to go through Kathleen and John's finances and get everything in order, while Kathleen and Ryan spent the afternoon at the hospital.

Ryan walked ahead of her into the kitchen from the garage. She felt she needed to go to her bedroom and freshen up. She was tired and knew her hair was a mess, but instead she followed Ryan into the kitchen.

Patrick greeted them. "Well it's about time. I thought you were going to be back by dinner." He stopped at the counter. "You look like you need a drink?"

"Oh God, yes." Kathleen dropped her keys and purse on the counter. "Sorry we are so late. It's been a long day. John had a bad reaction to some new medication, but he is stable now. Where's everyone."

"The kids are in bed and Jean and Connor are in the office. How about you Ryan, drink?"

"No thanks, I've got an early flight tomorrow and I need to finish packing."

"Connor and I will be flying home on Monday." Patrick pulled a bottle of white wine out of the wine cooler under the kitchen counter and poured Kathleen a glass. Ryan made his way out to the patio door to the guesthouse.

"Good night Ryan." Patrick said after the door closed. "Sleep well." He turned to Kathleen he asked, "You okay?"

"Copacetic, after mea culpa. Aren't you having anything?" Kathleen asked.

"I'm drinking Scotch. My glass is in the family room. I just came in for some more ice.

"Any success?"

"I'm doing great with the Scotch, but haven't got a clue what they are up to in the study."

"Well I'll go check."

On her way to the office she made a quick check on the children, both were asleep. When she entered John's office, a room she seldom visited, Connor was standing, looking over Jean's shoulder.

"Is there any money left?" Kathleen asked with a chuckle, dropped in a wingback chair and sipped her wine. "Did I spend all my allowance?"

"This is not a joke." Jean answered. "It would be a lot easier if you had paid a little attention to what was going on, we have more questions then there are bills."

"It can't be that complicated."

"It's not complicated. John is good at managing his money. However, there is so much missing information. His paycheck goes into one account from which he paid the utility bills and puts the rest into your house account. There's no mortgage or car payments, on a cop's salary you two are doing pretty darn well. Does he pay all the bills out of his account?"

"How should I know?"

"Not good." Jean continued. "It's obvious that there are more assets than we can find records for. Have you got a clue as to what is in the bank or in investments, any statements?"

"John takes care of everything."

"Well dear sister, now that he is in the hospital, in a coma, his salary will stop. You need to call human resources Monday and check on sick leave and filing for workman's comp. I haven't found any papers, insurance document, savings information, health directives, power of attorney or tax returns. As meticulous as John is, all his records have to be somewhere and we assume they are in the safe. Do you have the combination?"

"No."

"Do the two of you have a safety deposit box anywhere?"

"Not that I know of."

"What about Zach? He may know."

"Oh Zach, do we have to get him involved?" Kathleen angered. "I bet he knows about the divorce. I bet he was in on the whole thing."

"Well we will need to get in touch with John's attorney."

"Can't we just get someone to open the damn safe? Call a locksmith."

Connor finally spoke up. "I think we need to talk to Zach and considering John was preparing to file for a divorce, John's attorney, before we resort to safecracking." He turned to the bookcase. "Sometime men will write the combination of their safe in the front of their favorite book." He started to look at the books. "Jesus, does he actually read these or are they just for show?" He pulled a book off the shelf, opened to the flyleaf, and quickly stuck it back. "Nope, not in *War and Pease,* read that in high school English. How many hundreds more?"

"Listen Sis, if John recovers you're screwed." Jean raised her voice in frustration.

"Okay, okay, I'll call Zach in the morning. Right now, I need another glass of wine. Care to join me?"

"Jean can, I'll keep looking for the combination."

Kathleen stood and strolled to the door. "Maybe I'd be better off if he didn't recover."

CHAPTER 25

THE RIGHT COMBINATION

INT.-MICHAELS KITCHEN-MORNING-FEBRUARY 13, 1999

Kathleen, in her bathrobe, sits at the breakfast table
with a cup of coffee watching Jean fix herself a bowl
of cold cereal. Jean is already dressed in a blue
blouse and tan slacks.

                    JEAN
          Are you sure I can't fix you some-
          thing.

          No thanks. I just need to nurse my
          coffee for now.

Jean refreshed her coffee then carried it and her cereal to the table and sat.

"Thank God, Patrick and Connor took Ryan to the airport. I would have never made it. I didn't think I drank that much wine last night."

"Well you had a right too. If it were me, I'd be drinking more than wine. Thinking over the papers we found last night, I don't understand how you lived on John's salary. Does he have something going on the side?"

"John? You kidding, Mister Dudley Do-Right himself, no way. His father left him the house free and clear and some sort of trust."

"What trust?"

"I don't know. It was setup when his father was killed. That's all I know. He takes a monthly allowance and more if we need something special. "

"Do you know anything about it? Did he add you when you got married? Do you have any idea how much money is involved? Did you sign prenuptials when you got married?"

"No, I not the stupid. You don't need to talk so loud, I'm sitting right here. I told you the trust was setup before we were married. If I remember correctly, it started with a couple of million dollars. Of course, that was before he bought out his sister part of the house, built the guesthouse and renovated the house and pool. I don't know how much is left. That's all I know."

"Okay, okay, but do you know anything about the rest of your finances?"

"John takes care of that. He tried to keep me informed at first, but I just wasn't interested. I look to see if we're getting some money back from the IRS when I sign our tax returns. We usually just have to pay, plenty."

"Well we've got to get into that safe and Connor didn't find the combination. We've got to know what's going on, before you find yourself and the kids out in the street."

"All right, I'll call Zach . . . as soon as I finish my coffee."

"Why Zach?"

"I know he had something to do with the trust."

"I can't believe you. You've been in enough law classes that you know more than the basic. Why haven't you looked into this?"

"I trusted John."

Jean just shook her head. "Don't you know you can't trust anyone, especially John?"

"I am finding that out."

*   *   *

Kathleen managed to waste another hour fixing breakfast for the children, taking a shower and getting dressed before closing herself in John's office. Apparent by the disarray of the bookshelves, something John would never tolerate, Connor has spent quite some time looking for the combination. The leather desk chair let out a faint squeak of disapproval as she sat. She sensed her invasion into John's private space and for a moment, she contemplated retreating to the bedroom to make the call. *What am I afraid of? Certainly, it wasn't Zach. He's never seemed a threat to me. More like an uncle by marriage, someone who's family, but not really. Someone you think you know, but don't.*

With one last stall, she straightened the desk and put away the checkbooks before she reached for the phone. She knew the number by heart. After all, it was John's home away from home. She dialed and took a breath. "Hello, Zach, this is Kathleen."

"Hi, is everything okay?"

"I'm doing fine, I have a question."

"Are you at the hospital? Have you seen John? They moved him out of ICU this morning."

"You have got to be kidding. Dr. Hayward said it would be next week at best." Stunned by the news, Kathleen's hands began to tremble.

"He must be doing better. They moved him today, that's got to be a good sign."

"Let's hope. Listen Zach, I'm trying to keep things going here. You know, pay the bills and stuff. And well, I guess John has all the things I need locked in his safe, you don't happen to know the combination?"

"Gee Hon, I don't know . . . I mean he's never told it to me, but now that you mention it, he did give me an envelope some years ago to keep in case of an emergency. But, honestly, I don't know where it is at the moment. I'll have to go digging."

"It's real important."

"I can imagine. His attorney might have it. Do you want his number? But that won't help until Monday.

"Aaron? I have his number."

"Well I'll start looking for that envelope and see if I can find an emergency contact number for Aaron, but those guys are hard to get to outside the office."

"Please do what you can."

"I will. Are you going to the hospital?"

"Yes, in about an hour."

"Well if I find anything I'll get in contact immediately."

"Thank you Zach, you've been a great help."

"Give John my love, I'll be in tonight. And give Steven and Katie my love too."

"I will." Kathleen held the headset in both hands and let out a sigh of relief. She suddenly sensed someone behind her and turned, it was Jean. "Well that's done?"

"Any good?"

"Maybe, he says John gave him an envelope some time ago in case of an emergency."

"Well does it have the combination?"

"He's got to find it first."

"Is he telling you the truth or just stalling? Can you trust him?"

"He's been like a father to John all these years, of course I trust him."

"Well I don't."

*   *   *

Zach took his address book from his old role top desk in the family room, looked up Aaron's home number and dialed. "Hello Aaron, Zach James, I got the call we've been expecting from Kathleen Michaels. She's asking if I have the combination for the safe."

"Oh is she, I've been wondering when she would get around to that. How is John doing?"

"No real change. But they did move him out of ICU."

"Well that's encouraging. So about the combination, did you give it to her?"

"No, told her I'd look for it. That John had given me some contact information in case of an emergency, but I hadn't looked at it."

"Well you might as well give her the combination. I'm sure there isn't anything in there she shouldn't know. I don't think John keeps much in the safe other than extra checks and bank ledgers. I have the originals of the trust papers, his will, the divorce and other documents in our vault."

"I will. I just wanted to touch bases with you first. I'll give it to her this evening. Is there anything I should know?"

"You've seen it all. Don't you have copies of everything?"

"Yeah, I do."

"She needs to keep the house running, I am surprised she's waited this long. She'll need to get with the city on how they will handle the matter, disability, insurance, liability and all. With the situation as it is, I can't adviser her, but she has a house full of lawyers."

"Can she change anything?"

"The will? No. With the trust, only you, Alvin or John can. And that takes two of you."

"Well, considering her family, they will go over everything with a fine-tooth comb."

"I know. John warned me years ago. I assure you there are no loopholes."

"Good." Zach gave a faint sigh of relief.

"So go ahead and give them the combination, let them look through everything. I'll give her a call Monday, saying you asked me to call. Offer her my assistance. We'll play it by ear."

"Okay, thanks for your help. I'll keep my eyes and ears open. Have a good weekend."

"Thanks, I will, and I will keep you informed. Goodbye."

"Goodbye."

Zach hung up the phone and wrote on a piece of notepaper, *John Michaels' safe combination, 10R, 21L, 37R*, Zach's own birthdate. Steve had set the combination when he purchased the safe, so neither would forget it.

*   *   *

After dinner, Connor had volunteered to watch the kids while the rest went back to the hospital. The front part of the house was dark when they came in through the garage. Kathleen dropped her purse and keys on the counter and called. "Connor, kids, where is everybody?"

"Back here, in the office." Connor answered

Kathleen headed for the office, leaving Jean and Patrick in the family room. "What's going on?" Kathleen stood at the door and surveyed the mess. Dumped on the desk, were all the contents of the drawers from the cadenza and desk. The empty drawers haphazardly stacked upside-down on top. "What are you doing?"

"I was looking for the combination. I found a box with a pen and a little slip of paper with the number, 06-13-77 and though it was the combination. I tried it, but it wasn't. Then I remembered reading some-where that people will sometimes write important information on the underside of draws. No luck."

"Here's the combination." Kathleen handed Connor a slip of paper. "Zach came to the hospital and gave it to me."

"Where did he get it?"

"John gave it to him in case of an emergency. He forgot he had it."

Connor immediately went to the safe and started turning the dial. Kathleen picked up the box with the pen and recognized the number. It was the date of John's father's death.

Just then, Steven appeared at the door. "I told him to stop, stop messing up Dad's office, but he wouldn't listen to me." He looked at Connor kneeling in front of the safe and rushed at him. "You bastard, get away from there."

Steven thru himself at Connor and knocked him over. He jumped on top of him and started beating on him with his fists. "That's my father's you have no right snooping in my father's stuff."

"Quit that!" Kathleen shouted grabbing his wrist. "He is only trying to help us."

Steven glared at his mother. "You lying bitch, let me go."

Kathleen slapped him across the face. Shocked by her action, she immediately put her arms around him, hugged him and began to cry. "I'm sorry, I'm sorry."

"Let me go." Steven fought her.

Kathleen released her grip and Steven stepped back. "You have no right to do this. My father will be home soon. He will be angry with the mess. I'm going to tell Dad what he did." Steven wailed and hurried out of the room.

Through her tears, Kathleen, helpless, watched her son flee from her in anger.

"Got it open."

"Leave it." Kathleen shouted.

"What?" Conner asked.

"I said, leave it."

"But Sis, this is important."

"Get out!" She yelled. "Look at the mess you have made. Get out and leave me alone."

Connor stood slowly and retreated.

Kathleen began fitting the draws back in the desk. Tears ran down her cheeks as she straightened up, trying to figure out what went where. It didn't take long for Jean to show up at the office door.

"What's going on?"

"Look at what our asshole of a brother did."

"Let me help you."

"I told Connor and I'm telling you leave me alone. Now!"

After straightening the office, she sat in John's reading chair. She felt confused, did she ever love him, she wondered. Did she want him well and home or dead? *What have I done?*

*   *   *

The sun streaming through the window woke Kathleen. In her lap was the box holding his fountain pen. She touched it with her index finger. She closed the ageing box carefully with the scrap of paper tucked inside and returned it to its proper place.

"Can I help you with anything?" Zach's voice startled her. She ran to his arms and started to cry. He held her like a father and she felt safe.

"Jean called this morning, said you were having a rough time."

"There is just so much. I know I haven't been . . . . I don't deserve this. He doesn't deserve this. And the kids . . . ."

"Nobody deserves this, but sometimes things like this happen, for no apparent reason. They just happen." Zach walked her to the wingback chair.

"Can you stay a minute? I'd like to talk."

"Sure, what about?" Zach sat in the desk chair.

"John——and Steven, at least John's out of ICU, but other than a few less wires and tubes, he has not changed. What if he doesn't get better?" Kathleen wiped her eyes with a tissue.

"Let's not think that way right now."

"But we have to, what if . . . . Zach, what if he doesn't come out of this? What if he never regains consciousness? Do we just let him go on . . . on that machine forever?"

"No I guess not, but we are not at that bridge yet. You need to talk to Ryan. He is better equipped to answer that question."

"Is he, just because he's a Priest? He barely knows John." Kathleen blew her nose. "It's starting to take its toll on Steven. He got mad at Connor last night. We had some words. I——I slapped him. Hard, in anger. I slapped my own son's face. He doesn't understand the gravity of the situation. I wish you would talk to him."

"I will. Is he in his room?"

"I think so."

*   *   *

"Steven, can we talk." Zach asked standing in the doorway to the bedroom. Steven lay on top of the made bed with his face to the pillow. At first, there was no response. Zach was about to ask again when Steven turned over and looked at Zach.

"He is coming home, isn't he?"

"We don't know."

"Nobody knows anything. He's got to come home. Make him come home."

"I wished I could, but right now he can't." Zach sat on the corner of Steven's bed. "He is out of the ICU. You can visit with him all you want now. Would you like me to take you to the hospital?"

"Oh yes, can we go now?"

"Sure, let's go."

*   *   *

Zach stopped at John hospital room door and let Steven go on ahead. He stepped quietly up to his father's bed as if he were trying not to wake him. Tears filled his eyes. He just stood and looked at his father. The respirator was the only sound.

"You can touch him, hold his hand."

Steven reached out and touched John's arm, then took his unresponsive hand and held it.

"I miss you . . . . I want you to come home . . . ." He watched his father, apparently looking for any sign of recognition. "I need you to come home."

Zach leaned against the door case and watched silently. Several minutes past then Steven gave his father hand a shake as if trying to wake him. After a short wait, he shook it again. "Wake up Dad, pleases wake up."

Steven looked up when Zach shifted and shook his head, no. "If you want to you can go on home, I'll wait here until Mom comes and go home with her,"

Just then, a nurse came in to check on John. "How is he doing today? You must be his son, as handsome as your father." She turned and winked at Zach. "I'll put the side down. You can sit and hold his hand better that way. He would like that."

"Do you truly think he knows I am here?"

"Yes, yes I do." The nurse insisted.

Zach smiled then said. "I'll go. Have a good visit."

"Thanks Uncle Zach."

*   *   *

Kathleen came in through the garage door. Steven pushed past her and hurried to his bedroom. Kathleen was a little surprised to find Jean, Patrick and Connor sitting in the family room. "Well you look like a happy group."

"We went through everything in the safe." Connor began. "We found another checking account with a substantial balance in John's name and papers indicating additional investments, all under the Michaels Family Trust, and several of thousand in cash."

"Do you have any idea what John's worth?" Jean asked before answering her own question. "Millions, Happy Valentine's Day dearie."

Patrick stood, went to the bar and refreshed his drink, before he turned to Kathleen. "No will, no copy of the trust and no advance directive, only a letter stating that if anything happened to him you should contact Aaron Futter, his attorney and Zachery James."

"So what do we do now?" Kathleen asked.

"Well, Connor and I have to fly back to Chicago tomorrow. You need to contact Mr. Futter. Jean will represent you. We have to get all the information on this trust. Moreover, find out just how much John has stashed away."

"Millions, stashed away?" Kathleen questioned. "I thought he spent most it. You sure, you think it's millions. That skunk. Do you think Zach knows?"

"Undoubtedly." Connor answered.

"That snake, I can't trust any of them."

CHAPTER 26

PULLING THE PLUG

```
INT.-JOHN'S OFFICE-AFTERNOON-February 21, 1999
Steven, seated at his father's desk holds John's an-
tique fountain pen. A tear runs down his cheek and he
wipes is away with the sleeve of his shirt. Katie
appears at the open door. Steven glances up momentari-
ly and then turns his attention back to the pen, clos-
es the box and returns it to the drawer.

                    KATIE
         What are you doing?

                    STEVEN
         Just thinking.

                    KATIE
         About Dad?
```

Steven avoided eye contact and didn't answer. Depressed from the day spent at his father's bedside he wasn't in the mood to talk. Katie had visited for a short time the day before. For her the hospital visits were difficult, so her mother started limiting them. He sensed his sister move closer and closer and realized she wanted to sit in the chair with him, so he slid over so she could. Together they sat for a long silent moment.

"Is Dad dead?" Katie finally asked.

"No! I was with him all day."

"Did he say anything? Did he wake up and look at you?"

"No, of course not, he's in a coma."

"I heard Auntie Jean say he is dead. It's just the machine making him breathe and making him look alive, but he is already dead."

"She is lying!" Steven shouted, sprang to his feet and darted aimlessly across the room. "It's not true, she's lying." He whorled back to Katie in anger, "It's just not true. Dad will wake up any day now and be alright."

"Then you need to tell her."

"I will, the minute they get home."

Katie leaped out of the chair, hurried to Steven, put her arms around him, and leaned her cheek against his chest. "I don't want Daddy to be in a coma any more. I want him to come home."

Steven held his sister close. "So do I."

After a bit, he felt his sister begin to fidget and start to pull away. She looked up with a smile and announced, "I'm gonna go play with Amanda."

She hurried out of the room and he returned to the desk chair. Just as he was about to sit, he heard his mother and Jean's voices, and realizes they are on their way to the office. He hesitated a moment then decided to duck into the closet rather than face them, but the instant the magnetic latch of the closet door clicked shut, he changed his mind. It was too late. Through the louvers in the doors, he could see his mother sit in the wingback chair. He decided to stay put. He didn't want to try to explain why he was in the closet.

Jean closed the office door and then sat on the desk chair with her back to the closet. "We need to talk a little business."

"Don't we sound serious all of a sudden?" Kathleen pushed a loose lock of hair from her eyes. "What's up?"

"That's what I've been trying to figure out all week, no thanks to John's attorney or Zach."

"I though Zach was being more than helpful. He got all the papers together to file for John's disability and checked up on the insurance."

"That no big deal, but I can't help thinking he knows more about John's finance that he lets on. I've tried all last week to meet with John's attorney."

"I thought you had a meeting with him Thursday?"

"I do."

"So what is the problem?"

"I think he is stalling and Zach isn't talking either. I don't think we should trust him."

"Well we know that. But isn't the attorney going to release the funds I need to keep things going for now?"

"For now, but I haven't been able to get any information about how this trust is setup. Who's in charge and most important what is your share, if any. I had to threaten a subpoena to get Thursday's meeting."

"Well?"

"Listen Sis, we need to know what's in that trust, if John has a will and just what he is worth. This house and property is worth three million dollars alone and God know how much the property across the creek is worth, millions I'll bet." Jean paused as if expecting an answer. "I can't believe you never discussed this with John."

"It never seemed that important."

"Well it is now."

"How so?"

"Wakeup Kathleen, Your husband is dead."

"You don't know for sure, the doctors insist that there is some brain activity. There is a chance."

Steven wanted to scream, he clamped his hand over his mouth in case he couldn't control himself. Framed by the louver slats he watched his mother face react with amazement. She spat out the words, "No he's not." Her eyes turned cold. She glared at her sister.

"Face it Sis, he's in a coma that he's never coming out of. Turn off the machine and it's over, he's dead. Right now, you are still his wife. If he comes out of it, you are history. No matter how he has setup the trust or will, I can't help but believe you are better off as his widow."

The impact of Jean's words seemed to push his mother back in the chair. Tears filled her eyes.

"Don't tell me you're crying. He was planning to divorce you."

"It just hit me, to think of him as dead."

"Well pull yourself together. Jake will be here Wednesday. He'll go over John's situation again with the doctor. He'll get the real details and tell us the truth. I think we know his verdict. I've talk to him. He doesn't see any hope. He thinks we need to just pull the plug and be done with it."

"I'll bet Ryan doesn't think that way."

"We'll see — he's coming back with Connor on Friday."

"The whole damn family, that just what I need. I just got rid of them."

"We are here to help, that's all."

Kathleen raised her eyebrows. "Help or meddle? I've got to think about this."

Kathleen rose up slowly out of the chair like a ghost, stepped to the bar and poured a glass of Scotch. "Maybe you are right. Maybe it's time to pull the plug." She downed her drink. "Want one?" she asked, while refilling her glass.

"I think I'll get some wine. This room is depressing. Come on. Join me in the family room."

"Gladly."

Sure his mother and Aunt Jean were gone Steven emerged from the closet, drop in the desk chair and pulled up to the desk. Hesitant, he reached for the phone and dialed. His heart raced, anger, confusion and fear flooded his thoughts. He waited for what seemed an eternity for an answer.

"Hello." At last, the familiar voice answered.

"Hello, Uncle Zach, it's Steven."

"What's wrong?"

Steven was temporarily at a loss for words, then he blurts, "Aunt Jean and Mom are going to kill him."

"Wha——Who? What are you talking about?"

"Dad, they are going to pull the plug on Dad and let him die."

"They can't do that."

"Yes they can. Uncle Jake is coming Wednesday and is going to do it, shut off the breathing machine. I heard them say it."

"Steven, listen to me, they can't do that. I have the Power of Attorney for your father's health decision. Do you understand . . . do you understand?"

"I think so."

"You father is safe. You father has seen to it that your mother cannot do anything."

Steven gave a sigh. "Is that because of the divorce?"

"You know?"

"Dad told me after Christmas. He told me all about it. Told me I had to keep it a secret, I couldn't even tell Katie."

"You poor kid, I should have known John wouldn't keep a secret from you."

Hot tears began to roll down Steven's cheeks. Relief, the great burden shared.

"Steven, are you still there?"

"Yes."

"Don't worry. Nothing is going to happen to your father. I have been watching, I had some questions I needed to answer for myself. I will take care of you, Katie and your father. Nothing will happen to him. He will come home to you, understand."

"How——when?"

"I can't answer that right now, you just have to believe. In the meantime keep your eyes and ears open, if there is anything you think I need to know, call me, anytime——understand?"

"Yes."

"Don't let on that you know anything, play dumb, but keep watch."

"Can I tell Katie?"

"Not yet, she's a little too young to understand, let's keep it between you and me for now."

"Thank you Uncle Zach."

"I'm sorry I didn't confide in you sooner. I know you are going through hell, we all are, but we will make it. Now Son, anything you need, let me know."

"I will."

"Good, get some rest, I'm on the way to the hospital. From now on, I will keep you abreast of everything. Goodnight Son."

"Goodnight Uncle Zach, I love you . . . and tell Dad I love him too."

"I will. Goodnight."

Steven heard the click, but continued to hold the phone to his ear until he heard the dial tone. He quietly opened the desk drawer and took out the tattered box with the fountain pen. Through a blur of tears, he traced the shape of the pen. "Dad, talk to me."

*   *   *

"I see it as hopeless." Jake's cold words added a chill to the already cold and gloomy day.

Jake had arrived early at the San Jose airport, rented a car and went straight to the hospital. Now he sat on the sofa in the Michael's family room giving Kathleen and Jean his grim report. "I don't find any kind of response, and even though I am not a neurologist, I can see he is in an irreversible coma and should be taken off life-support. However, for some strange reason his doctor won't agree."

"Do we need his permission? I'm his wife, isn't it my decision."

"Unfortunately no. Oddly, there's no apparent advanced directive naming you his power of attorney. So, when in the course of treatment a patient is placed on a respirator, they cannot be taken off as long as there is a heartbeat without a court order."

"So what do we do?" Kathleen asked.

"I will need to document my finding. And being our good Dr. Hayward, does not agree, I'll have to get a second opinion and possibly a hospital review. Once we have that, we request a court order to take him off the respirator."

"How long will that take?"

"It depends, maybe a month or so, if there are no objections, but if there are objections it could take a long time. Cases like this can stretch on for years. Some have made it all the way to the Supreme Court."

"Well who can object?" Kathleen looked at Jean for a moment then back to Jake.

"His doctor, the city, patient rights groups, Zach." Jake started to snicker. "Even our own beloved brother, The Reverend Father Ryan, can throw a monkey wrench in the gears."

"That crazy, why should Ryan object, why should anyone object."

"I disagree. Between Connor, Patrick and myself we can handle the legal crap, Jake the medical and I'll take care of Ryan." Jean got to her feet. "I think we all need a drink."

"A good stiff one." Jake added.

"Kathleen and I meet with John's lawyer tomorrow afternoon." Jean said while she fixed them all a round of Scotch and soda. "Maybe he will finally shed some light on the subject. Then we can hash it all out. You, Jake when Connor gets here the two of you can start on Ryan."

"Oh joy."

*   *   *

"I am sorry that we couldn't have this meeting sooner. I was in court and it was held over. I hope it wasn't too much of an inconvenience. I have had copies made of everything so you can go over the documents in detail. Since you asked about it, I assume you have seen a copy of the divorce papers Mr. Michaels had my son draw up. However, you know they are no longer relevant and I did not include them."

Kathleen and Jean sat across the desk from Aaron. Once the cordialities were exchanged, an icy chill filled the room.

"The Michaels Family Trust was set up for Mrs. Steve Michaels, John and Tess by Mr. Michaels and became a permanent trust when he was killed, in the line of duty. The idea for the trust came from Mr. Steve Michaels' years before his death. I was his attorney, one of my first clients, and he wanted to make sure his family was taken care of in case something happened to him. He carried considerable life insurance. It seemed he had a premonition—."

"Yes, John told me the whole story, many times." Kathleen wanted Aaron to get on with out the stories."

Aaron frowned and cleared his throat. "Yes. Well it is simple. The majority of the life insurance along with the house and property were placed in a trust, managed by Mrs. Michaels, Reverend Dr. Patterson and Mr. Zachery James. Through the years the monies have been invested and reinvested and have grown. Some was used for education and other expenses. After Sarah past, John took her place as a managing trustee. Later John bought out his sister Tess's interest in the house when she wanted to move to New York, but the house and land is still in the trust. Tess is still an heir."

"No, John never added you to the trust only Steven and Katie."

"Is that legal? Kathleen asked Jean.

"I'm afraid so."

"When Rev. Patterson died, Alvin Zapped was appointed to the board of trustees. John has managed it well. The trust is now worth at least fifty-five million dollars."

"Oh my God!" Kathleen gasped. "Did you say fifty-five million?"

"Yes. However, I must inform you Mrs. Michaels, only Teresa Marie, Steven Seamus and Katie Elizabeth are named beneficiaries."

"What does that mean?" Kathleen asked.

Jean leaned over to Kathleen and whispered, "You're screwed."

Aaron made a strange sound and quickly covered his lips with his hand. Kathleen was sure he was covering a chuckle.

"Does Mr. Michaels have a will?" Jean asked.

"Yes, but as you know, with him still being alive, I am not authorized to give you a copy."

Jean stood abruptly and picked up the folder of papers from Aaron's desk. "One last question. Was John's will revised recently?"

"Yes, this past December."

"Come on Kathleen, let's go. I believe we have all the information we are going to get from Mr. Futter at this time."

*   *   *

Ryan and Conner arrived on Thursday evening and the five went to work. The consensus was the trust and will be damned. The way forward was to pull the plug. After all, Kathleen was the children's mother and John would never do anything to deprive his children. Jake was able to get a second opinion that agreed with his, and had convinced the hospital administration to go along. On Friday, Connor met with a friend from law school that was now a judge in Santa Clara County Superior Court and got the court order needed. Everything was set for Monday morning at ten o'clock. The only thing that was a little iffy was Ryan, but Jean was convinced he would be a problem.

"So everyone is in agreement?" Jean asked, turning from the family room window.

Kathleen quickly put her finger to her lips and then pointed to the children. Katie was playing with a Barbie doll while Steven sat on the raised hearth poking at the fire. It was still daylight but a cold rain had moved in late morning. Kathleen and Ryan took the children to see John before they met up with Jake, Jean and Connor at old Saint Joseph's

Catholic Church, now a Basilica, in downtown San Jose. Ryan insisted they all attend Mass. The Monsignor was a friend of Ryan's from seminary. The rest of the family came on home after the service except for Ryan. He stayed to spend some time with his classmate.

Kathleen noticed that Steven stayed unnaturally close all day. His behavior had been perplexing since the incident with Connor. Now he started acting clingy.

Because of the children, small talk sprinkled with hints of conversation had seasoned the afternoon meal, a large Irish style roast with plenty of potatoes and carrots. When Ryan got back to the house that afternoon, he seemed a bit more agreeable with the plans. Now that they had retired to the family room for brandy, they all were eager to hear what Ryan had to say. Kathleen was about to suggest that the kids go somewhere else to amuse themselves when Katie asked to be excused to play in her bedroom.

"Sure dear, nobody is making you stay in here."

Katie gave Steven a quick glance, picked up her doll and accessories and scurried off to her room. Steven kept his focus on the fire. No one spoke. Jake picked up the decanter of brandy and refreshed everyone's glass. He stopped at Kathleen and made a gesture with his head toward Steven.

"Steven?" Kathleen asked. "Don't you have something you would rather be doing?"

"No."

"I think you would be happier doing something besides sitting with us old folks."

Steven sat a moment longer as if in deep thought. "I guess I could go work on my science report, but it's not due until the end of the week."

"Why don't you go do that son?" Jake encouraged. "It's better than waiting 'til the last minute." He returned the decanter to the side table and stood looking at Steven.

Steven put another log on the fire and pocked it a couple of times before returning the poker to the rack. They all seem to give a collective sigh when he finally left the room.

The wind pushed the rain against the window for a moment, which made the storm sound worse than it was. The fire popped and startled Kathleen.

"As I started to say, I believe that everyone is in agreement." Jean said.

Everyone's attention turned to Ryan. "Yes, I agree. I believe it will be best for everyone. I believe that in all actuality, John is dead. We will all go to the hospital at ten tomorrow and I will administer Last Rites. Then we will, as you say, pull the plug.

CHAPTER 27

AN ACT OF COURAGE

```
INT.-HALLWAY OUTSIDE FAMILY ROOM-CONTINUOUS

Steven is setting on the floor beside the doorway that
leads from the family room. He is crying. He has been
listening to the conversation in the family room.
Voices of Kathleen, Jean, Jake, Conner and Ryan are
heard in the family room.

                    KATHLEEN (O.S.)
          Anyone up for desert?

                    RYAN (O.S.)
          Oh heaven sakes no.

                    JEAN (O.S.)
          I don't think anyone is ready for de-
          sert.
```

Steven struggled to his feet and silently made his way to his father's office, closing the door behind him. He wiped the tears from his eyes, picked up the phone and dialed. "Hello."

"Uncle Zach, they are going to do it."

"When?"

"Tomorrow morning at ten."

"Sit tight I'll take care of it. Now Son, are you all right?"

"Scared."

"Don't be. I told you I will take care of it. Continue to act as if you don't know anything. Don't let anyone know you have talked to me. I don't want them mad at you. Do you understand?"

"Yes. I love you Uncle Zach."

"And I love you too. Be brave, it will all work out."

After hanging up the phone, Steven took the worn box with his father's fountain pen from the desk draw. Holding the pen in the palm of his left hand he traced it elegant shape with the tip of his finger, it had captivated him ever since his father first showed it to him years ago and told him the story of it mysterious origins. He had inspected it several times, as had others for some sort of maker's mark or manufacture. Its' beautifully turned rosewood and elegant inlay were from the hand of a true artisan. Steven wept. Since the shooting, the pen had become a point of contact with his father. Holding the pen, he felt closer to his father than holding his lifeless hand in the hospital.

From the time his father told him about the divorce, Steven's inside have been tore apart. He suspected there were problems between his parents and hoped they would work things out. Even after the shooting, he had hope. That was until this past week. Hearing Jean discuss his father as if he was a commodity disgusted him. Saying that Kathleen would be better off if his father were dead, killed all the love he once had for the O'Malley family. Now with his mother agreeing to pull the plug on his father, his love for her was dying too. He could not see redemption in any of them.

He had wrestled with his father's words about our lives being scripted before we are born and that everything we experienced in life has a purpose. Something we are to learn. Though he could see no good or meaning in anything that was happening around him, just holding the pen seemed to give him hope. Unlike the relics and trappings of the Saint Joseph's Basilica, this pen in his hand put him in touch with God.

Steven wasn't sure how long he was lost in his thoughts when he heard the doorbell. The gray afternoon sky that filtered through the office window was gone, replaced by an eerie yellow haze from the backyard security light. He quickly put away the pen, went to the office door, and cracked it open. From the entry, he heard someone unlock and open the front door. The hall was dark. A crack of light crept under Katie's bedroom door and a dim glow outlined the opening to the family room.

"Zach, what a surprise, we weren't expecting you." Steven could hear his mother's voice, plainly. "Is there something wrong?"

"Are you busy? We need to talk?" Zach's voice was sharp.

"Let me tell the family, and then we can use John's office. Steven's heart pounded. He thought of the closet, should he chance it or make a dash to his bedroom across the hall.

"What I have to say concerns all of them too."

"Oh? Well come in. They are all in the family room."

Steven could hear movement. "Zach has something he wants to talk to us about." Kathleen announces.

Steven began to creep down the dark hall as Zach started to speak.

"Good evening Jean, Patrick . . . Conner, good to see you again. Doctor, Father O'Malley."

"What honors us with your present?" Ryan asked.

Steven peeked around the corner to see everyone standing looking at Zach.

"Please sit. I won't take much of your time." Zach said.

"May I offer you a brandy?" Jake asked, remaining standing.

Zach stood near the breakfast bar that separated the kitchen from the family room. Everyone focused on Zach. Steven felt safe to watch from the hall.

"No thanks, but please help yourselves."

Jake took a seat next to Jean.

I'll only be a minute. I'm on my way to the hospital to see John. I stopped by a friend's home to drop off some papers and since I was in the neighborhood, I thought I'd stop."

Zach appeared to study each face one by one. There was a long awkward moment. Steven peered around the opening, He knew Zach saw him, but gave no sign of his presence to the others.

"I had a late lunch with my old friend Teddy today. We had an interesting conversation about John. It seems he knows you too Conner."

"I'm sorry, but you have me at a disadvantage. I don't believe I know anyone in the area named Teddy."

"Sure you do Connor, you met with him Friday. Teddy Bradshaw . . . or maybe you only know him as Judge Teddy . . . ah, Judge Theodore Bradshaw, of the Santa Clara County Superior Court."

Steven suddenly felt a wave of anticipation. Everyone in the room stared at Zach.

"I stopped by here to give you a copy of this." Zach opened the manila envelope he was carrying and pulled out the contents and began to read. "'Advanced Health Care Directive, Part 1: Power of Attorney for Health Care, Designation of Agent. I, Jonathan Zachary Michaels, appoint, Zachary Albert James, as my agent. If Zachary Albert James cannot serve, I appoint, Alvin Jason Zapa, as my agent.'" Zach looked up. Everyone was riveted on him.

"Let me continue. 'When effective, the authority of my agent is effective when my primary physician or another authorized health care provider determines I am incapable of making informed decisions regarding my health care. However, when this document is signed——'.'"

"We all know and understand the provision of an Advanced Health Care Directive Mr. James" Conner interrupted, his distain crackled in his voice.

"Oh I am sure of that. So, since all of you know the provisions of an Advance Health Care Directive, I declare. At this time that I don't believe John is terminal or in a state of permanent unconsciousness, and therefore as his legally appointed agent I wish to inform all of you that John's life-support will not be turned off or withheld tomorrow as you planned. Is that understood?"

There was dead silence. Zach returned the documents to the envelope and handed them to Connor. "Just in case it is different in Illinois here is your own copy."

"Why didn't you give us this before?" Jean snapped.

"You didn't ask."

Jake went to the bar and poured himself another drink.

"So," Zach continued, "since everyone is free tomorrow. Instead of gathering at the hospital at ten to pull the plug on John, you Kathleen are requested to meet with John's attorney Aaron and me to discuss how we will proceed from here. The rest of you are invited to come along, I assume you are all interested. Now if you will excuse me, I am on my way to the hospital."

Conner jumped to his feet. "You can't just dump this on us and leave. I have questions?"

"I will answer your questions tomorrow . . . at ten, until then have a good night. I'll show myself out."

Zach was gone before they could stop him. Steven pulled away from the opening so he wasn't seen. He leaned his back against the wall, chuckled for a moment, and then quietly hurried to his bedroom. From his window, he could see Zach get in his pickup. Steven waved. He wasn't sure if Zach could see him. But as Zack turned his pickup around, he switched the headlights off and on twice. Steven watched the tail lights move down the street and disappear.

The muffled voices grew louder, each talking over the other until it was just noise. For a few minutes, Steven lay on his bed and tried to catch what they were saying, but the angry racket was unintelligible. He thought he should sneak back down the hall and find out what plans they were hatching now, so he could warn Zach. Instead, he took off his clothes, crawled under the covers and turned off the light, knowing that Zach had everything under control.

He wished he could be at the meeting in the morning with Zach, but he had school.

*   *   *

Angered at the arguing over how Zach found out what they were planning, Ryan finished his brandy, picked up and went to bed. Kathleen sat on the sofa and watched the O'Malley's start a slow boil. It reminded her of the old days at home.

It didn't take long for the five of them to finish the bottle of brandy and start another. Connor and Patrick got into an argument over how Zach learned about their plans. Jean was convinced that Ryan was the snitch.

She argued, "Why else would he suddenly change his mind, when only yesterday he called pulling the plug, murder."

"Yeah." Patrick chimed in. "He was the only one that wasn't here all day. He probably met up with Zach this afternoon and blabbed the whole thing. Then he pretended to go along with us, knowing that Zach was going to stop it."

Connor bounced unsteady to his feet. "I'm going to confront that bastard, right now. He's not going to make a fool of me that way."

"Wait a minute." Jake shouted. "You ever think he has the place bugged?"

"Which place?" Connor asked.

"This place. Zach's a retired cop. Maybe he bugged the place to keep tabs on us."

Standing straight, Connor appeared to be considering the idea. He spun around and pointed at Jake. "That's illegal."

"Da."

Now it was Jean's turn. "I'll bet you that's it. He's got the place bugged."

"Well I can assure you that the study is not wired. I've gone over every inch of the room looking for the safe combination."

"One or two well-placed bugs in this room would be enough." Jean started at the mantle, examining everything.

"Yeah." Jake giggled at Jean's search. "And if he is tapped into the security cameras outside, you wouldn't be able to fart without him knowing it."

"You are right dear brother, you are absolutely right." Jean staggered toward Jake and hovered over him. "Come on help me. All of you help me find the damn bugs."

Kathleen stood in the middle of the room. "When I find out how Zach knows what's going on in my house I'll stop it once and for all."

*   *   *

Steven was dress and ready for school when he came into the family room. It was a disaster. Knickknacks flung everywhere. Pictures on the wall skewed. He couldn't imagine what happened. He was about to run to his mother's room when something moved on the sofa. It was Jake.

He slowly sat up and blinked at Steven. "Hey Kid, you missed the party.

"What happened?" Katie asked.

"Oh we just got a little of our Irish up last night."

"Come on kids. Grab some pop tarts or something to eat and I'll drive you to school." Kathleen stood in the kitchen.

"What's happening Mommy?" Katie looked at the mess confused.

"We had a little party last night. Let's get going or you will be late. Go get in the car, I'll be right there. Jake, look alive. Get the others up and start straightening up this mess, the housekeeper will be in later today, but I don't want her to see this, she might just quit."

*   *   *

Conner looked down at his watch and fought back a yawn. Zach took the hint. The meeting had drug on well over and hour. The outcome was obvious to everyone, but Jean still wanted to argue.

"I'm not sure Kathleen should accept these conditions. She is John's wife and the mother of his children. She should be entitled to mor——."

"You don't seem to understand," Zach interrupted. "There is no negotiation here. John has put me in charge of both the Michaels Family Trust and made me his health care agent. I assure you that Kathleen is far better off, if John lives than dies. She can either live under the conditions I've put forth or go to court, which will change nothing."

"That's enough Jean." Conner snapped. Kathleen looked at him, shocked. "Under the circumstances, for now, I guess I'll have to agree with Zach. Let's get the hell out of here."

Kathleen looked down at her note pad. "All household expenses paid by the trust including food and the kid's needs, whatever John's disability pays goes in my account for me to use as I see fit."

"What about medical, especially long term care?" Jean asked.

"I told you, all medical expenses not covered by John's insurance will be paid by the trust. All John's expenses will be paid by the trust as long as he is incapacitated. If he dies, I assure you the provisions are far less favorable." With that, Zach closed the folder in front of him and stood. "We will put this all in writing. Now I have a lunch date and Aaron has business to attend too. Good-day all of you."

CHAPTER 28

A NEW WRINKLE

INT.-MICHAELS' KITCHEN-AFTERNOON-MARCH 3, 1999

Kathleen is alone. She has gathered some ingredients
and has start fixing dinner. She picks up the remote,
changes the channel to a local news broadcast, and
then returns to her preparations. Jake enters from the
patio through the family room door and crosses to the
breakfast counter and sits on a stool.

> KATHLEEN
> Where have you been?

> JAKE
> Stayin' out of people's way. Are they
> gone?

> KATHLEEN
> Yeah, they headed for the airport a
> little after eleven.

"Good, they were all in a foul mood after Monday, especially Jean."

"Weren't we all? Coffee?"

"No thanks."

"I'm glad to get the house back. You sure I can't get you something. I have beer?" Kathleen didn't wait for a response, but went to the refrigerator and got a bottle of beer and sat it on the counter for Jake.

"A true lady after me heart?"

"So, where did you go?"

"I spent some time with John . . . and then had a meeting with his doctor."

"Hayward? Why?"

"Well I had to answer some questions for myself. After what Zach said, I felt there was something I was missing. I knew Doctor Hayward would not hold out hope if there were none. So I had to know. He showed me all of John's tests, including a new EEG from yesterday. There is definitely brain activity and signs of improvement."

"Oh great, he's going to get better and then kick me out."

"Don't be so sure of that. He is improving, how fast and how far is unknown. He needs you and will continue to need you for a long time."

"I don't love him, and after finding the divorce papers, it is obvious he feels the same."

"Put that aside. If he wakes up chances are ten-to-one he will suffer long-term disability."

"What? Are you thinking of me taking care of him? Oh no, not on your life, I'm not going to play nurse."

"Think of your children. Are you ready to give them up?"

Kathleen thought a moment then answered hesitantly. "No."

"So what I'm suggesting is, if he wakes up, work out a compromise. And if he doesn't, play it cool."

"Compromise?"

"Compromise isn't so bad, we all do it. Look at Mom and Dad. Their faith wouldn't let them get a divorce, so Dad opened an office in New York and plays house with his mistress, only comes back to Chicago for Easter, a few weeks in the summer and sometimes, special occasions. Now Conner is following Dad's example. Ryan's got his buddies in Key West and Jean, Jean's got, 'no opinion' Patrick."

"So what's your compromise?"

Jake held up his beer.

"Beer?" Kathleen asked.

"Beer, wine, whiskey vodka, gin, you name it——booze. In med-school I wanted to be a surgeon, that's where the money is, but then I found out I'd have to get up at four in the morning with a rock steady hand." He ran his hand through his hair, made a goofy face and pretended to shake. "Hell, you can't get drunk the night before and do brain surgery the next morning. So I compromised, Nine to five, Monday thru Friday, with a half day off on Wednesdays, my hours at a good ole clinic. The pay is not as good and there's certainly no fame. But no one cares if I come in a little dragged out. If my hand shakes a little when I write out a prescription, fine, all doctors have lousy handwriting. No questions, as long as I keep handing out pills."

Jake finished his beer and held out the empty. "You got another one handy Sis?"

"Yeah, sure . . . ." Kathleen was in deep thought. She distractedly got Jake another beer. "Yeah, I'm getting your drift, compromise. Hell, life is nothing but a compromise anyway. Might as well get what you want out of it."

"Now you're talkin'."

Kathleen leaned on the counter and smiled at her brother. "So what is on your agenda for the rest of the week?"

"I thought I would drive up to San Francisco tomorrow, maybe spend a night or two and then drive down the coast to Monterey. I'll get back here on Monday or Tuesday. Then fly back to Chicago Thursday, that's if you can stand one more O'Malley around a little longer."

"You know Jake you are always welcome. You have a way of making life a little more interesting." Kathleen returned to the sink. "I envy you. I'd love to spend a long weekend in Frisco."

"Well come along."

"I wish, but the kids and all, I can't. Compromise, you know."

"Well that's up to you, keep dreaming, it might happen."

Keep dreaming, Kathleen wistfully peels a potato.

"Is Steven home?" Jake asked, interrupting Kathleen's thoughts.

"He is in his bedroom doing his homework as far as I know. Why?"

"I've got a couple of things I want to talk to him about."

"Guy things?"

"Maybe."

*   *   *

Steven had just finished his math homework and was thinking about going over to his friend Skip's house to shoot some hoops when there was a knock at his bedroom door.

"Got a minute?" Jake asked from the hall. Before Steven could answer, Jake opened the door and stuck his head in. "Can we talk? It's so damn quiet around here with everyone gone, it's like a morgue."

"Yeah, come on in, what's up?"

"Your Mom's busy fixing dinner so I thought we might hang out a little." Jake stood awkwardly for a moment and then pointed to the Steven's bed. "Mind if I sit."

Steven grabbed his jacket and books off the foot of the bed. Jake sat and crossed his leg in front of him. Steven nervously hung his jacket on the hook on the back of his door. He and Jake had never spoken much, just jokes and stupid stuff. He liked Jake's loud, touchy, aggressive manner, but now was wary of him. After what the family tried, he didn't trust any of them.

"You're sure getting tall, how old are you now?"

"Thirteen, in September."

Jake patted the foot of the bed indicating he wanted Steven to sit. "Come-on, sit down."

Steven sat at his desk.

"You're filling out good for your age. You could pass for fifteen easy. When my boys hit their teens, they were scrawny pimple bags, even now in their twenties they haven't improved much. You take after you dad's side of the family." Jake smiled and leaned toward Steven. "I remember the first time I met you dad. He looked like a movie star . . . especially up against the O'Malley clan." Jake smirked and chuckled. "Ryan had to do penance for a month after your father shook his hand." Jake dropped his legs over the side of the bed. He leaned forward, and acted buddy-buddy. With a hushed secret telling kind of voice, he said, "yep, your Old-man is a real handsome man . . . you are too . . . taking after him."

Steven guessed Jake was complimenting him, but he couldn't help but wonder what he wanted. He felt trapped and wanted to run.

"You know," Jake, turned serious. "You should have seen Jean, Patrick and Conner Sunday night. They searched this whole house for bugs, they were sure Zach had the place bugged. That he was listening in on everything going on in the house. I admit, I wondered how Zach knew what was going on, and then I thought . . . if I believed someone was planning to pull the plug on my father what would I do?" Jake sat back and grinned.

He knows. Steven felt the anger rise up inside him. *What's he up to?*

"Don't worry, I didn't say anything." Jake slapped Steven's leg. "I got to admire you kid, I'd never stuck up for my father, never wanted to. What's more, I believe you were right. I met with your father's doctor yesterday and look at a new EEG, your dad's brain activity in increasing—slowly, but increasing. In fact, Dr. Hayward is thinking about starting him on a muscle stimulation program that might help bring him around." Jake paused and looked Steven in the eyes. "Son, your dad is getting better and maybe coming home sooner that you think."

Steven felt the tears start to run down his cheeks.

"I don't want you to say anything to anyone for a few days. Dr. Hayward wants to run some more tests before he gets everyone's hopes up, but I believe you can keep a secret, are you with me on this?"

It took Steven a moment to find his voice. "Yes—yes, I won't tell anyone."

"Not even Zach?"

"Not even Zach." Jake looked him in the eyes. "Want you to ease up on you mom a little too. She's trying. If you have got questions come to me, or call me, here's my private number."

Steven took Jake's card and wiped the tears from his face with his hand. At last, he felt a glimmer of true hope. He couldn't help but wonder why the sudden change in Jake. *Could he be trusted.*

*　　*　　*

Jake made his trip to San Francisco and returned on Tuesday. He had call Zach the next morning and asked him to meet with him at the hospital. Zach had thought that Jake had gone back to Chicago with the rest of the family the week before, but Jake explained he had stayed behind, took a drive down the coast, and had been doing some soul searching. Zach doubted the guy even had a soul. It angered him when Jake said he had met with John's doctor and had him run additional tests, and now wanted to talk to him.

Zach stopped in the hall outside John's room, he knew Jake was already there waiting. *What kind of a stunt he is trying to pull now.* Zach marched into the room as if he owned it. "What's this all about?" Jake reached out his hand to greet Zach, but Zach ignored it. "This better be good."

"Look Zach, I know I can be a jackass, and this time, big-time. I apologize. I was wrong, completely and totally wrong. I had my head up my ass, where it usually is."

Zach was taken back. An old cartoon came to mind that had circulated around the precinct years ago. It was a drawing of a guy with his head stuck up his ass, bumping into things blindly. His mood changed. Zach had to chuckle. "Apology accepted." Zach said, and stuck out his hand. Zach's attention quickly turned to John. "Any change?"

"That's why I called you here. Doctor Hayward was right John's brain activity is increasing. During a coma, the brain is disorganized in the way it functions and responds. Each coma patient can have a different levels and types of brain functions. Parts of John's brain are still shut down and not processing information, however his prognosis is improving. For the past two months, focus has been preventing infections, providing nutrition, and maintaining the patient's physical health. It's time to start physical therapy to prevent bone, joint, or muscle deformities, but the stimulation can also aid brain organization and help bring John out of his coma."

"So why are you telling me this and not Doctor Hayward?"

"I asked him to let me tell you. Zach, I want to be on your side."

Zach looked at Jake. *Can I trust him? Maybe a little.* "Well then, he needed to start physical therapy."

"It isn't that simple. The hospital has limited staff or facilities for the kind of therapy John needs. However, there is a facility nearby."

"Let's transfer him."

"Again, it isn't that simple. The facility is a convalescent hospital. John is stable enough to go there, but some of their therapy is considered experimental and isn't covered by John's insurance."

"I don't give a damn about what's covered. If it can possibly help John, let's do it. Money is not an issue."

"I told Doctor Hayward that would be your reaction."

"How soon can he be transferred?"

"There are a couple of more tests that will need to be run and their doctor will want to examine him. And he must have a permanent feeding tube surgically put in before he can be transferred. If all goes well and he is approved, he can be transferred in a week or two."

"Does Kathleen know about this?"

"No, but I hinted to Steven that his father was improving and may start a new program. I didn't want to get ahead of Doctor Hayward. I thought you might want to break the news."

"This is exciting, and yes, I'd like to do that."

"I thought so. I took the liberty of asking Kathleen to come to the hospital. She should be here any minute."

"You're a gutsy little Irishman, maybe you're not that big a jackass after all."

"A regular ole leprechaun, but it's not magic. John's not out of the woods yet. Oh and the convalescent hospital is just blocks for the house, Steven can stop in on his way home from school, not a forty minute drive like to here."

Zach hugged Jake. "Thanks."

"Don't thank me, it's your loyalty and Steven's tenacity that has kept it from a much different outcome." Jake grabbed his jacket from the chair. "I'm going to scoot before Kathleen gets here. I don't want her to know I'm involved."

Jake started toward the door then stopped. "I was thinking, maybe you need to give her a break, you know, our father kept a mistress openly most of her life, I'm a drunk, Ryan's gay, Conner's a bum like our father and Jean, she is totally fucked-up. I tried to convince John not to marry Kathleen, but he had such hot nuts that he couldn't think of anything but screwing."

"I know, I tried too, but it didn't do a damn bit of good."

"She going through a lot, and no matter what you think of her, she is a decent mother."

"Well she's not much of a wife."

"I know, but that's between John and her, not the kids. She needs a break in more ways than one. The past few months haven't been easy on anyone, and she is in the thick of it. When I told her I was spending a few days in Frisco, she expressed how much she would like a long weekend in the City. I offered to take her along, but she wouldn't leave the kids."

"So your suggesting — ? Maybe we need to cut her some slack." Zach turned to John and looked at his peaceful face. *If you would just wakeup.*

"Think about it Zach. Just a weekend to get away."

*   *   *

After Jake left, Zach pulled a chair next to John's bed and sat holding his hand. He lost track of time.

"Jake said you wanted to see me."

Kathleen's voice startled him. He quickly stood, nervously. They had not spoken since the meeting at Aaron's office. "Hi, yes — come in. Would you like to sit-down?"

"I'll stand thanks." Her tone was sharp.

"There have been some marked improvements."

"That's what Jake's said."

"It appears that Doctor Hayward wants to start physical therapy. They will transfer him to a convalescent hospital in a few weeks. It's quite near your home."

"That would be nice."

"It's near to Steven's school."

"That would be nice for Steven."

"I'm sorry for the way things came down. John is like a son and I wasn't ready to give up on him."

"I understand. It was getting crazy. Jean kept saying it was useless and we needed to put an end to it and Conner was flipping out about the bill and all. And I — I was so tired I didn't think."

"I understand." Zach took her hand and led her to the chair. "I've been thinking. Maybe you need to get away for a few days. Go to the City for a few days. A long weekend. Katie and Steven can stay with us. Take John's credit card, go first class, do some shopping, whatever, I will authorize it, no limit."

"Really? You would really do that for me. You don't know how much I need a break. Thank you and your wife." Kathleen began to cry.

"Call me when you decide the date." Zach started for the door. "I'll talk to you later."

*   *   *

Kathleen pulled to a stop, looked at her watch, one-thirty, she smiled. It had taken her two weeks to get her holiday arranged. The drive from Cambria Park was uneventful. She had avoided Friday afternoon traffic by leaving early. A sharply uniformed valet opened her door, she stepped out and handed the young man her keys.

"Will you be staying with us?" He asked.

"Yes, until Monday."

"Do you have luggage Miss——?"

"Michaels, Kathleen Michaels, and yes."

The young man turned to his station. She noticed his broad shoulders and the slight curl to his blond hair. With a tingle of excitement, she watched him write down her name, and then signal to a bellman. Kathleen stepped back and took a deep breath of the cool afternoon air. From her vantage point on Nob Hill, she could see the fog already creeping in through the Golden Gate. She stood sophisticated and composed, waiting for the bellman. Inside she was as giddy as a schoolgirl. The bellman, another handsome young man in his perfectly tailored uniform, went quickly about his business. *Where do they find these guys?* She admired more than his speed. Once he had her bags on his cart, he directed her toward the gleaming glass and brass doors of the century old hotel, still the most elegant landmark in San Francisco. The doorman, in red tails, tipped his top hat and held the door for her. Followed by her bellman she walked regally across the vast lobby. There were guests sitting on the sofas and lounge chairs, chatting over afternoon tea or cocktails, she looked for a familiar face. Her eyes quickly scanned the grand staircase that through the years has been graced by kings, queens, presidents and celebrities of every kind.

At the desk, an attractive woman, looked up her reservation on a computer and quickly checked her in. "Will you need one or two keys mam?"

Kathleen hesitated a moment. "Two please. And will the bellman please take my bags up to my room? I'm meeting someone in the lounge."

"Yes ma'am." She slipped the two plastic key cards in a folder and handed them to her. "Room 603, welcome to the Fairmont, enjoy your stay."

"Oh I'm sure I will." She tucked the keys in her purse and took a ten-dollar bill, folded it and turned to the bellmen. "Please take the luggage to my room 603, I'm meeting someone." Then she discreetly put the bill in his white gloved hand.

"Yes ma'am." The young man said politely and slipped the money in his front jacket pocket. He turned. His high-waist burgundy jacket framed the tan slacks that slinked over his firm butt as he walked. She watched him make his way toward the elevators.

"Drooling over the eye candy?" A deep male voice spoke softly behind her.

She turned quickly. "Scott."

CHAPTER 29

ON THE WAY TO REHAB

INT.-JOHN'S HOSPITAL ROOM-AFTERNOON-MARCH 29, 1999

Steven sits beside John's bed. The nasal feeding tube was gone, replaced by a permanent tube directly into his stomach. His IV too was gone and a much smaller ventilator connected to his tracheotomy tube assisted his breathing. His hair is trimmed and he is freshly shaved. He lies peacefully asleep.

Steve is holding his father's hand weeping.

                    STEVEN
          Dad (beat) come back to us. You have
          to wake up. I need you. You know how
          it was when your father died. I can't
          do it without you, please.

Zach comes in with two large, lidded paper drink containers in his hands.

                    ZACH
          I thought you might like a cola.

                    STEVEN
          Yeah, thanks.

Zach sets Steven's cola on John's bed table. Steven remained with his back to Zach. He wipes his face with a tissue. Zach sat quietly in a chair near the window. After Steven gained control of himself, he slid his chair back and turned it so he can see both Zach and his father. Zach took a straw from his shirt pocket and handed it to Steven. "He sure looks better without all those tubes and crap."

"Yeah, better." Steven draws in a deep breath. "I just want him to wake up."

"We all do." Zach doesn't say any more for several minutes.

They both watch John, lifeless except for his slow steady breathing assisted by the ventilator. Occasionally John takes an involuntary swallow or shows a slight twitch in his face. When he first saw movement by his father, he thought they were sure signs he was conscious, but has come to accept them as just spontaneous movements. "I wonder if he dreams."

"It's hard to know." Zach paused. "I just had a good talk with Doctors Hayward and Gupta. Everything is on schedule for the transfer on Tuesday."

"Who is Gupta?"

"Your dad's new neurologist, he will be taking over John's care. And there is other good news. I have hired a private full-time registered nurse for your dad, Nurse Rube Garcia. Both doctors recommended Garcia for excellent credentials, experienced with brain injury patients and certification in acupuncture, therapeutic massage and physical therapy. And fortunately, Nurse Garcia has just become available."

"I guess that's nice, if it helps."

"Come on Steven, you can't let yourself get down now, just when things are beginning to look up."

"What's a private nurse going to do?"

"Nurse Garcia will work with you Dad eight hours a day Monday through Friday, caring for him, doing physical therapy, muscle stimulation and rehabilitation. Garcia will start Monday, here at the hospital, review all John's records and get him ready for the transfer and then stay with him through the move, be with him in the ambulance and then get him settled. What's more, when your dad is ready to come home, Nurse Garcia will work with him at home, on a long-term contract."

An image of an older Mexican woman in a white nurse's uniform flashed in his mind.

"Honestly, you think he'll be coming home?"

"Yes Son, I do."

Steven jumped to his feet and grabbed John's hand. "You hear that Dad, you're coming home."

"Now let's not get too far ahead of ourselves, we have a lot of work ahead of us."

Steven turned and gave Zach a hug. "I love you Uncle Zach."

"Well look at the time, your mother has probably bought out half the City by now. I hope she has a good time."

"I hope so too, she was excited about getting away."

"I bet you Aunt Nadia has dinner ready and she and Katie are sitting at the table waiting for us."

"Yeah . . . but I want to tell Dad goodnight."

Zach nodded and stepped out the door. Steve leaned over his father and kissed his forehead. "Goodnight Dad, sweet dreams."

*   *   *

"Is that you Mom?" Steven questioned from the family room at the sound of the door from the garage closing.

"It's me. Can you give me a hand?"

Steven put down his book and hurried through the kitchen. "What do you need?"

He immediately saw how happy she appeared. His old Mom had come home from San Francisco.

"There's a suitcase and a bag in the back of the car. Would you bring them to my bedroom please?"

Steven pulled the suitcase from the trunk of the car and a large shopping bag from the backseat. He pushed the button and paused long enough to make sure the garage door was closing unobstructed. Once in the bedroom he dropped the bag in a chair and hoisted the suitcase onto the foot of the bed. "Have a good time?"

"I had a wonderful time. How about you, do anything special?"

"We all went out to dinner and a movie Saturday night. Mom, Dad is looking good. They took out his——."

"I know. I stopped by the hospital on my way home. He is looking very good."

"They're transferring him tomorrow."

"I know Steven." She smiled and ran her finger through his hair. "It seems Zach has everything under control."

"I'm so excited."

Holding his chin, she looked in his eyes. "But you can't get your hopes up to high."

"You're right." Steven sat on the foot of the bed and sighed. Kathleen went into her walk-in closet and Steven took the moment to snoop in the shopping bag. It appeared to be only women's clothing. He started to open a smaller bag tucked under some tissue paper.

"I'm sorry Son but I didn't get you anything." She said, stepping out of the closet with a change of clothes in hand. She kicked off her shoes on her way to her bathroom. "I didn't do any shopping except in a boutique at the hotel, they were having a sale. Didn't even leave the hotel."

Steven sat on the bed for a minute. Raising his voice so she could hear, he asked, "Do you really want Dad to get better?"

His mother didn't answer and he was about to ask again when she stepped out of the bathroom and scowled at him. Steven could see she wasn't happy about the question.

"Sure I do, why do you——."

"The truth Mom, the truth."

Kathleen dropped the things she had in her hand on a chair and approached Steven. Standing in front of him, she pushed a lock of hair out of his eyes. "You need a haircut."

"You are not answering."

She kissed his forehead, took his hand and sat beside him. "Son, I know I can't fool you. You know that if your father gets better, he will probably go through with the divorce. I have thought long and hard about that. I've concluded that I want it too. But I can assure you, I still love your father. Even though our marriage is over, I still love him and want him to get well. I promised Zach that I would stay and take care of you and Katie. And I swear I love both of you and that will never change."

"I love you too Mom, no matter what, I love you."

"If the time comes that your father recovers to the point that he can competently make decisions for himself and direct his affairs, I will willingly accept a divorce without a fight. And at that time I will accept your and Katie decision on who you want to live with."

Steven was pleased by her answer and relieved that she spoke the truth.

"While we are on the subject, from now on, what goes on in this house, stays in this house, understand?"

What? Her smile had faded. Her eyes flashed with irritation. Steven knew from her expression he was about to be scolded. *What does she know?*

"From now on young man, if you have a problem, you come to me. No more running to Zach when you don't get your way. No more listening in on phone calls or eavesdropping. If I find out that, you are tattling to Zach, there will be hell to pay. I mean like, you are out of here. Do you understand?"

"Yes." *She knows. Jake!*

"I made a mistake not including you and Zach in our decisions, and I am sorry. Forgive me?"

"Yes."

"Good. Now give me a hug."

Kathleen put her arms around Steven in an embrace, but he only halfheartedly responded. He let her words sink in. His mother's weekend away had made a big change in her. Good and bad, he wondered if it was a bluff. Would she actually kick him out? Steven wasn't ready to find out, at least not for the time being.

Kathleen's moment of tenderness quickly ended. He began to creep toward the door. She stood and viewed her image in the full-length mirror.

"Where is your sister?"

"Down the street——playing with Pattie."

"Why don't you go and tell her to come home. I'll finish changing and we can go get pizza."

Her tender moment disappeared. She walked directly to the phone and dialed.

Steven stopped outside the bedroom door, out of his mother's sight.

"Jean . . . ? Tell me Sis, I need some help. What can I do to turn the table on Zach? There has to be some way to take back control of my home. What's my ace in the hole?"

Steven turned and ran to the front door. Once in the open-air he hesitated. A chill of fear went up his spine. It wasn't his old Mom. It was a mother he didn't know.

*   *   *

"Where am I, it's so dark and empty? What am I doing in this bed?"

"Keep the camera rolling." The director said on the dark movie set. A single spotlight illuminated the scene. "Think, what do you see? Look hard into your mind."

"It seems familiar. But that light is in my eyes, I can't see. Where am I? I can't make it out, too dark.'

"Who are you? Think, think hard." The director, spoke in a hush tone.

"I'm lost, completely lost. Can I see the script, just for a second?"

"Stay in character, try to go on without it. You are doing fine."

"Give me the line, please?"

"There is no line. You are in a coma trying to wake up."

"My name, I'm drawing a blank. I'm so tired, can't we break."

"Keep going we are almost there. If we quit now we have to scrape the whole project. "

"A clue, just one clue."

The script girl stepped out of the shadows and held up the script.

"Is it mine?" He asked. "But I don't know who I am."

"Look at the script. Look at the title."

"*The Incarnation——*. I can't make out the name, it's too dark." The script girl turned her flashlight on the cover of the script. "*The Incarnation of Jonathan Michaels*,' that's me, I'm John——."

"Keep rolling."

*   *   *

Steven hurried at a half run the five blocks from his school to Southwood Manor. By the time of his last class, he was so excited he couldn't concentrate. He had walked home from school passed the Manor several times since he learned of his father's transfer. Today, his father was really there.

He pulled the front door open and to his surprise, the convalescent hospital's lobby wasn't at all, as he imagined. Instead of a large sterile room with patients restrained in wheelchairs sitting mindlessly in front of a TV, blasting infomercials, it was like a small sitting room of a nice hotel. Most of all, to Steven, the place smelled fresh, not the sick and antiseptic odors of the hospital. Steven stepped up to the receptionist and asked to see his father.

"Mr. Michaels is in room 15, through the main door and turns left, and then follow the corridor, the room will be on your right. Are you John's son?"

Steven smiled, "Yes . . . Thank you."

The hall was busy, but not the way Steven thought it would be. There was one nurse walking with a patient in the hall, but there were no patients sitting unattended. In one room he passed, there were two patients exercising with a large ball and in another, a man was watching TV as he peddled an exercise bike. When Steven got to room 15, the door was closed. Steven knocked lightly.

"Come in." A male voiced answered.

The room was large, bright and no hospital-look. The bed was angled slightly away from the door and on the opposite side was an oversize sliding glass door. Beyond, there was a courtyard with walkways running between raised gardens and benches, connecting the private patios. Across the courtyard, was a bed rolled out on the patio, Steven could see the patient watching two children play.

The wall with the hall door had a huge mirror, reflecting the light and gardens. In front of the mirror were two padded armchairs with an end table between them and a vase of flowers. The wall opposite the head of the bed had built-in cabinets, a TV, and a door that opened into a bathroom.

"I'll be with you in a second." The orderly in dark blue scrubs said, stopping whatever he was doing only long enough to peek out the bathroom door. The man appeared to be in his twenties, with dark short-cropped hair and radiant smile.

Surprised to see that the TV was on, Steven stepped closer to his father. The voices of an afternoon talk show chattered from a wall speaker near the bed. Steven took a closer look at his father, he appeared different, he was still in a deep sleep, but his face seemed softer, calmer and somehow happier.

"You must be Steven. Your father has been telling me about you." The man stood at the foot of the bed.

Steven jerked around. "What?"

"I didn't mean to startle you. I'm Ruben Garcia, but everyone just calls me Rube."

"He talked?" Steven didn't know which was the greater astonishment. His father talking or that Rube was a man.

"Oh, no, not yet . . . but your look, your same gentle soul, you just have to be his son." Rube reached out and shook Steven's hand. "We've spent the last couple of days getting to know each other."

"But I don't understand."

"Take off your backpack and have a seat. Would you like something to drink, water, soda?"

"Soda, please," Steven replied. He watched Rube open a large cabinet door that was in fact a refrigerator.

Rube has a round face, with a perpetual, genuine, infectious smile. He wasn't very tall, sort of a stocky teddy bear. "Cola?" He asked.

"Yeah, fine."

"Anytime you want anything, help yourself." Rube handed Steven a can of cola and sat next to him. "I have a philosophy. When you want something to happen, act as though it has already occurred and it will manifest. We want your father to come out of this coma. So instead of seeing, treating him like a vegetable, we have to see and treat him as if he were well. Talk to him, not at him. Include him in our conversations. Ask him his opinion. What TV program does he want to watch, if he wants the lights on or off? It will build our faith, stimulate his brain, and help him reconnect to the here and now. He is in there. We just have to reach him."

"Do you truly believe he will wake up?"

"As much as you do. I know how you stood up for your father. I know the battles you are facing. You and your sister are the keys to you father's recovery."

"So what do we do?"

"I have started a daily regimen. We start our day at seven when I come in. We shave and bathe while watching the morning news. Have breakfast, assisted by a feeding tube. Then we spend some time on the commode before dressing for the day. After that, we go across the hall and workout in the gym. When we are through there, we rest a bit, either watch some TV, read the paper or a book or if the weather is nice take a stroll in the garden. After lunch is more physical therapy, followed by an early dinner and then get ready for bed and some more TV. Lights out is at nine."

Steven was in awe at the man's exuberance. "What can I do?"

"Come by tomorrow after school and I'll show you, then on weekends you can come in when I'm not here and fill in around the regular staff."

"Great, next week is spring break. I can spend days with you."

"Us, Steven, for now on, it's us."

CHAPTER 30

LOCKED IN

INT.-MICHAELS KITCHEN-PALM SUNDAY-MARCH 28, 1999

Steven sits on a stool at the kitchen breakfast bar eating a bowl of cold cereal. There is a fresh pot of coffee in the coffeemaker. Kathleen enters in a stylish green dress, putting on earrings. She pours herself a cup of coffee and silently goes about adding milk and sugar. Not wanting to stare, Steven pretends to keep his focus on his bowl of cereal. Kathleen leans against the counter and sips her coffee. She looks at the clock, which read 8:30 AM.

                    KATHLEEN
Well you're up early for a Sunday
morning.
                    STEVEN
I'm going to spend the day with Dad.
                    KATHLEEN
Again, you were there all day yesterday and after school every day last
week, you can't pine away every day
at that hospital. It's not healthy,
you've got to get out in the fresh
air and do things with your friends.

"Not healthy," Steven snapped back. "Dad's there all alone, that's not healthy."

"Don't you think I don't know that? I've stopped by while you were in school and met your mister, 'us' and 'we', Nurse Jube — Hube . . . Rube, whoever. A bunch of positive words and high hopes isn't going to help your father any more than four months in the friggin hospital has."

"So I suppose I should write him off like you. And just go on about life like he doesn't exist?"

"Do what you want. Believe what you want. You know where I stand."

No I don't. Steven wanted to scream, but knew it was useless. He pushed at the last few flakes of cereal floating in his bowl. He wished she would leave and go wherever she wanted, but she didn't, she just stood, leaning against the counter and sipped at her coffee.

"I'm going out today." She finally said. "You need to look after your sister."

"Are you going to church?"

"Don't take that tone with me, I have had enough. A friend is coming by to pick me up and take me to brunch. I will get home when I damn well please. This house is not going to be my cage and you're not going to be my jailer and keep me locked in."

"But Mom."

"Katie is your responsibility today. You can stay here or take her with you, that's up to you."

*   *   *

Katie had pulled her chair closer to her father's bed so she could hear the TV without it blasting. She had been giggling and laughing practically in their father's ear since they got to his room and Steven turned the channel to cartoons. Steven got a cola for himself and settled in the other chair. Katie was preoccupied.

Her laughter brightened the room. The giggles that so often annoyed, him made him happy. He studied his father's face. It seemed different today. *Was that an eye twitch?* For a second he though he saw movement in his father's eyes. Is it just Katie, or is Dad laughing too. Steven fixed his watch on every detail of John's face. There was another flicker of eye movement. For an instant, Steven was sure his father's eyes moved under his eyelids, just a little, but movement.

It was so brief, he wondered if what appeared to be happening was real, or the false reading of his overly hopeful imagination.

The hours passed. Steven saw no more movement than an occasional involuntary swallow and twitches, which were normal. The weekend staff nurses came in frequently and checked on John. Suctioned his airway, repositioned him and made sure, he hadn't soiled his bed. When it came time for his noon feeding, Steven took Katie to the corner hamburger stand. They took their time. Katie finished all she wanted of her lunch and worked it off in the play yard.

Nearly two hours later, they returned to John's room. Katie soon fell asleep in the chair. One of the nurses brought her a blanket and Steven watched both his sister and father sleep. Quietly, he kept a peaceful vigil over his little family. He too dozed, though he fought it. The morning's conversation with his mother, repeated in his head, *This house is not going to be my cage and you are not going to be my jailer and keep me locked in.*

*   *   *

That evening Steven fixed Katie and himself a repeat of his morning cereal for dinner. At nine, Katie went to bed. Steven started to worry when at ten o'clock their mother was not home. He was about to call Zach, but decided if there was nothing wrong, his mother would be livid. Instead, he simply turned out the lights in the house, turned on the entry and porch lights and went to bed.

Steven had been reading for about an hour when he heard a car pull up, he quickly turned out his light. Car doors opened and closed and a short time later, he heard the front door opened. Steven started for his bedroom door to check when he heard his mother's voice.

"Good the kids are in bed. Come on in."

Steven stood at his open bedroom door. In light of the entry, Steven caught the glimpse of a man following his mother toward the family room.

"Fix us a drink Honey, while I check on the kids."

Steven hopped back in his bed. The hall light flicked on. He pulled the cover up and pretended to be asleep. His mother stopped at his door a moment and then pulled it closed. He heard her open and close Katie's bedroom door. Shortly after that, she turned off hall light.

From his bed he could hear the strange man's and his mother's voices, but there words were muffled and he could not make out what they were saying. He thought about going down the hall and spying on them, but decided it was too risky. He strained to hear a name or put together the few words he could make out between their laughter. From somewhere inside, he felt he knew who his mother's visitor was, although he had never met, Scott.

He had fallen asleep, when his mother's laugh coming from the entry hall startled him. He looked at his clock, 4:44 a.m. The sound of the front door opening followed with another laugh, and bits and pieces of his mother's and the man's, goodnights. Steven stood and peeked out his bedroom window. He saw the man and his mother walking toward the car parked in the driveway. Halfway there they stopped and the man turned and gave his mother a kiss. Steven closed his eyes.

When he heard the car door, he looked out the window again. His mother stood, watching the car back out of the driveway and drive up the street. She stood a long moment and then returned to the house. Steven crawled back into bed.

He tried to sleep but couldn't. Images of his mother and the man he was sure was Scott plagued his mind. Would she be so brazen as to take another man into his father's home? He argued a losing battle with himself. He wanted to call Zach, he needed to talk to someone, but he remembered the promise made. There was no doubt of his mother's betrayal of his helpless father. He decided for now, he would simple play the game alone.

*   *   *

Steven pushed his way through Southwood Manor's lobby door and was surprised to see Zach talking with the receptionist. Zach looked up at the sound of the door. "What are you doing here so early?" Steven asked.

"Nadia and I are flying to Phoenix for a family Easter gathering, I told you we were going." Zach glanced at his watch. "Might I ask why you're here at six in the morning?"

"I couldn't sleep." Steven fought back bursting into a rant about his mother's visitor, instead he pasted a smile on his face. "I thought I would spend the day with Dad, it's spring break."

"Nurse Rube came in early. He's going over the weekend reports right now and asked if I could give him some time to get your dad's day started."

"I guess it's a little early."

"Have you had breakfast?"

"No."

"Why don't we go down the street and grab a bite while we wait."

"Sure." Steven reluctantly agreed. He wondered if or for how long he could keep his secret. Zach seemed to have a sixth since about secrets. Could he keep this from him, when he didn't want too? Then he remembered the good news. "Dad opened his eyes yesterday, at least he tried."

"Come on let's go, you can tell me all about it over breakfast." Zach said, and walked Steven to the door.

*   *   *

"Good morning John, how are we this beautiful morning?"

Who's that? The voice brought John out of the endless fog in which he had been drifting. *Where are you?*

"Let's get some light in here."

John heard the metallic sound of something sliding followed by a burst of red light.

"It's time to wake up Mr. Michaels, the sun is shining and the birds are singing, it's Monday, March, twenty-ninth, nineteen-ninety-nine. Your son and Zach have come to see you already, but I told them to wait until I got you ready."

Who is this chatterbox? Why can't I see? What does he mean its March, twenty-ninth. It's New Year's Eve . . . isn't it? John felt the blanket pulled off him and tried to grab it, to no avail. *What's this guy doing? Quit it, you have no business pulling up my shirt.*

"Good you didn't poop-poo, last night. Let's get you out of this nightgown and cleaned up for your visitors."

Strong hands reached around John's neck, untied his gown and slid it off him. John sensed his nakedness. *Who the hell are you? Touch me and I'll knock the crap out of you. You hear me?* Suddenly he realized, though he thought he was talking, there were no sounds coming out of his mouth. John felt a vibration of the bed and the mattress rise behind him. *What's going on?* A panic began to grip him.

John began to calm when he felt the warm washcloth on his face. Through the man's constant babbling, John started putting pieces together. He had been shot New Year's Eve and had been in a coma since then. But why couldn't he see and why couldn't he move. *Hey I'm here. I can hear you. Why can't you hear me?*

Eventually the man lowered the bed to flat and rolled him on his side, it was then John was able to open an eye ever so slightly. There in front of him was a man lying in a bed, and behind him, another man stood. It took a moment to realize he was looking in a mirror and that he was the man on the bed. *Oh God, what's happened to me?* John's mind reeled trying to put together what he saw. *What happened? What's happening?*

Try as he might he could not communicate. The man went about shaving him, feeding him through a tube in his side and dressing him in two-piece pajamas. By the time, the man was finished, John was exhausted and though he fought it, felt himself drifting off to sleep.

*   *   *

Steven had burst into his story about John to Rube the moment they got back from breakfast. Rube listened intently as Steven explained how his sister was laughing at cartoons, when he thought he saw movement in his father's eyes.

"I'm telling you." Steven was emphatic. "I was sure he opened them, he was trying to look at us.

"I believe you. Why don't you and Zach sit down? There is no reason why he isn't awake. "What you saw is to be expected. He might just open his eyes and start talking at any time."

"See, I told you Uncle Zach, he is waking up. He is going to be all right."

"However," Rube continued. "His waking might be real confusing for him at first. He will probably have no memory of the shooting or anything that has transpired since then. Even parts of his memory from before the shooting may be gone. That is why I talk to him as if he were awake, give him the date every day and tell him what has happen to him. Sometimes there is a slow awaking and hearing the date and the news of the day, helps a patients orientate them self. It helps lessen the shock and confusion."

"Now do you believe me Uncle Zach?" Steven questioned, standing.

"I believed you Son. I just want you to calm down. You've got to take a deep breath."

"Zach's right, the waking process may take several days."

Steven heard their words but heeded them little. He stood by John's bed with his gaze fixed on his father's eyes.

Zach gave Rube information on where he could be reached before saying his goodbyes. Steven acknowledged Zach without averting his eyes from his father. He finally sat back down. Rube went about his business. Steven was determined to keep his watch. He held his father's hand and stroked his arm from time to time, all the while talking softly, encouraging his father to wake.

Steven refused to leave and join Rube for lunch, so Rube went alone and brought him back a sandwich when he returned. At a little after three, Steven turned the TV to a cartoon channel. His eyes were heavy and he was about to fall asleep when he noticed his father's eyes begin to move back and forth ever so slightly under his eyelids. Steve sat up. "Dad, Dad . . . it's me Steven. Are you awake? Rube, Rube, come look."

Before Rube could get there, John's eye's slowly opened a crack.

"Rube!" Steven shouted.

Rube came to the bedside. "Call your father, softly."

"Dad, Dad, can you hear me. Dad, look at me, over here."

They both stood over John, watching for any response. His eyes were open enough that Steven could see most of his pupils. They stared straight ahead.

"Dad——please——look, look over here?"

Gradually almost imperceptible at first, John's eyes looked at his son. Steven froze. Tears burst forth and ran down his cheeks. A tear formed in John's eyes and then they slowly closed.

"Did you see it? He looked at me. He looked at me.

Steven sat by his father's side the rest of the day. From time to time, he tried to get his father to open his eyes again, but was unsuccessful. He stayed on after Rube went home for the night, in case his father woke. Sometime after ten that night, Steven fell asleep in the chair.

*   *   *

It was dark again. John didn't like the dark. He remembered how happy he was seeing his son's beautiful face, radiant and full of joy. John again struggled to open his eyes. Slowly the dimly lit room came into focus. He had to concentrate to make his eyes turn to the left. There he was, his son, curled in a chair, half covered with a blanket. He tried with all his might to call out to him. To make a sound, any sound, anything to let him know he was awake.

The clock on the wall glowed softly, two-twenty. John smiled in his heart. His son was there with him. A peaceful joy came over him. He watched over him as the hours past.

*   *   *

Steven woke with a start to a noise.

"Have you been here all night?" Rube asked. His voice between a scold and concern.

Steve struggled to wake up. His body ached. He tried to blink away sleep when Rube turned on the overhead light. "I guess I fell asleep." He finally answered embarrassed. Suddenly he jumped to his feet. "Dad!"

John's eyes were open about halfway and focused on Steven. Rube came immediately to the opposite side of the bed.

"John, this is Rube. I'm your nurse. Can you hear me? If you can, I want you the blink your eyes once. Blink your eyes."

There was a moment hesitation and then his eyes slowly closed and opened. Steven stood trembling with tears dripping off his chin.

"John, listen to me." Rube continued speaking slowly. "Are you in pain? If you are in pain, I want you to blink once. If you are not in pain, I want you to blink twice."

John's eyes looked forward as if he was looking over his body. Steven held his breath. John's eyes closed and opened once, held steady a moment and finally blinked again.

Steven thru himself on his father, hugging him and crying, tangling himself in the ventilator hose.

"Easy Steven you don't want to hurt you dad."

Steven straightened back up and took his father's hand. John's eyes turned back to his son. He blinked once again on an otherwise blank face.

"Steven, listen to me. I know you won't want to do this right now, but I want you to go home, get cleaned up and have something to eat. You have been here over twenty-four hours."

Steven immediately began to protest.

"Steven, I will give you ten more minutes, and then I need some time alone with your father. I called Dr. Gupta yesterday and he will be here at ten. I need to get your father fed, bathed and ready. I need to run some tests as well."

"I won't be in the way."

"Please son, give us a little time. Dr. Gupta and I believe your father may be locked-in, has Locked-in Syndrome. Awake but unable to move. The sooner we know the better. Please, give us until at least ten-thirty."

Assured that his father was awake, Steven agreed, reluctantly.

CHAPTER 31

AWAKENING

EXT/INT.-MICHAELS BACKYARD-9:30 A.M.-March 30, 1999

Steven creeps across the patio, checking for any signs
of activity in the house. He cautiously approaches the
sliding glass door that leads to the family room. He
looks to see that there is no one inside. He enters and
scans the kitchen. Morning coffee has not yet been
brewed, it's a good sign that his mother isn't up. He
moves quickly and silently to his bedroom, where he
kicks off his shoes, slides off he pants and pulls his
tee shirt over his head. He stuffs his shirt and pants
in the hamper by the door, checks the hall then stops.
He turns and pulls the cover down on his bed and messes
it to look like he had slept in it. He goes to the
bathroom and shuts the door.

SOUND EFFECT: SHOWER

                                                    CUT TO:

STEVEN'S BEDROOM

Steven is in his underpants, a bath towel draped across
the foot of the bed. He puts on a fresh pair of jeans
and then pulls on a dark blue Star Wars tee shirt. He is
suddenly aware of another presence and turns to the
door.

Kathleen is standing in the bedroom doorway leaning
against the casing. She is in her nightgown and robe and
appears to have just crawled out of bed.

                        KATHLEEN
            What time did you get home?

"Ah — nine-thirty." Steven avoided eye contact with his mother.

"I didn't hear you come in."

So far, the lie seemed to be working. *Now don't blow it. Be cool.* "I didn't want to wake you."

"I left your dinner in the microwave. You didn't touch it."

"Oh, ah . . . I grabbed a burger."

"Are you heading back there today?"

"That's what I planned."

"Well I want you home by five for dinner, you understand?"

"Yes Mom."

"Is there anything happening? Any change?"

"No." *Another lie, it's getting easier.*

The coffee maker beeped. "My coffee is ready. Remember, five o'clock, or I'll have your hide." She grumbled and then headed for the kitchen.

Relieved that she was gone, Steven hurriedly put on his socks and shoes and made up his bed. He was hungry but didn't want to hang around long enough to eat, beside his mother was in the kitchen and she might have more questions. He checked his pockets, sufficient cash to buy a breakfast muffin on his way back to Southwood Manner.

He took a deep breath before leaving his room. He headed for the front door. Once out the door, he felt free, out of the cage. Before he pulled the door closed, he yelled, "Bye Mom, see you at five."

*   *   *

Dr. Gupta stood over John. He looked up and smiled when Steven entered the room. He had a warm smile. "You must be Steven, Pleased to meet you." The doctor reached out and the shook Steven's hand. His handshake was firm. He was a small man, impeccably dressed in a gray suit and in spite of his Indian appearance, spoke without a noticeable accent.

"How is he doing?" Steven asked.

"Well, very well."

It was obvious that he wasn't ready to say more. Steven looked at Rube and he nodded his acknowledgement of him. The doctor listened to John's abdomen with his stethoscope. "Fine, that's fine. Rube, I want you to start him on a saline nebulizer every four hour for now. Keep his feeding on the same schedule and slowly increase to fifteen-hundred calories a day, as he can tolerate it. That should be all."

Rube made notes in John's chart, while the doctor talked.

"Now young man will you come with me?" Dr. Gupta motioned toward the door.

Steven stepped backward out the door and then followed the doctor. The doctor didn't say anything until they reached the lobby and took a seat in the corner.

"I want to talk to you in private a moment before we talk in front of your father."

"Why, what's wrong?"

"I have good news, but it may not be exactly what you want to hear. You father is awake and aware of where he is and what has happened to him. But——your father cannot move. He is totally immobilized, except his eyes. He has what is called, Locked-in Syndrome."

Steven listened intently, but couldn't hold back his tears. His voice quivered when he spoke. "What does that mean?"

"Locked-in Syndrome is a relatively newly diagnosed disorder and not well understood. You father is awake but cannot move or communicate verbally, he is completely paralyzed in nearly all the voluntary muscles in his body apart from his eyes. It most often it is the result of a stroke or as with your father, traumatic brain injury to the base of the brain and brainstem. Unfortunately, patients rarely recover full mobility. That does not mean he can't live a long and productive life, with help."

Steven broke down. The doctor took hold of Steven's hand and comforted him. It took a long time for Steven to process his feelings and finally pull himself together.

"In the next few weeks I know you will have many questions. If Rube can't answer them, call me, if I am busy at the time, leave me a message and I will get back to you." He handed Steven his card with a phone number hand written. "It's my cell phone. It's important that you stay as positive as you possibly can when you are with you father. He is going to have many questions about what has happened to him and what is going to happen. Answer him as honestly and the best you can. If you have to cry, cry with him, there will be times when that's all anyone can do."

Steven stood. "Thank you doctor."

"It's going to get better. By the way, he is responding, he might be ready to come home in as little as a month or two. Rube and I know about your situation with your mother. Rube has a call into Zach. I think it would be best to wait and let Zach or Rube explained what is happening to your mother."

"Thanks again."

"You are a courageous young man. I have confidence in you. I'm going to have to leave. When you are ready, go to your father."

*   *   *

Steven sat alone in the lobby. He had lost all track of time. "How are you doing?" Rube asked. Steven hadn't notice his approach.

"Okay. How is he? Does he know?"

"Yes, Dr. Gupta explained it and I've been talking to him. We are not holding anything back. He wants to see you. Are you ready?"

"I think so." Steven stood and they walked back to John's room together. Steven stopped outside the door. "Have you talked to Zach?"

"Yes, he's very happy, but he is concerned about you. I told him you were doing okay. He wishes he could be here with you. He wants you to call him before you go home."

"I will."

Steven stepped inside John's room and stood a moment. When John looked up at him, Steven smiled. He went to the side of his father's bed, leaned over and gave his father a long hug.

"I was talking to your father about communication. We agreed that one blink is yes or true, two is no or false and moving his eyes from side to side is, I don't know or I don't understand. We also agreed that to communicate a word, he would spell it by someone reciting the alphabet slowly and he would shut his eyes when he got to the right letter. Letter by letter he would spell the word. He would prefer we asked good yes or no questions. Sort of a game of twenty questions"

"Oh, Dad I'm so glad you are awake."

John blinked once.

"Well, I guess one blink can mean, I agree, too." Rube said.

Steven laughed. "So then, two blinks will mean I disagree."

"John, I talked to Zach. He is spending Easter with his family in Phoenix and will not be home until Tuesday, unless you need him."

John agreed.

"He also said, he doesn't think anyone else should know about your waking or your condition, until he is back. He wants to talk to your Attorney Aaron Futter first."

John looked at Steven. "I agree with Zach."

John indicated he didn't understand, but finally agreed.

"Should I tell Katie or wait and let Zach tell her?" Steven asked

"Steven, you asked two questions?"

"Oh, right——well ah——should I tell Katie?"

John indicated no, and then rolled his eyes.

"I think your dad is kidding you about your double question."

Steven chuckled. He then sat quietly and just looked at his father. After a while, John slowly closed his eyes.

"It's been a big day. He is tired, let's let him rest. I think you should go home and get some rest too."

"You're right." Steven looked at his watch, four-thirty. *Where has the time gone?* "I promised mom I'd be home by five. I'll see you in the morning."

*   *   *

Steven was quiet during most of their dinner, but started teasing his sister when she said she wanted to color Easter eggs. After dinner, he and Katie did the dishes and chatted about Easter's past.

"I'm glad you are in a better mood this evening. Something you want to tell me about?" Kathleen questioned when she brought in her dirty coffee cup to the kitchen.

"No——nothing, nothing at all."

"I'm getting my hair done Thursday. I'm expecting you to take care of your sister."

"Thursday? All day?"

"Yes all day, and don't roll your eyes."

"Good, we can color Easter eggs. Mommy, can we go to the store tomorrow and get eggs and egg coloring dye."

"I don't see why not. Do you want to come shopping?"

"Ah——oh no, I've got plans."

*   *   *

That evening, while Katie and his mother watched TV, Steven searched the encyclopedia for information about Locked-in Syndrome, but found nothing. The next day he spent the day with Rube. He had hundreds of questions and Rube tried to answer them in front John. They agreed that if Steven had a question John would probably have the same.

Rube spent time planning John's therapy and setting goals. Their plans included getting John's bowels on a regular schedule, teach him to breathe without the ventilator, at least during the day and hopefully control urine flow. Rube couldn't assure them that these things were all possible. He cautioned the control or activation of involuntary muscles vary among Locked-in Syndrome patients. They agreed they should try.

Steven spent Thursday being a good brother and helping Katie color and decorate five dozen Easter eggs. After lunch, he took her to Southwood Manner where she sat in the bed next to her father and watched cartoons, and they all laughed.

Steven and Katie returned home at four o'clock and he put the casserole his mother had prepared the evening before, in the oven. She told them she would be home by five. Katie set the table and they waited for their mother to get home.

Kathleen pulled in forty-five minutes late. Both Katie and Steven helped bring in several bags of groceries. They waited dinner while Kathleen put away the perishables and quickly made a salad. It was seven o'clock when they finally sat down for dinner.

"I am planning Easter dinner at two o'clock." Kathleen looked at Steven. "I want you home and dressed in your Sunday best by noon. We are having a guest for dinner."

"Do we know them?" Katie asked.

"No, it's an old friend from Chicago."

Steven didn't look up. *No! She's got to be kidding.*

"His name is Scott, Scott Hanson."

Steven stared at his plate. He didn't want his mother to see his anger. He felt his face flush. For the next few minutes, he poked at the food on his plate and wondered what he should do.

"I want you to be on you best behavior. Steven, do you hear me?"

"What?"

"I said I want you to be on your best behavior."

"Oh——yeah."

"I'm not kidding. You act up and you will live to regret it."

"Excuse me." Steven took his plate to the kitchen, scraped it in the trash, put it in the dishwasher and went to his room.

He lay on his bed, his thoughts muddled. At first, he considered calling Zach, but ruled that out then. Suddenly he knew what he would do.

*   *   *

The next morning he went to Southwood Manner and told his father before Rube arrived. It was a struggle but John was able to communicate his decision. It wasn't what Steven wanted to hear. John wanted Steven to do nothing. Steven tried to argue, but found it useless. Sunday he was to be a perfect gentleman. John insisted that his son not do more than listen, learn what he could and be wise.

They also decided not to tell Rube and when he came in Steven tried to stay out of his way. After he finished his morning routine, Rube got himself a cup of coffee and Coke for Steven and sat down beside him.

"Okay you two, what's the secret, or aren't I suppose to know."

Steven looked at his father. "Is it all right to tell?"

John blinked his permission with a yes.

Steven took a deep breath. "Mom is having her boyfriend to dinner for Easter——at our house."

Rube stood and took Steven in his arms. Steven's body shook as he cried. Rube just held him and let him cry.

When Steven finally gained his composure, Rube sat him back in his chair. "So, what have you and your father decided to do about it."

"Dad doesn't want me to do anything. He wants me to go to dinner, be a gentleman and play dumb."

John instantly signaled, "No."

Steven chuckled slightly. "I added the dumb part."

"Well, I think your father is right. I know it's going to be difficult, but I'm sure you're man enough to handle it."

Steven sighed. He knew he was out gunned. He reached for the remote and flipped some channels, settling on an old movie.

Before lunch, Rube excused himself to run his usual errands. Steven knew the movie probably motivated him to leave. So John and Steven settled and watched TV for a while.

"Knock, knock, can I come in?" Alvin stood at the door grinning with a huge bouquet of flowers in his arms.

"Alvin, come in." Steven jumped up to greet him.

"Look who I met at the airport." Alvin pulled Tess into the room. She carried a potted Easter lily.

"Who are you sir." Tess teased. "Where is my nephew Stevie."

"It's me, Aunt Tess."

"No." She kissed him on the cheek. "You've grown up. My God, you're better looking than your father."

"Dad, look who's here——." Steven panicked. "I——I——."

"What's wrong Steven?" Alvin asked.

"I wasn't supposed to tell anybody."

Tess put the Easter lily on the table. "Tell us what?"

"Dad's awake."

"What." Alvin dropped his flowers. "When?"

"A couple of days ago."

"Why didn't you tell us?" Alvin rushed to the side of the bed. "How are you doing? Feeling okay buddy?"

"He can't talk. He can't move either. He can only communicate with his eyes, it's call Locked-in Syndrome."

"Well that's the shits."

Steven got the giggles. He tried to explain their eye language, giggling through most of it."

"It's charming." Tess said. "Imagine what a wonderful world it would be if all men could only communicate with their eyes."

That got both Steven and Alvin laughing.

"I heard the laughter down the hall." Rube said coming through the door. "I thought you must have found something really great on TV. Hi, I'm Rube, John's nurse."

"Hi, I'm Alvin and this is John's sister. Tess."

Rube filled them in on the details of John's condition. Alvin leaned over the bed and watched John's eyes every time he communicated. At times, he got within inches of his face, studying his eyes. He eventually asked John to make a series of eye movement.

"I can do it. It will take some time, but I can do it."

"What can you do?" Tess asked.

"Set up a computer and interface so John can operate a computer, communicate, write emails and even play games. You'd like that wouldn't you buddy? We got it in prototype already in our Seattle lab. I'll go up there next week and start putting it together."

The five sat around all afternoon and chatted. Every so often Alvin would go off on a tangent on how he could make something else work for John on the computer. The subject finally got around to Kathleen and Scott. Alvin and Tess had several ideas on how to deal with the situation, but none of them were legal. They eventually settled on the same answer John gave. Play it cool for now.

That afternoon, when things got quiet, John spelled out, "Thanks for laughs."

Alvin had to leave to catch up with his family for the Holiday. Assuring John before he left, he would be back for a visit before went back to Seattle. Tess planned to spend the weekend with friends in San Francisco and then on to LA for business. However, before she left she asked to be alone with John.

After that, she insisted on driving Steven home so she could say hello to Katie and drop off the Easter baskets she brought from New York. They included a Compaq MP3 player and color Game Boy for both Katie and Steven.

On Saturday, Steven tried again to change his father's mind and stay with him on Sunday or go to Alvin's, anywhere but home. He finally realized his father wisdom and accepted the challenge. "I guess I'm locked-in for Easter Dinner."

CHAPTER 32

THE EASTER GUEST

INT.-JOHN'S HOSPITAL ROOM-EASTER-APRIL 4, 1999

John is in a bright pajama top. The head of his bed is
elevated and pillows are behind his back propping him
halfway on his left side. There is an Easter lily on
the bed stand with a festive, 'Happy Easter', helium
balloon attached and several Easter cards stand around
the lily. The balloon floats inch from the ceiling.
There is a bouquet of mixed flowers on the end table
between the chairs. The blinds are wide open and sunlight streams into the room.

Steven sits on a chair close to the bed. He is wearing
a blue dress shirt, a little large for him and black
slacks that are about two inches to short making his
white socks obvious. He looks up at the clock anxiously. The time is eleven-fifteen.

STEVEN

I guess I have to be going soon. I
wish I could just stay here.

Steven looked up at his father, he rolled a sign he wants to communicate something. Steven stood and picked up the pad and pencil from
the nightstand and starts reciting the alphabet. "A, B——." John blinks.

"A, B, C, D, E——." He blinks again.

"B . . . E, be?" Steven asked.

"Yes." John confirms.

Steven and John continue the laborious process of spelling out the next word. When they got to the letters BRAV, Steven calls out, "brave?"

"Yes."

"Be brave." Steven read the words again and then put down the pad and kissed his father's cheek. "I will Dad, I will, Happy Easter."

*   *   *

Kathleen stopped Steven at the front door. "Is that what you're wearing?"

"Other than jeans and tees, these are the only things that fit."

She looked at his feet. "High waters . . . . Don't you at least have dark socks, and where did you get that shirt?" "Dad gave me the shirt. He said it was too small for him." Steven started to button the too large collar."

"No leave it open——I can't believe how much you've grown since Christmas. And what about dark socks."

"No dark socks."

"Well get some from your father's draw."

Steven started across the kitchen. "What's wrong, why are you walking like that?"

"My dress shoes hurt my feet, they're too small."

"Well, while you're in his closet, see it you can find a pair of father's shoes that will fit."

*   *   *

When Steven returned into the family room wearing his father's black shoes and socks, Kathleen was checking Katie's Easter dress, a soft yellow and white pastel floral. "Come here and let me see." Kathleen looked her son over from head to foot before stepping behind him. She tugged at the shoulders of his shirt to straighten it. "A couple of inches taller and put some meat on your butt and you'll be in your father's pants too."

"Are you going to see Dad today?"

"I hadn't planned on it."

"You haven't been there all week."

"I've been busy——and it's depressing——besides he doesn't even know I'm there."

"But he is——."

"Enough. I'll stop by next week, when you are back in school."

Angered by her attitude, Steven was still thankful she interrupted him before he said too much. He was about to go to his room, when the doorbell rang.

Kathleen stood tall, checked herself in the entry mirror and then turned to the kids and asked, "How do I look?

"You're beautiful mom." Katie answered.

Steven didn't say anything.

Kathleen glared at him, "Remember I expect you to be on your best behavior." She then turned to the door with a flourish.

Steven noticed she paused with her hand on the doorknob until there was a second ring before opening it.

"Hello, Hello." She quickly greeted the man at the door with a hug and a kiss on the cheek. "Come in, come in."

The man took off his wraparound sunglasses and stepped into the entry. He was a tall slender man. He wore a silvery gray suite that shimmered and an open collar dress shirt the same color as Steven's.

"This is my daughter Katie. Katie, this is Mr. Hanson."

"Hello Katie." He bent his knees so he was at her level and took both her hands in his. "Pleased to meet you. My, aren't you beautiful——like your mother."

Katie giggled and suddenly turned shy.

"And this is Steven, Mr. Hanson."

The man stood and stuck out his hand. It looked huge. Steven slowly raised his hand to shake it. The man grabbed Steven hand in a viselike grip. A pain shot up his arm and he tried to pull away. "Pleased to meet you Steven. You can call me Scott."

Steven's eyes began to water. He looked up at Scott's face. He had a ruddy complexioned and a large nose. Their eyes locked and Scott's thick lips turned up in a grin.

"I've heard a lot about you."

In agony, Steven fought not to show he was in pain. He tried to squeeze Scott hand back, but he was defiantly no match. Just when he thought, he couldn't possibly endure any more, Scott's grip tightened. Steven throat started to vibrate with a cry for mercy when Scott released his bone-crushing grasp. Pain continued to shoot up his arm and his hand throbbed

"You are quite the little man, but you need to work on the handshake." Scott looked up at Kathleen. "They're both on the quiet side."

"Oh, they will talk your ear off once they get to know you. Did you bring your things?"

"They're in the car."

Steven thought it would be a good time to slip away to his room, but just when he started down the hall, his mother grabbed the back of his shirt.

"Steven."

Caught, he turned around and looked at his mother. She still had hold of his shirt.

"Will you get Scott's things out of his car and take them to the guesthouse. The blue room is made up for him.

"Here's the keys——my suitcase is in the trunk—— it's got wheels." Scott made a lifting gesture.

Steven took the keys. He was pissed at the way Scott treated him and that he was staying in the guesthouse. *What would happen if I dropped his suitcase in the pool? He would probably deck you little man, wheels and all.*

*   *   *

Steven poked at his desert, some sort of a pudding his mother called a trifle, as Mr. Know-it-all, raved about how great it was as if he were starving. That was the way he was about the entire dinner. *I guess when you live out of a suitcase any home cooked meal tastes wonderful.* And talk, this guy never shuts-up. For the last three hours, he's bragged about how good a salesman he was, how many countries he'd been to, all the famous people he has met and how much money he made. Steven was sure that Scott never actually flew on Mick Jagger's private jet or played polo with Prince Charles as he claimed, yet his mother hung on his every word, or at least she appeared too.

Steven took a spoon of the pudding and looked at it. He was fed-up, with food and the big man. He hoped Scott would hurry and finish his epic story about selling mining equipment to some Maharaja in India, so he could be excused from the dinner table, when it happened. Kathleen excused Katie and him to clear the remaining dishes, while she and Scott finished the last of their wine. Finally, Kathleen came into the kitchen to check on their progress. Of course, Scott was on her heels. If there was one thing Steven was sure Scott knew nothing about, it was doing dishes.

"Do those last two pots and the roaster by hand and let them dry on the counter." Kathleen instructed. When you are done you can go play for a while, but remember there's school tomorrow." Then she turned to Scott and asked, "Honey, will you go fix us a brandy, while I fresh——."

Her eyes met Steven's. He felt himself flush. His mother stood stone faced. Scott silently departed to the bar in the family room. Steven turned his back on his mother and returned to washing the last of the dishes. Kathleen stood behind him a minute, he expected her to say something, but instead she hurried toward her bedroom.

Steven rinsed off the last of the pots, stacked them and drained the sink. His stomach churned. "How dare she?"

"Are we done?" Katie asked.

Steven didn't answer. He made it into the bathroom in time to spill the contents of his stomach in the toilet. He convulsed long after his stomach was empty. With his hollow insides finally calmed, he washed his face in cold water.

*　　*　　*

For several hours, Steven consoled himself in his father's office. He thought of calling Zach, but remembered his mother's threat and going to see his father was equally out of the question. He would be wise. He would, *be brave.*

The afternoon disappeared into darkness. Katie came to the office and sat with him for a while, she was bored with playing by herself and Scott monopolized the TV. At eight, she kissed her brother and hurried off to bed.

Around ten, the TV was turned off. Steven quickly turned out the desk light and was about to sneak across the hall to his bedroom. He paused and listened at the door to make sure the hall was clear when he heard the family room door open. Rushing back to the window, he saw his mother and Scott walk across the patio to the guesthouse. The light came on in the sitting area and then the bedroom.

About twenty minutes had past when the great room's lights went out. Steven waited and watched, expecting to see his mother return to the house, when she didn't he thought he would sneak out and see if he could see anything. He was no more than a few steps from the house when Amanda decided that he came to play with her. She ran to him and jumped up on him with a ball in her mouth. He could not dissuade her and every effort only excited her more. It was when she dropped her ball and let out a bark, he knew his attempt at spying with her as a partner, were useless. He quickly ushered her in the house and let her in Katie's room. Upon his return to the family room door, the bedroom lights were out.

Steven left the lamp in the family room on low and turned out the lights in rest of the house, before returning to his own room. Naïve as he was he knew enough to have a clear idea of what was going on in the guesthouse. Long into the night, his mind raced with images, a waking nightmare rolling repeatedly until finally in the small hours of the morning he surrendered to the solace of sleep.

*   *   *

Hunger woke Steven early. The sun was up but his alarm had thirty-five minute to go before it was to sound. He slid on a clean pair of jeans and a blue and red stripped t-shirt, paid his tribute to the bathroom and headed for the kitchen. With two pop-tarts and a large bowl of cereal under his belt, he ventured in to check on his mother. Her bedroom was room empty and bed not slept in, he knew where she had spent the night. He quietly slipped out the side door and to the backside of the guesthouse. Stealthily he worked his way around the side of the building and up to the bedroom window. He crouched and was about to peek in when an iron hard hand grabbed his right ear and ripped him to his feet.

"What do you think you are up to?" Scott asked. His hushed deep voice hissed from his thick lips only inches for Steven's other ear. Scott's hot, cigarette-smelling breath swirled around his face. Pain poured like molten lava down the side of his face.

In the searing agony, Steven couldn't talk.

"Spying on me and your dear Mother?"

Scott pulled up on Steven until he danced on his toes. He thought Scott would surly rip his ear from his head. Dangling Steven by the ear, Scott reached around with his left hand and grabbed Steven's crotch, squeezing his genitals in his vice like grip. The unexpected pain forced out what little breath he had left.

"If I ever catch you spying on us again I'm gonna have these little marbles of yours fed to the fish." Scott's slow deep voice growled in Steven's ear. "Do you understand? I'm from Chicago and I've got guys there that for a few fin will grab you when you least expect it. Take you over to Santa Cruz, rip these little jewels right off, and toss them in the ocean. Got it?" Scott increased his grip on Steven's genitals. "I asked — you got it?"

"Yes." Steven could barely squeak out the word.

"But they won't stop there. They will slice you up in little pieces and feed the rest of you to the fish too. They won't leave a trace, they are professional and you father's cop friends will never figure it out. You will have simply disappeared. Now, do you understand me boy."

"Yes."

"What's going on out here?" Kathleen asked from the bedroom.

Scott released Steven's crotch, quickly grabbed him around his chest, and then drug him toward the door.

"Look what I caught coming back from my run, a peeping Tom, or in this case a peeping Steven."

Steven struggled and Scott twisted his ear more. Steven let out a yell.

"We've been having a little talk about what happens to snoopy kid and snitches in Chicago. Now he wants to apologize. Don't you boy?"

Steven pushed back with his last once of defiance. Scott screwed his ear more. Excruciating pain forced him onto his knees. "Now apologize boy. Apologize to your mother for spying on her."

"I — I apologize."

"I said Apologize for spying and snitching." Scott was unmerciful.

Steven let out a yell of agony before he got out the words "I apologize — for spying and snitching." He begged for mercy. "Oh God help me Mom?"

"Why? You've been getting too smart for your own good lately."

Scott pushed Steven away and he collapsed into the flowerbed. Scott calmly walked Kathleen back into the guesthouse. His mother didn't even look back.

Steven lay among the shrubs in anguish for several minute. Using the wall for support, he struggled to his feed. Half staggering, half dragging himself to the house. Pain shot down his legs with each step. Several times, he thought he would pass out. In his bathroom mirror, he expected to see blood. His throbbing ear was bright red and swollen, but not bleeding. It felt like his ear was on fire. He splashed cold water on it, but the cold intensified the pain. He opened his pants and checked himself. There was no other visible damage or swelling, just pain. A kind of pain he had never before experienced. In his bedroom, he lay down. He had never been physically abused in his life, never as much as a spanking. Except the slap, his mother gave him for talking back. He felt humiliated, frightened, dirty and alone.

The alarm clock sounded. It was time to get up for school. He wondered if he could he make it?

CHAPTER 33

GREAT EXPECTATIONS

```
INT.-HALL OUTSIDE JOHN'S HOSPITAL ROOM-SAME DAY

Steven, coming from school with his backpack, stands
in the hall and examines his ear in a wall mirror. His
ear is distended and purple. He puts a baseball cap on
sideways, pulling the bill down to hide his ear as
much as possible. Steven walked slow, obviously in
some pain, enters the room.

CAMERA FOLLOWS STEVEN INTO JOHN'S ROOM

John is propped in his bed. Rube is preparing a feed-
ing bag for John's afternoon meal.

Steven drops this backpack in the first chair and
moves toward the corner chair. He tries to appear
happy. Rube continues his prep work.

                    STEVEN
      Hi Dad. Hi Rube, have a nice Easter?

                    RUBE
      I did, as a matter of fact, I did.
```

Steven sat in the corner chair with his bad ear turned toward the wall.

"I took my mother to Mass." Rube didn't look up from his work. "Then we all had a big family dinner at my sister's home, complete with egg hunt for the kids and all." Rube picked up the prep tray and turned. "How was yours?"

Steven didn't say anything. "You roll your eyes like your father. I know what it means, not so good." Rube proceeded to the same side of the bed that Steven is sitting and put the prep tray on the bed stand. "Excuse me——why are you sitting in the corner?"

"Am I in your way?"

"No, but you are usually bouncing around the room like a Ping-Pong ball."

Rube hung the food bag from a hook above the head of the bed and after cleaning and checking John's feeding tube, connected it. Once he seemed satisfied with the flow, he turned to Steven. Steven saw his curious look and averted his gaze. Rube gently lifted Steven hat.

"What happened?"

After trying out several excuses at school during the day, he finally settled on, "I got hit with a soccer ball this morning at PE."

"That must have been some soccer ball. Who kicked it, Rivaldo? Let me fix you an icepack." Without a moment's hesitation, Rube pulled an icepack from the refrigerator. Icepack ready in hand, Rube turned to give it to Steven, but looked at John and stopped. John indicated he wanted to say something. "Here you put this on your ear. Your dad has something to say, I'll get the note pad."

Steven slowly placed the icepack to his ear. It stung a little at first then soothed. Rube began the process of going through the alphabet. The first word was, SEE. "You want to see his ear?"

Steven stood and showed his father his ear. John rolled his eyes. Steven sat back down and put the icepack back on his ear. There was a long break after that. Steven sat with his icepack and held his father's hand with the other. The feeding bag emptied like an hourglass. Rube cleaned up and tucked the permanent tube under John's shirt. The time was approaching four-thirty and as much as he didn't want to go, Steven knew he had to get home.

Just as he stood, John started to roll his eyes again. "I think you father has something else to say."

The letters came slowly, READ GREATER EXPECTATIONS. That was all. "I think it *Great Expectations,* Dickens novel. He wants you to read it."

John spelt out GREATER again. "Greater, he wants you to read *Greater Expectation*." Rube said with a wink. "Here put some of this on your ear when you go to bed." Rube handed Steven a tube of ointment.

Steven kissed his dad's forehead. "I'll read it, now goodnight."

Steven turned and walked slowly out of the room. His genitals still pained when he walked. He tried not to show it, but Rube looked at him suspiciously. Once well down the hall he turned back, Rube was standing at the door watching him. He hurried on and around the corner, before stopping for a breather.

*　　*　　*

From the street corner, Steven could see that Scott's rental car was gone. Rather than coming in the back way, as usual Steven came in the front door, hoping to bypass his mother, but the minute he turned to go down the hall she came out of Katie's room. She looked up at him, a concerned look came to her face.

"Shit, did you go to see your dad looking like that?

"Yeah."

"Was Zach there? I bet you told them all what happen."

"No, Zach wasn't there and no. I told them that I got hit by a soccer ball in PE."

"Well keep to your story. I don't want you blabbing to Zach that Scott did it or that he spent the night. Scott wouldn't like it, and as you found out, he plays rough. And I assure you, he means what he said."

"I know." Steven headed to his room, but hesitated at the door. "Could you take me to the book store?"

"Not tonight, maybe tomorrow afternoon. Why?"

"I ah——I need to read a book for school."

*　　*　　*

The next day, when Steven got to his father's room, Zach was sitting by the bed. He stood the moment Steven entered. Immediately Steven realized that everyone was staring at his ear.

"How is it doing?" Rube asked, taking a closer look.

"Still sore but better——only hurts when you touch it." Steven leaned away.

"I won't." Rube raised his hands like a bank teller in and Old Western holdup.

Zach was the next to examine it close-up. "I won't touch it either. I just want to look. A soccer ball did that?" Zach looked at Steven suspiciously. "Your dad thinks Scott did that to you. Is he right?"

Steven looked at his father. He knew he couldn't hide anything from him. He felt tears well up in his eyes and fear in his chest. He didn't want that to happen.

"Will you men excuse me? I need to make some phone calls." Rube was gone before anyone could speak.

"Let's sit." Zach insisted. "Pull your chair so your dad can see you."

Steven pulled his chair to the foot of the bed and Zach moved his chair next to it.

"We know there is more to this then a bruised ear, for some reason you don't want to tell us. Rube said you walked like you were in pain yesterday. Did he hurt you somewhere else?"

Steven sat silently, occasionally glancing up at his father, but avoiding Zach scrutiny altogether. He was too embarrassed to tell them the rest.

"We know this is difficult for you, but we want to help. Did Scott threaten you? Did he threaten harm if you told us?"

"Yes. He said he would have me cut up and fed to the fish by his Chicago buddies, and nobody would ever know who did it."

"What aren't you to tell us?"

"Scott——." Steven remembered the feel of Scott's hands, hard with a grip like iron. He remembered the pain. He finally spit out the words. "Scott spent the night in the guesthouse. Mom spent it with him."

"Are you sure?"

"Absolutely."

'Is he there now?"

"No, he left yesterday."

"Does your mother know he did this to you?"

"Yes, see saw him. He made me get down on my knees in front of her and apologize for spying on her——them."

"Do you feel safe at home for now?"

"Yes. Mom said that she warned me. I got what I deserved. She's not mad at me anymore. I think it's okay. Just don't let her know, you know.

"I won't. If he comes back, stay away from him. You can come here at any time and can call me. How about your sister do you think she is in danger?"

"No. It was me they were mad at. I was spying on them."

"If at any time you think she is in danger bring her here too."

"I will."

Zach looked up at John. John spelled, BOOK, and gave a questioning sign.

"Dad wants to know if I read the book." Steven explained. "No, I didn't have time to get a copy yet.

"Book, what book."

"Dad wants me to read a book, 'Great Expectations.'"

John then spelt out MY BOOKS.

"Your books, is there's a copy in your office?"

John blinked yes, and then letters, ER.

"Yes Dad, Great — er."

*　　　*　　　*

Steven came in quietly through the family room door. Katie was watching TV. He glanced in the kitchen. "Where's mom?"

"She's in her bedroom."

"Oh—well I'm going to be in Dad's office if she is looking for me."

Katie nodded but didn't look up from the TV. On his way to the office, he dropped off his backpack in his bedroom. He began searching the shelves the moment he got in John's office. Many of the books were out of order after Conner search. Steven tried to put some of the books back in there proper places. Things like home repair mixed with law books. The classics that were once in their own section were now scattered among the various other books. Steven guessed that there were over two thousand books in his father's collection. *This might take a while.*

He still hadn't found it when Katie called him for dinner. They ate at the kitchen counter. Kathleen had heated prepackaged frozen lasagna and fixed a green salad. She seemed preoccupied, which pleased Steven. During dinner, Steven remembered that there was another bookcase full of books in the guesthouse. If he didn't find it in the office, he would search there next.

Once dinner was over, he resumed his hunt and in a short time found success. In the corner of a lower shelf, at the end of a collection of books on the Old West, the brown leather volume blended in so that he almost missed it. The small gold leaf letters read *Greater Expectations*, as his father had insisted and across the bottom, the name Michaels.

Steven carried the book reverently to the desk and opened the cover. On the flyleaf, he was surprised to find it inscribed, 'To Steven Michaels, may the joy of this day be forever in your heart. Love Granny'. Shocked at first, Steven soon realized the inscription was to his grandfather Steven. And that is was not a novel at all, but a diary.

He turned the page and began to read. 'July 15, 1963. Yesterday was my son John's Christening. The birth of my son was the greatest day of my life. I will never forget it. He is my joy and my life and truly my Greatest Expectation. My hope for him is that he will be whatever he chooses and to that end, I will try to provide all the building blocks I can. I will never fill him with falsehoods, but let him explore life unfettered. My Goal is to provide him the ~~money~~, the opportunities, love and freedom to be his own man and someday experience the joy of fatherhood, and if in his script, a son of his own.

'I am proud of my profession, but would hope John do more and be more.

'August 13, 1963, made an offer on a new home today. Excited, I believe this is a once in lifetime buy. Also opened a bank account in John's name, for his college education.

'September 1965, brought Theresa, named for her Granny, home from the hospital, mother and daughter doing fine. I was afraid I couldn't love a second child as much as I do John. I was wrong. I love my whole family'.

The rest of the page was blank and so was the next. From there on the writing was in his father's hand.

'Steven Michaels died June 12, 1977, killed in the line of duty.' Below that a broken heart was drawn.

On the next page, John told the story of how the spirit of his father visited him and told him about his death and that, 'What we learn and what we do with what we have in this life is the reason we live. On the other side we are spirit, on earth spirit and body unite. This is where we can experience love, joy and happiness.

'We come to experience good as well as, pain, grief, sorrow and death, that we may live. The sages of old called it the perfecting of the soul. Your pain and sorrow can destroy you or make you a better man. It's your choice. Embrace life, all of it, the good and the bad.'

John wrote that he questioned his father's spirit and about his own future, but he said he was not at liberty to tell him. He went on to tell him to get up and face life and all its challenges. 'Live each day as though it's the first and last day of your life'.

John also questioned his fathers' spirit about the pen, if it was from him. His father said, 'No it's not from me, its origin was unknown, but take good care of it. You will need it someday'.

Steven was so intent on his reading that he didn't hear Katie come in to tell him goodnight.

"Where is Mom?" Steven asked.

"In her room."

Steven walked his sister to her room, helped her in bed and kissed her. "Goodnight Sis."

"When will Daddy come home?"

"Soon, I believe he'll be home soon."

Steven went to the kitchen and got a soda, turned out the lights and returned to his father's office and his reading. John was much more faithful at making entries. He wrote about coping with his father death, school and his mother's death, that he studied in Europe a year and loaning Alvin money to start his computer game business. There was a gap between then and the next entry. It was in the fall of 1986. He wrote, 'November 4, 1986. Met a girl while studying in the library tonight. Wow'. He was apparently a senior at Stanford and he was really excited about this girl. And then again, he wrote, Saturday, 'Nov. 10, 1986. Kathleen spent the weekend, best sex ever, totally spent.'

For the next several pages, John wrote a series of poems extolling the glory of sex. It embarrassed Steven to think, his father would write such words about his mother. Then there were several short entries about his trip to Chicago and Kathleen's 'weird family', especially Jake. Then on March 11, 1987, he wrote. 'Kathleen announced she is pregnant. Bittersweet, not ready to be a father, hoped to wait a few years, but when you play with fire you sometimes get burned. Excited to be a father, feel betrayed, not sure, but think Kathleen had another man in our apartment. I was warned.'

There were references about going to Reno to get married, the remodeling of the house and some strange remarks about the cost of sex and love and the folly of youth.

Then on September 29, 1987, he wrote. 'Steven Seamus Michaels was born at 5:28 this morning, the greatest day of my life.'

Steven read well into the night. John included entries about getting a vasectomy because Kathleen not wanting more children. The furor when Kathleen still got pregnant. John expressed his joy over Katie's birth and the growing chasm between him and Kathleen, and his regrettable decision to staying with Kathleen for the sake of the kids. Steven didn't understand all the words his father used, but he got the meaning. Then there was a remark about Scott and Kathleen and that Scott was the other man from the beginning. Finally, the day after Christmas 1999, John wrote about his decision to file for divorce, quit the force and sit for the bar exam that coming February.

Steven closed the book, opened the desk draw, took out the fountain pen, and took them with him to his room. He pulled out his bottom dresser drawer and put them in his secret hiding place under the drawer for safekeeping.

CHAPTER 34

TIT FOR TAT

```
INT.-SOUTHWOOD MANOR LOBBY-AFTERNOON-APRIL 7, 1999

Steven enters the front doors and walk passed the
receptionist. She stops him.

                    RECEPTIONIST
          Steve, do you mind waiting a moment?

Steven stops. There is a look of concern on his face.
The receptionist picks up the phone and dials.

                    RECEPTIONIST
          (Into the phone) Steven's here.

                    STEVEN
          Is there something wrong?

                    RECEPTIONIST
          Rube will be with you shortly
```

Steven waits anxiously at the hall door. Rube came through the door and motioned toward the corner chairs. "Let's have a seat over here."

"Is there something wrong with Dad?"

Nothing serious, he just had a rough night and he is sleeping now. I didn't want to wake him."

"What happened, is he okay?"

"He is doing fine, just things caught up with him a bit last night. It started with an itch. He tried to communicate with the night nurse but couldn't and had a panic attack. It's not uncommon for someone in his condition. They called me in and I gave him a sedative. I stayed with him and he calmed down. Dr. Gupta was in this morning, they had a talk, and then I called Zach. He spent the morning and they talked for a long time. He is doing fine now, just sleeping, naturally. He hasn't needed any more sedative. I don't want to disturb him right now. I hope you understand."

"I think so."

"Zach said he would be back to talk to you. I expected him to arrive before you got here."

"Can I see him?"

"Just peek in." Before Steven could move, Rube put his hand on Steven's arm. "He hurt more than your ear, didn't he? He hurt you down there. I could tell it by the way you walked. Your father saw it too. You're still hurting. Do you need to see a doctor?"

"I don't think so. I'm feeling better."

"If you need too, Dr. Green is here. He'll be discreet."

"Thanks, but I'll be Okay. Can I see my dad now?"

"Go ahead, but don't wake him."

*   *   *

By the time, Steven returned to the waiting room Zach was sitting with Rube.

"Is he still asleep?" Rube asked.

"Yes." Steven wondered how much he told Zach.

"I'll wake him before I go home." Rube stood. "To make sure he doesn't need anything. That will give him two more hours. I'll go sit with him, let you guys talk out here."

Zach stood and gave Steven a hug before they sat.

"Your dad got feeling a little helpless, which is to be understood. He was frustrated about Scott being at the house. He was sure he did more than twist your ear and so do I. Rube told me. I'm sorry Son. We need to tell your father and that you are all right. Don't keep things from him. He's got a keen nose and can smell trouble. Keeping secrets will upset him."

"I understand. I was just too embarrassed. I won't do it again."

"Your dad wants me to tell your mom that he is awake. Do you want to be there?"

"I've got mixed feelings. It might be better if I'm not there, but I would like to be the one that tells Katie, if it's all right."

"I'll check with your mother. I asked her to meet me here tomorrow morning at ten."

"Uncle Zach, please don't say anything about my ear and——or that I said anything about Scott?"

"I won't for now, but your safety, is very much my concern and your father's too."

"I understand."

Steven sat silent a moment and then remembered. "I found the book. He was right. It was Greater Expectations. It's sort of Grandpa's and Dad's diary. I read it all last night. I learned a lot."

"Why don't you go on home and get some rest and be prepared to talk about it with your dad tomorrow."

"I will." Steven jumped to his feet and checked in a moment of pain then grabbed Zach and gave his a bear hug "I love you."

*   *   *

The next afternoon, Zach was sitting with John when Steven got there. "Hi, Dad, how are——." Steven caught himself and rephrased to a yes or no question. "Are you okay today?"

John blinked, "Yes."

"How did she do?" Steven asked Zach.

"Okay I think. I'm not sure she fully believes us. She seemed a bit skeptical. It'll have to sink in a bit."

"Something will have to sink in, someday."

"Aren't' you being a little hard on her, she is your mother."

"Well——." He put his hand to his ear without thinking. When he realized what he did, he grimaced.

*   *   *

Time has slipped by and Steven stayed later then had planned. It was a little after six when he came through the back gate. Amanda greeted him with a ball in her mouth. He tossed it across the patio and the two played catch for a few minutes. Steven entered the house quietly, he knew he was late for dinner and his mother would be irritated. Katie was watching TV alone in the family room.

"Where's Mom?"

Katie pointed to the bedroom. There was no sign of dinner waiting in the kitchen.

"Did you eat?"

Katie shook her head no.

Steven sat on the sofa next to her and she cuddled up to him. He wondered what was going on. It wasn't like his mother to ignore Katie, no matter how angry she got at him for being late. The two sat together in front of the TV for about twenty minutes before he gathered enough courage to check on his mother. He didn't have too. Moments before he got up, his mother came out of the bedroom with an empty wine glass in hand and went to the wine cooler. She pulled out a bottle of white wine and started to open it. She had some difficulty with the corkscrew, but eventually got the bottle open. Once open, she filled her glass, and took it and bottle back toward her bedroom. When she got almost to the door, she twisted back blurry eyed and glared. "Steven, you're in charge, if you two want dinner you're going to have to fix it yourself." She then staggered to her bedroom and closed the door.

She's drunk. He had seen her tipsy before, his father too, but never like that. He asked Katie what she wanted for dinner. She wanted cold cereal, the sweet chocolate kind. After they ate, Steven stayed with his sister in the family room. She watched TV and he did his homework. At bedtime, he tucked her in, and went on to bed to read.

A short time later, his mother came in. "How long have you known your father was conscious?" Some of her word slurred.

"Two weeks."

"Why didn't you tell me?"

"We didn't know at first because he didn't move and the we——."

"I am fed-up with all this we shit. All these damn secrets and sneaking around. Do you hear me? I don't know what the fuck you, Zach and you father are up too, but I'll find out. I will put a stop to it." She hung on the door casing. "Do you hear me?"

"There's nothing up. Dad showed signs of consciousness. It took time to diagnose. We——we didn't want to say anything until we knew for sure."

"There you go with the we, we, we again. You sound like a damn pig. Stop it. Locked-in Syndrome, bullshit. I've never heard of such a thing. I don't believe it. I think you bunch of pricks are trying to pull something on me."

"It's real, it——."

"Enough bullshit. You keep it up mister and you'll have more than a sore ear to whine about. Are you hearing me?"

"Yeah, I hear ya." *The neighbors too.*

She slammed the door.

*   *   *

On Friday, Steven stopped by to check on his father, but he was asleep, so he didn't stay. He decided not to say anything about what his mother said the night before to Rube, or anyone. That afternoon, his mother acted as if nothing had happened. He figured she didn't remember what she had said. He hoped that was the case, just the wine talking, however he was cautious with his words.

Saturday, he knew his mother wanted to do some shopping so Steven volunteered to take care of Katie. After she drove off, Steven walked Katie to Southwoods Manor. It was a beautiful morning. On their way, Steven began to explain their father's condition. That he was awake but couldn't move or talk, that he could only move his eyes and blink. He wasn't sure if she understood everything he was trying to tell her as she skipped along. She seemed to have withdrawn some into her make believe world since the shooting. Steve knew it was her way of coping.

At the Manor, she ran ahead to her father's room. Steven helped her lower the side rail and she climbed up onto the bed and peered at her face in front of her father's face, only inches away and stared into his eyes. Steven wasn't sure what she was looking for or expected to find.

"Yep." She said finally. "He's awake." And proceeded to crawl in to the crook of her father's arm and turned the TV to cartoons.

Steven left her there most of the day. She would tell her father things about school, home or Amanda during commercials. Steven had explained that one blink of Dad's eyes meant yes and two no. She thought it was a great game. Occasionally, she would get up close and look deep into his eyes, satisfied that he was still awake. It was a wonderful day for Steven. He was sure it was for his father and sister too.

*   *   *

Steven arrived on Sunday morning to find his father was asleep. Katie's visit tired him and he napped most of the day. He wanted to discuss his thoughts with his father but couldn't. He decided it was probably better to keep them to himself. To be content, for now, just to be close.

That afternoon Zach arrived. Not wanting to disturb John, they went out on the patio to talk. It was the first time that they had to discuss the diary. Zach knew of the diary, but never read it, so he could only answers questions about firsthand knowledge.

When John woke, they moved back inside. Zach made a comment to the fact that he wasn't sure that all of the reading was appropriate for Steven, especially that it contained graphic depictions of Kathleen and John's early relationship. Steven assured him that he was mature enough. Zach kidded back that, "I don't know if the Michaels men are ever mature enough, when it came to matters of sex."

Steven blushed, John rolled his eyes, and Zach just laughed.

"I can't help but wonder what your mother is up to." Zach finally admitted.

"What makes you think she is up to something?"

"I've known her too many years and seen her work."

*   *   *

Steven spent his afternoon with his father as usual and busied his evenings with homework to avoid his mother as much as possible, the days past quickly. To his knowledge, his mother never, went to visit his father. At home, Kathleen seemed preoccupied, spending a good deal of her time in her bedroom, often on the phone to Jean and Scott. If she thought Steven was within hearing, she got quiet and mysterious. Steven didn't care anymore.

Thursday afternoon, Steven arrived to find his father sitting in a wheelchair with Zach in a chair beside him. At first he stood speechless with his mouth open, and then yelled. "He's up, in a chair!"

"We've been working on this for several days." Rube explained. "A little at a time, he wanted to surprise you."

"And he's off the ventilator too. How——?"

"As long as he is positioned properly and we watch him, his diaphragm is able to work without it."

Steven bounded to his father and hugged him gently. "I'm so proud of you."

"And something else son." Zach paused and grinned. "Dr. Gupta thinks he could go home in a week or two."

"We will have to work out some details, but Zach thinks that the exercise room could be used as a bed room. It's already got a full bath with a walk-in shower that will accommodate a roll-in handicap chair,"

"And there's the therapy tub too." Zach added.

"Yes!" Steven gestured with excitement and then stopped. "Who will take care of him?"

"I will care for him during the day and we'll need attendants at night to monitor him, but since the exercise room is practically part of the master bedroom, Zach thinks that your mom could also monitor him at night."

There was a momentary silence. "Mom——?" Steven looked at Zach. "You have to be kidding?"

"You're right."

"She seemed to be having problems with him being conscious. I don't know how she would handle Dad coming home."

"Well Rube is willing to stay nights in the guesthouse. We'll just have to hire night attendants and a nurse to fill in on the weekends. She can't object to that. It's your father's house."

"You get to tell her." Steven said, pointing at Zach.

"I will call her now. Your dad wants to go home."

"John will be taken care of completely." Rube added. "She won't have to do anything."

Steven chuckled. "Do you think that will make her happy? She doesn't do anything now."

*   *   *

Zach arrived at the house at seven. Steven greeted him at the door. "She is in the living room. On the phone to Aunt Jean. It's the third time since I got home. She asked me if I knew about Dad coming home, I told her I found out today. She wanted to know what I thought about it. I said, I thought it would be great."

"I want you in on this."

Zach followed Steven into the family room. Kathleen quickly ended her call.

"Have a seat. Would you like a drink?"

"No thanks." Zach sat in a club chair across from the sofa and Steven settled on the footstool.

Kathleen looked at Steven. "I guess you know all about this." She took a sip of wine and put the glass back on the coffee table. "I have been thinking over your proposal and here are my terms. If I consent to John being brought home with the staffing and plan you put forward, I want my allowance to be increased to five thousand a month. In addition I want a fulltime housekeeper and a new car."

"I don't believe you are in the position to make such demands."

"Oh aren't I. Well, just let me tell you exactly what position I am in. Now that John is awake he is well within his rights to file for a divorce, but while adultery may still be grounds for divorce in some states, it is not a crime in California. However, since John is a total invalid, there is no way he can care for the children and I will demand full physical custody, understood?"

Zach's eyes darted to Steven and then back to Kathleen.

"Maybe you would like that drink now."

"I don't think so."

"Well, talk it over with John. Those are my terms. Oh yes, if I stay, I will be his wife in name only, since I have no other rights, I want independence. I want control of my life. To have the guests I want and entertain whom I please and not necessarily platonic. I am sure you both know what I mean."

CHAPTER 35

THE HOUSEGUEST

INT.-JOHN'S ROOM-2:30 P.M.-APRIL 30, 1999

The exercise room, off the master bedroom connected to John's bathroom and walk-in closet. It's a large airy room with big windows on one wall and double French doors on another, that open onto a terrace overlooking the backyard. The exercise equipment except for a treadmill had been removed, only it and the mirrored wall were left, a workstation with sink, under-counter refrigerator and overhead cabinets have been added. A hospital style bed has been moved in along with a nightstand, bed table, hoist, commode and wheelchair. There are two armchairs with a small low table between them in one corner and a small desk and chair.

Zach is checking on George, the handyman's work. He is installing a new locking doorknob on the mirrored door between John's exercise room and the master bedroom. Two movers finish assembling the bed. Zach signs for it and they leave.

> GEORGE
> There you go. Locks from the bedroom side and here are the keys, four alike just as you asked, keyed dif-ferently than the French doors. Seem strange though, she gonna lock her husband out of his bedroom.

                         ZACH
          She doesn't want the nursing staff
          having free run of the house when
          she's not home.

"I got the power and cable run for the TV up there in the corner. I'll pick up the bracket and mount the TV on Monday morning. Should be done by noon." George stepped to the French doors and looked out. "Sure is a beautiful place." He looked back at Zach. "The wheelchair ramps off the veranda are done, one to the front of the house and the other by the door to the family room. Seem strange that this part of the house is three feet higher."

"When John did the remodel and added this section he wanted a balcony, but this area was zoned for single-story only. Also the heating and air for the house and the pool heater and filters where on this side. So John had a basement dug for all of that and raised the floor for the bedroom and exercise room as high as he could without changing the roofline so he could have his balcony."

"I wondered about the basement, you don't see them much in this part of the country, Dandy wine cellar down there too, handy with the access off the kitchen. You know, those steps from the bedroom to the kitchen are wide enough that I could put a ramp that way. So they could roll the Mister right down into the kitchen, garage or rest of the house, but the Missis didn't take to that idea at all."

"No, she doesn't want the house to look like a converted convalescent hospital."

"I can see that." George stepped back inside. "They did a lot of entertaining."

"The wife has a big family."

"Sure is nice. Well. I'm done for now, see you Monday, and if you think of anything else that needs fixin' let me know."

"Thanks George, I sure will."

Zach watches George walk down the ramp, giving it one more inspection before he left. Zach looked in the bathroom. John's toiletries were still there. The large shower awaited and professional hydrotherapy tub that John had to have, but never used, stood ready. As if this day was planned. All of John's clothes were still in place in his walk-in closet, just as he left them. Zach turned out the light and closed the door.

Kathleen was standing at the bedroom doors. "I saw George leave. Those ramps don't look too grotesque, I guess." She checks the new lock on the door. "Good. Do you have the keys?"

Zach reached in his pocket and pulled out the keys. "Here, both keys as you requested."

She put out her hand and Zach dropped the two keys on her palm. She scrutinized them and then eyed Zach, before closing her fingers around them. Zach took an envelope from his day planner that was on the counter and handed it to Kathleen.

"The letter you requested, stating the agreement."

She grinned slightly and nodded. "Good."

She left without another word, closing the door behind her. He heard the click of lock.

Just then, he spotted Rube through the windows, coming up the ramp. He carried a large cardboard box. "The ramp looks great."

"George did a good job. You need any help with that?" Zach offered.

"No, but thanks, this is it for now."

Rube came in the open French doors and put the box on the new counter, then turned to observe the rest of the room. "I'm glad you left the treadmill, it'll help me keep in shape to run after John."

"Kathleen insisted it stay. She said she uses it."

"Good, she can visit with John while she exercises."

"Don't count on it. So, how is John, excited?"

"He can't wait. And you finding that used handicap-equipped van, what a gem. It would take months to get a new one equipped. He wants to come home in it."

"That's what I got it for. Give him a little freedom." Zach gestured to the room. "Well, what do you think, is it going to work?"

"We'll make it work. The linen service is meeting me here in an hour and by the end of the day, I will have everything ready for Monday morning."

"Here is the key to the house doors, I didn't tell Katheen I was give you them, and here's guesthouse key. You're in the left bedroom. And here's the——a key to——." Zach pointed to the new lock on the door between the rooms. Rube smiled. "In the event you need it."

*   *   *

Welcome Home balloons filled with helium bobbed, directing the way. Rube rolled John up the new ramp. Both Katie and Steven stayed home from school for the long awaited homecoming. Flowers and more balloons festooned John's new room.

John rolled his eyes to indicate how happy he was to be home. Rube turned the wheelchair around slowly so John could see everything. It was when Rube rolled him back outside where he could see his backyard and Amanda came to greet him that his eyes filled with tears. Just then, the phone rang and Kathleen quickly excused herself.

"I think we better think about getting you into bed." Rube finally said.

John blinked, "NO."

"Going to be argumentative now that you're home? All right, another fifteen minutes."

Steven and Katie stood on each side of John holding his hands. Zach walked back into John's room, he could hear Kathleen talking on the phone, but couldn't make out what she was saying and she shortly hung-up. He waited for her, but she didn't return. Curious, he stepped to the open door and looked into the bedroom. She had gone to another part of the house.

The kids and Zach stayed outside on the deck while Rube put John to bed. It took almost an hour to get him changed and settled in his new bed. In that time, Kathleen had not returned.

Zach was about to cross through the bedroom to the kitchen to see where Kathleen was, when he realized that it wasn't a good idea and went around outside and in through the open the family room door. She was sitting on the sofa, watching television.

"Knock, knock. Mind if I take the kids to dinner?" Zach asked.

"No, I don't mind."

"You are welcome to come."

"No thanks, I'm waiting for a call. Take your time."

*   *   *

After dinner, Katie had crawled in John's bed and Steven sat along-side, all watching TV together. Rube was pleased with the sight. "I will check back later. I'm going to get settled in."

"You are in the green room, on the left side." Katie instructed. "The other is for Mommy's friend."

"Thanks."

Rube had put his things in the guesthouse bedroom that morning. Now he had the time to unpack.

In setting up the agreement to take care of John at his home, Kathleen wanted a qualified caregiver on the premises at night if one was needed. Rube agreed to move into the guesthouse, subletting his own condominium. He would work a five-day week on a sort of split shift. Under Rube's direction, Zach hired a part-time registered nurse, Lam Huang, to work weekend days or if Rube needed time off. For nights, Zach hired two attendants, both men, both pre-med students. They would work rotated ten to six a.m. shifts.

Rube unpacked and put away his things and then checked out the great room of the guesthouse. The kitchenette was intended for guests to make coffee and snacks. Zach had made sure there was enough food for a few days, but after that, Rube would have to stock it himself. The cooking facilities were more than adequate for Rube, and he was pleased that there was a dishwasher. Zach told him it was unlikely Kathleen would welcome him at the dinner table. He didn't care, he wasn't any more found of her than she was of him.

Rube had time to kick back, relax and watch some TV. From the guesthouse, he had a full view of John's room and the rest of the backside of the house. At ten, he went back to the main house to orient the attendants. Both would work the first night.

Katie had already gone to bed, but Steven was still sitting with his father. Rube began their orientation.

*   *   *

Kathleen lay on her bed starring into the dark. It was after midnight and she still couldn't sleep. Four months had elapsed since the shooting, but it seemed so much longer. Even with the door closed and locked, she could hear the ventilator. Quietly, but constantly reminding her that man she called her husband was home again. It seemed to get louder. She began to imagine it was a voice, John's voice, saying slowly, *I hate you.* Repeatedly it spoke. *I hate you. I hate you.* With each cycle, it mocked her. Her nerves frayed. The time passed and she couldn't sleep. Finally, she got up. In the eerie glow of the security light, she stepped out on the deck and to the window of John's room. The attendants sat reading. Their light illuminated John's face softly. She studied it. It had changed little in their thirteen years of marriage. She remembered the first night they made love. Gradually the voice of the ventilator changed. *I love you. I love you.* It spoke. *I love you.* She was repulsed by the thought of crawling in his bed beside him now. She knew she never really loved him.

Suddenly he jerked. His breathing became erratic. The attendant sprang to their feet. One of the attendants suction his trach and in seconds John was breathing normally again.

She stepped away from the window, unseen. Back in her bed, she determined to ignore further noises from John's room. Before she willed herself to sleep, decided that tomorrow she would buy earplugs and get her doctor to write a prescription for sleeping pills.

By Friday, the routine set in. Kathleen made her adjustment and was sleeping through the night, with a little help from her wine, earplugs and pills. Rube had the weekend nurse come by and introduce herself. She was a tiny Vietnamese woman that lived a few blocks away. Kathleen was a little uneasy about the new nurse being on the premises for the weekend.

*   *   *

Friday night Steven and Katie stayed up to watch a rented movie on the family room VCR. They went on to bed and Kathleen stayed and watched TV until about eleven. She had checked the house and was preparing for bed when the phone rang. Her first though was it was Rube calling to check on her. She reluctantly picked up the phone.

"Hello sexy, what are you up to?"

"Scott, what——or should I ask, why are you still up?"

"I was thinking about you and that invitation."

"And that's keeping you up?"

"That you do baby, you keep me up. All the time."

"Oh Scott, you say the nicest things. So what about the invitation, you gonna do it?"

"Sooner than you think."

"I wish you were here now."

"That's why I called. I just got in from Australia, my flight got delayed and I missed my connection. I'm stuck here in San Francisco. Is the guesthouse available? I'm renting a car now. Be there in an hour."

"The guesthouse is sort of in use."

"John's home?"

"Yes, but I always have a place in my bed for you."

"Well keep it warm for me. I'm on my way."

"I will leave the front door unlocked. We don't want to disturb the rest of the house."

*   *   *

Kathleen slipped the phone back on her nightstand. She quietly glided to the changing room and donned her favorite negligée before going to the front door and unlocking it. She turned a lamp on low in the family room, got a bottle of Scott's favorite wine, two glasses and took then back to her bedroom.

She poured a generous glass, set it on her nightstand, and then put the other glass and the bottle on the opposite nightstand. She leaned back against several pillows, sipped her wine and awaited her houseguest.

She woke when she felt someone crawl into bed. She had dozed. The lights were out. She felt his warm body cuddle next to her. Her fingers ran down his bare chest. "Mm Scotty——what took so long?"

"How did you know it was me?"

"I would know you anywhere."

*   *   *

Kathleen woke to a sound coming from John's room. She looked at the clock, eight, time for Nurse Huang to start work. Scott was still asleep, a trail of his clothes were strewn from the bedroom door to his side of the bed. Her negligée tossed on the chair. She grinned impishly, pulled back the covers and began tickling his navel ever so lightly with the nail of her little finger. He stirred. She continued. He smiled. She made larger circle over his abs. His grin broadens.

"I'll give you all day to stop that."

"Do you think you are up to it?"

He rose up, leaned over and kissed her on the lips.

The bedroom door open and before Kathleen could say anything Steven came it. He was looking at the label on a bottle of laundry detergent.

"Mom, will this work——shit."

Steven froze wide-eyed. Kathleen saw him rapidly glance around the room then to John's door and back at Scott.

"Hey squirt——don't you know how to knock?" Scott rolled on his back. "You better get used to seeing me around. I'm moving in."

"Ah——." Steven back hastily out of the room.

CHAPTER 36

CUCKOLDED

```
EXT.-COFFEE SHOP RESTAURANT-11:30 AM-MAY 9, 1999

The restaurant is extremely busy with Mother's Day
Breakfast. He spots Rube's car pull in to a parking
place. Rube and Steven get out and start toward the
restaurant. Zach greets them, a concerned look on his
face.

                         ZACH
          Good morning, sorry I couldn't get
          back with you yesterday. We went to
          Tracy to visit Nadia's mother.

                         RUBE
          I understand. Man this place is buzz-
          ing this morning.

                         ZACH
          I reserved a table. They should call
          us any minute. What's so secretive
          that I couldn't just meet you at the
          house?
```

Rube glanced around and then at Steven. "Do you want to tell him or should I?"

"I will." Steven spoke up. He eyes down cast. He pushed a pebble off the sidewalk with his foot.

Zach looked at Rube. He stood silent. "What's wrong? Something with John?"

"No." Steven finally forced out the words. "Scott's moving in."

"What?"

Steven looked up at Zach. His once innocent blue eyes filled with hate. His face was as expressionless as his father's. "Scott, he is moving into our house. He is going to live there, with my mother."

"Ah shit! So that's what she was up to. Damn it, what wrong with that woman?"

Several of the people standing near looked at Zach, showing their displeasure at his language with all the children around. A little girl gigged nervously and a redheaded boy answered, "I don't know."

Zach quickly gained his composure and gave an embarrassed, apologetic grin to the small crowed around them. "I wish they'd hurry with that table." He muttered through tight lips. He felt as if someone just stuck a knife in his chest. He now understood Steven's pained look. Inconspicuously as possible, he slipped a nitro pill from his pocket, turned his back and popped it under is tongue. Then thought of what John must be going through.

Rube put his hand on Zach's Shoulder and asked, "Are you all right?"

Zach knew his action hadn't escaped Rube's sharp medical eye. "I'm okay, just wish I could sit down."

"Take some deep breaths." Rube said. He stepped between Zach and Steven at the same time took hold of Zach's wrist. Zach realized he was checking his pulse. "Why didn't you say something?"

"Just some angina, my doc says nothing serious. It's expected at seventy-one. Any more news to tell me?"

The hostess announced that their table was ready and they followed her to a booth. The restaurant swarmed with activity, but the service was quick. A cheery young waitress served them drinks and took their order. Throughout the wait, Steven didn't talk. During the few minutes Steven left to use the restroom, Rube told Zach about Steven walking in on his mother and Scott in bed. Zach just shook his head.

After the server brought their meals, it was apparent none of them had much of an appetite. Each just picked at their meals silently.

"I should have guessed that she was up to something when she started dictating her terms. Do you think your father knows?"

"I don't think so, the bedroom door was closed and he didn't give any indication he knew."

"I spent some time with him this morning, alone, in case he did want to communicate anything without Steven's presence." Rube added, "He didn't appear to know about Scott, but he did express his concern about Steven seeming stressed."

"Well he's going to find out sooner or later. Meanwhile, how are you doing Son?"

"Okay, I guess."

"Any ideas on what we should do?" Rube asked.

"I don't know if there is much, but I'll call Aaron this afternoon."

"What do we do with John?" Rube asked.

"He has to know immediately. I'll tell him, this afternoon. If that's all right with you Son?"

Steven nodded, yes.

"Can I get anything else for you gentleman?" The waitress asked, "More coffee?"

"I think we are all fine. Can we have our check?" Zach asked.

The waitress pulled the check from her apron pocket and placed it on the table. "You can pay up front."

Zach pulled some bills from his wallet, dropped it on the table and picked up the check. He was about to stand when he saw the hostess coming in their direction, she was followed by Kathleen and Scott. Kathleen paused at their table. "My, fancy meeting you gentleman here." She glared a moment, "Celebrating Mother's Day?" She added with a snicker, before they followed the hostess to their table.

*   *   *

They drove back to the house, Steven road with Zach. He took the opportunity to ask Steven in private, how he was doing. Shaken, he assured Zach he was doing okay. He just wanted some space. He knew they needed to be more concerned about his father.

Katie and Nurse Huang greeted them. Katie wanted to stay with her father instead of going to breakfast. Rube tactfully encouraged Katie to introduce Nurse Huang to Amanda, and escorted them to the patio.

Steven and Zach stood on each side of John's bed. John looked back and forth between the two, then rolled his eyes questioning and spelled out. "WHY SAD?"

Zach looked at Steven and took a deep breath. "I'm not going to beat about the bush, Kathleen has moved Scott in."

John look at Zach a moment then rolled his eyes confused. "IN?"

"Here, she moved him in here, your house." Zach's pain and desperation was apparent in his voice.

John turned his eyes to Steven. Steven's head was down but after the silence grew on, he looked up. Zach watched the unspoken communication, each comforting the other. Steven took his father's hand. In that solemn moment of father and son camaraderie, there were no tears.

John suddenly turned his eyes to Zach and spelt out, "NO ANGER, NOT WORTH IT."

"Oh Dad what are we going to do?"

"NOTHING NOW, I WILL THINK."

Steven leaned over and rested his cheek on his father's chest, hugging him. Zach knew how mush John wanted to hold his son. He remembered the love John had shared with his father Steve and now shared with his son.

John turned his eyes to Zach. 'SMILE, ALL SMILE.' And then he added, 'TELL KATIE.'

Katie, Rube and Nurse Huang came back in chattering about how smart Amanda was. Amanda pushed passed them before the door closed and ran to the bed. She put her front paws on the bed and started licking John's hand. Zach thought for a second that he saw John's finger move, as if he was trying to pet her. He knew that was impossible, just wishful thinking.

Zach asked Katie to help him take Amanda back to her kennel. Amanda jumped down and ran about enjoying the company. Zach sat on the corner of a lounge and told Katie that he had something to tell her.

"What is it Uncle Zach?"

"Well your mom's friend Scott, he is going to come and live here."

"Oh, that's okay. I saw him and Mommy getting ready to go out this morning, but I decided, he's not gonna be my Daddy." She looked at the family room door. "Can I go watch cartoons now?"

*   *   *

The overhead light clicked on in John's room startling him awake. Nine-thirty the clock read. *What's going on?* His eyes adjusted to the brightness.

"Hello John, did I wake you? You see, Kathleen's taking a bath, so I thought I'd give you a little visit." Scott stepped into John's view. He wore a white t-shirt and a pair of pajama bottoms, John recognized as his. "We haven't been introduced, but I feel I know you, like a brother. Through the years Kathleen has told me all about you."

Scott walked around the foot of the bed to the other side, staring at John's eyes. "Too bad about your little accident, it kind of puts you at a disadvantage. But hear Kathleen talk, you were at a disadvantage all along." He leaned forward looking closely into John's eyes. "I hope you're in there." His thick lips twisted into a sneering sort of smile. "I first learned about you when you were still a student at Stanford. Kathleen told me she picked you out to be her husband. 'Not too bad looking,' she said. 'Smart, with plenty of money and not much family,' she said. Did you know she did a background check on you as a part of her Criminal Investigation class? She had it all planned. Waited for you to show up for your usual Tuesday night study session at the library and flirt with you. Toyed with you, to get you hot and bothered before she invited you for coffee."

Scott suddenly jabbed two fingers in John's ribs. John's eyes slammed shut a moment from the pain. The ventilator paused and readjusted its rate. When he reopened his eyes, Scott was at the foot of the bed.

"So, you can feel . . . pain. Good" Scott looked around. "You need a bar in here." He moved close to John. "It was a setup you know. Inviting you back to her place for drinks, pretending her roommate was home. Then the next date, her friends showing up at the movies, and then after that her father showing up, it was all in her plan. She would get you so horny that when you finally got a little, you would think you were in love. Fool. Would you like a little spumoni, Mr. Gorgeous? Oh, that's right you can't swallow it, can you? Yeah, I know about that bite scar too and just how and when she gave it to you."

Scott walked back up the other side of the bed. John knew it would be another half-hour until the attendant got there. His only hope was

Rube would see the light on in his room and come investigate. Scott drew near again, John felt his hot breath against his face. He didn't fear him, but prepared himself for what might come next.

"She had it all planned except, getting pregnant. That she didn't plan. I was there the day she found out. She was thinking about an abortion. You know, she never wanted children. But, you caught wind that she might not be the most faithful wife. That's why she told you about being pregnant. To save her plans. Being pregnant was probably the only time she ever told you the truth. Sorry about my sloppy housekeeping that day. Knotty of me to drop that condom wrapper. If you didn't use the common kind you probably would've never known it wasn't yours."

Scott ferociously trusts his gathered fingers into the flaccid muscle of John's chest in the exact place where Kathleen had left her mark. John tried not to show any reaction.

"That's why she made you go for your little snip-snip. Thanks to you, she made me get one too. I should have done it years before. I wouldn't still be paying child support on my last couple of fuck-ups. Then when she got pregnant the second time she was furious. She would have terminated it, but Father Ryan got wind of it before she could, and stopped her."

Scott moved around the bed. His hands clenched and opened repeatedly. John was sure he was about to get more abusive. "I hear you haven't been much of a lover boy the past few years. Did it just dry up and fall off." Scott started to lift the covers. "I bet I——."

A light came on in the bedroom. Reflected in the mirrored door John could see Kathleen sit on her bed.

"Well isn't that interesting." Scott looked in the mirror. "A regular ringside seat. Regretfully we have to end this little chat. I'm wanted elsewhere. But I'll be right next door. Goodnight, Mr. Hoover. Ring-a-ding. Enjoy the view."

Scott turned off the overhead light on his way back into the bedroom, but left the door open at just the right angle. Obviously, Scott planed further humiliations. He pulled off his t-shirt and slid off his pajama bottoms before he crawled onto bed and snuggled up next to Kathleen. John didn't want to watch, but the rage building inside him forced his eyes open to see Kathleen reach up to turn off the light.

"Leave it on." Scott said.

"If you insist, you exhibitionist."

Scott laughed.

John could close his eye but not his ears. Their raucous lovemaking, clearly staged for his benefit, seared into his mind. The torture of the mind is greater than the destruction of the flesh. The cuckolding complete, the last splinter of love burned mercilessly from every fiber of his being. He pleaded to the Infinite, for the numbing of the mind, but it would not come.

They were still at it when the night attendant came on. He quickly went to the bedroom door. John knew he couldn't help but see the pair as he discreetly closed the door. John kept his eyes closed when the young man checked him. He heard his muttering something about it being a nutty place.

Through the night, John's anger built. The wheel of blame spun, its spokes, the memories of a lifetime. Images connected, fell apart and connected again. Every time more bizarrely. Pictures from the past mixed with nightmares and fears for his children. Anger ate at him, the cancer that eats a man's soul in little painful bites. There was no off switch to be found. Finally, his exhausted mind collapsed, only to wake sometime later, haunted by a new demon to torment him. Revenge, not the noblest of traits. It plagues even the lowest of beasts.

John woke in the early light to begin his plot. He decided he would destroy Scott and Kathleen and wreak his revenge. He thought of his guns locked in the gun safe in his closet, poison, setting fire to their bed, electrocution, the list grew. His thoughts of revenge had no reason or rational. *There has to be a way.* John made up his mind that he would find a suitable manner to dispense the justice they deserved. He told himself he had to be logical, go over every method of murder he ever studied. *By God, I'll find a way.*

*　　　*　　　*

Rube noticed that John's heart rate was elevated the moment he stepped through the door. Not high enough to set off the alarm, but definitely an indication he was stressed.

"Good morning John, how was your night?" Rube checked John's vitals. "Not as good as we would hope. Are you upset about something?"

"YES."

"Do you want to talk about it?"

"NO."

"Suit yourself. But if you don't calm down before breakfast I'm going to give you something to help you relax a bit." Rube went about his morning routine of getting him up. He was putting a shirt on John when Steven came in through the French doors. Rube finished buttoning John's shirt.

"Good morning Master Steven, on your way to school, running a little late?"

"Yeah, but I wanted to leave this with Dad." Steven moves to his father's bed. "I had a strange dream about it last night. I don't have time to tell you about it right now, but I remember reading in you diary, that you wrote that Grandpa told you, 'take care of it, you will need it someday'." Steven pulled the box with the fountain pen out of his backpack and put in on the bed stand in front of his father. "Here, I got ta go, see you after school." Steven hurried out the door and down the ramp.

Rube came over to the bed and could see John's eyes fixed on the box. John's heart rate, which had been lowering, jolted up on the monitor. Rube stood quietly a moment. John became teary-eyed. Slowly his heart rate lowered and he began to calm.

"Do you want me to open the box?"

"YES."

Rube opened the box carefully and looked at the striking pen inside. He slowly lifted the pen out of the box and laid it on the stand. "That's beautiful. My grandfather collected antique pens, but I've never seen one quite like that."

John' looked up at him and then back at the pen. Suddenly Rube spotted the slightest of tremor in John's right index finger. It was a wonderful sight, but Rube didn't bring it to John's attention just yet. He wanted to make sure it was what he thought and not an involuntary movement, before he got anyone's hopes too high.

"Would you like to hold it?"

"YES."

Rube placed the pen in John's hand and gently curled his index finger around it. John's eyes followed Rube's movements.

Rube stepped back and then went to his workstation to prepare a mild sedative. He administered it with John's morning feeding. John drifted off to sleep with the pen still in his hand.

CHAPTER 37

SILENT CACOPHONY

```
EST.-MICHAELS' PATIO-AFTERNOON-MAY 10, 1999

Zach, Rube and John in his wheel chair, are sitting
near the pool. Steven comes around the side of the
house and is pleased to see them. He approaches, drops
a backpack on the ground and pulls up a chair.

                    STEVEN
          What's going on?

                    ZACH
          Not much...how was school?
```

Steven shrugged, but didn't say anything. He looked up to the house. "He still here?"

"No." Rube answered. "He left for the airport about ten this morning."

Amanda ran up to Steven with her ball. He took it and threw it for her. She ran off after it and eventually returned. Steven threw it again in the opposite direction.

Zach felt the situation with Scott was really eating at Steven and John also. He knew something had to be done, and soon. "Not a very talkative bunch."

"Uncle Zach did you ever read Dad's diary?"

Zach glanced at John before answering. "No, he's never showed me what he's written, but I had read what his father had written, though it wasn't much."

"Dad did better." Steven reached out and took his father's hand. "Some of Dad's stuff gets quite personal. And kinda dirty in some places." He looked up at his father and laughed. "But it's one thing in the writing, that's confusing."

"Oh, well maybe I can help. At least I'll try."

"What was meant by the phrase, it's in the script?"

"Well, let me see, your grandfather Steve, talked about it a little when we were partners. I tried to explain it to you father right after he was killed, I don't know if I did a good job, but he never mentioned it again. He probably thought I was touched." Zach looked at John for a moment.

"You see your Grandpa Steve had a belief that before we are born, we choose the life we are going to live. That we come here to Earth, to experience something we can't in the spirit life. That our life and everything that happens to us here on Earth, is all written down in a scroll or script before we are born and it is kept on the other side, heaven."

"I've heard of that. I believe it's part of the Gnostic's beliefs." Rube added. "There is a church just up the street in Campbell, which teaches that philosophy."

"I don't think that Steve was connected with them, he was a Presbyterian, and maybe that's where he got some of his ideas about predestination. However, I think his Granny, his father's mother, had something to do with his beliefs too. She was kind of a psychic. I remember she made a pronouncement at the gathering after John's christening, that John had chosen a difficult life."

Zach looked over at John and took his other hand. Your dad didn't talk about it much, but every now and then, he would express the views. Do you remember any of this John?"

"YES."

"Steve's last words to me when he died, was to, 'tell John to remember the script.' I did that at his father's funeral, and again some months later. He was having a rough time. I think that's when his mother gave him Steve's diary. That's about all I can tell you." Zach looked at Steven. "Does that answer your question?"

"Kinda——. Has Dad's pen got anything to do with it?"

"Not that I know of, only thing I know about it, is that it showed up at his christening, but nobody knew who sent it. No one had any idea from where it came."

Steven knelt on one knee in front of his father and asked, "Is it all right if Uncle Zach reads your diary now?"

". . . YES."

Steven stood, opened his backpack and took the diary out. "Since I found it, I've not wanted to leave it where others could get their hands on it. Conner just about tore Dad's office apart looking for something. I think it might have been this."

"I'll read it and make sure I get it back to you." Zach took the diary, stood and looked toward the house. "Rube said your mom went grocery shopping, I'll go before she gets back."

Zach left. When he got in his pickup, he carefully placed the book on the seat beside him. "I've got to do something about Scott." He said, starting the engine. *Maybe I can just shoot the bastard and claim I thought he was an intruder.* Zach drove off deep in thought. Through his years of police work, he had seen cases of it several times. An unsuspecting husband comes home, discoveries his wife's lovers sneaking around and plugs the son-of-a-butch, no charges, just a man defending his home.

Maybe I can get them both. Say, I was visiting John one night, heard an odd noise coming from Kathleen's bedroom, saw a stranger, though he was attacking her and shot him, but the bullet went through him and got her too.

What a shame. I was just trying to protect her and the children, Your Honor.

Now how do I set it up? I can't tell John. Can't tell anybody. Got to keep silent about this.

*   *   *

"Hi guys." Alvin came in the side gate. He had walked from his home. "I waved at Zach at the corner, but he didn't even notice me. He looked as if he was a million miles away. Something wrong?"

Rube saw Steven glance at his father before turning to him. He knew he was elected to tell Alvin the latest.

"Scott's moved in."

Alvin looked at the guesthouse. "But you——."

"Into Kathleen's room." Rube added.

"Ah shit, what's next?"

"I don't think it can get much lower." Steven answered.

Alvin reached over, pulled Steven into his arms and held him. "We'll get this straightened out real quick. John buddy, how are you doing, okay?"

"YES."

Alvin let Steven go and sat in a chair next to John. "I wished I had better news, but the prototype is, well it's a prototype. It works, but it's not practical——yet." Maybe by the end of the month. Right now, it's too big and clunky. And damn temperamental, but that part fits your personality, right John?"

Steven knew Alvin was attempting a joke, but nobody laughed. Alvin lifted his eyebrows, quirked his mouth and sighed.

"Tracking eye moment is tricky." He continued. "The camera has to be aligned perfectly, attached to the head. It isn't uncomfortable and needs to be realigned every few minutes. Right now spelling out words as you are doing is faster. But we are getting close."

"Is there any other way?" Rube asked.

"Steven Hawking interfaces to his computer by twitching a muscle in his cheek. We are trying for an interface with the eyelid, but there is too much involuntary movement with the eyelids.

"Twitch, some kind of movement, you say? That's interesting." Rube looked at his watch. "It's getting late. I need to get John back to his room. Excuse us. It's been an interesting conversation."

*　　*　　*

John was back in his bed and Rube began to prepare John's evening feeding, while it was warming, he unlocked the meds drawer and looked at accumulating bottles of pills. Dr. Gupta had prescribed a number of sedatives and pain medication that could be injected or added to John's feedings but John needed fewer than anticipated, yet the prescriptions were on automatic refills and just kept coming. The bud of an idea entered his thoughts. Rube opened the second draw, the locked drawer with the vials of injectable sedative and narcotics. John rarely needed them but the doctor wanted them on hand just in case.

If he were to lace a bottle or two of wine with a hefty dose of sedative, it would knockout Kathleen and Scott. Then he could then inject Scott with a cocktail that would stop his heart. The coroner would think he just had a cardiac arrest. *Unfortunate guy, the cigarettes, booze and dope finally got to him.* Rube picked up a syringe. *I could stick Kathleen instead. Or just stick them both.* He put the syringe back, closed and locked the draw. *Now keep quiet and figure out the lethal combination that won't show up in their blood after they are dead.*

*   *   *

Steven walked Alvin home taking Amanda with them. By the time he returned and fed Amanda, his mother and Katie were back. During dinner, his thoughts were preoccupied. His mother talked and he half listened, only speaking to her when he had to. He only paid attention when his mother mentioned that Scott would he back Thursday and that she was picking him up at the airport, so he needed to get home right after school to watch Katie. The housekeeper refused to babysit.

Dinner ended uneventfully and the dishes were taken to the kitchen. Steven spent an hour on homework before going to tell his father goodnight. He circled around out the family room door and in the French doors. Cutting through the bedroom was forever off limits as far as he was concerned.

From the door to the bedroom, John appeared to be asleep. The night attendant would arrive shortly. So he didn't stay long, when he kissed his father's forehead goodnight, he noticed the fountain pen was on the bed table near the bed. He ran his fingertips over it and it felt warm. He recalled that it always felt warm to the touch. Suddenly everything became a bit eerie and he left the room quickly to the safety of his own bedroom.

Once in bed he began to think, was something he could do to get rid of Scott. At first, nothing logical occurred to him, but eventually he remembered an old movie where a son poisoned his stepfather to save his mother from an abusive situation. *Could that be the solution?* He thought about possibilities well into the night. He knew he didn't dare confide in anyone, but where would he find out about poisons. What kind he could use and where a twelve-year-old could get his hands on it.

The next morning he made a quick internet search that indicated pesticides were a ready source of poison in and around the home. He remembered the garden shed was full of all sorts of bottles and containers marked poison. When his mother went to pick up Scott on Thursday, he would slip the key out of the key box in the laundry room and check out the shed.

* * *

John woke about five that morning. He thought he heard a strange noise. Maybe it was the night attendant. He usually sat behind him reading and fighting sleep at this time in the morning. The room was quiet the only sound came from his ventilator, a sound now so familiar that he rarely paid any attention to it.

He thought of all the years that he was the protector. From the time of his father death, he checked the locks at night, secured the house, slept with an ear tuned to any strange sound in the night. *What worth was he now? Was there really a preordained plan for everyone's life? Was all this part of some mystical script? What a comedy. A few feet away in that closet are my guns. I could end this whole thing with Scott and Kathleen in seconds, but I can't reach them, can't even pull the damn trigger.*

In a shaft of light coming from the attendant's reading light, he could see the pen on the bed stand. It appeared luminous in the darkness. He wanted to hold it in his hand. With every fiber of his being, he wanted to touch it.

He lay in the dark, the ventilator mocking him until sleep returned.

* * *

Punctual as always Rube's greeting woke John. His eyes fluttered against the light. "How was your night?" He asked, starting his morning routine.

Rube came into focus when he took the monitor clip from John's left index finger and hung the cord over the side of the bed. *Crappy as usual, but what good is to complain?*

"Wonderful as always?" Rube picked up the washbasin he prepared and brought it to the bed table. He gave John a strange look. "Have you been writing letters last night?"

John followed Rube's gaze. The pen was laying by his hand.

"It must have fallen off your bed stand."

*   *   *

Thursday afternoon Steven hurried home, waving to Rube through the window. He checked in on Katie and then hurried to the laundry to grab the garden shed key. The shed door creaked when he opened it. It had been sometime since it was visited by anyone. He stood a moment to let his eyes adjust to the dim light. Obvious immediately was that nearly all the bottle, bag and containers, from rose dust to snail bait carried the labeled, poison. Then in the dim light he made out the shape of his father old VW in the corner. He forgot it was even there. *Maybe someday I could fix it up and drive it. Dad could help.*

Then he remembered why he was there. He quickly scanned the selves for the most potent poison. One small bottle caught his attention. The label was faded and hard to read, so he carefully lifted the bottle for a closer look.

"What are you doing?" Rube asked.

The bottle slipped from Steven's hand, crashed to the floor, and burst, spattering his pants and filling the shed with a foul odor, forcing him to back out the shed door.

"I——I was looking for something for ants. I've got ants in my room."

Rube reached in, garbed a container, and backed out quickly. "What a stink. Here, try this, it's ant pounder. Use it sparingly or you'll be sleeping in the guesthouse with me. It says odorless but it's not, none are."

"Thanks, I'll clean it up."

"We'll leave it for a few days, for the smell to dissipate and then I'll have George take care of it, he'll know how to do it safely. Right now you better get in and take a shower."

"Okay, thanks."

Steven locked the shed and returned the key. He knew now that garden pesticide wouldn't work because of the smell. He stripped to his underpants and put his clothes in the washing machine, turned it on and added a double measure of detergent.

After a long shower, he thought he could still smell insecticide on him. Dressed, and doused with aftershave, he went to John's office. The internet had led him to the pesticides and insecticides and that turned out a bust so he would try another source. Although he had never seen one, he thought that there might be a book on poisons among his father's books. The search began.

*   *   *

Scott drove the Michaels' silver Ford SUV. Kathleen, in the passenger's seat, she had picked Scott up at the San Jose airport, a much more convenient airport, especially for domestic flights. Scott had emptied out his small apartment in Chicago, retuning his rented furniture and dumping the rest, bringing only his clothes and necessities. Kathleen knew he always lived a minimal lifestyle but not that transient. All of his belongings, four suitcases and a dozen boxes, fit in the back of the SUV.

Almost overshooting the driveway, Scott pulled to an abrupt stop before hitting the garage door. "Not used to the size of this thing. I usually drive smaller cars, when I drive."

"Well you better get used to it. You're not driving my new Beamer."

Scott opened the SUV's door and glanced over at Kathleen. "Steven over his pout, or his he still pissed?"

"Still a little pissed I think. Sort of been getting the silent treatment from him all week. All of them have been pretty quiet."

"Isn't that too bad." Scott said sarcastically. He stepped out, opened the hatchback, and pulled out the smallest of the four suitcases, before grabbing two heavy coats and a briefcase off the back seat. He followed Kathleen to the front door.

"Steven," Kathleen called opening the door.

"Yes Mom." He met them in the hall.

"Will you help unload the SUV?"

"Yeah." He was less than enthusiastic in his response.

Scott started toward the bedroom while Kathleen put her purse on the entry table.

*   *   *

Steven came in with a box under his arm and dragged a heavy suitcase that didn't have wheels. "Take them to my bedroom."

He stopped and scowled at his mother.

"He is putting his clothes in my closet. I don't think you father wants to share."

"What's that smell?" Scott stopped and looked at Steven.

"I don't know." Kathleen sniffed about trying to find the source. "It smells like bad perfume mix with fingernail polish remover."

"I used some aftershave when I got out of the shower." Steven said and started towards his mother's bedroom.

Kathleen looked at Scott and shook her head. "Don't drink it, whatever you do."

Katie brought in a shaving kit and small suitcase, proud of her effort. Scott chattered on about his customer base having shifted to the West Coast and Pacific Rim and it being more convenient to live in California then in Chicago while he and Steven unloaded the rest of the SUV. Kathleen noticed that Scott was trying to engage Steven in conversation, but try as he might, he couldn't get a word out of Steven. Everything from the SUV was now in the bedroom. Steven turned to leave when Scott pulled a bottle of men's cologne out of his shaving kit.

"Hey squirt, try this next time, that stuff you're wearing would repel a skunk."

Scott tossed the bottle to Steven. He muttered a thanks and left.

Scott and Kathleen spent the next few hours unpacking. As it got late, Scott offered to take everyone to dinner, but Steven declined, saying he had lots of homework to do. Kathleen glared at Steven. When Scott and Katie were out of the door, she grabbed his arm.

"I expect a real attitude adjustment out of you young man by the time we get home. I've had enough of your moping and this silent shit. Do you hear me? Or you'll get more than a sore ear to be pissy about. I'll really give you something to really mope about."

CHAPTER 38

THE CROSSING POINT

```
INT.-JOHN'S BEDROOM-8:30 AM - MAY 17, 1999

Rube is well into his morning routine. John is sitting
on the commode and Rube is making up John's bed. Rube
finished up with John, the camera sifts to the bedroom
door that opens slowly and quietly Scott steps into
the doorway and stands.

The cameras pulls back to reveal Rube lifting John
back in bed.

                    SCOTT
          Pretty strong there. I thought you
          had a hoist for that.

                    RUBE
          We do but it's mush faster this way
          at least for me.
```

Scott leaned against the doorframe. "How do you know when he needs to take a shit? Does he tell you?"

"In John's situation, we set up a routine. The involuntary systems work with little input from the brain. So when I sit him on the commode nature takes its course. It doesn't mean we don't have accidents, but we are doing quite well."

"Oh, well good. My guess his shit dose stink." Scott reached for a cigarette and prepared to light it.

"I'm going to ask you not to smoke in here. We have oxygen tanks and cigarettes could blow the place up. You probably shouldn't smoke in the bedroom next door either, especially if the door is open."

"Yeah, and smoking's not good for me either."

"I didn't say that."

Scott grunted and started to leave. "I almost forgot. Kathleen wanted me to tell you she'll be driving me to the airport, SFO, she'll be gone for a few hours, in case she's not back before the kids get home. I've got to make a sales pitch in Brazil. See you all next week." He left shutting the door.

"Jerk, as if anyone cares." Rube grumbled to himself. He heard the lock click on the bedroom door.

"Well after that wonderful visit from the nice man, are you ready for a yummy breakfast?" Rube hung the feeding bag and started to connect it. "Let's see, blueberry pancakes with maple syrup. Would you like an egg with that sir?"

John rolled his eyes.

Rube got the pen out of the nightstand, placed in on the bed table, and pulled up a chair.

"While you enjoy that great breakfast I spent so much time preparing, we need to talk. I have noticed something over the last several days. When I've place this pen on the table I've seen a tremor in your right index finger. I'm convinced it was more than a spontaneous twitch. Have you felt anything?"

"NO." John blinked.

"Well, I want you to concentrate on moving your finger." John focused he eyes on his finger. "Now try to move it, try to move your index finger."

Both men sat fixed on John's finger, but after several minutes, there was no movement. "Don't get discouraged, keep trying." The feeding bag emptied, but there was still no movement in his finger. "You keep trying." Rube disconnected the bag and cleaned up the sink. When he returned to John's bedside, he saw a tear forming in the corner of John's eye.

"Stop——I want you to stop trying to move your finger. I want you to look at the pen instead of your finger." He moved the bed table so the pen was directly in front of John, close to his chest. "Now, look at the pen.

Forget about your hand and your finger. Just concentrate on the pen. Think about only the pen. Think about how it felt in your hand. Remember the other day when you held it. Remember how it feels, its weight, its shape in your hand. Now think about writing with it. Think of it as an extension of your finger, your hand, your mind. Now remember when you used it and wrote in your diary. See it in your mind, and extension of your finger. See the book, Greater Expectations. Think John——think——. Now slowly look at your hand."

John's eyes focused on his hand. "See what is happening, it's moving, your finger is moving. Small ups and downs. See it. Now write a circle."

Both men stared at John's finger. It moved up and down several more time and stopped. Rube held his breath. Then it happened. John made a small circle with his finger.

"Yes!" Rube yelled and began dancing around the room shouting, "Yes." He started singing, "Johnny's making circle."

*   *   *

John spent most of the day practicing his circles. By afternoon Rube was pleased to see his progress and determination. Katie and Steven came through the side gate together. Steven stopped by Katie's school, only a few blocks out of his way, to walk her home. They seemed to Rube to spend more time together when Scott was around.

"Hey kids, your mom's not home. She took Scott to the airport."

"Good," Katie said and started to walk off.

"Wait a minute. Come in here, your dad wants to show you something."

Rube had Katie and Steven stand by the bed and instructed them to watch John's hand. At first nothing happened then slowly after a couple of twitches, John started making his circles.

"Oh Dad that's neat." Steven cheered and then hugged his father.

Katie got excited too, but Rube suspected it was more from Steven and his excitement than understanding her father's achievement.

*   *   *

John woke. It was one-thirty-five. He hated the night and the way the clock mocked him, slowly ticking away the hours. It was when he felt most alone, most vulnerable, most helpless. He knew that only a few feet away, behind the screen a nurses-aid sat, reading or watching TV, but it might as well be another world if he needed them for something.

He turned his attention to his hand. He had spent much of the day repeating his exercise. Up, down and round and round he wrote his little circles on his bed sheet. First one way and then the other, he was gaining control of his finger. It helped him from thinking of other things. He felt the sheet under his fingertip slip by with each circle.

John noticed that before Scott had left on his latest trip, he had been paying more attention to him. Checking in on him several times a day, he probably hoped to find him alone or dead. While thinking about Scott, John realizes his finger was moving differently. He barely could see it at first, moving forward and back, forward and back, in his anger he had replace the image of the pen with an image of his gun, and he was squeezing the trigger. *If I had my gun. The next time that ugly bastard pokes his head through the door. I'll blow it off. That's it——that's it. Now, how to get my guns?*

*   *   *

It had been a pleasant week-and-a-half with Scott away. Rube called Alvin with the news. He let out such a yell on the other end of the phone that hurt Rube's ear. With John moving a finger, Alvin now had something to work with. He would bring a new computer and interface when he flew down Friday. They decided to make it a surprise and not tell John until he got there.

Scott's return earlier that Wednesday morning quickly brought back the clouds. He and Kathleen decided to celebrate with dinner and a mid-week movie. Before they left for the evening, Kathleen ordered in a pizza for Steven and Katie's dinner, which went largely untouched.

After dinner, John demonstrated his steady progress of his finger movements.

Katie, watching her father, asked. "Why don't you tie a pencil on his finger and let him write what he wants to say?"

Steven looked at his dad and then at Ruby. "Great idea. But instead of a pencil and string, I'll call Alvin about a computer interface, first thing after breakfast. I mean if that's all right with you Dad."

"YES."

Steven and Katie grabbed hands and started dancing around the room.

"Wait a minute." Rube interrupted. "I've already called Alvin a week ago. He has been working on the interface. He'll bring it here Friday. We were going to keep it a secret until he got here.

*   *   *

Later that evening Steven was in John's study. He had found an older book on household poisons that had belonged to his grandmother. He didn't recognize the names of lot of the products, but found antifreeze interesting. At around eight, the phone rang and he answered it.

"Hello, Steven? This is Uncle Jake, is your mother there?"

"No, she went to the movies."

"Alone?"

"No, she went with Scott."

"Oh . . . ah is he from around there?"

"No, he's one of your people from Chicago."

"From Chicago . . . ? It isn't Scott Hanson, is it?"

"Yes, do you know him?"

"Unfortunately. Is he visiting?"

"No, he lives here now."

"Does he live near you guys?"

"No, he lives here, in our house." There was a long silence on the other end of the phone. "Hello, Uncle Jake, are you still there?"

"Yeah Son, I'm still here. When did this happen? When did he move in? Is he staying in the guesthouse?"

"He moved in Mother's Day weekend——he's sleeping in Mom's bedroom."

"Oh for Christ sake——. Are you and your sister all right? I guess your dad knows. I'm sorry Son."

"We are all okay Uncle Jake, but I don't know when they'll be home, I'll tell Mom you called."

"No! Don't Son. Don't tell them I called. I will call her at another time. So don't tell her I called or that I know about Scott. Now you take care, okay, and don't tell anyone I called. Okay?"

"Okay"

"Good night Son, and remember not a word to anyone."

"Goodnight Uncle Jake." Steven hung up the phone slowly. *Why is he so suddenly concerned about Katie and me?*

*   *   *

Kathleen sat quietly on the family room sofa. It was Friday, the second day Scott was out shopping, for himself. She knew he liked to dress nice, but not that he was quite so self-centered. Insisting he had no casual wear for California.

She took a sip of wine when the phone rang. She was expecting Scott when she answered. "Hello dear, get home I'm missing you."

"You are? That's nice."

"Ryan? Why are you calling?"

"Dear sister, you should get caller ID. And as for why I am calling, your greeting spoke quite eloquently."

"Zach, that son-of-bitch, did he call you?"

"He did not. No one called me. Jake told me——. I suspected something was up when Jean got back and did her imitation of a clam. Sis what can I say."

"Nothing——say nothing."

"You know I can't do that. For your children's sake, for John's sake and most of all your own sake, I must speak."

"The kids forsook me when they went to Zach. John forsook me when he drew up the divorce papers. What I am doing now, is for my sake."

"What you are doing is an abomination before God."

"I don't give a damn. It's my life, and what I do is not yours, not the kid's, Zack's, Jake's, Conner's or Jean's and it certainly not God's business."

"Please Kathleen listen to me, what you are doing is wrong."

"I'm not going to listen to you. Goodbye." Kathleen poked the off button and threw the phone across the room.

Within seconds, the phone started to ring. Scott came through the door on the second ring. He looked at Kathleen and the phone on the floor. It rang again. "Don't answer it." She said.

He stood in the entry. On the fifth ring, the answering machine on the kitchen counter clicked on with its generic greeting.

"Kathleen," Ryan's voice came from the recorder, "for the love of God Kath——."

Kathleen pulled the plug on the answering machine. She calmly re-filled her glass. The phone in the bedroom and office, still connected, began to ring. "Want a glass of wine?" She asked Scott. The phone continued to ring.

"Sure." He dropped his armload of bags on a chair and joined her in the kitchen. They lifted their glasses and clicked them. "What are we toasting?" The phone finally stopped ringing.

"Ryan."

"I gather Ryan's not happy about something." Scott went back into the family room and picked up one of his bags. "Let me show you what I got."

"Bring them in the bedroom."

*　　　*　　　*

Rube followed Alvin through the French doors. Both men had their arms full of boxes. "Wait until you see what I've got for you. I've been putting this together since Rube called last week."

"Did I hear the house phone ring? Isn't Kathleen in there?"

"YES." John's blinked.

Rube went to the phone and checked, "There's a dial tone." He looked at John and shrugged his shoulders. "Oh well, that's her business, I'm not supposed to answer it anyway. I'll get the last of the stuff Alvin, you can get started."

It was dark, when Alvin finally declared he was ready for a test run. Rube and Steven had made a run for pizza around six while Katie stayed with Alvin. Kathleen and Scott drove off soon after the kids got home. Saying only that they were going out and there was stuff for dinner in the refrigerator.

Alvin powered up the new computer and waited for it to boot. Katie and Steven sat on the floor beside Rube. The three munching pizza, drinking soda and watching Alvin, as transfixed as if they were watching a 'B' movie, where the mad scientist was about to bring his creature to life. It made a couple of odd sounds. Between each dialog box, that read either to WAIT or NEXT, Alvin typed on the keys. He was so busy he hardly noticed the intensity of his audience.

He had tried to explain during the assembly and boot up that John's finger movement on a touch pad would control this computer. "Unlike the previous idea, that would have tried to read John's eye movement. John could use the computer to do anything a normal computer could do and more. This computer will convert finger movement into synthesized speech, similar to the one Stephen Hawking used. You will be talking like a genius as soon as I get the interface to recognize your finger movements."

At around nine, Steven saw Katie to bed. Mike the night attendant came on at ten. He was curious about what Alvin was doing. By eleven, Alvin had no more success than a few occasional signals from the pad. Steven excused himself and went to bed. Alvin worked on for another two hours, until Rube convinced him it would be better to start fresh in the morning. Alvin called it a night and Rube walked him to his car. Just as he was pulling away from the house, an SUV came weaving down the street. Alvin pulled to the right to give the driver a wide berth. When the vehicle slowed to turn in the driveway, Rube realized it was Scott and Kathleen.

*   *   *

Alvin worked all Saturday trying to attune John's finger movement to the computer. By midafternoon, they had only minimal success. Rube finally suggested that Alvin give John a rest.

Rube and Alvin sat on the patio near the guesthouse, had a soda, and enjoyed the sun. Alvin was tired, but determined to make it work.

"I don't understand the problem." Rube admitted. "He was doing so well moving his finger, even spelling out words."

"I see two problems, one is the movement is weak, but when I turn up the sensitivity the other problem is the movements aren't consistent enough for the computer to recognize."

"You know, when I first saw he was getting movement in his finger, I tried to have him repeat the movement while we watch. He couldn't. I had him visualize moving his finger as if he was writing with his old fountain pen. That's when he was successful. Wait a minute, it was the pen, when I put the old fountain pen in front of him, that when he started controlling his finger."

Alvin Jumped to his feet. "It's worth a try. I'll get a stylus"

"Wait. It only worked with the fountain pen."

"Where's the pen?"

"In his room."

*   *   *

Within less than hour, John had mastered, yes, no and maybe, along with single words and simple sentences. He also was able to navigate into other parts of the computer and use the pen like a mouse or to type words. Alvin tried a stylus, but John could only make the pen work.

Alvin had Rube gather the kids and Nurse Huang at the foot of John's bed.

"Hello . . . everyone . . . how . . . are . . . you?" John's synthesized voice came through the computer's speakers. Gee Dad, it's like it said in the diary, the pen did come in handy for something.

"We did it guys. I'm going home to crash. You keep playing with it. It will get easier and you'll get faster. I have some things I need to do in the morning, but I'll be back tomorrow afternoon to check on your progress."

*   *   *

John spent hours that evening working with the computer. Even after Rube checked in on him at nine, he was still at it.

"You are going to wear it out." Rube joked.

"Then . . . I . . . get . . . new . . . one." John said back in his synthesized voice.

"If it makes you happy, get a dozen."

"I . . . might. Goodnight . . . Rube."

"Goodnight John."

*   *   *

John played with the computer until he fell asleep. The next morning he made a list of the things he needed or wanted done. When Steven came to visit his father, John put him to work. He had Steven adjust the computer monitor, higher, lower, right, left, this way and that, until he was satisfied with the position. Then he had Steven mark each joint, screw and knob, even spotting the floor for where the wheels of the computer stand and the bed stood, so if either moved he could have it quickly put back into their exact positions. Steven was in his glory along with John. Together they work with Velcro strips to more a comfortable attachment for the pen to John's finger.

John was busy telling Nurse Huang what to do, until she threatened to unplug his computer. He hoped she was kidding. She acted as if she was happy to be able to do things the way John wanted. John never hesitated to tell her how grateful he was for all her work.

By afternoon, John was beginning to slow in his demands. He finally admitted he was tired and wanted a nap before Alvin arrived. Both Nurse Huang and Steven seemed pleased. Nurse Huang darkened the room. John put the computer in sleep mode, but refused to give up his pen.

*   *   *

John sensed a presence in the room. He opened his eyes enough to get a peek. If it were Scott or Kathleen, he would pretend to be sleep. Gathered at the foot of the bed were Katie, Rube, Alvin Zach and Steven. When he opened his eyes fully, they smiled. John woke his computer and asked with his mechanical voice, "Why . . . the . . . shit . . . eating . . . grins?"

Nobody said a word, but slowly stepped aside to reveal a gleaming powered wheelchair with a big red ribbon tied on it. Alvin sat in it and leaned back, with his hands on the armrest. Suddenly the wheelchair started to move. Using just the tip of his right index finger, he made several complete turns in the middle of the room then headed out the door. Whizzing around the side of the building, he spun around, came back in, and right up to John's bed.

"Your chariot is ready." Alvin looked at him and beamed. "It had its own computer and the same interface as other computer. You like it?"

"Holy . . . gees . . . I . . . love . . . it."

CHAPTER 39

COCKTAILS IN THE MORNING

EXT.-TENNIS COURT MICHAELS' HOME-JUNE 7, 1999

John is learning to use his new wheelchair with Alvin
coaching. Rube is standing back. There is a line of
small orange cones across the court. John starts to
maneuver the wheelchair between the cones, but runs
over the third cone. Amanda is jumping joyously around
John.

                    ALVIN
          Come on Andretti, you can do better
          than that. You're forgetting every-
          thing you learned yesterday.

                    JOHN'S SYNTHESIZED VOICE
          Fuck . . . you. Get . . . out . . .
          of . . . my . . . way.

Alvin sat up the cone as John got ready to try the course again.

"The next thing you know he will want to play soccer." Rube shouted.

"Great . . . Father's . . . Day . . . in . . . two . . . weeks. The . . . kids . . . and . . . me. Against . . . you . . . Ruby . . . Zach . . . and . . . the . . . dog."

"Well I'm out of here." Rube said. "I've got work to do. I can't stay out here and play all day."

Alvin saw John stop and his eyes follow Rube walking to the house. "Great . . . guy."

"He sure is, you were lucky to find him."

Lucky? Yeah . . . I . . . am . . . lucky.

The house phone rings. Alvin looked then remembered that Kathleen was home.

"Too ... early ... for ... Scott."

"Where is he this week?"

"Jap ... an."

*   *   *

Kathleen picked up at the beginning of the fourth ring. "Hello."

"I thought you might be out, or just not answering your phone."

"It depends on who you represent today." Kathleen stepped out the patio door and sat in the first chair.

"I represent myself and no one else. I may not understand completely. But I neither condemn nor commend."

"Well Sis, at least you are not like the others. I can't believe Jake would stab me in the back." She watched John make it through the slalom course without knocking over a cone.

"I thought you might like to talk about it."

"It?"

"I didn't mean to sound that way. I just thought you might like an ear to bend."

"Yeah, thanks for thinking of me." Kathleen sees Alvin sit on the court beside John's wheelchair.

*   *   *

Alvin sat near John watching Kathleen on the phone and then asked, "Are you all right with this situation?"

No ... hard ... to ... talk ... before. Don't ... know ... how ... I ... feel. Some ... days ... want ... to ... kill ... them. Other ... days ... I ... wish ... they ... would ... just ... go ... away.

"Zach said that Kathleen threatened to take the kids."

*   *   *

"The marriage is over, was over for a long time. You know, Scott and I go way back, but ... we both agree he's not the marrying kind. He even admits it, sometimes."

"I thought you were thinking of something like this when you called in March and ask if you had an Ace in the hole."

Kathleen watched John and Alvin out of the corner of her eye. "I'm afraid my Ace is slipping away."

*   *   *

"Now ... I ... have ... hope."

Alvin looked up at John. His paralyzed body hadn't changed nor was there any transformation to his expressionless face, only his eyes seemed a bit brighter, but there was an invisible energy radiating from his very being. The two men sat quiet in the morning sun.

Alvin's attention snapped back to the present when he heard Kathleen close the slider behind her after going into the house.

John watched Alvin glare.

"I wish I could fix it. I wish I had an answer. It's harder than hell to sit here and see the crap they are pulling."

"You ... have ... giving ... me ... answer. I'll ... fix ... now."

"Care to elaborate?"

"Can't ... yet.

"Well I've got some more work to do. I'm going to dump all your files off your office computer onto your new one. I will also link the video feed from the security cameras, you can think about adding a few more cameras. Inside too."

"I ... see ... enough."

"I bet you do." Alvin stood. "You want to stay out here?"

"Yes ... here."

"Okay, stay. I'll tell Rube." Alvin took a step and then stopped." Is your password on the office computer still the same?"

*   *   *

John maneuvered his wheelchair near the pool in the sun. Amanda settled on a spot nearby in the shade. When he heard movement, he turned his chair around. George was doing something with the skimmer on the spa. George agreed to work three days a week, keeping up with the grounds and tending to the many odd jobs that John was coming up with constantly.

John's mind began to put together an idea. He had fantasized eliminating Scott even before he was shot. Since he had moved in, the fantasy has become a necessity. *If I can move the pen, I can squeeze the trigger. It's getting to a gun.*

John was deep in thought when George dropped a tool. He looked up at John and smiled.

"George ... please ... come ... here."

"Yes John. It's sure is good to see you up and about. What can I do for you?"

"I ... want ... you ... to ... get ... one ... of ... my ... guns ... for ... me."

"Yes Sir, no problem."

"You ... know ... where ... my ... gun ... safe ... is?"

"Yes, in your closet."

"Yes ... the ... combination ... is ... 4 ... right ... 11 ... left ... 63 ... right."

"Got it." George wrote it on his note pad he always carried in his shirt pocket.

"I ... want ... the ... Glock ... and ... a ... full ... clip.

George continued to write. "That's the small one?"

"Yes ... Don't ... tell ... anyone. Don't ... let ... anyone ... see ... you. No ... hurry ... when ... you ... get ... a ... chance."

Yes Sir, Mr. Michaels. He slipped the note pad in his pocket and smiled. "I'll do what you ask, today if I can."

John watched George go on about his business. At last, he had a plan. *Good thing I didn't tell Zach about Scott's ongoing night visit. Let him think it has past. Now I can finally take care of it.*

*   *   *

At noon, Rube insisted that John come in out of the sun. He put him in his bed and fed him his noon nourishment. "You don't want to get a sun burn. You will have a real itch you can't scratch."

John watched with anticipation as Alvin moved the computer monitor into place and put the tough pad under his hand. John had kept the pen in his hand when Rube transferred him into bed.

"You've learned to grip the pen darn well with one finger." Rube noted. "You have some real motivation."

"I've put on all your programs and transferred your files. It might take some experimentation to learn how to interface with some of the software, but everything should work with your pad. The surveillance icon will take you to the security camera feed. And you're connected to the internet through high-speed DSL instead of a phone modem. You are wired to the World."

"Thanks . . . Alvin . . . you'll . . . never . . . know . . . what . . . this . . . means."

"Don't mention it buddy. Now I've to run. I have to catch a plane for Seattle."

*   *   *

Steven slipped quietly in the front door, dropped off his books in his bedroom and went out the patio door. George was finishing vacuuming the pool. He looked up when Steven approached. He finished reconnecting the automatic sweeper. "Hi, the monthly maintenance is done, the pools ready for summer. Last week of school, I bet you're glad."

"Yeah, sort of."

"That new wheelchair of your father's is a humdinger. It even talks. He was out here most of the morning running around with it."

"Great. Ah George, where's the best place to buy antifreeze?"

"Auto store, of course. But not much need for antifreeze around here, especially this time of year." George answered with a chuckle.

"Ah — well you can use it in summer as a coolant."

"Yep, you got me. Any particular brand you looking for?"

"What do you use?"

"Whatever's on sale, but you won't find sales this time of year. I try to get a 50-50, it's usually the best deal."

"Thanks."

"And, stay away from the ethylene glycol, it's poisonous. Check the labels. You want to get propylene glycol instead."

"Thanks for the information, I didn't know that."

Steven went back in the house and to John's study. On the computer monitor was a note from Alvin, telling him that he copied his father's file to his new computer and that the computer was now hooked-up via router to high-speed internet. That he didn't need dialup, just click on internet icon. He did and typed in ethylene glycol.

Thanks George, I might have made a big mistake.

*   *   *

In no time, John had navigated to the word processing program and started a document to Aaron. Asking him, with his new mobility and ability to communicate, if he should go ahead and file for divorce, and would he be able to keep Steven and Katy.

By the time Zach arrived that afternoon, he had a three-page document full of what if questions and a list of all the things he could now do.

John lay patently, watching and waiting while Zach read the printout. Some of Zach's facial expression amused John. When he read, John tried to guess where he was in the document.

Zach lowered the papers and smiled at John. "You ought to be a lawyer."

"Maybe . . . I . . . will." John's synthesized voice came louder than he expected. He quickly turned down the volume.

"If you have questions I certainly don't have the answers. I will call Aaron in the morning and set up a meeting. Shall we invite him here?"

"No . . . way . . . I . . . will . . . go . . . to . . . him."

"That would be a great start. So you have been a busy boy today and Alvin has got you all hook up?"

"To . . . the . . . world."

Then email this to Aaron so he will have it before we meet."

George rapped lightly on the French door then came in with his tool bucket and stepladder. "I've come to fix that light in your walk-in, if I'm not interrupting anything."

"No, go ahead" Zach spoke up, then turned to John and laughed. "I got use to answering for you."

"That . . . is . . . fine."

George disappeared into the closet and pulled the door closed.

"Where is Steven, he is usually home from school by now?"

"Don't . . . know . . . haven't . . . seen . . . him . . . today."

"He's been kind of quiet lately, sort of preoccupied." Zach said.

"If you gentlemen will excuse me." Rube stood at the bed with a feeding bag. "I'll plug John into his dinner."

"Fine." John and Zach answered, simultaneously.

A few minutes later George came out of the closet. "There, I have that problem you asked me to take care of fixed. I'll see you in the morning, with the results, if that will be all right?"

"That . . . would . . . be . . . fine."

"How are we doing with George?" John watched Zach eye George suspiciously. He can only give us three days a week, but if you need more help, I'll try to find someone else.

"George . . . is . . . O . . .K."

*   *   *

The next morning, George found reasons to visit John three times, but each time Rube was with him. Shortly after eleven, Rube put John back in bed and prepared to make his weekly run for supplies and meds.

"I'll be back in an hour, I've told Kathleen and also George is around." Rube looked at John's monitor and saw that the security feed was on. "Now you can keep a watch on all the comings and goings. Certainly beats old movies on TCM."

Rube was gone about five minutes, before George came in. He moved quickly to the right side of John's bed, took the gun out of his tool bucket, and held it up for John to see.

John nodded. He saw it was loaded and the safety was on. "Pull . . . the . . . clip . . . and . . . check . . . that . . . it's . . . unloaded. You . . . know . . . how."

"Yes." George quickly did what John instructed, even pointing the gun at the ceiling and pulling the trigger. It snapped a metallic sound.

"Good. Now . . . put . . . it . . . in . . . my . . . hand."

George took the pen out of John's hand and moved his hand off the touch pad. He took another cautious look around. Then he placed the Glock, carefully in John's hand. John slipped his finger in front of the trigger. The gun was stable in his hand. It felt good. For years now, the mandatory time he spent at the range meant little. An obligation of the job, but today he felt the rush of holding a weapon again. The feel he felt when his father first took him to the range and taught him to fire his service revolver.

He took a deep breath and tried to hold it, fighting against the ventilator. For a moment he was afraid he wouldn't have the strength to pull the trigger? He wondered. He concentrated not on the gun in his hand, but an imaginary image of Scott, half-dressed, standing in the dim glow of the nightlights, at the foot of his bed. There was a long hushed pause.

Snap, the empty gun responded. George cocked it and John fired the empty gun again. He continued to fire it repeatedly with George's help.

"I know what you are thinkin'." George said quietly. "Self-defense, a man's got to protect himself and his children."

John practiced pulling the trigger several more minutes, but was unable to raise the muzzle. He had George fold a small towel and put it under his hand aiming the gun to a man's mid-chest. Snap. *It will work.*

"Got him in the heart. Always shoot for the heart." George coached.

They spent a few more minutes practicing and then George replaced the gun with the pen and touch pad. "Where do you want me to put it?"

"In . . . my . . . nightstand."

"Do you want it loaded?"

"You . . . can . . . but . . . want . . . to . . . practice . . . more."

"I understand, I'll help you practice every chance I get."

"Thanks."

John saw a movement on the monitor. It was Steven entering the front door, with his backpack and a large bag."

*   *   *

Steven hurried down the hall to his bedroom, dropping his backpack on his bed and set the bag with a gallon of antifreeze on the floor. He knew Rube was out, but still made a quick check of the house. He spotted George out the kitchen window. He was pushing a wheelbarrow past the guesthouse. *Safe.*

Opening the refrigerator, he pulled out the four bottles of sports drink that Scott had put there last weekend, knowing nobody else in the house would touch the stuff. Steven hurried to his bathroom. Put the bottles on the sink. Turned on the hot water, and rushed back to his bedroom to grab the antifreeze and his pocketknife.

With everything assembled, he began by filling the sink with enough hot water to cover the caps of the inverted bottles. Carefully, he used the knifepoint to coax the caps off the bottles without breaking the seal. He managed to get the caps off three of the four bottles without breaking a seal. He would put the one with the cracked seal in the back of the refrigerator, if Scott got that far, he thought, it wouldn't matter.

The next step was simple. Fill the bottles without spilling any on the labels. A funnel would have helped, but he didn't have time to look for one. He filled the first bottle halfway. The fluorescent green liquid looked close to the color of the sports drink. Now Steven took a deep breath, stuck his finger in the gallon jug, and wet it. Hesitantly he put his finger to his mouth. *The decisive moment.* He tasted the antifreeze and it was sweet, just as he had read, almost too sweet, but should work. With a swirl of the bottle, he checked the look of the liquid. It was a little thicker than the sport drink. *Should he dilute it and loose potency or chance that on his morning run, Scott wouldn't notice?* He decided on going with the liquid as it came from the jug.

When he finished, he carefully placed the four bottles back in the refrigerator exactly as he found them, making sure the lid he messed up was in the back. On his return to the bathroom, he heard a car in the driveway. He grabbed the jug and his pocketknife and darted to his bedroom. The door to his room accidently slammed, the same time his mother and Katie came through the front door.

*   *   *

"Steven was that you? What were you up too?"

Before Steven had to answer, the phone started ringing. Kathleen picked it up in the kitchen.

"Hello." Kathleen put her purse and a small bag on the counter.

"Hello, Mrs. Michaels?"

"Yes." At that moment, Kathleen spotted a jar of mustard, pickles and a carton of milk on the counter beside the refrigerator.

I'm calling from Mr. Futter's office. Mr. James left a message. He asked that he and Mr. Michaels could meet with Mr. Futter, on an urgent matter. I've tried to reach Mr. James unsuccessfully. Regretfully Mr. Futter will be out of town until next Wednesday. Will you give you husband the message and have him or Mr. James call me. I have an opening that Wednesday morning."

"I will give them the message."

"Thanks."

Kathleen held the phone to her ear after Aaron secretary hung-up. She wondered why John and Zach needed to see their attorney so urgently. The phone started beeping in her ear and she hung up.

She wrote down the message and then started for Steven's room, to find out what he was doing, thinking he was supposed to be in school.

*   *   *

John was distressed when Rube got back. He sent him to find out where Steven was. It was so unlike him not to check-in with him first thing when he got home. He also wondered why he was home in the middle of the day.

Rube was only gone a couple of minutes when he and Steven came through the French doors.

"I had minimum day today. And, tomorrow too, it the last day of school, you know." There was a bit of frustration in his voice.

"Sorry. Saw . . . you . . . come . . . home. Thought . . . something . . . wrong."

Steven leaned over and hugged his father. John was not altogether convinced that Steven wasn't trying to hide something. After all, he had been mysteriously quiet all week.

"Good afternoon everybody, it is sure a beautiful day." Zach's arrival changed the mood. "Are you still writing legal briefs today?"

"No . . . not . . . today."

"Oh, here." Steven pulled a sheet of notepaper from his pocket and handed it to Zach. "Mom wanted me to give you guys this."

Zach's smile disappeared. "Aaron secretary called, it seems Aaron is going to be out of town until next Wednesday. Now Kathleen knows."

*　　　*　　　*

"How about something to drink, Zach, a beer?" Rube asked.

"A beer would be great." Zach answered. He sat on a chair next to John.

Rube turned to the pool and caught Katie and Steven's attention. "You kids want something to drink too, cola, juice, sports drink."

"Cola." Katie yelled.

"Yeah, me too cola. Not a sports drink, none of those sports drink for us."

"Well Steven's emphatic. I guess he doesn't like sports drinks." Zach said with a chuckle.

"Different . . . every . . . day. Last . . . week . . . he . . . drank...two . . . in . . . one . . . day."

Rube went to the patio refrigerator for the drinks. As soon as he was out of earshot, John turned his wheelchair to face Zach.

"How . . . much . . . longer . . . we . . . wait? Want . . . them . . . out . . . now."

"I don't think we should do anything until we talk to Aaron. I know you know the law too, but we need to be positive. Kathleen has a covey of vultures on her side, one miss step and they will see you screwed."

"I'm . . . pissed." John turned his wheelchair and headed for his room.

Rube return with the drinks. "You two have words?"

"What a difference a week makes. He wants Kathleen and Scott out now."

"I don't blame him."

"We don't want to move so fast that the whole think blows up in our face."

"I know. Zach there is something you ought to know. I found a handgun in the nightstand beside John's bed, when I was cleaning today."

"Really, was it loaded?"

"No, but there was a clip with six rounds with it."

"Was it one of John's?"

"I don't know. I don't know much about guns. I just wonder how it got there."

"Well I don't think Steven put it there. I don't think John would put that kind of responsibility on his son. I wonder. Alvin could have got it out of the safe for him."

"What do we do? There is no way that John can get it out of the drawer and possibly use it."

Zach sat a moment. "Leave it where it is for now. Keep an eye on it and Steven. I've got to think about it. If it being there gives him some kind of security, I don't want to take it away."

"What if he wants to use it on himself?"

"John, no way."

The whizzing sound of John wheelchair interrupted the conversation.

"Sorry. Sometimes . . . I . . . get . . . so . . . frustrated . . . I . . . want . . . too . . . scream. I'll . . . give . . . it . . . a . . . couple . . . of . . . weeks."

*   *   *

"Come here Scott." Kathleen stood back from the kitchen window, watching what was happening by the pool. "I wonder what they are hatching now. I know they're up to no good. And it includes Aaron?"

"Maybe it's time for a little accident." Scott looked at Kathleen and whispered. "I could slip in between Nurse Huang going home and the night watchman. Disconnect the ventilator and put my thumb over his tracheotomy, in a few minutes it's all over. Reconnect the ventilator and when the attendant checks him, he'll find him dead."

"It's not that simple, there are consequences."

"Well it looks to me like they are up to something. We know what the consequences are now. We don't know what they will be in a month or so. I say we move first."

"Let me think about it. Give me a couple of weeks."

*   *   *

Steven sat at the kitchen counter eating a bowl of cereal. Saturday morning cartoons blasted from the family room, peppered with Katie's laughter.

"Katie, Katie, turn it down." Steven had to yell to get her attention. His nerves were raw and the noisy sound effect didn't help.

His heart pounded in his chest when the door from the master bedroom opened and Scott stepped out in his jogging gear. He kept his eyes on the bowl in front of him, doing his best to hide his nervousness. Scott took his time to put on a pot of coffee. Steven's heart skipped a beat when Scott went out the backslider, without his usual bottle of sports drink. He wanted to yell, you forgot your drink.

Through the window, he could see Scott steadied himself with the back of a patio chair. Stretch his legs and then start to trot in place. Then he stopped. Steven could hear his heart beat in his ears. A sweat broke out and he began to tremble. Scott returned to the kitchen. Open the refrigerator and grabbed a bottle of sports drink. He looked at Steven. Steven diverted his gaze. *Did he suspect something?*

"Hey squirt, you'll have to come with me sometime, that's if you can keep up."

Scott's taunt lingered in Steven's head. He waited for the slider to closed, but when it didn't he looked up. Scott was gone.

Steven stirred the soggy flakes once more, and then picked up his bowl, took it to the sink and dumped it down the garbage disposal. Suddenly he felt someone behind him. He instantly knew. He twisted around. Cornered by the counter he stood face to face with Scott, his eyes filled with rage. The open bottle in his left hand and the front of his tee spattered with florescent green liquid.

"You dirty little bastard." Scott bellowed.

Steven saw Scott's right arm and shoulder pull back. The movement seemed in slow motion. A huge fist came straight at his head. He froze. It hit. His head recoiled backward. Strange colored lights flashed. He saw the ceiling and he knew he was falling. The back of his head slammed on the granite counter. Everything went black.

CHAPTER 40

CONSEQUENCES

INT.-THE MICHAELS KITCHEN-CONTINUES

Steven is unconscious on kitchen floor, a small trickle of blood oozes from the corner of his mouth. Scott stands over him in a rage, panting.

Kathleen rushes into the kitchen.

> KATHLEEN
> What in the hell have you done?

Kathleen drops to one knee and leans over Steven.

> SCOTT
> The little bastard tried to poison me.

> KATHLEEN
> (Hurries to the open slider in a panic and yells)
> Rube, Rube, come quick.

Rube, sitting on the guesthouse patio, alerted by Scott's strange actions and the commotion, jumped to his feet when Kathleen yelled. He ran all out to the house. Kathleen stood at the door and pointed Rube to the kitchen.

"What happened? Rube asked, kneeling beside Steven and taking hold of his hand.

"I decked the little bastard." Scott shouted standing beside Steven.

Steven stirred. Rube checked his pulse at the wrist. Steven opened his eyes, looked up at Rube, and then past him. Fear came over his face. Rube followed Steven's stare, he is looking up at Scott.

"The bastard tried to poison me so I decked him. I think he hit his head when he fell."

"He a twelve-year-old boy." Rube turned back to Steven. "Lay still." Steven's eyes still fixed on Scott.

"Thirteen soon."

"Stand back." Rube commanded Scott. "Now Son, just lay still." He checked Stevens' eyes. Scott hadn't moved. "I asked you to stand away." Scott still stood over Steven. Rube rose to his feet. He was a head shorter than Scott was. "Now, I'm telling you, leave."

Kathleen immediately stepped between the two men. Scott looked at them, turned and started to the bedroom, but stopped at the door. "This is not the end of this. I sell heavy equipment that uses ethylene glycol. I know what it smells like, looks like and tastes like." Scott held up the half-full bottle of sports drink. "I know what's in this bottle and what this much can do to a man. It can kill him. And I know who put it in here."

Rube ignored Scott and knelt back down. Scott grunted and went to the bedroom.

"Look at my finger." Rube moved his hand from one side of Steven's field of vision to the other and back, Steven's eyes followed his finger. "Good, do you want to try and sit up?"

Steven nodded. Rube helped him into a sitting position. Kathleen handed Rube a warm, wet washcloth. Rube touched the cloth to Steven's lip. "Any loose teeth in there?"

Steven checked the inside of his mouth with his tongue. Gave a faint painful looking smile. "Nope."

Rube checked the back of Steven's head. There was no blood, but a knot was already forming. He helped Steven to his feet slowly and let him stand a moment.

"Steven, how could you do such a thing? You know better——."

Rube interrupted Kathleen with the lifting of his is hand. "Dizzy? Can you walk?"

"Yeah."

Rube slipped Steven's arm over his shoulder. Grabbed the back of his pants and walked him out the back door and to John's room. In the room, he sat him in a chair facing his father.

John's eyes were wide. "What . . . happened?"

Rube was already preparing an ice pack. "Do you want to tell him, or shall I?"

"I will." Steven sat a moment and drew in a breath. "I put antifreeze in Scott's sports drink bottles."

Rube handed Steven the ice pack. "Put this on the back of your head." Rube turned to John. "Scott figured it out with one taste and nailed Steven on the jaw. He hit the back of his head on the countertop when he fell. It knocked him out for a couple of minutes."

"Antifreeze . . . is . . . poison."

"I know. That's why I did it."

"Is . . . Scott . . . okay?"

"Yes — unfortunately." Rube answered hushed.

Just then, Scott and Kathleen came busting through the door from the bedroom. "Do you know what that——that——kid did? He tried to poison me. That's attempted murder. I've got the evidence right here." He stuck the bottle of sports drink in Steven's face.

"We'll take care of it." Rube stepped in front of Steven. "You assaulted a child."

"I had provocation. I ought to call the police."

"Call the police about what?" Zach asked standing in the open French door.

"That kid tried to poison me."

"Is that so? Let me get to the bottom of this, and if we need to, I'll call the police. Now Mr. Hanson, I think you need to go into the other room and cool down."

Scott scowled and looked at Zach and then at Rube. Hesitantly he backed out of the room and closed the mirror bedroom door. A moment later, the lock clicked.

Zach listened to Rube tell the story. Steven sat quietly and stared at the floor, holding the icepack to the back of his head. When he was finished, Zach sat quietly for several minutes. The laser printer cranked out several sheets of paper, but Zach didn't pay any attention. He finally asked Rube if would take Steven to his room so he and John could talk.

"Just let me grab those papers off the printer." Rube picked up the papers and looked at them briefly. Steven stood and Rube walked him out the door. Once out the door he saw that Kathleen and Scott were now waiting on the patio. Rube whispered to Steven. "Lean on me and don't say a word."

Scott glared at them. Steven kept his head down, letting Rube guide him into the house.

*   *   *

"Stall." John's synthesized voice came from the computer speakers.

Zach looked at John in wonderment, but before he could ask a question, Kathleen and Scott came up on the deck and stood glaring in the window. Zach asked them to come in. Scott followed Kathleen, stopped at the French door and flipped his cigarette in the flowerbed. They sat. Scott still carried the half-full bottle of sports drink, rolling it between his hands. Zach stood beside John's bed.

The laser printer spit out a sheet of paper. Zach remembered that John was the only one that could send anything to the printer. He acted as if he hadn't noticed.

"Now, why don't you tell me your side of the story?" Zach walked past the printer, pausing only long enough to look at the paper. In large print it read, 'Rube is fixing stuff. Keep an eye on my monitor'. It took a moment for Zach to realize what John was up to, and then he turned back to Scott. "Well, I'm waiting?"

"I was going out for my morning run and stopped in the kitchen for a bottle of sports drink, like I always do. The kid was sitting at the counter eating cereal."

"The kid, you mean Steven,"

"Yeah, he looked fishy, damn fishy. I pulled this bottle out of the fridge." Scott held up the bottle. "I saw him lookin' at me, strange. His hands were shaking. He was sweaty. I figured he was either sick or up to somethin'. When I got outside, I opened the bottle. The cap was still sealed. I took a swig. I knew when I tasted it. It was antifreeze, ethylene glycol. I've been around it long enough to know. I spit it out. That's when I knew what that little bastard was up to. I went back and decked him."

"Well that is where I have a problem. How do you know, Steven put antifreeze in you drink?"

"By the way he looked and he was the only one that could have done it."

"If what you allege is true, you are well within your rights to press charges against Steven."

Zach looked up at John's computer screen, big letters flashed, OK.

Zach turned to Scott. "What evidence do you have that Steven put the antifreeze in your drink?" Scott appeared to think a moment. "By now any fingerprints on that bottle would he gone. How do I know you didn't spike your own drink just so you could batter the poor kid?"

Scott stood and rushed to the bedroom door. He bounced off the mirror when he hit the locked door. He stumbled back and held his head for a second. Whirling around, he grabbed several rubber gloves from a box on the counter and darted out the French doors. Kathleen followed.

Zach turned to John and whispered, "Score." Then he hurried after Scott and Kathleen.

Scott was already at the refrigerator. He had the gloves on his hands and had pulled out a bottle of sport drink, opened it and smelt, then tasted it. He spun to the sink. He looked at Zach the instant he threw the bottle in the sink, "Sports drink." He bellowed and grabbed the second, checked it and slammed it in the sink.

Zach could see his anger grow. Scott's movements slowed and became forced, the look of a man defeated. He still pulled the last bottle out of the refrigerator and checked it. This time he let it drop out of his hand, into the sink. With a cold glare, he looked up at Kathleen. Without another word, he retreated to the bedroom. Kathleen scowled at Zach a moment, and then followed Scott.

*   *   *

"He's all right, he's a tough kid. Like his father. Rube picked up the gloves that Scott dropped. I sent him to my room. I think he will be safe there. He needs quiet and rest, but I don't want him to sleep for several hours. I need to make sure he doesn't have a concussion. I'll keep an eye on him."

"What did you do with the stuff?" Zach asked quietly

"George took it and will dispose of it."

"What would we do without George?"

"Can . . . Steven . . . stay . . . with . . . you . . . until . . . this . . . blows . . . over."

"I was thinking the same thing." Zach agreed. "What time is Alvin supposed to be here?"

"This . . . morning."

"Gee, he's missed all the fun." Rube kidded.

"That was a close call. We have to be on our toes. I know we talked about cutting the night attendant, but I don't think it's a good idea."

"I . . . agree. If . . . Aaron . . . says . . . the . . . divorce . . . is . . . a . . . go. I . . . want . . . them . . . out . . . ASAP.

"I don't want to be a wet blanket." Rube looked at Zach and asked, "What if it isn't a go?"

"I can't even think of it right now."

* * *

"This is a bunch of bullshit." Scott paces, puffing on a cigarette.

"Sit down." Kathleen patted the seat of a wooden lawn chair. She could see his frustration so she walked him to a secluded area near the creek. The house was far enough away she felt they were free to talk.

"I know the little bastard put the antifreeze in my drink. No proof, my ass, I'll never trust him again. If his tries something again, he'll end up dead or in the hospital. I will guarantee that." Scott finally took a seat.

"Come on Kay, let's fly this chicken coop. I make enough money. Let's move back to Chicago, get a downtown apartment and live. Here we can't even fart without the Gestapo smelling it. Let him file for divorce, you'll counter. So what, if he thinks he's got everything tied up? This is a community property state and you've been married thirteen years. You might not get half, but with a good lawyer, you'll get plenty."

"You think it's that easy?"

"I've been telling you to come fly with me for thirty years, it's not a better time, baby." He leaned over and kissed her. They lingered. "Or there is always the——." He held up his right thumb. "But then we are stuck with the brats."

"Let me think about it." Kathleen took a long look at her home, tantalized by Scott's suggestion. Just as the scales began to tip away from Scott's offer, John in his wheelchair came out of his room and down the ramp follow by his entourage of Zach, Alvin, Rube and Katie, heading for the pool.

"Let's go and have lunch somewhere." Kathleen suggested. "A long one."

*　　*　　*

Before the group had settled on the patio, Scott and Kathleen left without a comment.

"You would think we were disturbing them." Rube remarked.

"I'd like to disturb the hell out of her for good," Zach muttered, convinced that Katie was safely out of earshot. She were playing with Amanda at the shallow end of the pool. Amanda was trying to catch splashes of water that the she make just for her.

"So what do you think John, those new upgrades going to work for you?" Alvin asked. "You're fully linked to phone, TV, house system and the lighting in and around your room."

"Fine . . . thank . . . you."

"I can add more cameras. I brought them with me, small, inconspicuous, wireless and easy to conceal."

"Tempting . . . but . . . I'll . . . have . . . to . . . think."

"Got ya. Say, I'm taking my kids to Great America, Saturday. We are going for the day and staying until closing. We would love to have Katie and Steven join us, I'll pick them up Friday and bring them home Sunday afternoon."

"Sound . . . good . . . they . . . need . . . it."

*　　*　　*

With Alvin and Zach there Rube asked if he could slipped away for a hour or two, making the excuse that with the mornings excitement, be had neglected to do his dishes or make his bed.

In his room, he checked Steven and sent him out with his father. Then Rube pulled the cardboard box out of his closet, filled with vials of injectable sedatives and muscle relaxants. He was positive he could make a soup that could take out ten people. However, he knew he would have to knock them out first and with Scott and Kathleen now suspicious, he would have to be doubly careful. He had tested five different oral sedatives. Placing a dose, large enough to knock someone out, in a glass of wine and tasting it. To his surprise, the one supposed to be most effective was the least detectable.

Over the past several weeks, he had slipped several bottles of Kathleen favorite white wine out of the house, careful to wear gloves when he handled the bottles. Scott would drink anything, but seemed to favor reds, so Rube copped a few reds too. He decided he could crush the pills, mix the powder with a small amount of water and inject it through the cork and they would never suspect his tampering. He would prepare well in advance. And when the time was right, he would place the wine in the wine cooler, lye low and hope they didn't start hitting the bottle to early.

Suddenly Rube's stomach churned, he thought he would vomit. Could he really go through with such a diabolical plan, he wondered? All of his life he had dedicated himself to saving life, healing and nursing. Could he go against all he believed in to help someone he has only known a couple of months? He sat for a while, and then pushed the box back in his closet.

*   *   *

John woke about three thirty in the morning. He could see Roger, the night attendant in the mirror. He was in the recliner, watching TV and obviously fighting sleep. *What a hell of a job. Sit up all night and watch someone else sleep.*

Roger split the nightshift with Mike. Rube coordinated their night work to fit each other's schedule and their need to sleep. The job didn't need any particular skill, other than to stay awake, but the guys', being pre-med students, was a plus. John didn't know much more about the two young men, other than their names.

He wandered how Steven was doing staying with Zach. He was thankful that he hadn't asked Steven to help with what he had planned.

John marveled at his son's courage and guts to come against Scott. He understood the fear he must of felt. He could see the dread in his eyes whenever Scott was around. He seemed guarded even knowing Scott was in the house. Although John could never get it out of Steven, he suspected that there was more than a simple threat and a bruised ear between them.

Then it occurred to him, the phone interface. He would try calling George in the morning.

*   *   *

A small table lamp cast a warm glow across the antiquated room. Zach sat in his favorite chair in the living room. He lived in the same house with his wife Nadia for more than fifty years. Not much had changed in that time. They replaced carpet a few pieces of furniture and reupholstered others when needed. The room was like Zach, it never really changed much.

Steven had stayed with them before, but tonight it sparked memories of a young John, maybe it was because he looked so much like his father at that age, he was getting close to the same age as John, when senior Steve was killed. He knew he needed to act, and now. He had seen the courage in Steve and John, willing to stand and sacrifice everything. He knew what he must do. Come Saturday night, when the attendant went to dinner. He would take his gun, shoot Scott and Kathleen in their bed, and then take his own life. It would be over.

"Uncle Zach." Steven's voice, in the process of changing to manhood, startled him.

"What Son."

"I just want to thank you for what you did for me today."

"That was your father's idea."

"But you were part of it. You and Nadia are better than any real aunts or uncles I have."

"Even Tess."

"I forgot, Tess is great, but I hardly ever see her."

"Well thank you Son, that means a lot to Mother and me."

"Goodnight Uncle Zach." Steven hugged Zach and kissed him on the cheek.

"Goodnight Son." Steven was already gone, Zach's words hung in the empty room.

Zach sat a good deal longer going over his plans, rehearsing in his mind every detail. Questioning if he should enter through John's room. *That would be the most direct. What about John, what if I wake him or he is already awake? Would he try to stop me? How could he. What could he do?*

"Steve, I don't know if you are watching over us down here, or if you can hear me, but if you can. Pleases help me with this. I'm doing it for your son and grandson, but mostly for you. You were the best friend I ever had, and when you died a part of me died too. It was only through John and young Steven that I was able to go on. Accept what I'm about to do as my sacrifice, an act of love. Even if I face the fires of hell in eternal damnation for what I do, I do it without fear or reservation. I do it for you."

CHAPTER 41

THE BIG CHILL

```
INT.-AARON FUTTER'S OFFICE-11:15 A.M.-JUNE 9, 1999
```

Steven in his wheelchair and Zach, sits across the desk from Aaron.

Aaron is reading his notes and writing comments. Zach looks at the rows of book on the shelves behind Aaron.

> AARON
> And you said Scott first assaulted
> Steven, is that correct?

> ZACH
> Yes, grabbed and twisted the boy's
> ear, severely bruising it.

> AARON
> Anything else besides bruising his
> ear and making some threats, no other
> physical contact?

"I ... believe ... there ... was." The synthesizer mechanically spit out John's words. "But . . . I . . . can't . . . get . . . Steven . . . to . . . talk. Whatever ... happened ... scared ... him."

"Well John, you know the laws as well as I do. We can file a restraining order, but with both living in the same house and considering Kathleen and Scott's relationship, enforcing might makes it difficult. We can try to force Scott out by eviction, but that takes one to three months. Divorce is defiantly the way to go. Most of your assets are protected and you have a good case. There should be no alimony. However, California is a community property state and property you have purchased since your marriage falls under this law. Kathleen's attorneys, the court and we, will have to work out a settlement."

"Money . . . is . . . no . . . issue. It's . . . the . . . kids."

Zach could see frustration in John's eyes.

"I understand and I believe now that you can demonstrate that you can take care of children, full physical custody is probable, but legal custody is possible going to be split. She will get visitation also. A certain amount of the restrictions in the court orders may prevent Scott's contact with the children, but if they marry there isn't much we can do."

"I . . . understand. What . . . can . . . we . . . do . . . now?"

"You have to be kidding. Can't we get them out now?" Zach's anger grew and he knew what John was going through.

"Well most couples usually separate voluntarily before a divorce. We would have to have cause for a restraining order. However, since, with the exception of few last minute changes, the work is complete on the divorce. My son is here and I think I can have papers ready for John's signature, in say an hour. I can file them tomorrow, have them served Monday morning, and ask them to leave right then. Maybe she'll move out voluntarily when the papers are served, if not we can try making them an offer."

"And if they do refuse." Zach stood.

"Unless they do something in the form of a direct threat of physical harm, there isn't much you can do legally."

"Let's . . . do . . . it . . . I . . . sign . . . today. The . . . kids . . . can . . . stay . . . with . . . Zach."

Yeah, and if they don't move out Monday we'll get a restraining order. I'd like to see them refuse that offer." Zach stood. "We'll be back after lunch."

*   *   *

Kathleen pulled in the driveway next to George's pickup. He stood at the tailgate working on a large piece of metal. He turned to her when she got out of her car.

"Hi Miss Michaels, remember last winter when you smelt gas in the basement, but no one found the leak. Will I was checkin' it for Mr.

Michaels and found there was a hole in the burner of the furnace that heats the main part of the house."

"Fine, tell John and Zach when they get back."

"I would, but I've got to go, I need to take the burner to a repair shop all the way in San Bruno. Only guy I know that can fix this kind o' furnace."

"Well don't let me stop you."

"It's important that nobody turn on the main house heater until I get it fixed. It might take a week or two."

"Well nobody will be turning on the heat in June."

Kathleen took a shopping bag from the seat of the car and started to the front door. A delivery of six oxygen bottles, were sitting next to the door. Kathleen stopped and looked back at George.

"What are these doing here?"

"I guess they came when nobody was here."

"Put them away, I don't want them setting out here."

"Can't, the storage shed is locked and Rube's got the key. There can only be two tanks in the bedroom at a time."

"Well put them somewhere. Put them in the basement, you have the key for that, don't you?"

"Yes, Miss. Michaels."

Kathleen went into the house muttering. "Some handyman, damn fool. Why not buy a new furnace. He's as useless as a tit on a boar."

*   *   *

Rube didn't ask any questions while he loaded John in the van. Zach told him they needed to kill an hour, before John could sign the papers, so he suggested that they go for a ride. Just as Rube started to back out of his parking place, he noticed Alvin driving up. He got out of his car and came up to the van.

"Hi, guy's out for a drive?"

Rube rolled down the driver's window. "Just killing time."

"As long as that's all your killing."

Zach leaned over. "We are filing the divorce papers tomorrow."

"Great, get it over with."

"What are you doing here?" Zach asked.

"I have to see Aaron on some financial matter. I need to get in there."

"Do you want to meet us for lunch?" Zach asked. "We are coming back later. John is signing the divorce paper after lunch."

"I can't but I'll be over to the house about five. We'll talk then."

"The ... beer ... will ... be ... cold."

*   *   *

Zach went out to the patio, where Steven and Katie were playing. Rube put John back in his bed. His outing had exhausted him. He fell asleep before Zach came back.

When he did, he was noticeably quiet and just sat by John's bed. "I called Alvin and asked him not to come this afternoon." Zach spoke softly. "I think John's too tired. I told him to come by tomorrow."

John didn't wake. During that time, Rube fed John his evening meal and prepared him for the night.

Zach finally stood, took John's hand, leaned over, kissed his forehead, and then turned. "I've got to be going Rube. Nadia will be waiting dinner for me and Steven."

Rube had never seen Zach so solemn and thought it must have been because of the meeting with Aaron. He watched him walk unhurriedly down the ramp. Stop at the bottom and take a measured look around. He called for Katie and Steven and the three were off for the night.

Rube left a note for Roger telling him that John might need an antidepressant and that if he did, to call. After a final check of John and his room, he left. He knew what he had to do.

He was too anxious to eat. Since he started working for Zach, caring for John, he had never seen either man so despondent. He decided that tomorrow night would be the best time. He would solve that problem. He would put the drugged wine in the wine cooler early Saturday morning, and then that night, after they had passed out, and while Roger was on his meal break, he'd take care of them for good.

Tonight he would inject the bottle. Everything would be ready for tomorrow.

*   *   *

"Where's the boss?" Alvin asked, sticking his head through the doorway.

"He is with the kids, out by the pool. Zach dropped Steven off about noon." Rube Answered. "Hey Alvin, wait a minute, I want to talk."

"Sure thing, what's on your mind?"

"John's been a little down since the meeting with his attorney. He hasn't said anything, but I don't think it went that well. I thought you might have a word to cheer him up."

"You know, I was thinking the other day, what I would do if I were John. I can't imagine how helpless he must feel. You have given him life. I've tried to help with the computer, but you are the one that has kept him going."

"Thanks, but that's my job.

"I've known John a long time, tough, really tough, on the inside. I've seen him face things that would crush most men, me certainly. He will be all right. He is just reinventing himself. In another year, he'll have passed the bar and be a crusader for Persons with Disabilities or something like that. You wait and see."

"I don't know where you got your faith and positive outlook on life."

"John, I got it from John." Alvin turned towards the open French doors. "If he's down, I'll just have to go kick his butt." He strode out the door.

Rube finished straightening up and made a few notes in the log for Nurse Huang before joining John and Alvin. By the time Rube got there, it appeared Alvin has worked some sort of magic. Alvin and the kids were laughing and John has a sparkle in his eyes.

"Well are you kids ready? We are going for pizza tonight and then all day at the park tomorrow."

"Make sure you take a sweater or windbreaker." Rube advised. "We are supposed to get a cold front coming through. Look at the mountains, the fog is already pushing in over the top from the ocean."

Katie and Steven started running for the house. "Meet you out front." Alvin called as they left. "I'll be there be a few minutes." He turned and knelt beside John.

"I talked to Aaron yesterday. He thinks it's time to diversify a little and take some cash out of the company. He's convinced tech stocks are over sold and a big correction is coming. So now's the time." Alvin beamed. "A.J.S. is ready with another zero to be transferred to the

Michaels' family trust. Aaron is holding the money in an offshore account until the divorce is final. No matter was happens, Aaron assures me that Kathleen can't touch it."

"Another . . . five . . . million?"

"No John, a little more, this one has three zeros added, just like I promised. You and the kids will never have to worry about anything."

"Fifty?"

John looked at Alvin and he nodded yes. Rube wondered what Alvin meant, but knew it had to be good.

"Have you tried the phone?" Alvin asked abruptly.

"It . . . works . . . great."

"Good." Alvin took John's hand. "Remember what you taught me, it's all in the script." Alvin bounded to his feet. "Got to go."

"Good . . . bye . . . old . . . friend."

Alvin stopped at the family room door and turned back. "It isn't a question of what you have. It's what you do with what you got that matters."

Rube moved his chair closer to John. He sensed a change in him. The dark mood that was over him, had lifted. "You have a great friend in Alvin."

"You . . . don't . . . know . . . the . . . half . . . of . . . it."

"You'll have to tell me the whole story sometime."

"I'm not disturbing anything, am I?" Zach asked, approaching from the side gate. He pulled up a chair. "Did I see Alvin leaving with the kids?"

"You just missed them. I was telling John what a great guy I though Alvin was."

"You don't know the half of it."

Rube laughed a moment. "John just said the same thing."

"I won't be long. I came by to check on John and who was on the schedule for tomorrow night."

"Roger, he's on the same schedule as usual."

"I used to work those kind of hours when I was young, hell on body and mind."

Zach stepped over to John and took his hand with both his. He stood silent for several minutes, before he spoke. "I was reading the diary today. I guess I'm kind of a slow reader. A lot of memories there in just a few words, thanks for letting me read it."

Rube could see tears form in Zach's eyes. He wanted to leave but didn't want to disturb the moment.

Zach gently lowered John's hand to his lap and stepped back. "I know everything will work out just fine." A big smile came across his face.

Zach stood and by his stance, Rube knew he was prepared to leave. His parting words were to John. "Like your father said, it's all in the script."

*   *   *

John woke while Rube was getting ready to leave for the weekend, but he pretended to sleep. When he was gone, he began to run his plan through his head. *Tomorrow would be it.* Scott always came into his room on weekends to crow a little before they went to bed. He would have George come over Saturday, after Nurse Huang, went home and put the gun in his hand. *When the sun-of-a-bitch pops in, Brag! Bang! And when she comes to see what happen, bang, bang. In the dark Your Honor, I thought they were burglars.*

Now let's see how well this phone thing of Alvin works. "Hello . . . George?"

*   *   *

Rube has set his alarm for five. He dressed and made a pot of coffee. When brewed, he poured a cup, took it outside and sat at the cafe table near his door to wait for Roger to leave. A chill went through him, he didn't know if it was the nip in the morning air or his nerves, maybe both.

Right on time Roger departed. It was time. He went to John's room and checked through the window. His computer monitor was off. Rube didn't want John to see him plant the drugged laced wine.

Rube took his box of wine to the family room slider, unlocked the door and slipped quietly into the house.

*   *   *

That afternoon Rube's nerves were raw. He decided to sit out in the sun to warm up and relax. Shortly after Nurse Huang, returned from her lunch break he saw her pull the blinds in John's room then step out on the deck, look around and then sit in a chair on the patio in the sun. After a while, he joined her and asked how John was. He didn't want to see him today. He was afraid that John's sharp discerning eyes would detect his nervousness and suspect he was up to something.

He was relieved when she told him that John was tired and was taking a nap. "That's why I came out here, so I wouldn't disturb him. He seems kind of nervous or upset."

"Tell him I checked on him. I won't disturb him either. "

"Burr." Nurse Huang shivered. "You almost need a sweater today." She commented.

"Did you bring one?"

"No."

Rube went to the guesthouse and brought back a throw. "It can get surprisingly cool this time of year. When it starts to heat up in the central valley and deserts, we sometime get a strong onshore breeze, brings the fog in on the bay off the ocean. Look up there." Rube pointed to the coastal mountains that flanked the west side of the Santa Clara Valley. "Fingers of fog are already reaching their way over the top. We'll be fogged in by nightfall."

*   *   *

Rube forecast was accurate. When Nurse Huang left at eight, a wet fog had settled in. He had moved inside, sat on the sofa in the great room of the guesthouse, and watched the main house. His curiosity heightened when George came around the side of the house and went into John's room. Nurse Huang had left the blinds pulled and he couldn't see what George was doing.

He was about to go check, when Scott and Kathleen came out of the house. Kathleen carried plates of food and Scott had tall glasses and a bottle of wine. They cozied up to the fire pit and Scott ignited the flame. Rube's heart pounded. His plan was working. He sat in the darkened room and watched.

*   *   *

George placed the loaded gun in John's hand. It was cocked and ready to fire. John had been practicing aiming, using his pen as a gun and was confident he could hit his mark. He repeatedly told George over the past couple of days that he wanted the gun for self-defense.

The only concern he had was that the repercussion of the first shot might knock the gun out of his hand. He had George use a large rubber band to secure the gun in his hand. *This has got to work.*

"Goodnight." George said.

With the gun in his hand, John couldn't use the synthesizer. George smiled shrewdly, turned down the lights and stepped out the door.

He was set. And if Scott didn't make his usual visit before Roger came to work. He would pretend to be asleep and hope Roger wouldn't check under the blanket. Scott would definitely come calling during Roger's dinner break.

A moment later George opened the door and stepped back in. "Mrs. Michaels and Scott are sitting by the fire pit. I just thought you ought to know. I'll sit out here until the night nurse gets here.

No, no, no. John wanted to scream. There was nothing he could do but wait.

*   *   *

"Will you sit down? You are making me nervous." Kathleen grumbled at Scott. "If you want to do something, pour me some more." Kathleen turned on the portable radio she had brought, to a classic rock station.

Scott's hand trembled when he filled her glass, then his own.

"Are you cold?"

"Just a little anxious. I've never killed a man before." Scott put down the bottle and lit a cigarette.

"I am sure that John can't see us on the security camera here, it's pointed in the other direction." She pointed to the camera mounted under the eve." She turned up the music. "This will make sure he can't hear us talk either."

Scott took a couple of steps toward John's room and hurried back to the fire. "George is sitting on the deck outside his room."

"Well crap. It might be a long night. Why don't you get us another bottle, some more of these crackers and a blanket?"

*   *   *

Rube thought it was a bit odd that George was sitting on the deck. George being there at all was strange. Then he recalled that George had been acting a little weird all week. The thickening fog added to the peculiar atmosphere and so did Scott and Kathleen sitting in the dark by the fire. Rube began to feel a little more confident when Scott returned with another bottle of wine. He thought a glass of wine would go good right now, but settled for more coffee.

Roger showed up at ten-to-nine. George spoke to him briefly and then left.

*   *   *

John kept his eyes closed when the door opened. He peeked only enough to make sure it was Roger. He sensed him stop at the desk. The chair creaked. After several minutes, he heard him move to the foot of the bed and stand. When he moved to his right side, John started to panic. *No, don't check under the cover.* After what seemed an eternity, he felt Roger pull the blanket up a little and tuck it around his shoulders, before returning to the desk.

*   *   *

"Crap, Roger's already here." Scott flipped the butt of his cigarette in the fire.

"That's a gas fire."

"I know. Are we going to stay out here until one?"

"Why not? We can pretend we are camping."

"You know I don't like camping."

"Fill the glasses then come and cuddle up under the blanket. I know how to warm you up."

*   *   *

Rube thought that when Scott joined Kathleen under the blanket the drugs where finally taking effect. Nevertheless, when twenty minutes later Scott got up for another cigarette, he suspected something was wrong.

Aggravated, Rube turned on a lamp. Scott spun around and looked at the guesthouse. Five minutes later, he turned on the porch light and stepped out on the patio. He nonchalantly walked toward the fire pit.

"Good night for a fire."

"You are up kinda late?" Scott stared at Rube. The flames of the fire danced in his eyes.

"Couldn't sleep. I heard the music and saw the fire."

"We're having a celebration. I scored a huge sale in Hong Kong. Here, have some champagne. I'll grab you a glass." Before he could say no, Scott set down the bottle and hurried to the house.

Rube read the label in the flickering light, Dom Pérignon. He had only heard of it, but never tried it. Scott had returned with a champagne glass and another bottle.

"This will help you sleep."

I might as well get some sleep. Nothing else is likely to happen. Rube chuckled at himself. *Well there is always tomorrow night.*

Scott filled their glassed. "To Life."

"L'Chaim." Rube took a drink and they laughed.

By the second glass, Rube could feel the effects. He hadn't eaten all day and rarely ever drank. He excused himself and headed back to the guesthouse, a little unsteady on his feet.

*   *   *

Kathleen watched Rube meander back to the guesthouse and trip in the door. "That's one way to get rid of a nosey neighbor."

"Now we wait." Scott looked at his watch. "Two more lousy hours and freedom is ours."

"I can almost taste it. Come cuddle with me some more."

*   *   *

Zach recognized Roger's car parked on the street past the driveway. He pulled up behind Rube's Mustang and turned out his lights. From where he parked, he could see lights on in the main part of the house. It was twelve-forty. *Who is still up at this hour?* He released his seatbelt, un-holstered his revolver and laid it on the seat next to him. He zipped up his dark windbreaker, pulled down his cap, slouched in the seat, and waited for Roger to take his meal break.

*   *   *

Something woke Rube. Maybe it was the sudden silence or the need to pee. Rube sat on the edge of his bed. He was still dressed. The fire was out and it was silent. However, the family room and kitchen lights still blazed.

He reached to turn on the nightstand lamp when the master bedroom lights came on. A dark figure of a man stood near the low masonry wall that enclosed the guesthouse's separate patio. Rube froze. He slowly reached for the phone. A cigarette lighter lit, it was Scott.

He watched. A few minutes past, Scott was obviously cold. The fog had laid a wet blanket of dew across the yard. Lights from the house reflected in the wet. The desk lamp eliminated the blinds of John's room. Scott crouched when Roger stepped up to the French doors and peered out. He stepped out on the deck, put on a jacket and looked around a moment before closing the door and starting for the side gate.

Scott gave the remains of his cigarette a toss and hurry to the house through the patio door. Inside Rube saw him stop and do something at the wall near the bar. Whatever he was doing, seemed to frustrate him, he made a gesture at the wall and then turned out the light. He walked quickly through the kitchen on his way to the bedroom, turning out the lights.

Rube couldn't resist the call of nature any longer. He grabbed his robe and hurried to the bathroom.

*　　*　　*

At the sound of the door, John opened his eyes and checked the room to be sure Roger was in fact gone. The wait had been long and excruciating. *It shouldn't be much longer now.* John's heart pounded with anticipation. He felt the hard steel of the gun in his hand, his finger ready against the trigger. He thought back to the night when he almost pulled the trigger on Kathleen. *Damn fool. Should have finished it then.*

*　　*　　*

When Zach saw Roger walk to his car, he sat up and grabbed his gun. Adrenalin pumped, at last the time had come. He watched Roger get into his car and waited, but he didn't move. No taillights, he didn't start the car, the kid just sat there. Zach looked at the house. The lights in the front of the house went out. "Now Roger, go. Get your ass in gear and go." *He always goes to Denny's.* Roger finally started his car, but still didn't drive away. *What the hell is he doing?*

*　　*　　*

Scott came into the bedroom. Kathleen was already in her nightgown. The bed turned down. She sat on the side of the bed.

"What were you doing out there so long?" She asked.

"Freezing my balls off waiting for that jackass to leave. Jesus Christ, it's cold." He went to the thermostat on the wall.

"What are you doing?"

"Turning up the heat, I tried the thermostat in the family room but nothing happened."

"Wait! Don't! The heater's brok——."

CHAPTER 42

DEVASTATION

```
EXT.-NEAR ZACH PICKUP-NIGHT-CONTINUOUS

Zach is sitting in his pickup parked in front of the
Michaels' home.

Camera sees Zach through the windshield. He picks up
his gun.

FX A huge ball of fire lights up the night, seen re-
flected in the windshield.

Zach looks up. His mouth drops open.

SFX - Slightly delayed, EXPLOSION.

Zach ducks then looks back up. Flaming debris starts
to rain down over pickup.


                         ZACH
            OH MY GOD!


                                    FADE TO BLACK:
```

Zach rolled out of his pickup. Temporarily blinded by the fireball he stayed low beside his pickup. Out of the blackness, sparks, like shooting stars, descended. When he thought it was safe enough, he ran to the side of Roger's car and crouched. Fiery rubble still rained from the dark sky. Roger rolled down his window. Zach handed him his cellphone. "Call the fire department."

Staying low but determined, Zach started around the side of the house. The fog glowed crimson above him. There was another loud explosion. Zach tucked under the eve of the garage. Part of metal oxygen bottle dropped at his feet. He pressed on.

*   *   *

The concussion knocked Rube against the bathroom mirror. Toothpaste splattered. The door jammed. He struggled to open it, but it wouldn't budge. He would have to kick his way out. After several tries, the door split open. The windows where blown in and shards of glass covered the floor and bed from the blown in windows. Pieces of glass embedded in the walls, glisten, reflecting of the wall of fire outside. The heat pushed him back into the bathroom. The only exit was the bathroom window, but first he braved the heat enough to grab his cellphone off the nightstand. The heat intensified. He struggled out the small window. Outside, the building shielded him. Terrified and disoriented he managed to dial 911.

*   *   *

Zach approached the wooded gate. Steam rose from it. He kicked it open and the flames immediately pushed him back. He dropped to the ground and curled up against the wall at the next explosion. From where he was, he could see the metal shed where the oxygen tanks were stored. Steam rose from its' roof, but appeared secure for now. In the distance, he could hear sirens. Roger came up behind him.

"Go back, stay in your car. When the fire department gets here, tell them there are three people in the house and one in the guesthouse. I've got to see if I can rescue John."

*   *   *

Rube stayed low and peered around the corner of the guesthouse. The flames rose into the sky. It looked like the roof over the back part of the house was gone. He lay flat and crawled military style behind the masonry wall toward the inferno. If there were any chance of saving John, he would do it.

*   *   *

Zach worked forward, the heat nearly unbearable. When he got to the end of the garage, he could see John's room. It was entirely engulf. He buried his face in his arms and screamed. He knew there was nothing he could do. Exhausted, he went numb with grief. He knew if he stayed where he was, he wouldn't last, the fumes, heat and smoke, would overtake him. He no longer cared.

*   *   *

Rube was about to try a dash closer to the house. The sirens where getting louder and he could see red lights flashing in the trees. Suddenly there was a succession of blasts from deep within the flames, followed by burst of blue-white flashes. In his heart, he knew there was no hope of anyone surviving the inferno.

*   *   *

Zach felt a hand grab his ankle and start to pull. Rescued, but he was too dazed to help. In seconds, there were others, pulling, lifting and then carrying him to safety. An oxygen mask slid over his nose and mouth. Moments later, someone placed something cool and wet over his eyes. In the distance, he heard someone yelling turn off the gas main. Others repeated the call several times until somebody shouted. "I got it." Moment later the roar from the fire changed. The relay of voices repeated, gas off, powers off.

*   *   *

Rube felt safe behind the wall. He could see streams of water sprout from the front of the house and shower down on the flames, but they fought back stubbornly. He eventually worked his way back to the side of the building. It was cooler. He sat with his back to the cold stucco. He could hear Amanda barking in her kennel yard.

In the distance, off in the trees beyond the creek, vehicle headlights with flashing red and blue lights appeared. Ahead of them came firefighters, some with flashlights and others with hoses.

"Here, I'm over here." Rube started shouting. "Save the dog."

It wasn't long and two of the firefighters helped him to safety. The EMTs checked him. He asked about Zach and Roger. They didn't know. When they were certain he was all right, they drove him and Amanda to the main staging area and reunited him with Zach and Roger.

*   *   *

Zach was still on oxygen. He had first-degree burns on his hands and face, but insisted on being in on the action. In a state of shock, he sat on a gurney. With his legs draped over the side, he watched the firefighters work from two fronts.

Zach called Alvin and told him what had happened. They all heard the explosion and sirens. A decision was made to wait until Zach could be there to break the news to the children. Then Zach called his wife.

The fog lifted and a mild breeze began pushing it back to the bay. By sun raise, the fog was gone. The flame, gave way to black smoke eventually surrender into billows of white.

Roger brought Zach and Rube coffee and donuts that the neighbors furnished and then went back to his car, still hemmed in by fire and police vehicles. He carefully picked the debris off his car and waited for an opportunity to leave.

There was no need for words. Both Rube and Zach accepted John's fate. The question in Zach's mind was what had happened to cause such a huge explosion and fire.

About ten that morning, the chief started releasing some of the fire crews. The investigating officer took Roger's statement and released him. Still an extremely frightened young man, he told Rube and Zach he was going home. Rube thanked him and told him he would call him later that day.

"What next?" Rube asked.

Zach had ditched the oxygen mask, but still sat on the gurney with the oxygen tank next to him. "As soon as they can get in they will try to find and identify the bodies. The Coroner will call the shots after that."

Rube sat on the gurney next to Zach and quietly asked, "What were you doing here at one o'clock in the morning?"

Zach chuckled a little, smiled, leaned close to Rube and opened his jacket to reveal his gun. "I came here to kill Scott and Kathleen. I was waiting for Roger to go to dinner."

Rube sat a moment, looked at Zach, and then let out a faint almost sinister laugh.

"What's so funny?" Zach asked.

"I had planned to kill them last night myself. I had laced their wine with sedatives so when they passed out, I could to inject them with a lethal dose of drugs. They drank the wrong wine."

*   *   *

By noon, the temperature had climbed to the upper seventies. The EMT's released Zach, and he discreetly put his weapon wrapped in his jacket in his pickup. Rube leaned against his car holding Amanda's leash. Zach grabbed a couple of bottles of water and joined him.

"Holly crap!" Alvin exclaimed, stepping up from behind. "Unbelievable."

Zach turned. "Where did you come from?"

"I thought I'd walk over and see what's going on. The streets are blocked with the traffic and emergency vehicles. We were still up last night when we heard the explosion. The kids all wanted to jump in the van and see what it was. I am glad we didn't."

"How are they doing?"

"Okay I think. Steven's been watching the news but nothing's been reported so far, usually no local news on Sunday morning. He wants to walk over and check on his father."

"I wish I could get over there and talk to him. He will figure it out himself fairly soon."

"That's why I came over. I know I better break the news."

"I hate to put this burden on you."

"I can handle it."

Alvin waited a short time then took Amanda and walked back home.

*   *   *

The fire was out, only one engine crew stayed for mop up, but the fire investigator and police were still quite active. The Coroner told him that they found a body in the hospital bed. He was sure it was John, but the body was badly burned. An autopsy would determine positive identification. At that time, they were still trying to locate Kathleen and Scott's bodies. It appeared that the fire started in the basement, directly under the master bedroom. The floor had collapsed and made the investigation difficult. There was one more problem.

"It might become a homicide investigation. We found a gun in the hand of the man in the bed."

"A gun?" Zach asked.

"I don't know if it's been fired." The officer responded. "Wasn't Mr. Michaels paralyzed?

"Yes. Completely, except for his right index finger."

"Any ideas on how he may have come to have a gun in his hand?"

"No, none what so ever."

The officer hurried away with no further questions.

Zach looked at Rube and shook his head, no.

They removed John's body. Zach and Rube where given a few moments of privacy with John's remains before he was taken to the morgue. Then the Coroner allowed Zach and Rube to enter the backyard and see the full extent of the damage.

"It really looks like a bomb when off." Rube kept saying and shaking his head in disbelief. When Rube was confident nobody could hear, he whispered to Zach "I can understand why they are suspicious."

"Quiet. I want to know how he could get the gun out of the nightstand. I don't think John would have asked Steven to do it. And anyway he's been gone since Friday."

"Well, I'm sure neither Nurse Huang nor Roger would do it."

"That leaves you or me, Rube."

"Wait, George! George came by last night after Nurse Huang left. He was in the room for fifteen minutes or so, and then turned down the lights. He sat out on the deck until Roger arrived. No one went in the room after that accept Roger. This morning he told me John was asleep when he got there and didn't wake up all evening."

"Or he pretended to be asleep." Zach walked toward the pool. "John had made a comment about Scott coming in his room one night and harassing him. Maybe it was more than just once."

"Are you going to tell the Coroner?"

"Not for now. It will depend on what condition they find Kathleen and Scott. I want to talk to George."

      *   *   *

George fell apart on the phone when Zach broke the news. Zach questioned George at length about the gun and was satisfied with George's answers. Zach asked George to come over.

It was when George saw the damage and heard that the fire started in the basement that he told the Coroner about the burner being out of the furnace. Zach felt sorry for George. He was so confused and upset, thinking he might have had something to do with causing the fire.

It was while George was there that they found Scott and Kathleen's bodies. There was not much left of them, but enough to make a tentative identification and do a toxicology exam. The furnace was as George said it would be and the remains of the six oxygen bottles were where he said Kathleen told him to put them. Zach eventually felt comfortable enough with the situation to have George tell the story about the gun. The Coroner informed them that they had determined the gun had not been fired and reassured him that he didn't think it was his fault, and sent him home.

The Coroner wrapped up at five. He told Zach, off the record, that his preliminary finding indicated that, the furnace was the source of the explosion. The thermostat in the family room was on and apparently, the furnace filled the basement with gas. Furnace's that old didn't have a good safety system. When the furnace for the addition was turned on, the gas exploded, creating the fireball. He believed that the concussion probably killed all three of the victims instantly. "They didn't know what happened."

In the meantime, the entire estate was condemned and uninhabitable. Zach invited Rube to stay with him until he could get back in his own condominium. Zach helped him get some belongings out of the guesthouse for the night. City police would guard the property until private security was arranged.

After dropping Rube off, Zach had one more task to perform at Alvin's home.

*   *   *

In the morning sun, Steven and Katie stood beside Zack and looked at the burned out remains of their parent's bedrooms transfixed. Alvin had told them what had happened, they took the news with the steadfastness of two brave, but battered souls, all they did ask was to see the house. For five months, they had lived the uncertainty, refugees from a sorrowful and conflicted world. Watching them look over the devastation, it seemed to Zach that there was at last peace in their lives. Hand-in-hand they stood, with a solemn dignity that astonished Zach.

Zach left the kids a moment to check with the crew that had come to secure the estate. Rube was in the guesthouse packing his personal belongings. When Zach returned neither Steven nor Katie had moved.

Most of the patio furniture was unrecognizable, charred, twisted or melted curios of another time.

"Can I go to my room and get my dolls?" Katie asked.

"Not today." Zach knelt beside her. "The men are coming tomorrow. They have to make sure it's safe first. Then we can go in and take out all that you want."

"I don't want anything." Steven snapped, "I don't want to remember this place. Why didn't it all just burn up, as if it never was? Like I never had a mother or a father or anything at all, I want it to be as if it never was."

Steven turned and ran out of the yard. Zach followed until he saw him climb in his pickup and slam the door. When he returned to Katie, she held up one of Amanda's squeaky toys she had found.

"I don't want to forget. I don't ever want to forget my Mom or Dad, or anything about this place." She up righted one of the few recognizable chairs. "See it's still good. It's gonna be alright."

CHAPTER 43

WE SURVIVE

Tess arrived early the Tuesday morning after the fire, went straight to Alvin's home, and began to weave a most magical spell on Katie and Steven. The first thing she did was to ask the children to help her plan John's funeral. All three sat on Alvin's family room floor and began to choose the music. No suggestion was to bazaar. If Alvin had it on a CD, they played it, if not they sang it. Pop, classical, show tunes, TV commercials, they spent hours listening, singing and best of all laughing together. They even got Alvin and his wife and children to join in.

The next morning Tess took Katie and Steven and the three started making arrangements. Somehow, Tess managed for the funeral service at the old Presbyterian Church, the family once attended. Astonishingly they agreed to the service being conducted by a Unitarian minister, a high school classmate of Tess's, a woman pastor from San Francisco. Interment would be next to his parents that same day. However, by unanimous decision of the three, it would not be a police funeral, no processional of police cars to the cemetery. No flag draped coffin or uniformed color guard and definitely no twenty-one gun salute.

The funeral was Friday, a joyous celebration of John Michaels life, with hundreds in attendance. Kathleen's brother Ryan was the only O'Malley to attend. He was even called upon to offer a prayer. That afternoon he flew back to Chicago with Kathleen's remains for burial there.

During the interment Steven read an email, his father wrote him the day before the fire.

The week after the funeral, Tess, Katie and Steven talked about what to do with the house. They decided not to decide now, but wait until at least Christmas before any plans were made. They would all spend Christmas in New York and think about it then.

It was during that week that we got the news that Scott's family had his remains cremated and his ashes scattered at sea off the coast of Santa Cruz, California. Steven found it hilarious that Scott's ashes went to the fish.

In accordance with John's will and arrangement make years before, Alvin and Sandra were to adopt Steven and Katie and raise them as their own.

It had been two weeks of nearly constant going. On Saturday, Steven called and asked Zach to meet him at the house on Sunday, at ten, alone. Zach offered to pick him up, but Steven wanted to walk. The front of the house showed little effect of the fire, just some smoke damage around the garage doors. None of the front windows of the house had been broken, but the yard already showed the signs of no water or care. A chain-link security fence crossed the front lawn and circled around to the back.

Plywood sheets covered the guesthouse's windows. The patio rubble was gone, the cement swept, the pool drained, and the chain-link fence secured the open pit that once was the master bedroom. Boards covered John's windows, even though the roof was gone.

Zach found a place to sit on the low masonry wall in front of the guesthouse and waited for Steven. He took a copy of the email John sent to Steven and reread it. 'Steven, my father once told me, we come into this life to experience the good as well as, pain, grief, sorrow and ultimately death, that we may live. The sages of old called it the perfecting of the soul. Your pain and sorrow can destroy you or make you a better man. It's your choice. Embrace life, all of it, the good and the bad.

'My father believed that we choose our life here on earth before we are born, one incarnation of many. We choose this life in its entirety before we are born. In our time, the best example is a movie script. A framework of words and actions of a character that we like actors indwells and brings to life. The script is the matrix by which the soul is perfected and made one with God. God is not someone sitting on a thrown in a far off heaven. God is the life that indwells in all of us, good or bad. The purpose of this earthly journey is to experience it not as individuals, but as part of what we call God. Therefore embrace life, all of it, the good and the bad, it is all God.'

Zach slowly folded the paper back and put it between the pages of the book he brought for Steven. Bits and pieces of years of memories about this place sifted through his thoughts.

"Zach?" Steven called.

"Out in back."

Steven came through the gate, dressed in dark gray slacks and a burgundy dress shirt. He definitely was not the frightened boy of two weeks ago, but a handsome youth with poise beyond his years. All though the ordeal, from January on, Zach had marveled at Steven's courage and fortitude, today he saw the man it had forged.

"Good morning Uncle Zach, this is for you." Steven held out a card.

It was a Father's Day card with a special note, thanking Zach for being there when he needed him. Zach started to cry and turned away embarrassed.

"I didn't intend it to do that."

Steven sat next to Zach, silent. When he gained his composure, Zach thanked Steven and gave him a hug.

"Don't get your new pants all dirty."

"It's okay." Steven looked up at the house. "Two weeks ago, I said I didn't what to remember any of this. I know now, it's a part of me that I must never forget."

"The building inspector says the structure of the main house is not sound and will need to be razed completely, but the guesthouse is structurally sound."

"Can we fix it up and move Dad's books, art and other things in there until we decide about rebuilding?"

"I don't see why not." Zach handed Steven the book. "Then you can return this to the collection."

"*Greater Expectation,* It didn't get burned." Steven opened it. "There are still a lot of blank pages. I guess it's up to me to fill them in."

"And Son, the other day the Coroner gave me this. It was at the morgue with your father's belonging." Zach handed Steven his father's fountain pen. "Somehow it survived unscathed, only the box is gone. You had better take good care of it. You might need it someday too."

"Maybe I'll find the magic in it yet."

"The only magic in it, is what you believe is there."

"I think you are right."

CHAPTER 44

EVER AFTER

Gentle waves found their way upon the uninhabited beach and kissed the snow-white sand before they retreated back to the great azure sea. A stray breeze softly stirred the grasses that tufted the gradual slope that separated beach and land. Peace, a stillness spread across the trees, shrubs, and grasses that stretched to the horizon.

On the sand, a solitary figure walked near the edge of the waves. Khaki trousers rolled to mid-calf exposed bare feet. A breeze tugged at his unbuttoned blue shirt, the cuffs turned back on his arms, he casually strolled along.

Up the beach, a Yellow Labrador runs out from a dune and chases a wave back to the sea. A man in shorts and tee shirt, follow the dog. A wave rushed in catching the dog, it turned and ran barking. The dog spotted the man coming up the beach, appeared to recognize him, and ran toward him. He knelt on one knee to greet the dog.

"Hi Sandy, you remember me. It's been a long time hasn't it old boy?"

The exuberant Sandy laps at his hands and chin. Sandy's companion walked up to them and smiled. I heard you rapped, how did the shoot go?"

"Well, very well, but I'm glad to be back. I'm sorry your character exited the story so early in the story, I missed working with you."

"That was the way it was written. How is the kid doing playing your son?"

"Great, he's playing it low key, internalizing more than I did."

"Well he's got a long way to go."

"It is astounding how all the scripts intertwine and yet are so separate. There is one for every life. "

"That is the way it works. In this script, I played your father, in another you might play my father, or mother, a good guy or bad guy, or girl, who knows what we might try in the next script. Just remember, the tougher the roll the greater the reward."

"But you know, just playing the part the best you can is the greatest reward."

"You are right Anders, you are right. The true reward is in the doing."

"It's a shame we don't remember that while we are living it."

THE END

AUTHOR GENE STIRM

Gene Stirm fell in love with the arts at an early age and by high school, he was active in art and theater. Winning honors in display design and stage design, including the Bank of America Award for Fine Art. At that early age, he established himself as an artist, actor, director, and set designer. He gathered his friends together and started his own local theater production company, in Santa Clara, California.

Finishing two years of college, majoring in Theater Arts and with a number of personal and family conflicts, he chose to move to the mountains, the Sierra Nevada's. After a year of tramping the woods and trying to find himself, he figured he wasn't really lost, and focused his direction towards commercial art. By the time he finished art school, he had spent several years as an ER Technician, sign painter and restaurant owner and had been married and divorced.

With his college diploma at last in hand, he went to work for a weekly newspaper and commercial printing company in Central California. With the knowledge of printing now reinforcing his graphic art and design skills, he took a position as a studio artist at a full-service advertising agency. There, he participated in everything from typesetting, illustrations and photography to storyboarding, copywriting and was even involved with direct commercials for TV. Within two years he left the advertising agency and took the job of art director for Jostens Publishing, in Visalia, California,where he continue to study photography under Ansel Adams and even guest lectured at Ansel Adams Workshops in Yosemite.

Now married to Patricia, and with their daughter Malinda, they moving to Orange County, California, in 1978, and after managing two printing companies, doors opened in the area of menu design where he combined his restaurateur knowledge with art training and graphic experience. His work was in demand and he, with a partner, started Stirm/Collins & Associates, a menu design company, in Anaheim, with a client list that included The Fairmont Corporation, The Plaza NYC, The Beverly Wilshire, The Bel Air and Halekulani. Along the way, he filled in his spare time by teaching painting, floral design and photography, painted murals, designed sets for professional production in LA and Orange County, worked in clay, jewelry making and raised orchids. Gene, an ordained minister, was also active in his church and other ministries for several years in the Orange County area.

Upon selling the menu business, he returned to acting, and dabbled in filmmaking and screen writing with a special interest in documentary. His first documentary, *Dreams Forgotten*, won a VIC award in 2001. He is a member of SAG/AFTRA and has several TV and film acting credits.

In 2004, he and his wife moved to Tehachapi, California, where he continued his studies of Native American art and culture and Shamanism. In 2008 he received a Doctor of Shamanism Degree from ULC Seminary. It was at that time he began rewriting some of his screenplays into novels.

Gene has been connected with publishing, book design and editing most of his professional life. Writing credits include Impression, Josten's employee magazine; Award winning writer and editor of mineralogical bulletins. His first Novel, *Mystical Path To Mystique*, won Honorable Mention in the California Fiction Writer Challenge 2012. Other works include, *As A Shaman Dreams, The Art and Craft of Cover Design, Oscar Goes Camping*, co-authored with Chelley Kitzmiller, and writer-producer of the feature film, *Birthday Wishes*.

Gene's hobbies include jewelry making and lapidary, he is an award-winning Master Lapidary.

Mystical Path to Mystique
by Gene Stirm

After a bump on the head, Dave, a crusty two timed divorced, ex LA ad man turned maintenance man, starts seeing a ghostly image of an American Indian reflected in windows and mirrors. When he is fired from one more menial job on his long road to wreck and ruin, he makes a choice, get out of town. So he loads all his worldly possessions into the back of his pickup truck and heads to Northern California, to a piece of land he had inherited. On the way he picks up a mysterious hitchhiker, who takes him on the journey of a lifetime where all his hidden secrets are unmasked, and he is confronted by his past, his weaknesses and his fears. Can a simple act of forgiveness and letting go, actually bring happiness and fulfillment and could the beautiful widow he met at a rest stop be his soulmate, or is it all an illusion to be snatch away just when he finds hope? Find out as you join Dave on his Mystical Path to Mystique.

Trent, the hitchhiker and half Native American, slowly reveals the fact that he is a Shaman and Mystic Traveler sent to help Dave find his way. However, when his own romantic involvement distracts him, he must choose between personal passionate pleasure and a higher commitment in order to save Dave's life. And what of the ghostly Indian, is it a Spirit Guide sent to Dave or the effects of the bump on his head?

This mystical romantic adventure makes many twists and turns on its way to Mystique.

As A Shaman Dreams
by Gene Stirm

Before writing, before religious and dogmas, before priests, there were Shamans. The Shaman were the spiritual advisers, healers and sometimes head or leader of their clan. Shaman see beyond the ordinary by a process called Journeying, and Altered State of Consciousness, a dreamlike state where they visit the Spirit World. This book is a collection of photographs of Shaman Art from southwestern America with interpretations by a Shaman.

Author Gene Stirm, brings his unique blend of talent and insight to this photographic book of petroglyphs from southeastern California and Nevada. Artist, photographer, writer and Shaman, Gene has applied a Shaman's perspective to ancient artwork left on stone in the desert by early inhabitants of southwestern America.

www.ingramcontent.com/pod-product-compliance
Lightning Source LLC
Chambersburg PA
CBHW070904260626
47162CB00007B/2557